ANGELS and OUTCASTS

ANGELS
and
OUTCASTS

•

An Anthology of
Deaf Characters
in Literature

THIRD EDITION

Trent Batson

and

Eugene Bergman

EDITORS

GALLAUDET COLLEGE PRESS WASHINGTON, D.C.

Originally published as *The Deaf Experience*
© 1973, 1976 by Eugene Bergman and Trenton Batson
Gallaudet College Press, Washington, DC 20002
© 1985 by Gallaudet College. All rights reserved
Published 1985
Printed in the United States of America

Designed by Judith Bair
The cover is reproduced from a plate designed and engraved by
William Blake for *The Complaint, and the Consolidation; or,
Night Thoughts*, by Edward Young, 1797. "EXPLANATION: An
evil genius holding two phials, from one pours disease into the
ear of a shepherd, and from the other scatters a blight among his
flock; intimating that no condition is exempt from affliction."
(Roger R. Easson and Robert N. Essick, *William Blake: Book
Illustrator*, Vol. I [Normal IL: The American Blake Foundation,
Illinois State University, 1972], 16.)

Library of Congress Cataloging in Publication Data
Main entry under title:

Angels and outcasts.

    Rev. ed. of: The Deaf experience. 2nd ed. c1976.
    Bibliography: p.
    1. Deafness—Fiction.   2. Deaf, Writings of the.
I. Batson, Trenton W. II. Bergman, Eugene. III. Deaf
experience.
PN6071.D35A6 1985   808.83'1   85-20669
ISBN 0-930323-17-3

Gallaudet College is an equal opportunity employer/educational
institution. Programs and services offered by Gallaudet College
receive substantial financial support from the U.S. Department
of Education.

CONTENTS

ACKNOWLEDGMENTS

Grateful acknowledgment is made for permission to reprint the following materials in this anthology.

"At the Dances of the Deaf-Mutes" by Walter Toman. Reprinted by permission of The Chicago Review from *The Chicago Review Anthology*, Vol. 10, No. 3, 1959.

•

"Talking Horse" from *Rembrandt's Hat* by Bernard Malamud. Copyright 1968, 1972, 1973 by Bernard Malamud. Reprinted by permission of Farrar, Straus, and Giroux, Inc.

•

"The Key" by Eudora Welty. Reprinted by permission of Harcourt Brace Jovanovich, Inc., from *A Curtain of Green and Other Stories*, copyright 1941 and 1969.

PREFACE

This book, unique when it appeared in 1976, is still unique and therefore serves an important purpose for understanding deaf people and deaf culture. When it was first published, Gallaudet College did not have a college press; now it does and we are pleased that Gallaudet College Press decided to re-issue our book, newly tailored and spiffed-up for its reintroduction to the world. We hope that you will enjoy reading the stories of the deaf characters; we ourselves have known the characters for so long that they seem not mere characters but old friends.

PREFACE TO FIRST EDITION

In this book, you will find selected fictional and biographical works of the last century and a half which deal with deafness— that is, they all have deaf characters in them. This collection, then, is an extremely valuable tool for those who are interested in understanding deafness better because it is a unique collection and with it, one can study deafness in a totally new way. From these selections it is possible to know much about the attitudes in the western world toward deaf people, and how these attitudes have changed over the last one hundred and fifty years. The characters range from sweet to profane, from tyrannical to help- less, from good to bad, but they are all human, alive, in the midst of things. Far from being isolated from life, they are in the thick of it. In a sense their stories are stories of how they triumph over their affliction and arrive at self-fulfillment or painful self-under- standing. They are fully developed, living characters.

The book is divided into three parts: the nineteenth century, the twentieth century, and deaf authors of the nineteenth and twentieth centuries. Of these three sections, in many ways the most interesting (and certainly the most revealing about the deaf experience) is the third one because here we find genuine concern with aspects of the deaf experience. The accounts are written in the first-person mode, which is just as characteristic of them as it has been of black writers, from Frederick Douglass through Booker T. Washington, W. E. B. DuBois and James Weldon John- son, to Richard Wright and James Baldwin.

This preoccupation with the self, with one's own story, can be traced to the exposed existential position which members of a minority occupy in society. The blacks have their tale of oppres- sion and de facto second-class citizenship to tell, and so do the deaf. The deaf writer confines his imagination to the auto-biographical mode because to him the struggle for dignity and assertion of the self in the community is an overriding and passionately absorbing concern. This is perhaps best exemplified in Albert Ballin's autobiography, *The Deaf Mute Howls*, which incidentally is most recommended to the reader, whether hearing or deaf, because it states so clearly the misunderstandings burdening the deaf in the public eye, and it also reflects the depth of emotion which the deaf feel about their own language—sign language, which is still suppressed in many places the world over. This is not the first instance of linguistic oppression. As the psychologist Ursula Belugi pointed out, there were at least two previous known instances in human history: the suppression of the teaching of French in Prussian-occupied Alsace after the Franco-Prussian war, and of the teaching of Polish in Prussian-occupied western Poland during the same period. Let us say, however, that the rage which the Alsatians and Poles had then felt can hardly surpass the intensity of the feelings of the deaf about their own sign language, since to them it is also their lifeline toward self-fulfillment, and without it life to them is a living death. The vital importance of this language has long been recognized. Thus nearly a century ago a writer commented:

> . . . the greatest thing needful is to wake up the mind, to make it flow with life—the life of the soul. How is this achievable but with the language of signs? *This strange yet wonderful language possesses in fact almost the power of an autocrat over the mind tied and bound by the fetter of deafness*; it waves its magic wand and the fetters fall off: it acts the part of nursing mother, and behold the passive intellect is awakened to the power of understanding. (R. Patterson, *American Annals of the Deaf*, Vol. XXIII, 1878, p. 20.)

The vividness, immediacy and dramatic impact of this language are reflected in the following excerpt from an anonymous article in *The Arkansas Optic*, circa 1910:

> It is the language of the soul. It stirs the heart to the deepest depths of pathos; it convulses the frame with the merriest peals of laughter. I have seen again and again some Demosthenes of the deaf carry his audience in the sweep of

one fleeting moment from the agony of burning tears to the delight of enraptured smiles. (Brochure, Boston Society of the Deaf, printed by Herman Schultz. Boston, 1910.)

And Arnold H. Payne in 1937 acclaimed sign language as "far more expressive, facile and beautiful than the English of Shakespeare and the Bible." (Quoted by Edmund Critchley, in *The Language of Gesture*. London: E. Arnold, 1939.)

These particular qualities of sign language are illustrated by the following recent anecdote about a man who became interested in learning it:

But there is one thing he said that I will never forget. He wanted me to sign a poem of song so that he could get an idea of how the deaf enjoy them. I chose "The Star-Spangled Banner."

When I was through he stared at me for a while and then said: "I've heard it so many times but never understood it with feeling and meaning until now." (As narrated by Ed Holonya to Toivo Lindholm, in *The Deaf American*, September, 1970, p. 17.)

It has been conclusively demonstrated by the distinguished linguist William C. Stokoe and others that sign language is a distinct and autonomous language with its own specific rules of grammar and syntax. It is the native language of the deaf, not English, which is one reason for the relative scarcity of deaf writers, another being the suppression of instruction in sign language—since a man who has never received methodical instruction in his own language can hardly be expected to write well in another language. But read Ballin and find out for yourself what sign language means to the deaf.

Yet the autobiographical centering of narrative on conflict between the deaf individual and the hearing society does not mean that the deaf writer is so preoccupied with the problems of the deaf in society as to forego the luxury of writing about the subtler and finer aspects of human perception and feeling. The Frenchman Eugene Relgis, a deaf friend and disciple of Romain Rolland, has written a more or less veiled autobiography (one chapter of which is included in this book) which sheds interesting light on what deafness means to a sensitive and intelligent young man who senses more keenly than most the attendant humiliations and psychical tortures and yet succeeds in refining his powers of observation and imagination to a rare degree.

But Relgis' hero, while not unique, is not really representative of the deaf majority. The deaf Steppenwolf, the lone deaf outsider, is rarely encountered in real life in the United States. In Europe and elsewhere, for historical reasons there exists a sharp cleavage between deaf intellectuals and artists and the deaf man in the street, so that there such outsiders account for a much larger proportion of the deaf population. Relgis illustrates the danger of the isolation of the deaf intellectual from the community: toward the end of his fictionalized autobiography he loses his contact with reality so much that he resorts to the notorious miracle-cure motif and is thus perhaps the only deaf writer to give credence to a fallacy that has been foisted upon the public by misinformed hearing authors: if he had only associated with the other deaf a little more, if he had only studied the anatomy of hearing, he would have known that no cure is possible for those with a sensorineural hearing loss, i.e., for a majority of the deaf.

The truth is that most deaf people do not lead lives of isolation. On the contrary, they love to associate with one another to such an extent that clannishness is a byword for them even more than for other minorities, but it is a clannishness informed by a special zest. It is this other, much more prevalent type of the deaf, the joiner, the hustler, the go-getter with his thirst for an active enjoyment of life, that is represented in *No Sound*, the autobiography of Julius Wiggins, which is not surprising when we consider that, unlike the other classes of the physically handicapped, unlike the lame, the halt, the blind and all the other varieties, the deaf are distinguished by a special vigor and robustness. *No Sound* is of additional interest in that it is an unusually authentic literary depiction of the everyday life of the deaf, of their particular concerns and pleasures. Read Wiggins and you will understand a little more how the deaf live and what they are really like. The other two sections, divided historically, contain stories that are fascinating in the way they show the feelings of hearing people toward deaf people. The fantastic variety of roles we find deaf characters playing in this book suggests that deafness inspires strong reactions in hearing people—sometimes they feel threatened (for at times many hearing people see themselves as deaf—that is, as what they imagine deaf people to be—lonely, isolated, "strange"); or sometimes they feel suspicious (it is, for some reason, hard for a hearing person to *really* believe that someone else can't hear); or they feel somehow that there's something "wrong" about deafness (in earlier days it was firmly believed that knowledge of God could come only through the ear).

At the end of the book is a bibliography compiled by Dr. Daniel Nascimento of the English Department at Gallaudet. Taken as a whole, then, with its selections, introductions, prefaces and bibliography, this volume is a nearly complete survey of all the important western literature relating to deafness in the last century and a half. I use the word "survey" advisedly: we have obviously had to be highly selective in our excerpts and even in the titles cited in the bibliography and in the various introductions and prefaces we have also had to ignore many titles we felt would not materially add to our awareness of the deaf experience.

• ONE •

THE NINETEENTH CENTURY

INTRODUCTION

Nineteenth century stories with deaf characters show a marked contrast in tone to those written in the twentieth century. The deaf characters themselves are of a different sort altogether: they are pitiable rather than extraordinary. They are good, better than their hearing counterparts. Because they are outside of society, they have not imbibed of the evil within society, so are superior to their hearing counterparts. In general, they represent moral qualities that most people could not aspire to. They are beautiful (Sophy in "Doctor Marigold" and Camille in "Pierre and Camille") or strong (Gerasim in *Mumu* and Gargan in "The Deaf Mute"), they are resourceful, loyal, generous, sincere, etc. In short, to arouse sympathy in nineteenth century readers it seems that writers felt their characters must seem to be victims of injustice, and that they must be good.

The four fictional stories in this section are marvelous stories, and we learn a great deal about attitudes toward deafness during the last century from reading them. First, though it is apparent that the old notion that deaf people were uneducable had passed, it is also apparent that the potential for education to bring deaf people into society was not yet grasped. The only real hope for deaf people, judging from these stories, was to have hearing children, or somehow to marry a hearing person. Society, being less fluid than it is today, was not inclined to tolerate differences of any sort, and certainly not differences as great as not being able to hear.

And these four authors are no exception to this general intolerance: in their very idealization of their deaf characters, de Musset, Dickens, Turgenev and de Maupassant reveal their own inability to tolerate differences. If one cannot accept the racial

3

or ethnic characteristics of a group, but feels that one must try, a solution is to change those characteristics into ideal attributes or to pretend they don't exist. Thus, in America, during the years of black integration, white liberals either would pretend that blacks were just like whites ("I don't care if a person is black or white, or yellow or blue!"), or that blacks were somehow superior ("they've got more soul, more feeling"). We find what is perhaps a similar pattern in the four stories in this section: the authors, unwilling to deal with deaf characters who represented real deaf people, created ideal deaf characters.

It is a reaction that deaf people even today are probably aware of. They meet hearing people who are bending over backwards to be "liberal" and understanding, and so they treat the deaf person as if he is saint-like: patient, dedicated, reconciled to fate but resolved to overcome it, and so on. The deaf person senses this and realizes that he is trapped: if he doesn't act like a saint, then the illusion is destroyed and the hearing person's idealization changes to contempt. The hearing person is saying, "I will accept you, in spite of your deafness, but only if you are an ideal person." The hearing person would be horrified to hear that deaf people not only are not the saints he thinks they are but often have to exploit pity, have to lie and cheat, have to feign ignorance and so on, all just to get by in a world stacked against them. Anyone who has the odds against him has to resort to any means to get by, be they dishonest, dirty, or saint-like. If you're in a fight with someone bigger and stronger than you, you don't feel guilty about a little dirty fighting.

So, it may be true that suppressed people, be they black, or Jewish, or deaf, have to resort to ways of getting by that we don't like to admit or think about. However, if one is going to write about a person who is deaf, and if one lives in the nineteenth century when heroes had to be heroic, one had better ignore the realities of the situation. Thus we have Camille and Sophy and Gerasim and Gargan, all extraordinarily patient and good people. But are they representative of most deaf people (or of *any* people, for that matter)? Probably not, yet we can grasp much of what it was like to be deaf in the nineteenth century, and, in the twentieth, as well, for that matter, by reading about them.

Pierre and Camille
by Alfred de Musset

EDITORS' PREFACE

"Pierre and Camille" is a nineteenth century story written by a Frenchman, de Musset, who obviously had great sympathy for the deaf people of his time. The story reflects a great deal of awareness of the difficulties a deaf child faces in growing up in a hearing world, especially if the child has hearing parents.

De Musset correctly locates Camille's greatest problem: the attitudes (and ignorance) of others, especially those of her parents, toward deafness. Camille's mother and father feel overwhelming guilt; the father assumes he has been cursed by God and cannot see Camille without seeing her as a living accusation; the mother feels guilty also, and tries to compensate for Camille's deafness by sacrificing her own life. How Camille is able to emerge from such an oppressive environment of guilt to become a happily married mother is a feat that tests our credibility as much as it gratifies our heart.

It is clear from the story that most people of the time assumed that deaf people could not be educated—there was the common assumption, which we are all familiar with, that deafness automatically meant muteness also, but, in addition, it is clear that people felt *any* kind of language or communication was impossible, that somehow the mind was deadened to systematic thinking by the condition of deafness. As de Musset says: "Unfortunately, at this time, when

5

so many prejudices were destroyed and replaced, there existed a most pitiless one against those poor creatures known as deaf-mutes."

By pointing out such ignorance, de Musset accomplishes a world of good with this story. He reveals not only an awareness of the facts of deafness, and of attitudes toward deafness, but, also, something of the existential aspect of deafness for the deaf person: the sense of isolation, of frustration at seeing so much going on that the deaf person is necessarily excluded from. Camille feels this isolation so strongly at one point that she decides to wear the mourning clothes she had put on after her mother's death for the rest of her life, signaling her own spiritual death.

De Musset captures another aspect of the deaf experience that is subtle, elusive, but which may lie at the heart of the attitude of society toward deaf people. Because the handicap is invisible, there is a certain unbelievability about it: there is often a vague suspicion that the deaf person is just putting on, or if he is not, there is still the sense of it somehow being wrong, because the person is apparently normal, yet does not respond or act like other people. (Ernest Tidyman's *Dummy*, of recent vintage, contains statements by police officers wherein they refuse to believe that Donald Lang is deaf even though the evidence is absolutely conclusive. See especially pages 217-218.) Camille, as a baby, was perfect, it seemed, and beautiful; her mother thanked God (before learning of Camille's deafness) for sending her such a perfect baby. When the parents learn of her deafness, there is a horror for them in such knowledge, and neither can accept it, the father eventually running away, the mother committing suicide. There is something wrong, something unjust or cruel in the ironic combination of beauty and grace and the fact of deafness: for the father such a combination was so horrible that it "almost turned his brain."

We find in this story one of the earliest fictional accounts of the facts of the deaf experience and also an example of a theme running all through nineteenth century western literature: to be isolated from society is also to be free of its corruption. It is apparently because of this theme and the convenience of using a deaf character for it that much of the early literature about deafness exists, the deaf character being the one, of course, who is isolated and therefore superior. Camille is no exception. "Her reflective and melancholy air gave to her every movement, to her childish ways and poses, a certain aspect of grandeur; a painter or a sculptor would have been inspired by it." At another point: "Coquetry shows itself at an early age in women. Camille gave no indications of it." Or at another: "If her heart is in the right place, people will know it without it being necessary for her to put honey on the end of her tongue." (The implication is that Camille's natural goodness—her heart— is not spoiled by the hypocrisy of society, symbolized by the honey on the tongue.)

In these selections, we see a romantic assumption that the more "natural," less socialized a person is, the better and more virtuous that person is. We find similar characterizations in other stories in this anthology: Sophy in "Doctor Marigold" and Gerasim in *Mumu*. In the twentieth century, literature of isolation also uses deaf characters, but in this century such characters are conceived of as more typical than peculiar: i.e., twentieth century man, alienated and isolated in a non-human world, is the archetypal deaf man.

"Pierre and Camille" offers a lot to the person interested in the deaf experience, but even de Musset could fall into a typical hearing error. Toward the end of the story, as Camille sees the yet unrecognized form of her lover approach her window at night, she is frightened, but immediately she is supposed to be comforted because, after all, her uncle is in the next room, as Camille should know because his presence is "revealed by his *noisy* slumber." Some comfort to a deaf person!

Which only shows that de Musset was not perfect in this early attempt to deal imaginatively with the deaf experience. All in all, the story is a classic in the literature of the deaf experience, and it is only appropriate that we begin the anthology with it.

PIERRE AND CAMILLE

• I •

The Chevalier des Arcis, an officer in the cavalry, had left the service in 1760. Although still young, and with means amply sufficient to allow him to appear to advantage at the Court, he had tired of bachelor's life and the pleasures of Paris. He retired to a pretty country house near Le Mans. Here, after a time, solitude, which had at first pleased him, became distasteful. He found that it was a difficult task to suddenly change from the habits of his youth. He did not repent having left the world of gaiety, but, not being able to endure living alone, he determined to marry and find, if possible, a woman with tastes similar to his own, and fond of the quiet and sedentary life that he had decided to live.

He did not wish his wife to be beautiful, nor did he want her ugly. He desired the woman he chose to be educated, intelligent, and not frivolous. What he wished for, above all, was cheerfulness and a good disposition, which he regarded as being the first qualities a woman should possess.

The daughter of a retired merchant, who lived in the vicinity, pleased him. As the chevalier was not dependent upon any one, he did not worry about the social gap existing between a gentleman and a merchant's daughter. He asked the father for his daughter's hand, and the request was immediately acceded to. He courted her for a few months, and then they were married.

Never was a marriage celebrated under brighter or happier auspices. As he understood his wife better, the chevalier perceived in her new qualities and a uniform sweetness of disposition. She fell deeply in love with her husband. She lived but for him, thought only of pleasing him, and not regretting the pleasures that she had sacrificed at her age, she hoped that her whole existence might pass in this solitude, which daily became more precious to her.

The solitude, however, was not absolute. Occasional visits to the town and the regular calls of a select circle of friends, from time to time, diverted them. The chevalier was pleased to frequently see his wife's parents, so that it almost seemed to her as if she was still under the paternal roof. She often ran from her husband's arms to those of her mother, and in this way enjoyed a favor that Providence accords to a few, for it is rare that a new pleasure does not destroy an old one.

Monsieur des Arcis was no less gentle and kind than his wife; but the passions of his youth and the experience he seemed to have had with the affairs of this world, at times rendered him melancholy. Cecile, as Madame des Arcis was called, religiously respected these moments of sadness. Although on this subject she neither reflected nor thought deeply, her heart readily taught her not to complain of those light clouds that destroy all happiness as soon as they are noticed, and which amount to nothing if allowed to pass.

Cecile's family was composed of substantial people, merchants enriched by hard work, and whose old age was, so to speak, one long Sunday. The chevalier liked this contentment and ease, bought by labor, and willingly joined in it. Tired of the customs of Versailles, and even of Mademoiselle Quinault's suppers, he was pleased with these manners, somewhat noisy, yet fresh and new to him. Cecile had an uncle, named Giraud, who was an excellent man and a very agreeable guest. He had been a master mason, and latterly became an architect. During this time he had amassed a fortune which yielded an income of twenty thousand francs. The chevalier's house was very much to his taste, and he was well received there, although he sometimes appeared covered with plaster and dust. For, in spite of his age and his twenty thousand francs, he could not resist climbing on the roofs and handling the trowel. After partaking of one or two glasses of champagne at dessert, he would often say to the chevalier, "You are happy, my nephew, you have a good little wife and a comfortable house. You lack nothing, and there is nothing to be said; so much the worse for the neighbor who may grumble. I repeat that you are happy."

One day Cecile, hearing these words, and bending toward her husband, said to him: "Must it not be somewhat true, since you do not contradict him?"

Madame des Arcis, after a time, realized that she was pregnant. In the rear of the house there was a small hill from the top of which the whole country could be seen. The couple often strolled there together. One day, when they were seated on the grass, Cecile remarked: "You did not dispute my uncle the other day. Do you think, however, that he was altogether right? Are you perfectly happy?"

"As happy as man can be," answered the chevalier, "and I see nothing that can add to my happiness."

"Then I am more ambitious than you," answered Cecile, "for I could easily mention something that is missing here, and which is really necessary to us."

The chevalier thought it was a question of some trifle, and that she wished to make a detour in order to confide some woman's whim.

Jokingly he made a thousand guesses, and at each question Cecile's laughter redoubled. While still jesting together, they had risen and were descending the hill. M. des Arcis quickened his steps and, tempted by the rapid slope, urged his wife on, when the latter stopped, and leaning on the chevalier's shoulder, said: "Take care, my friend, do not make me walk so quickly. You sought a long way for an answer to the question I asked you; we have it here beneath my petticoat."

From this day it was almost their sole topic of conversation; they spoke of their child, of the care they would bestow on it, of the way in which they would rear it, and of the plans they were already making for its future. The chevalier wished his wife to take every precaution to preserve the treasure she carried. He increased his attentions and his love for her, and the whole time before the birth of Cecile's child was, for her, but a long and delicious intoxication, full of the tenderest hopes.

The time fixed by nature at length arrived; a child, as beautiful as day, came into the world. It was a girl, whom they named Camille. In spite of the general custom and even against the doctor's advice, Cecile wished to nurse the little one herself. Her motherly pride was so flattered by the beauty of her daughter, that it was impossible to separate them. It is true that rarely in a newborn babe had such regular and such remarkable features been seen; its eyes, especially, when they opened to the light, shone with wonderful luster. Cecile, who had been raised in a convent, was extremely pious. Her first thought, as soon as she was able to be dressed, was to go to church to render thanks to God.

The child soon began to get strong and develop. As she grew, they were astonished to find her unusually quiet. No noise seemed to disturb her; she was insensible to those thousand tender words that a mother addresses to her child; while she was being rocked and sung to, she would remain with fixed and open eyes, intently watching the light of the lamp, and seeming to hear nothing. One day, while asleep, a servant overturned a chair; her mother rushed up at once and noticed, with astonishment, that the child had not awakened. The chevalier became frightened at these indications, all too clear to be mistaken. As soon as he had carefully observed them, he understood to what misfortune his daughter was condemned. The mother wished in vain not to believe it, and by all imaginable means to turn away at her husband's fears. The physician was sent for, and his diagnosis was short and not difficult. They understood that poor Camille was deprived of the sense of hearing and speech.

• II •

The mother's first thought was to inquire if the misfortune was incurable, and the reply was that there had been a few cases which had been cured. For a year, in spite of the evidence before her, she continued to hope; but after having exhausted all the resources of science, they at length were compelled to abandon all hope.

Unfortunately, at this time, when so many prejudices were destroyed and replaced, there existed a most pitiless one against those poor creatures known as deaf-mutes. Noble spirits, eminent scientists, or men guided solely by a feeling of charity, had, it is true, protested this barbarity for some time. Strange to say, it was a Spanish monk who, during the sixteenth century, was the first to think of and attempt the task, then thought impossible, of teaching deaf-mutes to communicate thought without words. His example had been followed in Italy, England, and France at various times. Bonnet, Wallis, Bulwar and Van Helmont had brought forth important works, but they did not fully realize their good intentions. Some good had been accomplished here and there, unknown to the world, almost accidentally, and without any resultant benefit. Everywhere, even in Paris, in the most advanced civilization, deaf-mutes were looked upon as a kind of being separate from the rest of humanity, stamped with the seal of the wrath of Providence. Deprived of speech, they were given no credit for possessing the power of thought. The cloister for those who were born rich, abandonment for the poor; such was their lot. They inspired more horror than pity.

The chevalier gradually sank into the most profound melancholy. He spent the greater part of the day alone, shut up in his study or walking in the woods. When he saw his wife, he forced himself to appear tranquil and at rest, and attempted to console her, but without avail. Madame des Arcis was no less sad. A deserved misfortune may cause the tears to flow, usually too late and of no use; but a misfortune without reason benumbs the senses and discourages piety.

These two newly married people, made to love each other, in this way, commenced to see each other with pain and to avoid meeting in those same walks where they had so recently discussed a hope, so near, so peaceful, and so pure. The chevalier, involuntarily exiling himself to his house in the country, had thought only of rest; happiness had seemed to surprise him there. Madame des Arcis had only made a prudent marriage; love had come and was reciprocated. Suddenly a terrible obstacle came between them, and this obstacle was precisely the very thing that should have been their sacred bond.

What caused this sudden and tacit separation, more terrible than a divorce, more cruel than a slow death, was that the mother, in spite of the misfortune, loved her child passionately, while the chevalier, whatever he may have wished to do, in spite of his patience and goodness, could not conquer the horror that was inspired in him by this malediction of God that had fallen upon him.

"Can I, then, hate my child?" he often asked himself during his solitary walks. "Is it her fault if the wrath of Heaven has fallen upon her? Should I not only pity her, try to lighten my wife's sorrow, hide my suffering, and watch over my child? To what a sad existence she is doomed if I, her father, abandon her! What will become of her? God sent her to me thus; it is for me to be resigned. Who would look after her? Who would bring her up? Who would protect her? She has only her mother and me in the world; she will never find a husband and will never have a brother nor a sister. One unfortunate child in the world is sufficient. Unless I am utterly heartless, I should dedicate my life to helping her to endure."

Such were the chevalier's thoughts as he returned to the house with the firm intention of fulfilling his obligations as a father and husband. He found his child in his wife's arms, knelt before her, and held Cecile's hands in his own. He had been told, he said, of a famous doctor, for whom he was going to send; nothing was yet determined; marvelous cures had been effected. In speaking thus, he took his daughter in his arms and walked around the room with her. But horrible thoughts seized him, in spite of himself; the idea of the future, the sight of this silence, of the incomplete being, whose senses were dormant, the reprobation, the mortification, the pity, the contempt of the world, overwhelmed him. His face paled, his hands trembled. He returned the child to the mother, and turned aside to hide his tears.

It was at these moments that Madame des Arcis pressed her daughter to her heart with a sort of desperate tenderness, and that full look of maternal love, the most violent and the proudest of all. Never did she complain; she retired to her room, placed Camille in the cradle, and spent whole hours, mute like the child, in gazing at her.

This kind of passionate and somber exaltation became so strong that it was not rare to see Madame des Arcis preserve the most absolute silence for days at a time. In vain was she spoken to. It seemed as if she wanted to discover for herself what this darkness of the mind was in which her daughter was to live.

She spoke by signs to the child, and she alone knew how to make her understand. The rest of the household, even the chevalier himself, were as strangers to Camille. The mother of Madame des Arcis, a woman with a vulgar mind, rarely came to Chardonneaux, which was the name of the chevalier's estate, unless to deplore the misfortune that had fallen on her son-in-law and her dear Cecile. Thinking to show proof of her sympathy, she ceaselessly pitied the sad condition of this poor child, and one day she remarked: "It would have been better for her not to have been born."

"What would you have done if I had been like she is?" answered Cecile, almost angrily.

Uncle Giraud, the master mason, did not think it such a misfortune that his niece was mute.

"I have had such a loquacious wife," he would say, "that I look upon anything in this world, whatever it may be, as preferable. This little girl is certain not to indulge in idle talk, nor listen to it, sure not to annoy a whole household by singing old opera airs, which are all alike; she will not be quarrelsome, she will not abuse the servants, as my wife always did; she will not awaken if her husband coughs, or if he arises before her in the morning to attend to his business. She will not dream aloud, but will be able to settle an account, even if she only counts on her fingers,

15

and to pay, if she has the money, but without disputing, as do the merchants, over the least trifles. She will naturally know a very good thing, one which is ordinarily learned only with difficulty, and that is, that it is better to act than to talk. If her heart is in the right place, people will know it without it being necessary for her to put honey on the end of her tongue. She will not laugh in company, it is true; but, at dinner, she will not hear the foolish words spoken now and then. She will be pretty, intelligent and quiet; she will not be obliged, like the blind, to have a poodle to lead her. My faith! if I was young, I would marry her myself, when she grows up; and today, now that I am old and childless, I will gladly take her as a daughter, if, by chance, she annoys you."

When Uncle Giraud spoke thus a little cheerfulness reappeared, for the time being, between Monsieur des Arcis and his wife. They could neither of them help laughing at this good natured man, somewhat blunt as he was, but respectable, and above all, kind-hearted, and not wishing to see trouble anywhere. But the trouble was there; all the others of the family looked, with frightened and curious eyes, upon this misfortune, which was rarity. When they drove up in a coach from the ford of Mauny, these good people sat in a circle before dinner, trying to comprehend and to reason, examining everything with an air of interest, with composed faces, consulting each other in whispers as to what they should say, essaying now and then to turn away their common thought by a loud remark about a mere nothing. The mother remained before them, with her daughter on her lap, her breast uncovered, from which a few drops of milk still flowed. If Raphael had been of the family, the Madonna of the Chair might have had a sister; Madame des Arcis, quite unconsciously, was far from not beautiful.

• III •

The little daughter was growing rapidly; nature fulfilled her task in a melancholy manner, but faithfully. Camille had only her eyes at the service of her soul; her first gestures were directed toward the light, as had been her first glances. The faintest ray of sunlight caused her transports of joy.

When she commenced to stand up and walk a very marked curiosity made her examine and touch everything surrounding her, with a delicacy combining fear and pleasure, and mingling the vivacity of a child with the modesty of a woman. Her first action was to run toward anything new, as if to seize and take possession of it; but she usually turned around, when half-way, to look at her mother, as if to consult her. She then resembled the ermine, which, it is said, stops and turns back, if it sees that a little dirt or gravel may soil its fur.

A few of the neighbors' children came and played with Camille in the garden. It was strange to see her watching them talk. These children, of about the same age as herself, naturally attempted to repeat the words spoken by their nurses, and tried, by moving their lips, to exercise their intelligence by means of a noise which, to the poor girl, was only a motion. Often, to show that she understood, she would stretch out her hands to her little friends, who would draw back afraid of this different expression of their own thoughts.

Madame des Arcis did not leave her daughter. She observed, with anxiety, the small actions, the least sign of development in Camille. If she had been able to guess that the Abbe de l'Epee would soon come and bring light into this world of darkness, how great would have been her joy! But she could do nothing, and remained powerless before this evil of chance, which the courage and piety of a man was about to destroy. It is strange that a priest sees more than a mother, and that the mind that discerns should discover that which the suffering heart lacks.

When Camille's little friends were of an age to receive their first instruction from a governess, the poor child began to show a great sadness at not being given the same attention as the others. One of the neighbors had an old English governess who had great trouble in teaching a little girl to spell, and treated her severely. Camille was present during the lesson and watched her little companion with surprise, following her efforts with her eyes, and attempting, so to speak, to help her; she also cried with her when she was scolded.

Music lessons were, for her, the subject of still greater pain. Standing near the piano, she stiffened and moved her little fingers while watching the teacher with her eyes, which were black and very beautiful. She seemed to inquire what was going on, and sometimes struck the keys in a gentle yet irritated manner.

The impression that people or exterior objects produced on the other children did not seem to surprise her. She noticed things and, like the others, remembered them. But when she saw them pointing at these same things with their fingers, and observed that movement of the lips which was unintelligible to her, then her sorrow returned. She retired to a corner, and, with a stone or piece of wood, she almost mechanically traced in the sand a few capital letters which she had seen others form and which she attentively studied.

The evening prayer, which the neighbor had her children repeat every day, was to Camille like an enigma which almost resembled a mystery. She kneeled with her companions and joined her hands without understanding the reason. The chevalier saw in this a profanation: "Spare me that mockery."

"I take it upon myself to ask God's pardon," answered the mother one day. Camille early showed indications of possessing that strange faculty which the Scotch call second sight, that the followers of magnetism wish to have acknowledged, and which the doctors generally classify with the diseases. The little deaf-mute felt the approach of the ones she loved, and often went to meet them, without anything having forewarned her of their arrival.

Not only did the other children approach her with a sort of fear, but they sometimes shunned her with an air of scorn. It happened that one of them, with that lack of pity of which La Fontaine speaks, came and spoke to her for some time, looking in her face and laughing, asking her to reply. When these groups of little children danced, which they will do as long as they can on their little legs, Camille only watched them; already a half-grown girl, when the old refrain was sung:

"Enter in the dance
See how we dance. . ."

Alone and apart, leaning against a seat, she stood and followed the measure, balancing her pretty head, without attempting to mix with the company, but sad and gentle enough to inspire pity.

One of the hardest tasks this unfortunate soul attempted was to try to count with a little neighbor who was learning arithmetic. It was a very easy and short sum. Her companion was struggling with several numbers, somewhat mixed. The total did not amount to more than twelve or fifteen units. The neighbor counted on her fingers. Camille, understanding that it was wrong, and wishing to help, extended her two open hands. They had given to her the first and most simple ideas; she knew that two and two make four. An intelligent animal, even a bird, can count in one way or another, of which we are ignorant, up to two or three. A magpie, they say, has even counted five. Camille, under the circumstances, should have been able to count still more. Her hands only went as far as ten. She held them open before her little companion with such a good-natured look that one might have thought her an honest man unable to pay his debts.

Coquetry shows itself at an early age in women. Camille gave no indications of it.

"It is, however, strange," said the chevalier, "that a little girl does not understand what a hat is!" At these words Madame des Arcis sadly smiled.

"But she is beautiful!" said she to her husband; and, at the same time, she gently touched Camille, to have her walk in front of her father so that he could see her figure, which had begun to develop, and notice her childlike step which was still so charming.

As she advanced in age, Camille became passionately fond, not of religion, which she did not comprehend, but of churches, which she could see. Perhaps she had, in her soul, that invincible instinct which causes a child of ten to conceive and retain the project of putting on a woolen dress, to look for those who are poor and suffering, and to spend an entire life in this way. Many ordinary persons and even philosophers will pass away before one of them can explain such a mystery, but it, nevertheless, exists.

"When I was a child, I did not see God, I only saw the heavens," is certainly a sublime idea, written, as you know, by a deaf-mute. Camille was far from having so much power of thought. A rough plaster image of the Virgin, colored with white lead and blue paint, somewhat like a shop sign; a choir boy of the provinces, whose old surplice covers his cassock, and whose faint and silvery voice causes the window-panes to mournfully reverberate, without Camille being able to hear anything; the beadle's walk; the verger's airs— all attracted her attention; but who knows what makes a child raise its eyes? But what does it matter as long as the eyes are raised?

• IV •

"But she is beautiful!" the chevalier repeated to himself, and, in fact, Camille was beautiful. In the perfect oval of a regular face, upon features of an admirable purity and freshness, there shone so to speak, the light of a good heart. Camille was small, not at all pale, but very fair, and with long black hair. She was naturally of a gay and active dis- position; rarely sad, and almost indifferent to the misfortune with which she was afflicted; in her little pantomime, she was full of grace, spirit and energy in all her movements; she was singularly skillful in making herself understood; quick to grasp the meaning of anything; and always obedient when she comprehended. The chevalier, sometimes, like Madame des Arcis, remained watching his daughter, with- out speaking. Such grace and beauty, joined to so much misfortune and horror, almost turned his brain. He was often seen embracing Camille fondly, saying aloud: "I am not such a bad man!"

There was a path in the woods, in the rear of the garden, where the chevalier was accustomed to stroll after break- fast. From the window of her room, Madame des Arcis saw her husband coming and going between the trees. She hardly dared to join him. With a sorrow full of bitterness she watched this man, who had been to her more of a lover than a husband, who had never said a harsh word to her, to whom she had never spoken unkindly, and who no longer had the courage to love her because she was a mother.

She risked it, however, one morning. She came down in her dressing-gown, beautiful as an angel, her heart throbbing; she was excited about a children's party to be given at the house of a neighbor. Madame des Arcis wished to have Camille attend. She desired to see the effect that her daughter's beauty would produce upon her husband and the world. She had spent sleepless nights thinking of how she would dress her; she cherished the fondest hopes on this subject. "He shall be proud of her, and the others must be jealous of that poor little girl, once for all," she would say to herself. "She will say nothing, but she will be the most beautiful."

As soon as the chevalier noticed his wife coming toward him, he went to meet her, and took her by the hand, which he respectfully kissed with a gallantry which he had acquired at Versailles and which he had never forgotten, in spite of his natural good humor. They began by exchanging a few insignificant words, and then walked on together.

Madame des Arcis was wondering how best to broach to her husband the subject of taking her daughter to the party, and in this way to break a rule he had made, since Camille's birth, of no longer appearing in society. Even the thought of exposing his misfortune to the eyes of those who were indifferent or malicious, caused the chevalier to be beside himself. He had formally announced his intention on the subject. It was therefore necessary for Madame des Arcis to find an expedient, some pretext, not only for executing her design, but for suggesting it.

Meanwhile, the chevalier appeared to be thinking deeply. He was the first to break the silence. An unexpected business affair, which had just happened to one of his relatives, had greatly embarrassed the fortune of his family. It was important that he should interview those who were placed in charge of the matter. His interests, and consequently those of Madame des Arcis were in danger of being compromised through the lack of careful surveillance. Briefly, he announced that it was necessary for him to make a short trip to Holland, where he was to have an understanding with his banker. He added that the business was extremely urgent, and that he expected to leave the next morning.

It was only too easy for Madame des Arcis to comprehend the reason of this journey. The chevalier was far from entertaining the thought of deserting his wife; but, in spite of himself, he felt an irresistible desire to completely isolate himself for a time, if only to become more resigned. All real sorrow usually produces in man this need of solitude, just as physical pain does in the case of animals.

Madame des Arcis was at first so surprised that she could only answer with those commonplace remarks that one always has on the tip of one's tongue when one cannot express one's thoughts. She found this journey quite natural; the chevalier was right, she understood the importance of this matter, and did not oppose it. While she spoke, her heart was full of sorrow; she said she felt tired, and sat upon a bench.

She remained there absorbed in a profound reverie, her eyes fixed, and her arms hanging by her side. Up to that time, Madame de Arcis had experienced neither great happiness nor great pleasure. Although not a woman of marked intelligence, she was sensitive, and came from a family of tradespeople and knew what it was to suffer, somewhat from the imaginary tinge of commercialism. Her marriage had been quite an unexpected happiness, entirely a new felling; a light had flashed before her eyes in the midst of long, dreary days, and now darkness was again coming upon her.

She remained thoughtful for some time. The chevalier turned away his eyes, and seemed anxious to return to the house. He arose and then sat down again. At length Madame des Arcis arose and took her husband's arm; they returned together.

When the hour for dinner arrived, Madame des Arcis sent word that she was not well and would not be present. In her room was a prayer desk before which she remained on her knees until night. Her maid entered several times, having received secret orders from the chevalier to watch over her; she did not answer when addressed. Toward eight o'clock she summoned the maid, asked her for her daughter's dress, which was ordered for the party, and requested the carriage to be ready. At the same time, she sent a message to the chevalier that she was going to the party, and that she hoped he would accompany her.

Camille had the figure of a child, but most graceful and slight. Upon this lovely form, the outline of which was beginning to develop, the mother placed a simple new dress, and an embroidered robe of white muslin, little shoes of white satin, a necklace of American beads around her neck, and a wreath of corn-flowers around her neck; such was the attire of Camille, who proudly admired herself before the mirror and danced with joy. The mother, dressed in a long velvet gown, as one who did not expect to dance, held her child before the full-length mirror, kissed her again and again, and repeated all the time: "You are beautiful, you are beautiful!" When the chevalier entered, Madame des Arcis, without any apparent emotion, asked the servant if the carriage was waiting, and inquired of her husband if he was going. The chevalier gave his hand to his wife and they went to the party.

It was the first time Camille had been seen in public. She had, however, been often spoken of. Curiosity attracted all eyes toward the little girl as soon as she appeared. It was expected that Madame des Arcis would be somewhat embarrassed and anxious, but such was not the case. After the customary greetings, she sat down in the calmest manner, and while every one watched her child with a sort of astonishment or an air of affected interest, she allowed her to wander about the room without appearing to notice her.

Camille found her little friends there; she ran first to one, then to another, just as she had done in the garden. However they all received her with reserve and apparent coolness. The chevalier, standing at one side, suffered visibly. His friends came and praised his daughter's beauty; acquaintances and even strangers, approached him for the purpose of complimenting him. He felt that they were consoling him, and it was hardly to his taste.

However, a look which he could not mistake, the assurance of every one, gradually brought joy back to his heart. After having greeted nearly every one by gestures, Camille remained standing by her mother's knees. They had noticed her going from side to side; they expected something strange, or at least curious; she had done nothing only bow a pleasant "good evening," had shaken hands with some English girls, and had thrown kisses to the mothers of her little friends, all, perhaps, learned by heart, but gracefully and naively done. Having quietly returned to her place, everyone began to admire her. In fact, nothing was more beautiful than this living form, closed against the outside world, and from which her poor soul was unable to escape. Her figure, her face, her long curly hair, her eyes especially imcomparably brilliant, surprised everyone. At the same time that her eyes tempted to divine everything, and her gestures to express all, her reflective and melancholy air gave to her every movement, to her childish ways and poses, a certain aspect of grandeur; a painter or a sculptor would have been inspired by it. They approached Madame des Arcis, surrounded her, asked many questions of Camille by gestures; instead of astonishment and repugnance, there was a sincere good-will, a frank sympathy. Exaggeration, which always exists as soon as one neighbor repeats anything to another, soon disappeared. Never had such a charming child been seen; nothing approached her; no one was as beautiful as she. In fact, Camille had a complete triumph, which she was far from understanding.

Madame des Arcis comprehended it. Always outwardly calm, her heart throbbed and throbbed that night with the happiest and purest emotions of her life. Her husband and she had exchanged smiles, which compensated for the many tears she had shed.

Meanwhile, a young girl sat down at the piano and played some music. The children joined hands, took their places and began to execute the steps that the dancing-master had taught them. The parents began to compliment each other, to pass favorable remarks on the fete, and to speak of the gracefulness of their children. It was soon only a loud noise of childish laughter, jokes between the young men, talk about dress among the young girls, chatting among the fathers, sarcastic politeness among the mothers and, in short, a regular provincial children's party.

The chevalier's eyes never left his daughter, who, as one may imagine, did not join in the dance. Camille watched the fete with a rather sad expression. A little boy came and invited her to dance. In answer she shook her head; a few corn-flowers fell from her wreath, which was not very firm. Madame des Arcis picked them up, and, with pins, soon repaired the damage to the coiffure which she had made; but she looked in vain for her husband; he was no longer in the room. She asked if he had left, and if he had taken the carriage. They answered that he had walked home.

The chevalier had decided to depart without saying good-bye to his wife. He feared and avoided any annoying explanations; and, as it was his purpose to return very shortly, he thought it was wiser to simply leave a letter behind him. It was not altogether true that business required his presence in Holland; however, the journey might be beneficial. One of his friends wrote a letter to Chardonneaux urging his departure; it was a prearranged pretext. Upon returning, he acted as a man obliged, unexpectedly, to go away. He ordered his trunks to be packed in great haste, sent them to the town, mounted his horse, and departed.

However, an involuntary hesitation and a great regret took possession of him when he had left the house. He feared he had, too quickly, obeyed a sentiment that he might have conquered, and that he might cause his wife unnecessary tears, and moreover, that he might fail to find that contentment which, perhaps, really existed at home, if he only understood. "But who knows," he thought, "if I am not, on the contrary, doing a proper and sensible thing? Who knows if the passing sorrow my absence may cause will not give us happier days? I am overwhelmed by a misfortune, of which God alone knows the cause; I am withdrawing, for a few days, from the place where I suffer. The change, the journey, even the fatigue, will perhaps calm my emotions; I am going to occupy my time with things material, important, necessary; I shall return with a more tranquil and contented mind; I shall have reflected and shall know better what I must do. However, Cecile will suffer," he thought. But his mind was fixed, and he continued on his way.

Madame des Arcis left the party at about eleven o'clock. She had entered the carriage with her daughter, who soon fell fast asleep upon her lap. Although she was ignorant of the fact that the chevalier had so promptly executed his project of traveling, she suffered, nevertheless, at having left her neighbor's house alone. That which in the eyes of the world, is only an absence of regard, becomes an actual suffering to whoever expects the cause. The chevalier had been unable to endure the public spectacle of his misfortune. The mother had desired to show it, and thus attempt to conquer it.

She could easily have forgiven her husband a moment of sadness or bad humor; but one must remember that, in the provinces, such a manner of leaving one's wife and child is an almost unheard of thing; and, in such cases, the merest trifle, a cloak, for instance, which one may be looking for, when he who should find it is not present, has sometimes done more harm than all the good that the respect for conventionality should do.

While the carriage rolled slowly over the stones of a newly made road, Madame des Arcis, watching over her sleeping daughter, yielded to the saddest forebodings. Holding Camille in such a way that the jolting would not awaken her, she mused with that fervor that night gives to the thoughts, of the fatality that seemed to pursue her, even in the most natural joy she had just experienced at the party. A strange turn of mind made her think now of her own past and of her daughter's future. "What will happen?" she said to herself. "My husband leaves me; if he does not leave today, he will tomorrow; all my efforts, all my prayers, will only annoy him; his love for me is dead; his pity remains, but his sorrow is stronger than he or myself. My daughter is beautiful, but doomed to misfortune. What shall I do? What can I forecast or prevent? If I consecrate myself to this poor child, as I should, and as I am doing, I must renounce my husband. He flees from us, and looks upon us with horror. If I attempt on the contrary, to draw nearer to him, if I dare to recall his old love, will he not ask me to separate from my daughter? May he not wish to confide Camille to the care of strangers, and thus rid himself of a sight which troubles him?"

While meditating thus, Madame des Arcis kissed Camille.

"Poor child!" said she; "I abandon you! I, to buy the semblance of happiness which would, in turn, escape me, at the cost of your repose, perhaps, of your life! To cease to be a mother, in order to be a wife! If such a thing was possible, would it not be better to die rather than have to do so?"

Then she returned to her conjectures. "What is about to happen?" she asked herself again. "What will Providence ordain? God watches over all, and sees us as well as others. What will He do with us? What will become of this poor child?"

Some distance from Chardonneaux there was a ford to be crossed. For about a month there had been heavy rains, so much so that the river had overflowed and covered the surrounding meadows. The ferryman, at first, refused to allow the carriage on his ferry-boat, and said that they must unharness the team and that he would cross the stream with the people and the horses, but not with the carriage. Madame des Arcis, anxious to see her husband again, refused to get out. She ordered the coachman to drive onto the boat; it took but a few minutes to cross, and she had done so a hundred times.

In the middle of the ford the boat began to drift, carried by the current. The ferryman asked the coachman to help him or they would be driven over the dam. There was in fact, two or three hundred feet down-stream, a mill with a dam made of timbers, piles and boards fastened together, but now old and broken by the water. It was certain that if they allowed themselves to drift there would be an awful accident.

The coachman alighted from his box; he wished to lend a helping hand, but there was only one pole in the ferry-boat. The ferryman did all he could, but the night was dark. A mist blinded the two men, who relieved each other, now they used their combined strength in their effort to reach the shore.

As the roar of the water grew louder, the danger became terrifying. The boat, heavily laden, and driven against the current by two vigorous men, did not move very rapidly. When the pole was deeply imbedded and tightly held in front, the ferry-boat swayed from side to side, or turned around; but the current was too strong. Madame des Arcis, who remained in the carriage with the child, and was in great terror, opened the window.

"Are we lost?" she cried. At this moment the pole broke. The two men fell in the boat exhausted, their hands bruised.

The ferryman could swim, but the coachman could not. There was no time to be lost.

"Father Georgeot," said Madame des Arcis to the ferryman, "can you save us—my daughter and me?"

Father Georgeot looked at the water, then at the shore.

"Certainly," he answered, shrugging his shoulders with an almost offended look at such a question being addressed to him.

"What must we do?" said Madame des Arcis.

"Rest your weight on my shoulders," answered the ferryman. "Keep your dress on, it will support you. Place both your arms around my neck, have no fear, but do not cling too tightly or we shall be drowned. Do not cry out, you will only swallow water if you do. As for the little one, I will hold her with one hand, by the waist, above the water to prevent her being wet; with the other, I will swim on my side. The potatoes, in the field yonder, are hardly the distance of twenty-five strokes from here."

"And Jean?" said Madame des Arcis, referring to the coachman.

"Jean will swallow a little water, but will survive. Let him drift to the dam and wait. I will return for him."

Father Georgeot plunged into the water with his double burden, but he had misjudged his strength. He was no longer a young man; far from it. The shore was farther than he had calculated, and the current stronger than he had thought. However, he did his best to reach land, but was soon carried away. The trunk of a willow tree, covered by the water, which he had not observed in the darkness, suddenly stopped him. He had violently struck his forehead against it. The blood flowed and obscured his sight.

"Take your daughter and put her upon your neck or mine," he said. "I can do no more."

"Could you save her if you carried her alone?" asked the mother.

"I do not know, but I think I could," answered the ferryman.

Madame des Arcis did not answer, but unclasped her arms from around the man's neck, and sank into the water.

When the ferryman had placed little Camille safely on the shore, the coachman, who had been rescued by a peasant, assisted in the search for the body of Madame des Arcis. They found the corpse the following morning, near the bank.

• VI •

A year after this catastrophe, in a well-furnished room of a hotel, situated in the Rue du Bouloi, in Paris, the coaching district, a young girl in mourning was seated near a table, close to the fire. On the table was a bottle of ordinary wine, half empty, and a glass. A man, bent by age, but of an open and frank countenance clothed almost like a working man, was walking up and down the room. Occasionally he approached the young girl, stopped before her and looked at her with an air almost paternal. She then extended her arm, quickly raised the bottle, but with a sort of involuntary repugnance, and refilled the glass. The old man drank a little, then resumed walking, gesticulating all the time in a singular and almost ridiculous manner, while the young girl, sadly smiling, attentively followed his movements.

It would have been difficult for an observer to have guessed the relationship between these two people: the one motionless, cold as marble, but full of grace and distinction, expression on her face and in her every gesture something more than ordinary beauty; the other quite vulgar in appearance, his clothing in disorder, his hat on his head, drinking the common wine of an inn, and the nails of his shoes resounding on the floor. It was a strange contrast.

These two people were, nevertheless, united by a very true and tender affection. They were Camille and Uncle Giraud. This kind old man had come to Chardonneaux to the funeral of Madame des Arcis, when she had first been carried to the church, and then to her last resting-place. Her mother being dead, her father gone, the poor child found herself entirely alone in the world. The chevalier, on having left the house, distracted by his journey, called away by business, and obliged to visit several towns in Holland, had only heard very lately of his wife's death; almost a month had passed, during which time Camille remained, so to speak, an orphan. It is true, there was in the house a kind of governess, who had the care of the young girl; but the mother, when alive, would not permit any one else to have charge of her daughter. This position was a sinecure; the governess hardly knew Camille, and could be of no assistance whatever to her under the circumstances.

The young girl's sorrow, at the time of her mother's death, had been so violent that for a long time her life was despaired of. When the body of Madame des Arcis had been taken from the water and carried into the house, Camille accompanied this funeral procession uttering such heartrending cries of distress that the neighbors were almost afraid of her. There was, in fact, something terrifying in this being whom they were accustomed to see mute, gentle, and tranquil, and who suddenly emerged from her silence in the presence of death. The inarticulate noises that escaped her lips and which she alone was unable to hear, had something of the savage about them. They were neither words nor sobs, but a kind of horrible language which seemed to have been invented by sorrow. During a day and a night, these awful cries filled the house. Camille ran about, tearing her hair and striking the walls. In vain they attempted to comfort her; even force was useless. It was only exhausted nature that finally made her drop at the foot of the bed where the body of the mother was laid.

Almost as quickly she had appeared to regain her accustomed tranquility, and, so to speak, forget everything. She remained for some time apparently calm, walking all day at random, with a slow and heedless step, declining none of the attention they gave to her.

They thought she had recovered, and the physician who had been summoned was mistaken as was every one else; a nervous fever soon developed accompanied by the gravest symptoms. It was necessary to constantly watch over the sick girl—her reason seemed entirely gone.

It was then that Uncle Giraud resolved, at all costs, to

come to console his niece.

"Since she has neither father nor mother," he said to the members of the household, "I, her granduncle, declare myself, for the present, charged with caring for her and preventing any misfortune befalling her. I have always loved the child. I have often asked her father to give her to me to cheer my life. I do not wish to deprive him of her, she is his daughter, but for the time being I take possession of her. Upon his return, I will faithfully surrender her to him."

Uncle Giraud had not much confidence in doctors, for the very good reason that he hardly believed in illness, having never been sick himself. A nervous fever, especially, appeared to him a fancy, a pure derangement of ideas, that a little diversion should soon cure. So he had decided to take Camille to Paris. "You see," he again remarked, "that she is melancholy, poor child! She does nothing but weep, and she is right—a mother dies only once. But the daughter must not die because the mother has just departed. We must try to make her think of other things. It is said that Paris is a very good place for that. I do not know Paris, nor does she. I will take her there; it will do us both good. Besides if there is only the journey, it should be of great benefit to her. I have had trouble, like others, but every time I have seen a coach driver's pigtail wagging before me, I have been made more cheerful."

In this way Camille and her uncle had arrived in Paris. The chevalier, informed of the journey by a letter from Uncle Giraud, approved it. Returning from his tour in Holland, he had brought back to Chardonneaux a sadness so profound that it was almost impossible for him to see any one, even his daughter. He seemed to wish to avoid every living thing and even to try to hide from himself. Always alone, riding on horseback in the woods, he tired himself out physically in order, by sleep, to gain peace for his soul.

A secret and incurable sorrow devoured him. From the depth of his heart he reproached himself for having made his wife's life unhappy, and for having contributed to her death. "If I had been there," he said to himself, "she would be alive, and I should have been there." This thought, which never left him, poisoned his life.

He wished that Camille might be happy; he was ready, when the occasion arose, to make the greatest sacrifices with this end in view. His first thought, on returning to Chardonneaux, had been to replace, for his daughter's sake, she whom he had lost, and to pay with usury that debt of the heart which he had incurred. But the memory of the resemblance between the mother and her child caused him, in advance, an intolerable sorrow. It was in vain that he tried to deceive himself regarding this very grief, and that he wished to persuade himself that it would rather be a consolation to his eyes, an alleviation of his suffering, in this way to find again in his daughter's countenance the features of her for whom he wept incessantly.

Camille, in spite of all, was to him a living reproach, a witness of his fault and misfortune, which he did not feel strong enough to endure.

Uncle Giraud did not pay so much attention to it. He thought only of enlivening his niece and making her life as pleasant as possible. Unhappily, this was not an easy matter. Camille had allowed herself to be led away without resistance, but she had refused to join in any of the pleasures which the good man proposed. Walks, fetes, theaters, nothing could tempt her. In answer to everything she pointed to her black dress.

The old master mason was obstinate. He had rented, as we have seen, a furnished apartment in a hotel in the Messageries, the first one that the clerk had shown him, expecting to stay there only a month or two. He had now been there with Camille nearly a year. For twelve months Camille had declined all his proposals of entertainment, and, as he was at the same time as good and patient as he was obdurate, he had waited for a year without complaint. He loved this poor girl with all his heart, without knowing the reason, by one of these inexplicable charms that joins goodness to misfortune.

"But, after all, I do not know," he said, finishing the bottle, "what can prevent your coming to the opera with me. It costs a great deal of money; I have the tickets in my pocket; your year of mourning was ended yesterday; you have two new dresses, and, besides, you have only to put on your wrap, and . . . ."

He stopped. "The devil!" said he, "you hear nothing, and I had forgotten that. But what matter? It is not necessary in such a place. You will not hear. I will not listen. We shall watch the dancing, that is all."

So spoke the good uncle, who would never remember, when there was anything interesting to say, that his niece could neither hear nor speak. He chatted with her, in spite of himself. On the other hand, when he attempted to express himself by means of signs it was still worse; she understood him even less. So he had to follow the habit of talking to her as he would to any one else; in gesticulating, it is true, with all his force. Camille had come to understand this method of communication and found means to answer, in her own way.

Camille's mourning was not, indeed, at the end, as the good man had said. He had ordered two beautiful dresses made for his niece, and presented them to her with such a tender and supplicating air, that she threw her arms around his neck to thank him, and then sat down with the calm sadness that was habitual to her.

"But that is not all," said the uncle, "you must put them

on—these beautiful dresses. They were made to be worn and they are pretty." And, while speaking, he walked up and down the room holding up the dresses and exhibiting them.

Camille had cried sufficient for a moment of joy to be allowed her. For the first time since the death of her mother, she stood before the mirror, took one of the dresses which her uncle was showing her, looked at him tenderly, held out her hand and made a little nod with her head as if to say "Yes."

At this sign the good man Giraud began to leap about in his rough shoes, like a child. He was triumphing. The hour had at last arrived when he would accomplish his purpose: Camille was about to attire herself, go out with him, visit the opera, and see the world. He could hardly restrain himself at this thought; he kissed his niece repeatedly, calling out all the while for the maid, the servants, and everyone in the house. Her toilet completed, Camille was so beautiful that she seemed to realize it herself, and smiled at her own image.

"The carriage is waiting," said Uncle Giraud, imitating, with his arms, the action of a coachman whipping his horses, and, with his mouth, the noise of a carriage. Camille smiled again, took the mourning-dress which she had just taken off, folded it with care, kissed it, placed it in the wardrobe, and accompanied him.

• VII •

If Uncle Giraud was not elegant in his person he prided himself, at any rate, on knowing how to do things properly. What did he care if his clothes, always brand-new and much too large, for he did not wish to be uncomfortable, fitted him badly, that his hose was carelessly adjusted, and that his wig was drawn down almost over his eyes. But when he entertained others, above all, he insisted on the best and most costly of everything. And, in fact, he had engaged, for that evening, one of the best boxes, well in front, so that his niece might be seen by everyone.

Camille's first glance at the stage and the audience dazzled her, and no wonder; a young girl, hardly sixteen, brought up in the country, and finding herself suddenly transported into the most unbelievable dream. They were performing a ballet; Camille followed with curiosity the attitudes, gestures and steps of the dancers. She realized that it was a pantomime, and as she was accustomed to that, she endeavored to understand it. Every now and then she turned to her uncle, with an astonished air, as if to consult him; but he comprehended it hardly better than she did. She saw shepherds in silken hose offering flowers to their shepherdesses, angels fluttering and suspended at the end of cords, and gods resting upon clouds. She gazed at the decorations, the lights, the brilliancy of which charmed her, the dresses of the ladies, the embroideries, the feathers, all the pomp of a spectacle hitherto unknown to her with pleasing astonishment.

She herself soon became the object of an almost general attention. Her toilet was simple, but in the best of taste; alone, in a spacious box, by the side of a man as uncouth as was Uncle Giraud; beautiful as a star and fresh as a rose, with her large black eyes and her air of naivete she necessarily attracted all eyes. The men began to call the attention of each other to her, the women to observe her. Marquises approached, and the most flattering compliments, uttered loudly, according to custom of the time, were addressed to the new arrival. Unfortunately, Uncle Giraud alone gathered this homage, which he received with relish.

However, Camille, little by little, at first regained her tranquil air, then a feeling of sadness came over her. She felt how cruel it was to be isolated in the midst of that crowd. These people conversing in their boxes, these musicians whose instruments regulated the steps of the dancers, this great exchange of thoughts between the actors and the audience—all this, so to speak, made her again withdraw within herself.

"We speak and you do not," every one seemed to be saying. "We listen, we laugh, we sing, we love, we enjoy everything; you alone enjoy nothing, you alone hear nothing, you alone are but a statue here, the phantom of a being who but looks on life from a distance."

Camille closed her eyes to shut out this scene. She remembered that children's party where she had seen her companions dancing, and where she had remained quiet near her mother. Her thoughts carried her back to the home where she was born, to her unhappy childhood, her long suffering, her secret tears, her mother's death, and, finally, to that mourning she had just cast off and which she resolved to put on again when she returned to the hotel. Since she was condemned forever, it seemed better for her never to attempt to be happy. She felt, more bitterly than ever, that all her efforts to resist the malediction of Heaven were useless. Filled with this thought, she was unable to restrain a few tears, which Uncle Giraud noticed. He tried to find out the cause, when she gestured to him that she wished to leave. The good man, surprised and anxious, hesitated and did not know what to do. Camille arose and pointed to the door of the box, that he might bring her cloak.

At this moment she noticed beneath her, in the audience, a fine looking young man, very elegantly dressed, who held in his hand a small slate, on which he drew letters and figures with a little white pencil. Then he showed the slate to his neighbor, an older man than he; the latter seemed to comprehend at once, and promptly answered in the same way. At the same time, by opening and closing their fingers, they both exchanged certain signs which seemed to enable them better to comunicate their ideas.

Camille understood nothing, neither the drawings on the slate which she could see, nor the signs with their fingers which she did not comprehend; but she noticed from the first glance that the young man did not move his lips. Ready to depart, she hesitated. She saw that he communicated his thoughts in a manner different from every one else, and that he found means to express himself without that movement of the lips so incomprehensible to her, and which was the torment of her thoughts. Whatever this strange language might be, an extreme surprise, an invincible desire to know more of it, made her resume the place she had just left; she leaned over the edge of the box, and attentively watched what this stranger was doing. Seeing him write on the slate again and present it to his neighbor, she made an involuntary movement as if to catch it in passing. At this motion the young man turned around and, in turn, looked at Camille. Hardly had their eyes met when they both remained, at first motionless and undecided, as if trying to recognize each other; then, in an instant, they understood each other, and seemed to say with a look: "We are both mute."

Uncle Giraud brought his niece her cloak and operaglasses, but she no longer wished to depart. She had reseated herself, and remained leaning her elbows on the balustrade.

The Abbe de l'Epee had just begun to make himself known.

Visiting a lady in the Rue des Fosses-Saint-Victor, and touched with pity for two deaf-mutes he by chance had seen doing embroidery, the charity that filled his soul had been suddenly awakened, and was already working wonders. In the crude pantomime of these miserable and unfortunate beings, he had discovered the foundation of a valuable language, which he thought might become universal, better, in any case, than that of Leibnitz, who like most men of genius, had perhaps, in expecting too much, gone beyond his goal. But it was already a good deal to have seen its greatness. Whatever may have been his ambition, he taught deaf-mutes to read and write. He returned them to their places among men. Alone and without help, by his own efforts, he had undertaken to establish a colony of these unfortunates, and he was preparing to sacrifice to this project his life and his fortune, until the king should notice them.

The young man seated near Camille's box was one of the Abbe's pupils. Born a gentleman of a noble family, gifted with great intelligence, but afflicted with this semi-death, as it was then called, he had been one of the first to receive about the same instruction as the Comte de Solar, with this difference, that he was rich, and did not run the risk of dying of hunger, for lack of an allowance from the Duc de Penthievre. In addition to the Abbe's lessons, they had given him a tutor, who being a layman, could accompany him everywhere, and was charged with attending him and directing his thoughts; this was the companion who read from the slate. With great care and application the young man profited by these daily studies, which developed his mind in every way, the riding-school, the opera, the lecture, and the mass. Nevertheless, a little natural pride and a very pronounced independence of character struggled in him against this laborious application. He knew nothing of the difficulties which might have overtaken him if he had been born in a lower rank or even like Camille, in any other place than Paris. One of the first things they had taught him, when he began to spell, was the name of his father, the Marquis de Maubray. So he knew that he was different from other men both by the privilege of birth and by the affliction of nature. Pride and humiliation thus disputed, in a noble mind, which, happily, or perhaps necessarily, had remained simple.

This Marquis, a deaf-mute, observing and comprehending others, as haughty as any of them, who had also, together with his tutor, drawn his red heels through the great salons of Versailles, according to the customs of the time, was glanced at by more than one pretty woman, but his eyes never left Camille. She saw him very well, without appearing to look at him. The opera finished, she took her uncle's arm, and, not daring to turn around, went home pensively.

• VIII •

It is needless to say that neither Camille nor Uncle Giraud knew of the Abbe de l'Epee; still less did they have knowledge of a new science which enabled mutes to communicate thought. The chevalier might have known of this discovery; his wife certainly would have learned of it had she lived. But Chardonneaux was some distance from Paris. The chevalier did not subscribe to a newspaper, or if he received one he did not read it. Thus, a few leagues of distance, a lack of observation or death, could produce the same result.

Having arrived home Camille had but one thought; all of her gestures and means of expression were employed to convey to her uncle that she wanted above all a slate and pencil. The good man Giraud was not at all surprised at this request, although it was made to him a little late. He hurried to his room and, confident that he had understood her, brought back in triumph to his niece a little board and a piece of chalk, relics of his old business of building and carpentry.

Camille appeared to be delighted at having her desires gratified in this way. She placed the board upon her lap, and persuaded her uncle to sit down beside her; then she handed him the chalk, and took his hand as if to guide it, at the same time that her anxious eyes followed his movements.

Uncle Giraud well understood that she desired him to write something, but what? He did not know. "Is it your mother's name? Is it mine? Is it yours, you wish?" and to better explain himself, he pointed with his finger at the young girl. She nodded her head at once, and in large letters he wrote the name "Camille"; after which, satisfied with himself and with the manner in which he had spent the evening, supper being ready, he sat down at the table, without waiting for his niece, who was too tired to sit in her accustomed place at the head of the table.

Camille never retired before her uncle had finished his bottle. She watched him eat his supper, said good night, and then retired to her room, with her little board under her arm.

As soon as her door was locked, she attempted to write. Relieved of her petticoats and with her hair down, she began to copy, with great care and pains, the word which her uncle had just written, and to scrawl, with the chalk, all over a large table which stood in the middle of the room. After more than one attempt with several erasures she managed, fairly well, to reproduce the letters she had before her eyes. When it was finished, to assure herself of the correctness of her copy, she counted one by one the letters that had served her as models; she then walked around the table, her heart throbbing with joy as if she had gained a glorious victory. That word "Camille," which she had just written, appeared admirable to her, and should certainly express to her the most beautiful thing in the world. In this one word she seemed to see a multitude of thoughts, each one sweeter, more mysterious, and more charming than the other. She did not understand that it was only her own name.

It was July; the air was pure and the nights superb. Camille had opened her window; she stood before it, and from time to time, dreaming, her hair falling over her shoulders, her arms crossed, her eyes sparkling, and beautiful with that pallor which clearness of night gives to a woman, she looked out upon one of the most dismal sights that can be imagined—the narrow court of a long building occupied by a stage coach company. In this court, cold, humid, and unhealthy, no ray of sunlight had ever penetrated; the height of the structure, rising one floor above another, obscured this sort of cavern from the light.

Four or five large coaches, crowded together in a shed, seemed to offer themselves to whomever wished to enter. Two or three others, left in the court for lack of space, seemed to be awaiting the horses, whose noise in the stable served as their demand for hay continuously. Over a gate carefully closed at midnight to the tenants, but always ready to open noisily at any hour at the crack of a coachman's whip, heavy walls reared up, pierced with some fifty casements, behind which, after ten o'clock, no candle ever shone unless under extraordinary circumstances.

Camille was about to leave her window, when suddenly, in the shadow cast by a heavy coach, she seemed to see a human form moving, handsomely attired and walking slowly.

A thrill of fear came over Camille at first without her comprehending why, for her uncle was near, and the presence
of the good man was revealed by his noisy slumber; besides,
what thief or assassin would come and walk in that court
in such a costume as the man was dressed in?

However, the man was there, and Camille could see him.
He was walking behind the coaches, watching the window
at which she stood. After some moments, Camille felt her
courage returning. She took the candle, and stretching her
arm out of the window, suddenly lit up the court; at the
same time she glanced down, half-frightened, half-threat-
ening. The shadow of the coach was gone, and the Marquis
de Maubray—for it was he—seeing that he was completely
discovered, fell upon his knees, and clasped his hands as
he gazed at Camille in an attitude of the most profound
respect.

They remained thus for a few moments, Camille at the
window holding the candle and the marquis on his knees
before her. If Romeo and Juliet, who had only seen each
other one night at a masked ball, at their first meeting,
could exchange so many vows, which were faithfully kept,
let us imagine what might be the first gestures and glances
of two lovers who could only tell each other by their actions,
those same things, eternal before God, and which the genius of Shakespeare has immortalized on earth.

It certainly must appear ridiculous to mount two or three
steps in order to climb to the top of a carriage, stopping,
at each effort one is obliged to make, to inquire if one may
continue. It is true that a man in silk hose and embroidered
waistcoat runs the risk of a bad appearance when it is a
question of jumping from the top of a carriage to the ledge
of a window. All this is incontestable, unless one is in love.

When the Marquis de Maubray reached Camille's room
he began by saluting her as ceremoniously as if he had been

in the Tuileries. If he had been able to speak, perhaps he would have told her how he had escaped the vigilance of his tutor; by means of bribing a lackey, and been allowed to pass the night beneath her window; how a glance from her had changed his whole life; and, finally, how he loved only her in the world, and wished for not greater happiness than to offer her his hand and fortune. All this was expressed in his gestures; but Camille's bow, in return for his salutation, made him understand how useless such a recital would have been, and that it mattered little to her to know how he had managed to reach her, inasmuch as he was there.

The Marquis de Maubray, in spite of a certain audacity of which he had given proof in intruding upon the privacy of her whom he loved, was, as I have said, simple and reserved. After having saluted Camille, he vainly sought a way of asking her if she would accept him as her husband. She understood nothing of what he was attempting to explain. He saw on the table the board on which was written the name "Camille." He seized a piece of chalk, and by the side of this name he wrote his name, "Pierre."

"What is the meaning of all this?" exclaimed a deep bass voice. "Who ever heard of such a meeting? How did you get in here, monsieur? What are you doing in this room?"

It was Uncle Giraud who spoke thus, entering in his dressing-gown, with a furious air.

"This is a fine thing!" he continued. "God knows I was sleeping, but if you made any noise, it was not with your lips. What sort of being are you that you find nothing easier to do than climb up this wall? What is your intention? To spoil a carriage, break everything, make havoc, and after that, what? To dishonor a family! To throw shame and infamy upon honest people."

"This one does not hear me either!" cried Uncle Giraud disconsolately.

But the marquis took a pencil and a piece of paper, and wrote this note: "I love Mademoiselle Camille and wish to marry her. I have an income of twenty thousand livres. Will you give her to me?"

"It is only people who do not speak who can finish their business so quickly," said Uncle Giraud. "But," he cried after a moment's reflection, "I am not her father, I am only her uncle. You must ask her father's permission."

• IX •

It was not an easy undertaking to obtain the chevalier's consent to such a marriage. Not that he was not disposed, as we have seen, to do all that was possible to make his daughter's life more cheerful, but in the present circumstances there was an almost insurmountable difficulty. It was a question of uniting a woman afflicted with a terrible infirmity to a man stricken with the same misfortune; and if such a union was to bear fruit, it was probable that it would only bring one more unfortunate into the world.

The chevalier, having returned to his home, always a prey to the deepest grief, continued to live in solitude. Madame des Arcis had been buried in the park; a few weeping willows surrounded her tomb, and from afar indicated to passers-by the modest place where she reposed. It was toward this place that the chevalier directed his footsteps every day. There he spent long hours, with remorse and sadness, and giving way to all the memories that could nourish his grief.

It was there that Uncle Giraud came suddenly upon him one morning. The day after he had surprised the two lovers together, the good man had left Paris with his niece, had brought Camille back to Le Mans, and left her in his own house, there to await the result of the course he was about to take.

Pierre having been informed of this journey, had promised to be faithful and to remain ready to keep his word. An orphan for a long time, master of his own fortune, needing only his tutor's aid in conversing, his wish had no obstacle to fear. The good man was quite willing to act as his mediator and to try and consummate the marriage of the two young people, but he did not intend that their first interview, which seemed to him somewhat strange, should be renewed without the permission of the father and the notary.

As may well be imagined, the chevalier showed extreme astonishment at Uncle Giraud's words. When the good man started to relate that meeting at the opera, that strange scene, and still more peculiar proposal, he found it difficult to conceive that such a romance was possible. Forced, however, to recognize that he was being spoken to seriously, he immediately thought of objections.

"What do you wish?" said he to Uncle Giraud—"to unite two beings equally unfortunate? Is it not enough to have in our family that poor afflicted creature of whom I am the father? Must we add to our misfortune by giving her a husband similar to herself? Am I destined to see myself surrounded by beings shunned by the world, objects of scorn and pity? Must I pass my life with mutes, grow old amid their awful silence, and have my eyes closed by their hands? My name, of which, God knows I am not vain, but which, however, is that of my father, am I to leave it to unfortunates who can neither sign nor pronounce it?"

"Not pronounce it," said Uncle Giraud, "But sign it; that is another matter."

"Sign it!" cried the chevalier. "Have you lost your reason?"

"I know what I am talking about, and that young man knows how to write," answered the uncle. "I bear witness and can testify that he even writes very well and readily, as his proposal, which I have in my pocket, and which is very frank, can prove."

At the same time the good man showed the chevalier the paper on which the Marquis de Maubray had written those few words which expressed, somewhat laconically it is true, but clearly, the object of his desires.

"What does this mean?" said the father. "Since when can the deaf-mutes use a pen? What story are you telling me, Giraud?"

"My faith," said Uncle Giraud, "I do not know what to make of it, nor how such a thing can be possible. The truth is, that my intention was just to amuse Camille, and to see also myself the ballet at the opera. This little marquis happened to be there, and it is certain that he had a slate and a pencil, which he used very skilfully. I had always thought, like you, that when one was dumb it followed one could say nothing; but it is nothing of the sort. It seems that they have recently made a discovery by means of which all these people understand each other, and converse together to their entire satisfaction. They say that it is an Abbe, whose name I do not know, who invented this method. As for me, you will understand that a slate has never appeared of any use other than for roofing purposes; but these Parisians are so ingenious!"

"Are you serious in what you say?"

"Very serious. This little marquis is rich, and a good fellow; he is a gentleman and a gallant man; I will answer for him. Remember one thing, I beg of you; what will you do with that poor Camille? She does not speak, it is true, but that is not her fault. What do you wish her to become? She can not always remain a girl. Here is a man who loves her; that man, if you give her to him, will never be impatient with her on account of the fault she has at the end of her tongue; he knows what it is from his own experience. They understand each other, these children; they comprehend, without having any need to shout. The little marquis knows how to read and write; Camille will learn to do the same; it will not be any more difficult for her than for him. You fully understand that if I was proposing to marry your daughter to a blind man, you would be quite right to laugh in my face; but I propose a deaf-mute, which is reasonable. You see that during the sixteen years that this little one has been yours, you have never reconciled to her. How can you expect a man, made like every one else, to arrange matters if you, who are her father, can not take your part?"

While the uncle was speaking, the chevalier from time to time glanced towards his wife's tomb, and seemed to be reflecting deeply:

"To give to my daughter the use of her intellect!" said he, after a long pause, "will God permit it? Is it possible?"

At this moment the priest of a neighboring village entered the garden, coming to dine at the house. The chevalier casually greeted him, then, suddenly emerging from his reverie:

"Abbe," said he, "you sometimes know the latest news, and you receive the papers. Have you heard of a priest who has undertaken to educate deaf-mutes?"

Unfortunately, the person to whom this question was addressed was a typical country priest of the time, simple and good, but very ignorant, and sharing all the prejudices of a century in which there were so many and such fatal ones.

"I do not know what monseigneur means," he answered, addressing the chevalier as the seigneur of the village, "unless he is speaking of the Abbe de l'Epee."

"Exactly!" said Uncle Giraud. "That is the name I heard; I no longer remembered it."

"Well," said the chevalier, "what can we believe?"

"I can not," answered the priest, "speak with too much caution on a matter with which I can not claim as yet to be fully conversant. But I am led to believe, from what little evidence I have been able to gather on the subject, that this Monsieur de l'Epee, who appears, moreover, to be a very venerable person, has achieved the success he expected."

"What do you mean by that?" said Uncle Giraud.

"I mean," said the priest, "that the best intention may sometimes fail in the result. There is no doubt, from what I have heard, that the most praiseworthy efforts have been made; but I have every reason to believe that the pretension of teaching deaf-mutes to read, as monseigneur says, is altogether chimerical."

"I have seen it with my own eyes," said Uncle Giraud. "I have seen a deaf-mute write."

"I do not wish to contradict you in any way," answered the priest, "but learned and distinguished men, among whom I might mention doctors from the Faculty of Paris, have assured me in the most emphatic manner that such a thing was impossible."

"A thing one sees can not be impossible," replied the good man impatiently. "I have come fifty leagues with a note in my pocket to show it to the chevalier; here it is. It is as plain as daylight."

Speaking thus, the old master mason had once more brought forth his paper and had placed it before the priest's eyes. The latter, half astonished, half annoyed, examined the letter, turned it over, read it aloud several times, and returned it to the uncle, hardly knowing what to say.

The chevalier had not appeared to heed the discussion; he continued to walk in silence, and his uncertainty increased each moment.

"If Giraud is right," he thought, "and if I refuse, I am not doing my duty; it is almost a crime. An occasion presents itself whereby that poor girl, to whom I have given only the semblance of life, may find a hand that reaches out for hers in the darkness by which she is surrounded. Without emerging from that night in which she will always be enveloped, she can dream that she is happy. By what right shall I oppose this? What would her mother say if she were here?"

The chevalier's eyes were again directed toward the tomb; then he took Uncle Giraud by the arm, stepped aside, and said in a low voice: "Do what you wish."

"That is right," said the uncle; "I will go and find her and bring her here. She is at my house. We will return together shortly."

"Never!" answered the father. "Let us endeavor to make her happy; but see her again I can not."

Pierre and Camille were married in Paris, at the Church of the Petis-Peres. The tutor and the uncle were the sole witnesses. When the officiating priest addressed them in the usual form, Pierre, who had learned to know when he should bend his head as a sign of consent, acquitted himself very well, in a role which was, moreover, difficult to perform. Camille did not attempt to understand anything; she looked at her husband, and bowed her head as he did.

They had only seen each other to fall in love, and that was sufficient, one might say. When they left the church arm in arm, they were hardly acquainted. The marquis had a large mansion. Camille, after mass, stepped into a brilliant equipage, which she examined with childlike curiosity.

The home to which she was taken was no less a subject of astonishment. The rooms, the horses, the servants, which were all to be hers, seemed to her a marvel. It had been arranged that this marriage should be celebrated quietly; a very simple supper after the ceremony completed the festivities.

• X •

Camille became a mother. One day, when the chevalier was walking in the park, a servant brought him a letter written in an unknown hand, and in which was apparently a singular mixture of distinction and ignorance. It came from Camille, and was as follows:

"O my father! I speak, not with my lips, but with my hand. My mouth is forever sealed, yet I can converse. He who is my master has taught me to write. He had me taught like himself, by the same teacher who instructed him, for you know he was dumb like me, for a long time. I found it very hard to learn. He taught me, at first, to converse with my fingers, and then with written letters.

"There are all kinds of characters, expressing fear, anger, and everything else. It takes a long time to learn it well, and still longer to form words, on account of the letters which are more difficult, but at length it is accomplished, as you see. The Abbe de l'Epee is a very good and gentle man, the same as Father Vanin of the Christian Doctrine.

"I have a very beautiful child. I hardly dare allude to him before I know if he is to be like us, but I can not resist the pleasure of writing to you, in spite of our great concern, for you may well understand that my husband and I are very anxious, especially because we can not hear. The nurse hears well, but we are afraid she may be mistaken; thus we wait with great impatience to see if he will open his lips and move them, making the sounds of those who hear and speak. You may well imagine we have consulted doctors to know if it is possible that the child of two people as unfortunate as we are, should not be mute also, and they have told us that such a thing is possible; but we dare not believe it.

"Judge with what fear we watch this poor child all the time, and how embarrassed we are when he opens his little lips and we can not tell if they make noise or not. Be assured, my father, that I often think of my mother, for she must have been anxious about me as I am now, myself. You loved me well, as I also love my child; but I have been only a cause of sorrow to you. Now that I can read and write, I understand how my mother must have suffered.

"If you desire to please me, dear father, you will come and see us in Paris. It would be an occasion of joy and gratitude for your respectful daughter.

Camille."

After reading this letter the chevalier hesitated for some time. At first he could hardly believe his eyes and be convinced that it was Camille herself who had written to him, but he finally succumbed before such evidence. What should he do? If he yielded to his daughter and went to Paris, he exposed himself to a new sorrow, and all the memories of an old one. A child whom he did not know, it is true, but who was nevertheless the son of his daughter, might remind him of Cecile, yet he could not resist joining in the anxiety of that young mother awaiting a word from her child's lips.

"You must go," said Uncle Giraud when the chevalier consulted him. "It is I who effected that marriage, and I hold it good and durable. Will you abandon your own flesh and blood in time of trouble? Was is not enough—and I say it without reproach—to have neglected your wife at the children's party, in consequence of which she was drowned? Will you also desert this little one? Do you think to be sad is ample repentance? You are that, I admit, and even more so than is reasonable; but do you not think there are other things to do in the world? She asks you to go; let us start. I shall go with you, but I have only one regret, and that is that she did not invite me also. It was unkind of her not to have knocked at my door, which has always been open to her."

"He is right," thought the chevalier. "I made one of the best wives suffer unnecessarily and cruelly. I left her to die a fearful death, when I should have saved her from it. If I must be punished today by the sight of my daughter's misfortune, I ought not to complain; however painful this spectacle may be to me, I should court it and condemn myself to it. This chastisement is due to me. Let the daughter punish me for having deserted the mother. I will go to Paris and see this child. I have forsaken those I loved, and have removed myself from calamity; I wish now to feel a bitter pleasure in contemplating it."

In a pretty wood paneled boudoir, on the mezzanine of a fine house situated in the Faubourg Saint Germain, were seated the young wife and her husband when the father and uncle arrived. On a table were sketches, books, and engravings. The husband was reading, the wife embroidering, and the child playing on the carpet.

The marquis arose. Camille ran to her father, who kissed her tenderly, and could not restrain a few tears; but the eyes of the chevalier were immediately fixed upon the child. In spite of himself, the horror that he had formerly felt over the affliction of Camille, again came over him at the sight of the child who was about to inherit the malediction that he had bequeathed to him. He recoiled when they presented the child to him.

"Another mute!" he cried.

Camille took her son in her arms; although not hearing, she understood. Slowly raising the child before the chevalier, she placed her finger on his little lips, rubbing them gently as if to invite him to speak. The child permitted himself to be entreated for a few moments, then pronounced very distinctly these three words, which the mother had already taught him:

"Good morning, papa!"

"Now you see clearly that God pardons all, and always," said Uncle Giraud.

Doctor Marigold
by Charles Dickens

EDITORS' PREFACE

Doctor Marigold, for whom this story is named, is a "cheap jack," what we in America would call an itinerant peddlar, or perhaps a "medicine man." Cheap jacks flourished in England in the last century and sold general store items from the back of a cart. This particular cheap jack adopts a deaf girl after his real daughter dies and later arranges for her to be educated.

At the time of the story, deaf education had made only tentative starts in a few European countries and therefore this story of a deaf girl who is taught to read and write must have raised eyebrows even among the enlightened readers of Dickens' time. But Dickens had gotten to know some deaf people, and he was aware of the potential of education for deaf people. His appreciation of sign language is also evident from the story: "we all three settled down into talking without sound, as if there was a something soft and pleasant spread over the whole world for us." The story, then, was written with the genuine intention to understand deafness better.

Let us quickly add, however, that even Dickens, like de Musset, as interested in the plight of the deaf as he was, was still capable of rather obviously mistaken ideas in connection with the deaf. In the end of the story, Sophy returns to Doctor Marigold after living with her deaf husband for years, but, unbelievably, she still uses the signs that her stepfather had taught her years before! Sign language, like any other language, is highly fluid when not tied to a written standard like a dictionary. In those years by themselves, Sophy and her husband (who had already known signs when he met Sophy) would certainly have evolved a language of their own—it is highly unlikely that Sophy would even *remember* the system she had used with her father, much less use it.

But our most critical remarks about the story are not related to minor points such as these but to the character of Sophy herself. In her cloyingness, as depicted by Dickens, she is a typical depersonalized Victorian heroine. Like Camille, she is a "prop," not a person in her own right but a means of making others happy. Like Camille, who in a sense is a mere broodmare, the means of continuing the family of the hearing des Arcis, Sophy's apotheosis consists in giving birth to a hearing child. But, despite her one-dimensionality, Sophy is a little more actively involved in life than Camille. Before her marriage, Sophy had at least given meaning to the life of her adopted father and made him feel less lonely.

Thus we find that even one as sympathetic and enlightened as Dickens still could not conceive of deafness other than as a kind of curse, the only salvation from the curse being to have a hearing child. And, as long as deafness is viewed as a curse, those who are afflicted by it will view themselves as victims and, as such, more likely to accept the pity of hearing people, such pity, in the end, proving a more debilitating curse than the handicap itself.

("Doctor Marigold" has been edited and unnecessary portions deleted.)

DOCTOR MARIGOLD

• CHAPTER I: TO BE TAKEN IMMEDIATELY •

I am a Cheap Jack, and my own father's name was Willum Marigold. It was in his lifetime supposed by some that his name was William, but my own father always consistently said, No, it was Willum. On which point I content myself with looking at the argument this way: If a man is not allowed to know his own name in a free country, how much is he allowed to know in a land of slavery? . . .

I was born on the Queen's highway, but it was the King's at that time. A doctor was fetched to my own mother by my own father, when it took place on a common: and in consequence of his being a very kind gentleman, and accepting no fee but a tea-tray I was named Doctor, out of gratitude and compliment to him. There you have me. Doctor Marigold.

I am at present a middle-aged man of a broadish build, in cords, leggings, and a sleeved waistcoat the strings of which is always gone behind. Repair them how you will, they go like fiddle-strings. . . .

I courted my wife from the footboard of the cart. I did indeed. She was a Suffolk young woman, and it was in Ipswich market-place right opposite the corn-chandler's shop, I had noticed her up at a window last Saturday that was, appreciating highly. I had took to her, and I had said to myself, "If not already disposed of, I'll have the lot." Next Saturday that come, I pitched the cart on the same pitch, and I was in very high feather indeed, keeping 'em laughing the whole of the time, and getting off the goods briskly. At last I took out of my waistcoat-pocket a small lot wrapped in soft paper, and I put it this way (looking up at the window where she was). "Now here, my blooming English maidens, is an article, the last article of the present evening's sale, which I offer to only you, the lovely Suffolk Dumplings biling over with beauty, and I won't take a bid of a thousand pounds for it from any man alive. Now, what is it? . . . It's a wedding-ring. Now I'll tell you what I'm a going to do with it. I'm not a going to offer this lot for money; but I mean to give it to the next of you beauties that laughs, and I'll pay her a visit to-morrow morning at exactly half after nine o'clock as the chimes go, and I'll take her out for a walk to put up the banns." She laughed, and got the ring handed up to her. When I called in the morning, she says, "O dear! It's never you, and you never mean it?" "It's ever me," says I, "and I am ever yours, and I ever mean it." So we got married, after being put up three times—which, by the bye, is quite in the Cheap Jack way again, and shows once more how the Cheap Jack customs pervade society.

She wasn't a bad wife, but she had a temper. If she could have parted with that one article at a sacrifice, I wouldn't have swopped her away in exchange for any other woman in England. Not that I ever did swop her away, for we lived together till she died, and that was thirteen year. Now, my lords and ladies and gentlefolks all, I'll let you into a secret, though you won't believe it. Thirteen year of temper in a Palace would try the worst of you, but thirteen year of temper in a Cart would try the best of you. You are kept so very close to it in a cart, you see. There's thousands of couples among you getting on like sweet ile upon a whetstone in houses five and six pairs of stairs high, that would go to the Divorce Court in a cart. Whether the jolting makes it worse, I don't undertake to decide; but in a cart it does come home to you, and stick to you. Violence in a cart is so violent and aggravation in a chart is so aggravating. . . .

The worst of it was, we had a daughter born to us, and I love children with all my heart. When she was in her furies she beat the child. This got to be so shocking, as the child got to be four or five years old, that I have many a time gone on with my whip over my shoulder, at the old horse's head, sobbing and crying worse than ever little Sophy did. For how could I prevent it? Such a thing is not to be tried with such a temper—in a cart—without coming to a fight. It's in the natural size and formation of a cart to bring it to a fight. And then the poor child got worse terrified than before, as well as worse hurt generally, and her mother made complaints to the next people we lighted on, and the word went round, "Here's a wretch of a Cheap Jack been a beating his wife."

Little Sophy was such a brave child! She grew to be quite devoted to her poor father, though he could do so little to help her. She had a wonderful quantity of shining dark hair, all curling natural about her. It is quite astonishing to me now, that I didn't go tearing mad when I used to see her run from her mother before the cart, and her mother catch her by this hair, and pull her down by it, and beat her.

Such a brave child I said she was! Ah! with reason.

"Don't you mind next time, father dear," she would whisper to me, with her little face still flushed, and her bright eyes still wet; "if I don't cry out, you may know I am not much hurt. And even if I do cry out, it will only be to get mother to let go and leave off." What I have seen the little spirit bear—for me—without crying out!

Yet in other respects her mother took great care of her. Her clothes were always clean and neat, and her mother was never tired of working at 'em. Such is the inconsistency in things. Our being down in the marsh country in unhealthy weather, I consider the cause of Sophy's taking bad low fever; but however she took it, once she got it she turned away from her mother for evermore, and nothing would persuade her to be touched by her mother's hand. She would shiver and say, "No, no, no," when it was offered at, and would hide her face on my shoulder, and hold me tighter round the neck.

The Cheap Jack business had been worse than ever I had known it, what with one thing and what with another (and not least with railroads, which will cut it all to pieces, I expect, at last), and I was run dry of money. For which reason, one night at that period of little Sophy's being so bad, either we must have come to a dead-lock for victuals and drink, or I must have pitched the cart as I did.

I couldn't get the dear child to lie down or leave go of me, and indeed I hadn't the heart to try, so I stepped out on the footboard with her holding round my neck. They all set up a laugh when they see us, and one chuckle-headed Joskin (that I hated for it) made the bidding, "Tuppence for her!"

"Now, you country boobies," says I, feeling as if my heart was a heavy weight at the end of a broken sashline, "I give you notice that I am a going to charm the money out of your pockets, and to give you so much more than your money's worth that you'll only persuade yourselves to draw your Saturday night's wages ever again afterwards by the hopes of meeting me to lay 'em out with, which you never will, and why not? Because I've made my fortune by selling my goods on a large scale for seventy-five per cent less than I give for 'em, and I am consequently to be elevated to the House of Peers next week, by the title of the Duke of Cheap and Markis Jackaloorul. Now let's know what you want to-night, and you shall have it. But first of all, shall I tell you why I have got this little girl round my neck? You don't want to know? Then you shall. She belongs to the Fairies. She's a fortune-teller. She can tell me all about you in a whisper, and can put me up to whether you're going to buy a lot or leave it. Now do you want a saw? No, she says you don't, because you're too clumsy to use one. Else here's a saw which would be a lifelong blessing to a handy man, at four shillings, at three and six, at three, at two and six, at two, at eighteenpence. But none of you shall have it at any price, on account of your well-known awkwardness, which would make it manslaughter. The same objection applies to this set of three planes which I won't let you have neither, so don't bid for 'em. Now I am a going to ask her what you do want." (Then I whispered. "Your head burns so, that I am afraid it hurts you bad, my pet," and she answered, without opening her heavy eyes, "Just a little, father.") "O! This little fortune-teller says it's a mem-orandum-book you want. Then why didn't you mention it? Here it is. Look at it. Two hundred superfine hot-pressed wire-wove pages—if you don't believe me, count 'em—ready ruled for your expenses, an everlastingly pointed pencil to put 'em down with, a double-bladed penknife to scratch 'em out with, a book of printed tables to calculate your income with, and a camp-stool to sit down upon while you give your mind to it! Stop! And an umbrella to keep the moon off when you give your mind to it on a pitch-dark night. Now I won't ask you how much for the lot, but how little? How little are you thinking of? Don't be ashamed to mention it, because my fortune-teller knows already." (Then making believe to whisper, I kissed her, and she kissed me.) "Why, she says you are thinking of as little as three and threepence! I couldn't have believed it, even of you, unless she told me. Three and threepence! And a set of printed tables in the lot that'll calculate your income up to forty thousand a year! With an income of forty thousand a year, you grudge three and threepence. Well then, I'll tell you my opinion. I so despise the threepence, that I'd sooner take three shillings. There. For three shillings, three shillings, three shillings! Gone. Hand 'em over to the lucky man."

As there had been no bid at all, everybody looked about and grinned at everybody, while I touched little Sophy's face and asked her if she felt faint, or giddy. "Not very, father. It will soon be over." Then turning from the pretty patient eyes, which were opened now, and seeing nothing but grins across my lighted grease-pot, I went on again in my Cheap Jack style. "Where's the butcher?" (My sorrowful eye had just caught sight of a fat young butcher on the outside of the crowd.) "She says the good luck is the butcher's. Where is he?" Everybody handed on the blushing butcher to the front, and there was a roar, and the butcher felt himself obliged to put his hand in his pocket, and take the lot. The party so picked out, in general, does feel obliged to take the lot—good four times out of six. Then we had another lot, the counterpart of that one, and sold it sixpence cheaper, which is always very much enjoyed. Then we had the spectacles. It ain't a special profitable lot, but I put 'em on, and I see what the Chancellor of the Exchequer is going to take off the taxes, and I see what the sweetheart of the young woman in the shawl is doing at home, and I see what the Bishops has got for dinner, and a deal more that seldom fails to fetch 'em up in their spirits; and the better their spirits, the better their bids. Then we had the ladies' lot,— the teapot, tea-caddy, glass sugar-basin, half-a-dozen spoons, and caudle-cup—and all the time I was making similar excuses to give a look or two and say a word or two to my poor child. It was while the second ladies' lot was holding 'em enchained that I felt her lift herself a little on my shoulder, to look across the dark street. "What troubles you, darling?" "Nothing troubles me, father. I am not at all troubled. But don't I see a pretty churchyard over there?" "Yes, my dear." "Kiss me twice, dear father, and lay me down to rest upon that churchyard grass so soft and green." I staggered back into the cart with her head dropped on my shoulder, and I says to her mother, "Quick. Shut the door! Don't let those laughing people see!" "What's the matter?" she cries. "O woman, woman," I tells her, "you'll never catch my little Sophy by her hair again, for she has flown away from you!"

Maybe those were harder words than I meant 'em; but from that time forth my wife took to brooding, and would sit in the cart or walk beside it, hours at a stretch, with her arms crossed, and her eyes looking on the ground. When her furies took her (which was rather seldomer than before) they took her in a new way, and she banged herself about to that extent that I was forced to hold her. She got none the better for a little drink now and then, and through some years I used to wonder, as I plodded along at the old horse's head, whether there was many carts upon the road that held so much dreariness as mine, for all my being looked up to as the King of the Cheap Jacks. So sad our lives went on till one summer evening, when, as we were coming into Exeter, out of the farther West of England, we saw a woman beating a child in a cruel manner, who screamed, "Don't beat me! O mother, mother, mother!" Then my wife stopped her ears, and ran away like a wild thing, and next day was found in the river.

Me and my dog were all the company left in the cart now; and the dog learned to give a short bark when they wouldn't bid, and to give another and a nod of his head when I asked him, "Who said half a crown?" Are you the gentleman, Sir, that offered half a crown?" He attained to an immense height of popularity, and I shall always believe he taught himself entirely out of his own head to growl at any person in the crowd that bid as low as sixpence. But he got to be well on in years, and one night when I was convulsing York with the spectacles, he took a convulsion on his own account upon the very footboard by me, and it finished him.

Being naturally of a tender turn, I had dreadful lonely feelings on me after this. I conquered 'em at selling times, having a reputation to keep (not to mention keeping myself) but they got me down in private, and rolled upon me. That's often the way with us public characters. See us on the footboard, and you'd give pretty well anything you possess to be us. See us off the footboard, and you'd add a trifle to be off your bargain. It was under these circumstances that I come acquainted with a giant. I might have been too high to fall into conversation with him, had it not been for my lonely feelings. For the general rule is going round the country to draw the line at dressing up. When a man can't trust his getting a living to his undisguised abilities, you consider him below your sort. And this giant when on view figured as a Roman.

He was a languid young man, which I attribute to the distance betwixt his extremities. He had a little head and less in it, he had weak eyes and weak knees, and altogether you couldn't look at him without feeling that there was greatly too much of him both for his joints and his mind. But he was an amiable though timid young man (his mother let him out, and spent the money), and we come acquainted when he was walking to ease the horse betwixt two fairs. He was called Rinaldo di Velasco, his name being Pickleson.

This giant, otherwise Pickleson, mentioned to me under the seal of confidence that, beyond his being a burden to himself, his life was made a burden to him by the cruelty of his master towards a step-daughter who was deaf and dumb. Her mother was dead, and she had no living soul to take her part, and was used most hard. She travelled with his master's caravan only because there was nowhere to leave her, and this giant, otherwise Pickleson, did go so far as to believe that his master often tried to lose her. He was such a very languid young man, that I don't know how long it didn't take him to get this story out, but it passed through his defective circulation to his top extremity in course of time.

When I heard this account from the giant, otherwise Pickleson, and likewise that the poor girl had beautiful long dark hair, and was often pulled down by it and beaten, I couldn't see the giant through what stood in my eyes. Having wiped 'em, I give him sixpence (for he was kept as short as he was long), and he laid it out in two three-penn'orths of gin-and-water, which so brisked him up, that he sang the Favourite Comic of Shivery Shakey, ain't it cold?—a popular effect which his master had tried every other means to get out of him as a Roman wholly in vain.

His master's name was Mim, a very hoarse man, and I knew him to speak to. I went to that Fair as a mere civilian, leaving the cart outside the town, and I looked about the back of the vans while the performing was going on, and at last, sitting dozing against a muddy cart-wheel, I came upon the poor girl who was deaf and dumb. At the first look I might almost have judged that she had escaped from the Wild Beast Show; but at the second I thought better of her, and thought that if she was more cared for and more kindly used she would be like my child. She was just the same age that my own daughter would have been, if her pretty head had not fell down upon my shoulder that unfortunate night.

To cut it short, I spoke confidential to Mim while he was beating the gong outside betwixt two lots of Pickleson's publics, and I put it to him, "She lies heavy on your own hands; what'll you take for her?" Mim was a most ferocious swearer. Suppressing that part of his reply which was much the longest part, his reply was, "A pair of braces." "Now I'll tell you," says I, "what I'm a going to do with you. I'm a going to fetch you half-a-dozen pair of the primest braces in the cart, and then to take her away with me." Says Mim (again ferocious), "I'll believe it when I've got the goods, and no sooner." I made all the haste I could lest he should think twice of it, and the bargain was completed, and Pickleson was thereby so relieved in his mind that he come out at his little back door, longways like a serpent, and give us Shivery Shakey in a whisper among the wheels at parting.

It was happy days for both of us when Sophy and me began to travel in the cart. I at once give her the name of Sophy, to put her ever towards me in the attitude of my own daughter. We soon made out to begin to understand one another, through the goodness of the Heavens, when she knowed that I meant true and kind by her. In a very little time she was wonderful fond of me. You have no idea what it is to have anybody wonderful fond of you, unless you have been got down and rolled upon by the lonely feelings that I have mentioned as having once got the better of me.

You'd have laughed—or the reverse—it's according to your disposition—if you could have seen me trying to teach Sophy. At first I was helped—you'd never guess by what— milestones. I got some large alphabets in a box, all the letters separate on bits of bone, and saying we was going to WINDSOR, I give her those letters in that order, and then at every milestone, I showed her those same letters in that same order again, and pointed towards the abode of royalty. Another time I give her CART, and then chalked the same upon the cart. Another time I give her DOCTOR MARIGOLD, and hung a corresponding inscription outside my waistcoat. People that met us might stare a bit and laugh, but what did I care, if she caught the idea? She caught it after long patience and trouble, and then we did begin to get on swimmingly, believe you me! At first she was a little given to consider me the cart, and the cart the abode of royalty, but that soon wore off.

We had our signs, too, and they was hundreds in number. Sometimes she would sit looking at me and considering hard how to communicate with me about something fresh—how to ask me what she wanted explained,—and then she was (or I thought she was; what does it signify?) so like my child with those years added to her, that I half-believed it was herself, trying to tell me where she had been to up in the skies, and what she had seen since that unhappy night when she flied away. She had a pretty face, and now that there was no one to drag at her bright dark hair, and it was all in order, there was a something touching in her looks that made the cart most peaceful and most quiet, though not at all melancholy. . . .

The way she learnt to understand any look of mine was truly surprising. When I sold of a night, she would sit in the cart unseen by them outside, and would give a eager look into my eyes when I looked in, and would hand me straight the precise article or articles I wanted. And then she would clap her hands, and laugh for joy. And as for me, seeing her so bright, and remembering what she was when I first lighted on her, starved and beaten and ragged, leaning asleep against the muddy cart-wheel, it give me such heart that I gained a greater heighth of reputation than ever, and I put Pickleson down (by the name of Mim's Travelling giant otherwise Pickleson) for a fypunnote in my will.

This happiness went on in the cart till she was sixteen year old. By which time I began to feel not satisfied that I had done my whole duty by her, and to consider that she ought to have better teaching than I could give her. It drew a many tears on both sides when I commenced explaining my views to her; but what's right is right, and you can't neither by tears nor laughter do away with its character.

So I took her hand in mine, and I went with her one day to the Deaf and Dumb establishment in London, and when the gentleman come to speak to us, I says to him: "Now I'll tell you what I'll do with you, Sir. I am nothing but a Cheap Jack, but of late years I have laid by for a rainy day notwithstanding. This is my only daughter (adopted), and you can't produce a deafer nor a dumber. Teach her the most that can be taught her in the shortest separation that can be named,—state the figure for it,—and I am game to put the money down. I won't bate you a single farthing, Sir, but I'll put down the money here and now, and I'll thankfully throw you in a pound to take it. There!" The gentleman smiled, and then, "Well, well," says he, "I must first know what she has learned already. How do you communicate with her?" Then I showed him, and she wrote in printed writing many names of things and so forth; and we held some sprightly conversation, Sophy and me, about a little story in a book which the gentleman showed her, and which she was able to read. "This is most extraordinary," says the gentleman; "is it possible that you have been her only teacher?" "I have been her only teacher, Sir," I says, "besides herself." "Then," says the gentleman, and more acceptable words was never spoken to me, "you're a clever fellow, and a good fellow." This he makes known to Sophy, who kisses his hands, clasps her own, and laughs and cries upon it.

We saw the gentleman four times in all, and when he took down my name and asked how in the world it ever chanced to be Doctor, it come out that he was my own nephew by the sister's side, if you'll believe me, to the very Doctor that I was called after. This made our footing still easier, and he says to me:

"Now, Marigold, tell me what more do you want your adopted daughter to know?"

"I want her, Sir, to be cut off from the world as little as can be considering her deprivations and therefore to be able to read whatever is wrote with perfect ease and pleasure."

"My good fellow," urges the gentleman, opening his eyes wide, "why I can't do that myself!"

I took his joke, and gave him a laugh (knowing by experience how flat you fall without it), and I mended my words accordingly.

"What do you mean to do with her afterwards?" asks the gentleman, with a sort of doubtful eye. "To take her about the country?"

"In the cart, Sir, but only in the cart. She will live a private life, you understand, in the cart. I should never think of bringing her infirmities before the public. I wouldn't make a show of her for any money."

The gentleman nodded, and seemed to approve.

"Well," says he, "Can you part with her for two years?"

"To do her that good,—yes, Sir."

"There's another question," says the gentleman, looking towards her,—"can she part with you for two years?"

I don't know that it was a harder matter of itself (for the other was hard enough to me), but it was harder to get over. However, she was pacified to it at last, and the separation betwixt us was settled. How it cut up both of us when it took place, and when I left her at the door in the dark of an evening, I don't tell. But I know this: remembering that night, I shall never pass that same establishment without a heartache and a swelling in the throat; and I couldn't put you up the best of lots in sight of it with my usual spirit,—no, not even the gun, nor the pair of spectacles,—for five hundred pound reward from the Secretary of State for the Home Department, and throw in the honour of putting my legs under his mahogany afterwards.

Still, the loneliness that followed in the cart was not the old loneliness, because there was a term put to it, however long to look forward to; and because I could think, when I was anyways down, that she belonged to me and I belonged to her. Always planning for her coming back, I bought in a few months' time another cart, and what do you think I planned to do with it? I'll tell you. I planned to fit it up with shelves and books for her reading, and to have a seat in it where I could sit and see her reading, and think that I had been her first teacher. Not hurrying over the job, I had the fittings knocked together in contriving ways under my own inspection, and here was her bed in a berth with curtains, and there was her reading-table, and here was her writing-desk, and elsewhere was her books in rows upon rows, picters and no picters, bindings and no bindings, gilt-edged and plain, just as I could pick 'em up for her in lots up and down the country, North and South and West and East. Winds liked best and winds liked least, Here and there and gone astray, Over the hills and far away. And when I had got together pretty well as many books as the cart would nearly hold, a new scheme come into my head, which, as it turned out, kept my time and attention a good deal employed, and helped me over the two years' stile.

Without being of an avaricious temper, I like to be the owner of things. I shouldn't wish, for instance, to go part-ners with yourself in the Cheap Jack cart. It's not that I mistrust you, but that I'd rather know it was mine. Simi-larly, very likely you'd rather know it was yours. Well! A kind of jealousy began to creep into my mind when I re-flected that all those books would have been read by other people long before they was read by her. It seemed to take away from her being the owner of 'em like. In this way, the question got into my head: Couldn't I have a book new-made express for her, which she should be the first to read?

It pleased me, that thought did; and as I never was a man to let a thought sleep (you must wake up all the whole family of thoughts you've got and burn their nightcaps, or you won't do in the Cheap Jack line), I set to work at it. Considering that I was in the habit of changing so much about the country, and that I should have to find out a literary character here to make a deal with, and another literary character there to make a deal with, as opportunities presented, I hit on the plan that this same book should be a general miscellaneous lot,—like the razors, flat-iron, chronometer watch, dinner plates, rolling-pin, and looking-glass,—and shouldn't be offered as a single individual article, like the spectacles or the gun. When I had come to that conclusion, I came to another, which shall likewise be yours.

Often had I regretted that she never had heard me on the footboard, and that she never could hear me. It ain't that I am vain, but that you don't like to put your own light under a bushel. What's the worth of your reputation, if you can't convey the reason for it to the person you most wish to value it? Now I'll put it to you. Is it worth sixpence, fippence, fourpence, threepence, twopence, a penny, a halfpenny, a farthing? No, it ain't. Not worth a farthing. Very well, then. My conclusion was that I would begin her book with some account of myself. So that, through reading a specimen or two of me on the footboard, she might form an idea of my merits there. I was aware that I couldn't do myself justice. A man can't write his eye (at least I don't know how to), nor yet can a man write his voice, nor the rate of his talk, nor the quickness of his action, nor his general spicy way. But he can write his turns of speech, when he is a public speaker,—and indeed I have heard that he very often does, before he speaks 'em.

Well! Having formed that resolution, then come the question of a name. How did I hammer that hot iron into shape? This way. The most difficult explanation I had ever had with her was, how I come to be called Doctor, and yet was no Doctor. After all, I felt that I had failed of getting it correctly into her mind, with my utmost pains. But trusting to her improvement in the two years, I thought that I might trust to her understanding it when she should come to read it as put down by my own hand. Then I thought I would try a joke with her and watch how it took, by which of itself I might fully judge of her understanding it. We had first discovered the mistake we had dropped into, through her having asked me to prescribe for her when she had supposed me to be a Doctor in a medical point of view; so thinks I, "Now, if I give this book the name of my Prescriptions, and if she catches the idea that my only Prescriptions are for her amusement and interest,—to make her laugh in a pleasant way, or to make her cry in a pleasant way,—it will be a delightful proof to both of us that we have got over our difficulty." It fell out to absolute perfection. For when she saw the book, as I had it got up,—the printed and pressed book,—lying on her desk in her cart, and saw the title, DOCTOR MARIGOLD'S PRESCRIPTIONS, she looked at me for a moment with astonishment, then fluttered the leaves, then broke out a laughing in the charmingest way, then felt her pulse and shook her head, then turned the pages pretending to read them most attentive, then kissed the book to me, and put it to her bosom with both her hands, I never was better pleased in all my life!

But let me not anticipate. (I take that expression out of a lot of romances I bought for her. I never opened a single one of 'em—and I have opened many—but I found the romancer saying "let me not anticipate." Which being so I wonder why he did anticipate, or who asked him to do it.) Let me not, I say, anticipate. This same book took up all my spare time. It was no play to get the other articles together in the general miscellaneous lot, but when it come to my own article! There! I couldn't have believed the blotting, nor yet the buckling to at it, nor the patience over it. Which again is like the footboard. The public have no idea.

At last it was done, and the two years' time was gone after all the other time before it, and where it's all gone to, who knows? The new cart was finished,—yellow outside, relieved with vermillion and brass fittings,—the old horse was put in it, a new un and a boy being laid on for the Cheap Jack cart, and I cleaned myself up to go and fetch her. Bright cold weather it was, cart chimneys smoking, carts pitched private on a piece of waste ground over at Wandsworth, where you may see 'em from the Sou'-western Railway when not upon the road. (Look out of the right hand window going down.)

"Marigold," says the gentleman, giving his hand hearty, "I am very glad to see you."

"Yet I have my doubts, Sir," says I, "if you can be half as glad to see me as I am to see you."

"The time has appeared so long,—has it, Marigold?"

"I won't say that, Sir, considering its real length; but—"

"What a start, my good fellow!"

Ah! I should think it was! Grown such a woman, so pretty, so intelligent, so expressive! I knew then that she must be really like my child, or I could never have known her, standing quiet by the door.

"You are affected," says the gentleman in a kindly manner.

"I feel, Sir," says I, "that I am but a rough chap in a sleeved waistcoat."

"I feel," says the gentleman, "that it was you who raised her from misery and degradation, and brought her into communication with her kind. But why do we converse alone together, when we can converse so well with her? Address her in your own way."

"I am such a rough chap in a sleeved waistcoat, Sir," says I, "and she is such a graceful woman, and she stands so quiet at the door!"

"Try if she moves at the old sign," says the gentleman.

They had got it up together o'purpose to please me! For when I give her the old sign, she rushed to my feet, and dropped upon her knees, holding up her hands to me with pouring tears of love and joy; and when I took her hands and lifted her, she clasped me round the neck, and lay there; and I don't know what a fool I didn't make of myself, until we all three settled down into talking without sound, as if there was a something soft and pleasant spread over the whole world for us. . . .

• CHAPTER II: TO BE TAKEN FOR LIFE •

So every item of my plan was crowned with success. Our reunited life was more than all that we had looked forward to. Content and joy went with us as the wheels of the two carts went round and the same stopped with us when the two carts stopped. I was as pleased and as proud as a Pug-Dog with his muzzle black-leaded for a evening party, and his tail extra curled by machinery.

But I had left something out of my calculations. Now, what had I left out? To help you to guess I'll say, a figure. Come. Make a guess and guess right. Nought? No. Nine?

No. Eight? No. Seven? No. Six? No. Five? No. Four? No. Three? No. Two? No. One? No. Now I'll tell you what I'll do with you. I'll say it's another sort of figure altogether. There. Why then, says you, it's a mortal figure. No, nor yet a mortal figure. By such means you get yourself penned into a corner, and you can't help guessing a immortal figure. That's about it. Why didn't you say so sooner?

Yes. It was a immortal figure that I had altogether left out of my calculations. Neither man's nor woman's but a child's. Girl's or boy's? Boy's. "I, says the sparrow, with my bow and arrow." Now you have got it.

We were down at Lancaster, and I had done two nights more than fair average business (though I cannot in honour recommend them as a quick audience) in the open square there, near the end of the street where Mr. Sly's King's Arms and Royal Hotel stands. Mim's travelling giant, otherwise Pickleson, happened at the self same time to be trying it on in the town. The genteel lay was adopted with him. No hint of a van. Green baize alcove leading up to Pickleson in a Auction Room. . . .

I went to the Auction Room in question, and I found it entirely empty of everything but echoes and mouldiness, with the single exception of Pickleson on a piece of red drugget. This suited my purpose, as I wanted a private and confidential word with him, which was; "Pickleson. Owing much happiness to you, I put you in my will for a fypunnote; but, to save trouble, here's fourpunten down, which may equally suit your views, and let us so conclude the transaction." Pickleson, who up to that remark had had the dejected appearance of a long Roman rushlight that couldn't anyhow get lighted, brightened up at his top extremity, and made his acknowledgments in a way which (for him) was parliamentary eloquence. He likewise did add, that having ceased to draw as a Roman, Mim had made proposals for his going in as a converted Indian Giant worked upon by The Dairyman's Daughter. This, Pickleson, having no acquaintance with the tract named after that young woman, and not being willing to couple gag with his serious views, had declined to do, thereby leading to words and the total stoppage of the unfortunate young man's beer. All of which, during the whole of the interview, was confirmed by the ferocious growling of Mim, down below in the pay-place, which shook the giant like a leaf.

But what was to the present point in the remarks of the travelling giant, otherwise Pickleson, was this: "Doctor Marigold,"—I give his words without a hope of conveying their feebleness,—"who is the strange young man that hangs about your carts?"— "The strange young man?" I gives him back, thinking that he meant her, and his languid circulation had dropped a syllable. "Doctor," he returns, with a pathos calculated to draw a tear from even a manly eye, "I am weak, but not so weak yet as that I don't know my words. I repeat them, Doctor. The strange young man." It then appeared that Pickleson, being forced to stretch his legs (not that they wanted it) only at times when he couldn't be seen for nothing, to wit in the dead of the night and towards daybreak, had twice seen hanging about my carts, in that same town of Lancaster where I had been only two nights, this same unknown young man.

It put me rather out of sorts. What it meant as to particulars I no more foreboded then than you forebode now, but it put me rather out of sorts. Howsoever, I made light of it to Pickleson, and I took leave of Pickleson, advising him to spend his legacy in getting up his stamina, and to continue to stand by his religion. Towards morning I kept a look out for the strange young man, and—what was more— I saw the strange young man. He was well dressed and well looking. He loitered very nigh my carts, watching them like as if he was taking care of them, and soon after daybreak turned and went away. I sent a hail after him, but he never started or looked around, or took the smallest notice.

We left Lancaster within an hour or two, on our way towards Carlisle. Next morning, at day break, I looked out again for the strange young man. I did not see him. But next morning I looked out again, and there he was once more. I sent another hail after him, but as before, he gave not the slightest sign of being anyways disturbed. This put a thought into my head. Acting on it I watched him in different manners and at different times not necessary to enter into, till I found that this strange young man was deaf and dumb.

The discovery turned me over, because I knew that a part of that establishment where she had been was allotted to young men (some of them well off), and I thought to myself, "If she favours him, where am I? and where is all that I have worked and planned for?" Hoping—I must confess to the selfishness—that she might not favour him, I set myself to find out. At last I was by accident present at a meeting between them in the open air, looking on leaning behind a fir-tree without their knowing of it. It was a moving meeting for all the three parties concerned. I knew every syllable that passed between them as well as they did. I listened with my eyes, which had to be as quick and true with deaf and dumb conversation as my ears with the talk of people that can speak. He was a-going out to China as clerk in a merchant's house, which his father had been before him. He was in circumstances to keep a wife, and he wanted her to marry him and go along with him. She persisted, no. He asked if she didn't love him. Yes, she loved him dearly, dearly; but she could never disappoint her beloved, good, noble, generous, and I don't-know-what-all father (meaning me, the Cheap Jack in the sleeved waistcoat), and she would stay with him, Heaven bless him! though it was to break her heart. Then she cried most bitterly, and that made up my mind.

While my mind had been in an unsettled state about her favouring this young man, I had felt that unreasonable towards Pickleson, that it was well for him he had got his legacy down. For I often thought, "If it hadn't been for this same weak-minded giant, I might never have come to trouble my head and vex my soul about the young man." But, once that I knew she loved him,—once that I had seen her weep for him,—it was a different thing. I made it right in my mind with Pickleson on the spot, and I shook myself together to do what was right by all.

She had left the young man by that time (for it took a few minutes to get me thoroughly well shook together), and the young man was leaning against another of the fir-trees—of which there was a cluster,—with his face upon his arm, I touched him on the back. Looking up and seeing me, he says, in our deaf-and-dumb talk, "Do not be angry."

"I am not angry, good boy. I am your friend. Come with me."

I left him at the foot of the steps of the Library Cart, and I went up alone. She was drying her eyes.

"You have been crying, my dear."

"Yes, father."

"Why?"

"A headache."

"Not a heartache?"

"I said a headache, father."

"Doctor Marigold must prescribe for that headache."

She took up the book of my Prescriptions, and held it up with a forced smile; but seeing me keep still and look earnest, she softly laid it down again, and her eyes were very attentive.

"The Prescription is not there, Sophy."

"Where is it?"

"Here, my dear."

I brought her young husband in, and I put her hand in his, and my only farther words to both of them were these: "Doctor Marigold's last Prescription. To be taken for life." After which I bolted.

When the wedding came off, I mounted a coat (blue, and bright buttons), for the first and last time in all my days, and I give Sophy away with my own hand. There were only us three and the gentleman who had had charge of her for those two years. I give the wedding dinner of four in the Library Cart. Pigeon-pie, a leg of pickled pork, a pair of fowls, and suitable garden stuff. The best of drinks. I give them a speech, and the gentleman give us a speech, and all our jokes told, and the whole went off like a sky-rocket. In the course of the entertainment I explained to Sophy that I should keep the Library Cart as my living-cart when not upon the road, and that I should keep all her books for her just as they stood, till she come back to claim them. So she went to China with her young husband, and it was a parting sorrowful and heavy . . . ; and so as of old, when my child and wife were gone, I went plodding along alone, with my whip over my shoulder, at the old horse's head.

Sophy wrote me many letters, and I wrote her many letters. About the end of the first year she sent me one in an unsteady hand: "Dearest father, not a week ago I had a darling little daughter, but I am so well that they let me write these words to you. Dearest and best father, I hope my child may not be deaf and dumb, but I do not yet know." When I wrote back, I hinted the question; but as Sophy never answered that question, I felt it to be a sad one, and I never repeated it. For a long time our letters were regular, but then they got irregular, through Sophy's husband being moved to another station, and through my being always on the move. But we were in one another's thoughts, I was equally sure, letters or no letters.

Five years, odd months, had gone since Sophy went away. I was still the King of the Cheap Jacks, and at a greater height of popularity than ever. I had had a first-rate autumn of it, and on the twenty-third of December, one thousand eight hundred and sixty-four, I found myself at Uxbridge, Middlesex, clean sold out. So I jogged up to London with the old horse, light and easy, to have my Christmas-eve and Christmas-day alone by the fire in the Library Cart, and then to buy a regular new stock of goods all round, to sell 'em again and get the money.

I am a neat hand at cookery, and I'll tell you what I knocked up for my Christmas-eve dinner in the Library Cart. I knocked up a beefsteak-pudding for one, with two kidneys, a dozen oysters, and a couple of mushrooms thrown in. It's a pudding to put a man in good humour with everything, except the two bottom buttons of his waistcoat. Having relished that pudding and cleared away, I turned the lamp low, and sat down by the light of the fire, watching it as it shone upon the backs of Sophy's books.

Sophy's books so brought up Sophy's self, that I saw her touching face quite plainly, before I dropped off dozing by the fire. This may be a reason why Sophy, with her deaf-and-dumb child in her arms, seemed to stand silent by me all through my nap. I was on the road, off the road, in all sorts of places, North and South and West and East, Winds liked best and winds liked least, Here and there and gone astray, Over the hills and far away, and still she stood silent by me, with her silent child in her arms. Even when I woke with a start, she seemed to vanish, as if she had stood by me in that very place only a single instant before.

I had started at a real sound, and the sound was on the steps of the cart. It was the light hurried tread of a child, coming clambering up. That tread of a child had once been so familiar to me, that for half a moment I believed I was a-going to see a little ghost.

But the touch of a real child was laid upon the outer handle of the door, and the handle turned, and the door opened a little way, and a real child peeped in. A bright little comely girl with large dark eyes.

Looking full at me, the tiny creature took off her mite of a straw hat and a quantity of dark curls fell all about her face. Then she opened her lips, and said in a pretty voice, "Grandfather!"

"Ah, my God!" I cries out. "She can speak!"

"Yes, dear grandfather. And I am to ask you whether there was ever any one that I remind you of?"

In a moment Sophy was round my neck, as well as the child, and her husband was a-wringing my hand with his face hid, and we all had to shake ourselves together before we could get over it. And when we did begin to get over it, and I saw the pretty child a-talking, pleased and quick and eager and busy, to her mother, in the signs that I had first taught her mother, the happy and yet pitying tears fell rolling down my face.

Mumu
by Jvan Turgenev

EDITORS' PREFACE

Gerasim, the noble deaf hero of *Mumu*, can remain noble
only because he is outside of the society of the time due to
his deafness. Had he been a man of normal hearing, the
tragedies in the story would not have befallen him, but, at
the same time, his nobility would have been compromised.
His emotions and sentiments could remain pure and un-
sullied only as long as he lived in isolation, protected from
the chance of falling into the habitual obsequiousness of his
fellow peasants. Had he learned how to get his way (through
such obsequiousness, for example), he would probably not
have been thrust into the position of having to make such
infinitely painful decisions as he has to make in this story.
Had he learned of society's ways, he could have performed
as others did also, and his nobility would never have been
called into existence. And that is the very point of the story:
Turgenev assails the peasant-master system as a system that
corrupts both parties, the peasant *and* the master (or, in
this case, the mistress), and shows that the only way a
person could remain true to himself under the system was
to be in it but not of it.

The story is powerful and well-crafted. Characterization
is vivid. Yet, though the central character is deaf, there is
really very little of insight into the deaf experience in this
nouvelle beyond the mere fact of isolation and the emotional
strength such isolation requires. The suggestion that deaf
people are more noble than others is simply another example of the theme found in "Pierre and Camille" and

"Doctor Marigold": the romantic belief in the superiority of the "natural" man compared to the socialized man.

A question arises at the end of this story: why does Gerasim drown Mumu when he must know at that point that he will leave Moscow to return to the country? Couldn't he, we wonder, have simply taken the dog back with him to the village?

It would appear that Turgenev conceived of the world of Gerasim as a world in which no compromise was possible. It was a world of action, not words. Only with words can compromise be made.

Is Gerasim's world really a better world? Probably not, but it sure made the world of Moscow look bad.

MUMU

In one of the streets on the outskirts of Moscow, in a grey house with white columns, a mezzanine, and a balcony that was all warped and out of shape, there once lived a woman landowner, a widow, surrounded by a multitude of serfs. Her sons were in government service in Petersburg; her daughters were married; she rarely left the house; and she spent the last years of her miserly and weary old age in solitude. Her day, joyless and overcast, had long passed away, but her evening too was blacker than night.

Of all her servants the most remarkable person was the caretaker Gerasim, a man of well over six feet, of immensely strong build, and deaf and dumb from his birth. His mistress had taken him away from his village, where he lived alone in a little hut, apart from his brothers, and was considered to be almost the most punctual peasant to pay his tax to his landowner. Endowed with quite extraordinary strength, he did the work of four men; everything he put his hand to turned out well. It was sheer delight to watch him ploughing, when, leaning heavily on the plough with his huge hands, he seemed to cut open the yielding bosom of the earth alone and without the help of his poor horse; when, some time at the beginning of August, about St. Peter's Day, he plied his scythe, he did so with a shattering force that might have uprooted a wood of young birch trees; when, swiftly and without stopping for a minute, he threshed the corn with a flail of over two yards long, the elongated and firm muscles of his shoulders rose and fell like levers. His perpetual silence lent a solemn dignity to his unwearying labour. He was a fine peasant and, were it not for his affliction, any girl would have been glad to marry him. But now Gerasim had been brought to Moscow, a pair of boots had been bought for him, a long peasant coat had been made for him for the summer and a sheepskin for winter, a broom and a spade had been put into his hands, and he was assigned the duties of a caretaker.

He took a great dislike to his new life in town at first. He was used to working in the fields and to village life from his childhood. Shut off by his affliction from the society of men, he grew up dumb and powerful, like a tree that grows on fertile soil. Transported to town, he did not know what was happening to him; he pined and was bewildered, as a young healthy bull is bewildered when taken away from a meadow where the lush grass grew up to his belly, put in a railway truck, and whirled along, his well-fed body hidden in smoke and sparks and clouds of steam, whirled along with a clatter and screech of wheels; but where he is whirled to—God only knows! After the heavy work in the fields his new duties seemed a trifling matter to Gerasim; in half an hour he had everything done, and again he either stopped dead in the middle of the yard and stared open-mouthed at the passers-by, as though trying to obtain from them a solution of the mystery of his position, or suddenly retired to some corner and, hurling the broom or spade a long way away, flung himself on the ground face downwards and lay motionless for hours on end, like a wild beast in captivity.

But a man gets used to anything, and Gerasim too, in the end, got used to living in town. He had nothing much to do: all his duties consisted in keeping the yard clean, bringing in a barrel of water twice a day, fetching and chopping up logs for the kitchen and the house, keeping out strangers, and keeping watch at night. And it must be said in all fairness that he carried out his duties zealously: there were never any shavings or any litter to be seen lying about in the yard; if the old, jaded mare put at his disposal for fetching water got stuck in the mud in the rainy season, he had only to heave with his shoulder and he would shove aside not only the cart but the horse itself; if he started chopping wood, the axe fairly rang like glass, and logs and chips were sent flying all over the place; as for strangers, after he had one night caught two thieves and knocked their heads together in so rough a fashion that there was no need to take them to the police station afterwards, everyone in the neighbourhood began to show the utmost respect for him; even in the daytime, passers-by, who were not criminals at all but simply strangers, catching sight of the formidable caretaker, would wave him away and shout at him— as though he could hear their shouts.

With all the other servants in the house, who were a little afraid of him, Gerasim was not exactly on friendly, but rather on familiar, terms: he looked upon them as members of his own household. They made themselves understood by signs, and he *did* understand them, and carried out all the orders exactly; but he also knew his own rights, and no one dared sit down in his place at table. Generally speaking, Gerasim was of a strict and serious disposition; he liked order in everything; even the cocks did not dare to fight in his presence—or there would be trouble! The moment he caught sight of them fighting he would seize them by the legs, whirl them round and round in the air a dozen times, and throw them in different directions. His mistress also kept geese in the yard, but a goose, as everyone knows, is a dignified and sober-minded bird, and Gerasim felt a respect for them, looked after them and fed them; he himself bore a rather striking resemblance to a sedate gander. He was allotted a tiny box-room over the kitchen; he fixed it all up himself, according to his liking, made himself a bedstead out of oak boards on four wooden blocks—a truly Herculean bed! You could put a ton or two on it and it would not have bent under the load. Under the bed was a sturdy chest; in the corner stood a little table of the same strong structure, and beside the table was a three-legged chair, so squat and strongly built that Gerasim himself would sometimes pick it up and drop it with a self-satisfied grin. The little room was locked up by means of a padlock that looked like one of those cottage-loaves that have a hole at the top, except that it was black; the key of this padlock Gerasim always carried about on his belt. He did not like people to come to see him.

So passed a year, at the end of which Gerasim was involved in a little incident.

The old lady in whose house he lived as caretaker was a strict observer of ancient customs in everything and kept a great number of servants: in her house were not only laundresses, sempstresses, carpenters, tailors, and dressmakers, there was even a harness-maker, who also acted as a veterinary surgeon and doctor for the servants; there was also a house doctor for the mistress, and last, a shoemaker by the name of Kapiton Klimov, an inveterate drunkard. Kapiton was a man with a grudge against the world. He regarded himself as one whose true merits had never been properly appreciated, as a man of metropolitan education, who should not be twiddling his thumbs in some out-of-the-way suburb in Moscow, and if he did drink, he did so—as he himself expressed it with slow deliberation, smiting his breast—because he had to "drown his grief" in drink. One fine day his mistress had a talk about him with her butler Gavrilo, a man who, to judge only by his little yellow eyes and his nose like a duck's bill, seemed to have been marked out by fate itself to be a person born to command. The old lady was sorry to hear of the depraved morals of Kapiton, who the night before had been picked up somewhere in the street.

"What do you think, Gavrilo?" she said suddenly. "Ought we not perhaps to marry him off? Perhaps he'd settle down then."

"Why not indeed, ma'am?" replied Gavrilo. "Let him get married, ma'am. Sure to be a good thing for him, ma'am."

"Yes, only who'd want to marry him?"

"Aye, that's right, ma'am. Still, just as you please. He might, if I may say so, ma'am, still be of some use for something. Can't throw him out into the street!"

"I believe he likes Tatyana, doesn't he?"

Gavrilo was about to make some reply, but he shut his mouth tightly.

"Yes, let him ask for Tatyana in marriage," the mistress decided, taking a pinch of snuff with relish. "Do you hear?"

"Yes, ma'am," said Gavrilo and went out.

Returning to his own room (it was in a cottage in the yard and was almost entirely filled with iron-bound chests), Gavrilo first of all sent his wife out and then sat down by the window and sank into thought. His mistress's unexpected order had evidently confounded him. At last he got up and sent for Kapiton. Kapiton made his appearance. . . .

But before communicating their conversation to the reader, it would not be out of place to relate in a few words who this Tatyana was whom Kapiton had to marry, and why the butler was embarrassed by his mistress's order.

Tatyana, who was one of the laundresses we mentioned earlier (though as a trained and skilful laundress she was put in charge of the fine linen only), was a woman of twenty-eight, small, thin, fair-haired, with moles on her left cheek. Moles on the left cheek are regarded as an ill omen in Russia, a token of an unhappy life. Tatyana could not boast of her lot. She had been badly treated ever since she was a young girl: she had done the work of two and never known any affection; she had been poorly clothed and had received the smallest wage; she had practically no relatives—an uncle of hers, an old steward, had been left behind in the country as no longer of any use, and her other uncles were ordinary peasants—and that was all. At one time she was said to have been beautiful, but her good looks were all too soon gone. She was very meek, or rather, cowed; she was completely indifferent about herself and was mortally afraid of others; all she thought of was how to finish her work in good time; she never talked to anyone and trembled at the very mention of her mistress's name, though she scarcely knew her by sight.

When Gerasim was brought from the country she nearly fainted with terror at the sight of his enormous figure. She tried as much as she could to avoid meeting him, and even closed her eyes if she happened to run past him on the way to the laundry. At first Gerasim paid no attention to her; then he started grinning to himself when she crossed his path; then he began to stare at her in admiration; and at last he never took his eyes off her. She had caught his fancy: whether by the gentle expression of her face or by the timidity of her movements—goodness only knows! One day she was walking across the yard, carefully carrying her mistress's starched jacket on her outstretched fingers, when someone suddenly seized her firmly by the elbow. She turned round and uttered a frightened scream: behind her stood Gerasim. Laughing stupidly and grunting affectionately, he held out to her a gingerbread cock with gold tinsel on its tail and wings. She was about to refuse it, but he thrust it into her hand by force, nodded, walked away, and turning round, again grunted something very affectionately to her. Ever since that day he gave her no peace; wherever she went, he was sure to be there, coming to meet her, smiling, grunting, waving his hands, suddenly producir ribbon out of the inside of his smock and foisting it on ne., or sweeping the dust out of her way with his broom. The poor girl simply did not know how to behave or what to do.

Soon the whole household learnt of the dumb caretaker's extravagant behaviour; Tatyana was overwhelmed with chaffing remarks, broad hints, and innuendoes. But not everyone could pluck up courage to make fun of Gerasim to his face; he did not like jokes; and, as a matter of fact, they left her alone too when he was present. Whether she liked it or not, the girl found herself under his protection. Like all deaf-mutes, he was very quick-witted, and he understood perfectly well when they were laughing at him or her. One day at dinner the maid in charge of linen, Tatyana's superior, began tormenting her and brought her to such a state that the poor girl did not know where to look and was almost bursting into tears from sheer vexation. Gerasim suddenly got up, stretched out his enormous hand, put it on the head of the linen maid, and stared at her with a look of such grim ferocity that she just dropped her hands on the table. Everyone fell silent. Gerasim picked up his spoon again and went on drinking his cabbage soup. "Just look at him, the dumb devil, the wood goblin!" they all muttered in an undertone, while the linen maid got up and went out into the maids' workroom. Another time, noticing that Kapiton, the same Kapiton who has been mentioned earlier, had been chatting a little too amiably with Tatyana, Gerasim beckoned to him to come up, took him to the coach-house, and, snatching up a shaft that was standing in a corner by one end, shook it at him lightly but with unmistakable meaning. After that no one dared say anything to Tatyana. And all this did not get him into any trouble. It is true that as soon as she reached the maids' workroom the linen maid at once fainted and altogether acted so skilfully that Gerasim's rude behaviour was brought to his mistress's knowledge the same day; but the fantastic old woman only laughed, and to the linen maid's great chagrin made her repeat several times how he had pushed her head down with his heavy hand, and next day sent Gerasim a rouble. She regarded him with favour as a strong and faithful watchman. Gerasim was very much afraid of her, but he had great hopes of her favour all the same, and was intending to go to her and ask her for permission to marry Tatyana. He was only waiting for a new coat he had been promised by the butler—for he wished to appear decently dressed before his mistress—when this same mistress suddenly took it into her head to marry Tatyana off to Kapiton.

The reader will now easily understand the reason for the butler Gavrilo's confusion after his conversation with his mistress. "The mistress," he thought to himself as he was sitting at the window, "no doubt favours Gerasim (Gavrilo knew this perfectly well and that was why he himself treated him so well); but, all the same, he is a poor dumb creature. Should I inform the mistress that Gerasim has been courting Tatyana? But, on the other hand, it is quite fair, isn't it? For what kind of husband would Gerasim make? But then again, if that damned wood goblin (God forgive me!)

was to find out that Tatyana was being married to Kapiton, he'd be sure to smash up everything in the house. Aye, he would and all. You can't get any sense out of a fellow like him. Why, a devil like him (God forgive me!) simply can't be got to see reason—Oh, well. . ."

The appearance of Kapiton interrupted the thread of Gavrilo's thoughts. The shiftless shoemaker came in, put his hands behind him, and leaning nonchalantly against the projecting angle of the wall near the door, crooked his right foot in front of his left and tossed his head, as much as to say, "Here I am! What do you want?"

Gavrilo looked at Kapiton and drummed with his fingers on the jamb of the window. Kapiton merely narrowed his leaden eyes a little, but did not drop them; he even grinned brightly and passed his hand over his fair hair, which was sticking out in all directions. "Well," he seemed to say, "it's me—see? Me! What are you staring at?"

"A fine fellow," said Gavrilo, and paused. "A fine fellow, I don't think!"

Kapiton merely twitched his slender shoulders.

"Just look at yourself," Gavrilo went on reproachfully. "Have a good look at yourself. Well, what do you think you look like?"

Kapiton cast a serene glance upon his threadbare, torn coat, his patched trousers, examined with particular attention his boots, which were full of holes—especially the one against whose toe his small right foot was leaning so gracefully—and then stared at the butler again. "What about it, sir?"

"What about it?" Gavrilo repeated. "What about it—sir? What about it indeed! You're the spitting image of the devil himself, God forgive me! That's what you look like!"

Kapiton blinked rapidly. "You can call me names as much as you like," he thought to himself.

"Drunk again, weren't you?" began Gavrilo. "Again, eh? Answer me, man!"

"Seeing as how I'm in weak health," replied Kapiton, "I have certainly exposed myself to the influence of alcoholic beverages."

"In weak health, are you? You're not flogged enough, that's the trouble! Apprenticed in Petersburg too! You've not learnt a lot during your apprenticeship, have you? All you're good for is to eat the bread of idleness!"

"So far as that is concerned, sir, there's only One Who can judge me, the Lord God Himself and no one else. He alone knows what sort of man I am and whether or not I eats the bread of idleness. As regards the little matter of drunkenness, if you insist, sir, on bringing it up, it's not me but a pal of mine who is to blame for it. It was him who put temptation in my way and it was him who, in a manner of speaking, foxed me—gave me the slip, I mean, while I—"

"While you remained in the street like a fool. Oh, you dissolute fellow! But that's not why I've asked you to come," the butler continued. "What I want to talk to you about is this: the mistress"—here he paused a little—"the mistress wants you to get married. Do you hear? She thinks that you'll—er—settle down when you're married. Understand?"

"Course I understands, sir."

"All right, then. If you ask me, it is about time someone took you in hand properly. However, that's her business. Well? Are you agreeable?"

Kapiton grinned. "Matrimony's an excellent thing for a man, sir. I mean to say, sir, so far as I'm concerned, I'd be only too happy. With the greatest of pleasure, sir, I'm sure."

"Very well, then," said Gavrilo; and he thought to himself, "I suppose the fellow means well." "Only," he went on aloud, "the trouble is, you see, that the wife they've found for you isn't the sort you'd—er—like."

"Oh? And who is she, if I may ask, sir?"

"Tatyana."

"Tatyana?" Kapiton detached himself from the wall and stared open-mouthed at Gavrilo.

"Well, why are you so alarmed? Don't you like her?"

"Like her? Of course I like her, sir. She's a good enough girl. A hard-working, quiet girl. But you know perfectly well, sir, that that wood goblin, that damned hellhound of the steppes, is after her himself—"

"I know, my dear fellow, I know all about it," the butler interrupted him with vexation. "But, you see—"

"But, good heavens, sir, he's sure to kill me. Sure to. Swat me like a fly. Why, his hand—have you seen his hand, sir? It's—why, it's simply like Minin's and Pozharsky's.* And he's deaf too. If he hits you, he don't know how hard he's hitting! Swings his enormous fists about without realising what he's doing. And there's no way of stopping him, either. Why? Because, as you knows yourself, sir, he's as deaf as a post. That's why. And he has no more brains, sir, than the heel of my foot. Why, sir, he's just a wild animal, a stone idol, sir, worse'n an idol—in fact, just a block of wood. Why then should I have to suffer because of him now? Not that I care a damn, sir. I've got used to this sort of life; I've lost all I ever possessed; I've got all

---

* Cosmo Minin and Prince Dmitry Pozharsky were two Nizhny-Novgorod patriots who in 1611 raised a people's army and defeated the occupying Polish forces, thus bringing about the union of Russia under the Romanov dynasty. Cosmo Minin was a butcher who offered his property to the national cause of liberation, and Prince Pozharsky was the commander of the national levies.
—TRANSLATOR.

dirty and greasy like a tramp's kettle; but I'm a man for all that and not some worthless kettle."

"I know, I know. Don't go on about it."

"Dear, oh dear," continued the shoemaker warmly, "when's there going to be an end to all my troubles, O Lord? Oh, I'm a miserable wretch, and there's no end to my misery! What sort of life have I had—what sort of life—just think of it, sir! When I was a boy I was beaten by my German master; when in the prime of life I was beaten by my own kith and kin; and now that I've reached a ripe age that's the sort of reward I get—"

"Oh, you soul of a bast sponge, you! What are you carrying on like this for, for goodness' sake?"

"What for, sir? It's not a beating I'm afraid of. Let my master chastise me in private, but in public I expect him to give me a civil word, for I'm still a man, am I not? But who, I ask you, have I got to deal with here?"

"Well, clear out now," Gavrilo interrupted him impatiently.

Kapiton turned round and walked slowly to the door.

"But suppose he didn't come into it," the butler called after him. "You'd be agreeable yourself, wouldn't you?"

"I give my consent," Kapiton replied and withdrew. His eloquence did not desert him even in the greatest emergencies.

The butler paced the room several times. "Well," he said at last, "call Tatyana now."

A few moments later Tatyana came in very quietly and stopped on the threshold. "What would you like me to do, sir?" she said in a soft voice.

The butler looked at her intently. "Well, my dear," he said, "would you like to get married? The mistress has found a husband for you."

"Yes, sir. And who has she chosen for my future husband?"

"Kapiton, the shoemaker."

"Yes, sir."

"He's a shiftless fellow, that's true enough. But the mistress relies on you to see to that!"

"Yes, sir."

"There's one thing, though. That deaf-mute, Gerasim—he's courting you, isn't he? How did you manage to bewitch that bear, I wonder? I shouldn't be surprised if he killed you, a bear like that."

"He'll kill me all right, sir. Sure to kill me."

"He'll kill you, will he? We'll see about that. But what do you mean—kill you? He has no right to kill you, has he? You see that, don't you?"

"I don't know, sir. I don't know whether he has any right to or not."

"What a funny girl you are! You haven't made him any promise, have you?"

"I beg your pardon, sir?"

The butler was silent and thought to himself, "What a timid creature you are, to be sure!"

"Very well," he said, "I'll have another talk with you later. You can go now, my dear. I can see you're a truly meek creature."

Tatyana turned round, pressed her hand lightly against the frame of the door, and went out.

"Let's hope the mistress will forget all about this wedding tomorrow," thought the butler. "What am I so worried about? As for that mischief-maker, we'll call in the police. Ustinya Fyodorovna," he cried in a loud voice to his wife, "set the samovar on the table, will you, there's a good woman!"

On that day Tatyana hardly left the laundry. At first she cried a little; then she dried her tears and set to work as before. Kapiton stayed in a pub till late at night with some friend of a gloomy aspect and he told him in great detail how in Petersburg he had lived with a gentleman who would have been perfect, had he not been a little too strict about things and had he not suffered just a little bit from a flaw in his character: he was a hard drinker—and as for the fair sex, there was simply no holding him. . . . His gloomy friend merely nodded; but when Kapiton at last declared that because of a certain event he would have to lay hands on himself the next day, his gloomy companion observed that it was time they went to bed. And they parted surlily and in silence.

Meanwhile the butler's expectations were not fulfilled. The mistress was so taken by the idea of Kapiton's marriage that even in the night she talked only of that to one of her companions who was employed in her house for the sole purpose of distracting her when she suffered from insomnia and who, like a night cabby, slept in the day. When Gavrilo entered her room after breakfast with his report, her first question was, "And what about our wedding? Is it coming off?" He, of course, replied that it was coming off, all right, and that Kapiton would be coming to see her that very day to thank her. The old lady did not feel well, and she did not spend much time in attending to her business affairs.

The butler went back to his room and summoned a council of war. And indeed the matter called for a special discussion. Tatyana of course did not voice any objections, but Kapiton kept announcing in everybody's hearing that he had one head, and not two or three. Gerasim kept casting quick and stern glances at everybody and refused to budge from the steps of the maids' workroom and apparently guessed that some plot was being hatched against him. The people who had answered the butler's summons (among them was an old footman who looked after the sideboard, nicknamed Uncle Tail, whose advice was always respectfully sought by everyone, though all they heard from him was, "So that's how it is! Yes, yes, yes, yes!") began by locking up Kapiton in the little room where the water-filtering plant was kept. This was done as a precaution, in case of an unexpected emergency. They then tried to think what they had better do. It would, of course, have been easy to have recourse to force, but what if—heaven forbid!—there were an uproar and the mistress were upset—that would be a disaster! What then were they to do? They thought and they thought and at last came to a decision. It had been observed repeatedly that Gerasim could not abide drunkards. Sitting at the gates, he would turn away with disgust every time someone who had had a drop too many passed by with unsteady steps and with the peak of his cap over one ear. They therefore decided to teach Tatyana how to pretend to be drunk and then make her walk past Gerasim, swaying and reeling from side to side. The poor girl would not agree to this for a long time but she was persuaded in the end; besides, she realised herself that there was no other way of getting rid of her admirer. She went. Kapiton was let out of the little room; for, after all, the matter concerned him closely. Gerasim was sitting on the curbstone at the gates, prodding the ground with a spade. From behind every corner, from behind every window blind, people were watching him.

The stratagem succeeded better than they had hoped. On seeing Tatyana, Gerasim at first, as usual, began nodding at her and grunting affectionately. Then he looked more closely, dropped his spade, jumped to his feet, walked up to her, put his face close to hers. She staggered more than ever from fright and closed her eyes. He seized her by the hand, ran with her across the entire yard, and, going into the room where the council was sitting, pushed her straight towards Kapiton. Tatyana nearly fainted away. Gerasim stood still for several minutes, looked at her, smiled bitterly, and with a wave of the hand went, stepping heavily, straight to his cubbyhole.

He did not come out of it for the whole of the next twenty-four hours. The post-boy Antipka said afterwards that he saw Gerasim through a chink in the door, sitting on his bed, his hand pressed against his face, humming a song quietly and rhythmically, and only from time to time uttering grunts—he was humming, that is, swaying backwards and forwards, closing his eyes, and tossing his head as coachmen or barge-haulers do when they strike up their mournful songs. It gave Antipka the creeps, and he came away from the chink. But when Gerasim came out of his box-room the next day, no particular change could be observed in him. He only seemed to be a little more morose, and he did not take the slightest notice of Tatyana and Kapiton. The same evening both of them, with geese under their arms, went to pay their respects to their mistress, and a week later they were married. On the day of the wedding Gerasim did not show any change in his behaviour, except that he came back from the river without water, having somehow managed to break the barrel on the way; and at night in the stable he cleaned and rubbed down his horse so vigorously that it swayed like a blade of grass in the wind and staggered from one leg to the other under his iron fists.

All this had taken place in the spring. Another year passed, in the course of which Kapiton had at last become an inveterate drunkard and gone completely to seed and as one who was no longer good for anything was sent away with the provision carts to a remote village with his wife. On the day of his departure he did his best to pluck up courage at first, assuring everybody that, send him where they would, even, as the saying is, "where the peasant women wash shirts and throw their carpet flails up into the sky," he would not go under; but later on he lost heart, began complaining that he was being taken to live among uneducated people, and in the end grew so weak that he had not even enough strength to put his own cap on; some compassionate soul pulled it over his forehead, put the peak to rights, and slapped it from above. When everything was ready and the peasants held the reins in their hands and were only waiting for the words of farewell to be said in order to start, Gerasim came out of his box-room, went up to Tatyana, and gave her a parting gift—a red cotton kerchief he had bought for her a year ago. Tatyana, who up to that moment had put up with all the vicissitudes of her life with the utmost indifference, could no longer contain herself, burst into tears, and, before getting into the cart, kissed Gerasim three times, like a good Christian. He went to see her off to the toll gate, and at first walked beside her cart, but at the Crimean Ford he stopped suddenly, dismissed it all with a wave of the hand, and walked away along the riverbank.

It all happened towards evening. He walked slowly, looking at the water. Suddenly he thought he saw something floundering in the mud close to the bank. He bent down and saw a little puppy with white and black spots, which, in spite of all its efforts, could not scramble out of the water. It was struggling, slithering, and trembling with all its little, thin, wet body. Gerasim had a look at the poor little dog, snatched it up with one hand, thrust it into the inside of his coat, and walked back home with long steps. He went into his box-room, put down the rescued puppy on his bed, covered it with his heavy peasant overcoat, ran first to the stable for straw and then to the kitchen for a cup of milk. Carefully removing the coat and spreading out the straw, he put the milk on the bed. The poor little dog was not more than three weeks old, and its eyes had not long been opened; one eye still seemed a little larger than the other; it did not know how to drink out of a cup and just kept shivering and closing its eyes. Gerasim took hold of its head gently with two fingers and pushed its little nose into the cup. The little dog suddenly began lapping greedily, sniffing, shivering, and choking. Gerasim looked and looked at it, and then suddenly burst out laughing. All through the night he busied himself with it, kept it covered, rubbed it dry, and at last fell asleep himself beside it; and his sleep was quiet and joyful.

No mother could have looked after her baby as Gerasim looked after his nursling. (The puppy turned out to be a bitch.) At first she was very weak, feeble, and rather ugly, but as time passed she put on weight and improved in looks, and eight months later, thanks to the unremitting care of the man who had saved her, she was transformed into a very presentable little dog of the spaniel breed, with long ears, a feathery, upright tail and large, expressive eyes. She was passionately attached to Gerasim, and never let him out of her sight, always following him about, wagging her tail. He had even given her a name: dumb people know that their inarticulate noises draw the attention of other people, so he called her Mumu. All the servants in the house knew her and also called her Mumu. She was very intelligent and very affectionate with everybody, but she was attached only to Gerasim. Gerasim too was deeply attached to her, and he resented it when other people stroked her. Whether he was afraid for her or jealous— goodness only knows! She would wake him in the morning, tugging at the skirts of his coat; she would bring him by its reins the old horse that drew the water cart and with whom she lived in great amity and would accompany him to the river with an expression of the utmost gravity on her face; she kept watch over his brooms and spades, and never let anyone go near his box-room. He purposely cut a hole in his door for her, and she seemed to feel that only in Gerasim's little room was she complete mistress, and that was why when she went in she at once jumped onto the bed with an air of utter contentment.

She never slept at night, but she did not bark indiscriminately, like some foolish watchdog that, sitting on its hind legs and with its snout in the air and its eyes screwed up, barks just out of boredom, without rhyme or reason, at the stars, and usually three times in succession. No! Mumu's thin little voice was never raised without good reason: either some stranger was coming a little too near the fence, or there was some suspicious sound or rustle somewhere. In a word, she was a most excellent watchdog. It is true, besides her, there was in the yard a sandy-coloured old dog with brown spots, called Volchok, but he was never—not even at night—let off the chain, and indeed he was so decrepit that he never asked for freedom; he just lay curled up in his kennel and only from time to time uttered a hoarse, almost soundless, bark, which he broke off at once, as though realising himself how utterly useless it was. Mumu never went into the mistress's house, and, when Gerasim carried wood into the rooms always stayed behind, waiting for him impatiently at the front steps, pricking up her ears, and at the slightest noise behind the front door turning her head to the right and, suddenly, to the left.

So passed another year. Gerasim carried on with his duties as caretaker and was very satisfied with his lot, when suddenly an unexpected incident occurred. One fine summer day the mistress was walking up and down the drawing room with her lady companions. She was in high spirits; she laughed and joked; her lady companions too laughed and joked, though they did not feel particularly happy: in the house they did not like it very much when the mistress was in a merry mood because, for one thing, she demanded that everyone should respond immoderately and fully to her feelings and was furious when someone's face did not beam with delight, and, for another, because these out-bursts did not last long and were usually followed by a sour and gloomy mood. That day she seemed to have got out of bed on the right side. At cards she had four knaves, which meant that her wishes would come true (she always tried to tell her own fortune by cards in the mornings), and her tea seemed to her particularly delicious, for which her maid was rewarded by a few words of praise and twenty copecks in money.

The old lady walked up and down the drawing room with a sweet smile on her wrinkled lips, and then went up to the window. A flower garden had been laid out in front of the window, and in the very middle bed under a little rosebush lay Mumu, busily gnawing a bone. The old lady saw her. "Goodness gracious," she cried suddenly, "what dog is that?"

The lady companion to whom the mistress addressed the question began to dither, overcome, poor soul, by that anguished state of uneasiness which comes upon every person in a dependent position when he is not sure what to make of his master's exclamation.

"I—I d-don't know, ma'am," she murmured. "I believe it belongs to the dumb man—"

"Goodness me," the mistress interrupted, "it's a most charming little dog! Tell them to bring it here. How long has he had it? How is it I haven't seen it before? Tell them to bring it in."

The lady companion at once rushed out into the hall. "You there," she shouted to a servant, "bring Mumu in at once! She's in the flower garden."

"Oh so her name is Mumu, is it?" said the old lady. "A very nice name."

"Yes, ma'am, a very nice name indeed!" the lady companion was quick to assent. "Make haste, Stepan!"

Stepan, a sturdily built young footman, rushed headlong into the flower garden. He was about to get hold of Mumu, when she cleverly slipped between his fingers and, with her tail in the air, fled as fast as she could to Gerasim, who was at that moment standing outside the kitchen, shaking and scraping out a barrel, turning it round and round in his hands like a child's drum. Stepan ran after her and tried to catch her at her master's feet; but the agile dog would not let a stranger get hold of her and, bounding about, evaded his grasp. Gerasim looked on with a grin at all this commotion; at last Stepan got up, looking very vexed, and quickly explained to him by signs that the mistress wanted to have the dog fetched to her. Gerasim looked a little surprised, but he called Mumu, picked her up from the ground, and handed her to Stepan. Stepan brought her into the drawing room and put her on the parquet floor. The old lady began calling Mumu to her in a coaxing voice. Mumu, who had never before been in such magnificent rooms, got very frightened and made a rush for the door, but, pushed away by the obliging Stepan, trembled all over and flattened herself against the wall.

"Mumu, Mumu, come to me, come to your mistress," the old lady kept saying. "Come here, you silly little dog— don't be afraid. . ."

"Come, Mumu, come to the mistress," the lady companions kept repeating. "Come along!"

But Mumu looked wistfully round her and did not budge from her place.

"Bring her something to eat," said the mistress. "How

stupid she is! Not to come to her mistress! What is she afraid of?"

"She isn't used to you yet, ma'am," one of her lady companions said in a timid, sugary voice.

Stepan brought in a saucer of milk and put it down before Mumu, but Mumu did not even sniff at the milk, and still trembled all over, looking round as before.

"Oh, you stupid little thing!" said the old lady, and, walking up to Mumu, she tried to stroke her.

But Mumu turned her head convulsively and bared her teeth. The old lady quickly drew back her hand.

There was a moment's silence. Mumu gave a faint whine as though complaining or apologising. The old lady moved away and frowned. The dog's sudden movement had frightened her.

"Oh dear," shrieked all the lady companions at once, "she hasn't bitten you, has she?" (Mumu had never bitten anyone in her life.) "Dear, oh dear!"

"Take her away," the old lady said in a changed voice. "She's a bad little dog! Such a spiteful creature!"

And, turning round slowly, she went towards her private office, but she stopped, glared balefully at her lady companions, and saying, "Why are you following me? I haven't called you, have I?" went out.

The lady companions began waving their hands at Stepan frantically. Stepan snatched up Mumu and threw her quickly out of the door straight at Gerasim's feet, and half an hour later a profound silence settled over the house, and the old lady sat on the sofa, looking blacker than a thundercloud.

To think what trifles will sometimes upset a person! Even when evening came, the old lady was still out of humour. She did not talk to anyone; she did not play cards; and she had a bad night. She took it into her head that the eau de Cologne they gave her was not the same as what they

usually gave her, that her pillow smelled of soap, and she
made the linen maid smell all the bed linen. In short, she
was nervous and in a bad temper.

Next morning she ordered Gavrilo to be summoned an
hour earlier than usual. "Tell me, please," she began as
soon as the butler, not without some trepidation, stepped
over the threshold, "what dog was that barking in our yard
all night? It wouldn't let me sleep?"

"A dog, ma'am—what dog, ma'am?" he said in a not-
quite-steady voice. "Perhaps the dumb man's dog, ma'am!"

"I don't know whether it was the dumb man's or someone
else's, only it wouldn't let me sleep. And I really can't
imagine what we want so many dogs for! I'd very much like
to know that. We have a yard dog, haven't we?"

"Why, of course we have, ma'am. Volchok, ma'am."

"Well, why another one? What do we want another dog
for? Just making a mess of things. There's no one with
authority in the house, that's the trouble. And what does
that dumb fellow want a dog for? Who gave him permission
to keep dogs in my yard? Yesterday I went up to the window
and there she was—lying in the flower garden. Had taken
some nasty bit of rubbish with her and was gnawing it. And
I've had roses planted there!" The old lady paused for a
moment. "See that she isn't here today—do you hear?"

"Yes, ma'am."

"Today! You can go now. I'll send for you later for the
report."

Gavrilo went out.

Passing through the drawing room, the butler moved a
bell from one table to another just to keep things nice and
tidy, blew his ducklike nose quietly in the ballroom, and
went out into the hall. In the hall Stepan was asleep on a
chest in the attitude of a slain warrior in a battlepiece, his
bare legs stretched out convulsively from under his coat,

107

which served him for a blanket. The butler shook him by the shoulders and gave him some kind of order in an undertone, to which Stepan replied by something that was between a yawn and a guffaw. The butler went away, and Stepan jumped down from the chest, put on his coat and boots, went outside, and stopped by the front steps. Before five mintues had passed, Gerasim made his appearance with a huge bundle of firewood on his back accompanied by the inseparable Mumu. (The old lady had given strict orders that her bedroom and study should be heated even in summer.) Gerasim turned sideways towards the door, pushed it open with his shoulder, and pitched into the house with his load, while Mumu, as usual, stayed behind to wait for him. It was then that Stepan, taking advantage of the favourable opportunity, suddenly threw himself on her like a kite on a chick, pressed her to the ground with his chest, snatched her up in his arms, and, without even putting on his cap, rushed out of the yard, hailed the first cab he met, and galloped off to the game market. There he soon found a customer to whom he sold her for fifty copecks, on condition that he keep her tied up for at least a week, and took a cab home at once. But before he reached the house he got out of the cab and, going round the yard, jumped over the fence into the yard from the back lane.

However, he need not have worried: Gerasim was no longer in the yard. On coming out of the house he had at once missed Mumu; he could not remember a time when she failed to wait for him, and he began calling her in his own way. He rushed into his box-room, up the hayloft, ran out into the street—this way and that. She was lost! He turned to the servants, asking about her with the most despairing signs, pointing about a foot from the ground, outlining her shape with his hands. Some of them really did not know where Mumu had got to and only shook their heads; others did know and just grinned at him in reply; while the butler assumed an important air and began shouting at the coachmen. Then Gerasim just ran out of the yard and disappeared.

Dusk was already falling when he came back. From his exhausted appearance, his unsteady gait, and his dusty clothes, one could see that he had been running over half of Moscow. He stopped in front of the windows of his mistress's house, cast a glance at the front steps, on which about seven house-serfs were standing in a group, turned away, uttering once more Mumu's name in his inarticulate way. But Mumu did not answer. He went away. They all followed him with their eyes, but no one smiled or uttered a word. The inquisitive post-boy Antipka told them next morning in the kitchen that the dumb man had been groaning all night.

The whole of the following day Gerasim did not put in an appearance, so that the coachman Potap had to go for water instead of him, which made the coachman Potap rather disgruntled. The old lady asked Gavrilo if her order had been carried out. Gavrilo replied that it had. The next morning Gerasim came out of his box-room and began to work. He came in for his dinner, ate, and went out again without a greeting to anyone. His face, which, as with all deaf-mutes, looked expressionless anyway, seemed now turned to stone. After dinner he went out of the yard again, but not for long. He came back and went up to the hayloft.

Night came, a clear moonlit night. Gerasim lay, uttering heavy sighs and turning continuously from side to side, when suddenly he felt as though he were being pulled by the skirt of his coat; he trembled all over, but did not raise his head and even shut his eyes tighter; but a moment later he was again pulled by the coat, much more vigorously this time; he jumped up, and there was Mumu spinning round before him with the torn end of a rope round her neck. A drawn-out cry of joy burst from his speechless breast; he seized Mumu and hugged her tightly in his arms; in less than a minute she was licking his nose and eyes, his moustache and beard. He stood pondering for a while; then he climbed cautiously down from the hayloft, looked round, and, having made sure that no one could see him, made his way without incident to his box-room.

Gerasim had realised before that his dog had not got lost by herself and that she must have been taken away by his mistress's orders—the servants had, in fact, explained to him by signs that Mumu had snapped at her—and he decided to take precautionary measures of his own. First he fed Mumu with some bread, fondled her, put her to bed, and then spent the whole night trying to think how best to hide her. At last he decided to keep her in his room all day and only go to see her now and again, and to take her out at night. He stopped up the hole in the door tightly with an old overcoat of his and as soon as it was light he was out in the yard, just as though nothing had happened, even preserving (innocent guile!) the same despondent expression on his face. It had never occurred to the poor deaf fellow that Mumu might betray herself by her yelping, and indeed everyone in the house soon knew that the dumb man's dog had come back and was locked up in his box-room, but out of pity for him and his dog, and partly, perhaps, out of fear of him, they did not let him know that they had discovered his secret. The butler alone scratched the back of his head and gave it up. "Well," he seemed to say, "good luck to him! Perhaps it won't come to the mistress's ears!" The dumb man, on the other hand, had never before worked with such a will as on that day: he cleaned and scraped the whole courtyard, pulled out every single weed, got out with his own hand all the stakes from the fence round the flower garden to make sure that they were strong enough and then drove them in again—in a word, he took so much trouble and busied himself so industriously that even his mistress could not help noticing his zeal. Twice in the course of the day Gerasim went to see his prisoner by stealth; when night came, he went to bed with Mumu in his room and not in the hayloft, and only took her out for a walk in the fresh air at two o'clock in the morning. After walking about the yard for quite a long time with her, he was on the point of going back when a faint noise suddenly arose from the lane on the other side of the fence. Mumu pricked up her ears, growled, went up to the fence, sniffed, and started barking, loud and piercingly. Some drunkard had taken it into his head to bed himself down for the night there.

At that moment the old lady had just dropped off to sleep after a prolonged attack of nerves: these fits always overtook her after a too-hearty supper. The sudden barking woke her; her heart began to beat fast; and she seemed on the point of fainting. "Girls, girls," she moaned, "girls!" The frightened lady companions rushed into her bedroom. "Oh dear, I'm dying!" she cried, spreading her hands in an anguished gesture. "There's that dog again—that dog again! Oh, send for the doctor! They want to kill me! The dog, the dog again! Oh!" And she threw back her head, by which she wished to show that she had fainted. They rushed out for the doctor—that is to say, the household quack, Khariton. This doctor, whose entire skill consisted in wearing boots with soft soles, knew how to feel a pulse with the utmost delicacy; he slept fourteen hours out of twenty-four; and spent the rest of the time sighing and continually regaling his mistress with cherry laurel drops. This quack doctor came at once, waved some burnt feathers under her nose, and, when the old lady opened her eyes, at once

111

offered her a wineglass of sacred drops on a silver tray. The old lady drank them, but immediately began to complain again in a tearful voice of the dog, Gavrilo, her own fate, of being abandoned by everybody, a poor old woman, of no one's showing any pity for her, of everyone's wishing that she was dead. Meanwhile the luckless Mumu went on barking, Gerasim vainly trying to get her away from the fence. "There—there she goes again—again!" the old lady murmured and once more rolled up her eyes. The doctor whispered to a maid, who rushed into the hall, woke up Stepan, who rushed to waken Gavrilo, who in a fit of temper ordered the whole household to be roused.

Gerasim turned round, saw the lights and shadows moving about in the windows, and, with a foreboding of trouble in his heart, snatched up Mumu under his arm, ran back into his room, and locked himself in. A few minutes later five men were seen trying to break down his door, but, feeling the resistance of the bolt, they gave up. Gavrilo came running in terrible haste and ordered them all to remain there and keep watch till the morning. He himself rushed into the maids' workroom and through Lyubov Lyubimovna, the eldest lady companion, with whom he used to steal and falsify the accounts of the tea, sugar, and other groceries, informed the mistress that the dog had unfortunately come back from somewhere, but that tomorrow she would be done away with, and begged her to be so good as not to be angry with him and compose herself. The old lady would most probably not have composed herself so quickly had not the quack doctor in his haste given her forty instead of twenty drops. It was the strength of the dose of the cherry laurel drops that had its effect: a quarter of an hour later the old lady was already snoring and peacefully asleep. Gerasim was meanwhile lying in his bed with a white face, holding Mumu's mouth tightly shut.

Next morning the old lady woke up rather late. Gavrilo was waiting for her to wake up, in order to give the order for a decisive assault on Gerasim's sanctuary, while he prepared himself to resist a violent storm. But the storm did not break. Lying in bed, the old lady sent for the eldest of her lady companions.

"Lyubov Lyubimovna," she began in a soft and weak voice (she sometimes liked to pretend to be a lonely, persecuted martyr, which, needless to say, made all the servants in the house feel very uncomfortable), "you see how I suffer. Please, my dear, go and talk to Gavrilo. Surely some wretched little dog isn't dearer to him than the health and indeed the very life of his mistress! I shouldn't like to believe that," she added with an expression of deep feeling. "Go, my dear, be good enough to go to Gavrilo for me."

Lyubov Lyubimovna went to Gavrilo's room. What they talked about is not known, but a short time after, a whole crowd of people was moving across the yard in the direction of Gerasim's room; Gavrilo advanced in front, holding onto his cap with his hand, although there was no wind; beside him marched the footmen and cooks; Uncle Tail looked out the window and gave orders—that is, just waved his arms about; behind them all, small boys were skipping about and pulling faces (more than half of them were strange boys who had run in from outside). One man was on guard on the narrow staircase leading to the box-room; two more, armed with sticks, stood outside the door. They started climbing the staircase, occupying its entire length. Gavrilo went up to the door, knocked on it with his fist, and shouted, "Open up!" A stifled bark was heard; but there was no reply.

"Open up, I tell you!" he repeated.

"But he's deaf, sir!" Stepan observed from below. "He can't hear you."

They all laughed.

"What's to be done then?" Gavrilo asked from above.

"He's got a hole in the door," replied Stepan. "You'd better put your stick through it and shake it."

Gavrilo bent down. "He's stopped it up with some coat— the hole, I mean."

"Why not push the coat in, sir?"

Here again a stifled bark was heard.

"See, see, she's answering you," someone observed in the crowd, and again they laughed.

Gavrilo scratched himself behind the ear. "No," he said at last, "you'd better push the coat in yourself, if you like."

"Well, why not?"

And Stepan clambered up the stairs, took the stick, pushed the coat in and began shaking the stick about in the hole, saying, "Come out! Come out!" as he did so. He was shaking his stick about, when suddenly the door was flung open and the servants, Gavrilo at their head, rushed headlong down the stairs all at once. Uncle Tail shut the window.

"You there," Gavrilo shouted from the yard, "take care, I say! Take care!"

Gerasim stood without moving at his open door. The crowd gathered at the foot of the stairs. Gerasim looked down on all the crowd of puny people in their foreign clothes; with his arms akimbo and his red peasant skirt he towered like a giant over them.

Gavrilo took a step forward. "Now then, my dear fellow," he said, "don't you play any silly tricks with me!" And he began to explain to him by signs that the mistress demanded that he should hand over his dog to her, and that if he did not give Mumu up at once, there would be trouble.

Gerasim looked at him, pointed to the dog, made a sign with his hand round his neck as if tightening a noose, and glanced inquiringly at the butler.

114

"Yes, yes," Gavrilo replied, nodding. "Yes, certainly!"

Gerasim dropped his eyes, then suddenly shook himself and pointed again to Mumu, who was all the time standing beside him, wagging her tail innocently and pricking up her ears, as though curious to know what it was all about. He repeated the sign of strangling and smote his chest significantly, as though announcing that he would see to it himself that Mumu was destroyed.

"But you'll deceive us," Gavrilo said, waving his arms at him in reply.

Gerasim looked at him, smiled scornfully, smote his breast again, and slammed the door to.

They all looked at one another in silence.

"What's the meaning of this?" began Gavrilo. "Has he locked himself in?"

"Leave him alone, sir," said Stepan. "He'll do it, if he's promised. He is like that. If he promises something, he'll carry it out for certain. He's different from any of us as far as that's concerned. That's true enough. Yes, sir."

"Yes, sir," they all repeated. "That is so. Yes."

Uncle Tail opened the window and and also said, "Yes.".

"Very well, we shall see," said Gavrilo. "But the guard is to remain there all the same. Hey, you, Yeroshka," he added, addressing a pale-faced man in a yellow nankeen Cossack coat, who was supposed to be a gardener, "you haven't got anything to do, have you? Take a stick and sit down here. If anything happens, run to me at once!"

Yeroshka took a stick and sat down on the bottom step of the staircase. The crowd dispersed, except for a few men who were curious to see what was going to happen, and the small boys. Gavrilo went back home and informed his mistress through Lyubov Lyubimovna that everything had been carried out as ordered and that he had sent the post-boy for a policeman in case of need. The old lady tied a

115

knot in her handkerchief, sprinkled some eau de Cologne on it, rubbed her temples, had a cup of tea, and, being still under the influence of the cherry laurel drops, fell asleep again.

An hour after all this commotion the door of the box-room opened and Gerasim appeared. He had his Sunday coat on. He was leading Mumu on a string. Yeroshka got out of the way and let him pass. Gerasim went to the gates. All the small boys in the yard followed him with their eyes in silence. He did not even turn round, and only put on his cap in the street. Gavrilo sent Yeroshka after him in the role of an observer. Seeing from a distance that he had gone to an inn with the dog, Yeroshka waited for him to come out again.

In the inn they knew Gerasim and understood his signs. He ordered cabbage soup with boiled meat and sat down, leaning on the table with his arms. Mumu stood beside his chair, watching him calmly with her clever little eyes. Her coat was glossy: it was evident that she had just been thoroughly brushed. They brought Gerasim the cabbage soup. He crumbled some bread into it, cut the meat into very small pieces, and put the plate on the floor. Mumu began to eat with her usual refinement, hardly touching her food with her little muzzle. Gerasim gazed at her for a long time; two big tears suddenly rolled out of his eyes: one fell on the dog's craggy little forehead, the other into the cabbage soup. He covered his face with his hand. Mumu ate up half the meat on the plate and walked away from it, licking her chops. Gerasim got up, paid for the cabbage soup, and went out, accompanied by the somewhat perplexed glances of the waiter. Yeroshka, catching sight of Gerasim, darted round a corner, and letting him go on, followed him again.

Gerasim walked unhurriedly, without letting Mumu off the string. On reaching the corner of the street he stopped,

as though wondering what to do next. Then he set off suddenly straight in the direction of the Crimean Ford. On
the way he went into the yard of a house to which a wing
was being added and brought away from there two bricks
under his arm. At the Crimean Ford he walked along the
bank of the river, went up to the place where there were
two little rowing boats tied to pegs (he had noticed them
before), and jumped into one of them, together with Mumu.
A little old man came limping out of a hut, stood in a corner
of a kitchen-garden, and shouted at him. But Gerasim just
nodded and began rowing so vigorously that, though against
the current, he had in no time at all gone two hundred
yards. The old man stood there for a few minutes; then he
scratched his back, first with his left, then with his right
hand, and went limping back to this hut.

Meanwhile Gerasim rowed on and on. Soon Moscow was
left behind. Soon meadows, kitchen-gardens, fields, and
copses stretched on either side of the bank and peasants'
cottages appeared. There came a breath of the open country. He threw down the oars, put his head close to Mumu,
who sat before him on a dry cross-seat (the bottom of the
boat was full of water), and remained motionless, his powerful hands crossed on her back, while the boat was gradually carried back by the current towards town. At last
Gerasim sat up hurriedly with an expression of painful bitterness on his face, tied the bricks he had taken with a
rope, made a running noose, put it round Mumu's neck,
lifted her up over the river, and looked at her for the last
time. She looked at him trustingly and without fear and
wagged her tail slightly. He turned away, shut his eyes,
and opened his hands. . . Gerasim heard nothing, neither
the quick, shrill yelp of the falling Mumu nor the heavy
splash of the water; for him the noisy day was soundless
and silent as no still night is silent to us, and when he

opened his eyes again, little waves as before were hurrying over the river, as though chasing each other and, as before, rippled against the two sides of the boat, and only far away behind some wide circles were spreading out towards the bank.

As soon as Gerasim had disappeared from sight, Yeroshka returned home and reported what he had seen.

"Well, yes," observed Stepan, "he will drown her. There's nothing to worry about no more. If he promised. . ."

No one saw Gerasim during the day. He did not have his dinner at home. Evening came; they were gathered together to supper, all except him.

"What a funny fellow this Gerasim is, to be sure," a fat laundress remarked in a squeaky voice. "Fancy missing your supper because of some dog! Really!"

"Why, Gerasim has been here!" Stepan cried suddenly, scooping up the porridge with his spoon.

"How? When?"

"Why, two hours ago. Yes, to be sure! I ran across him at the gates. He was going out again, coming out of the yard. I was about to ask him about his dog, but he didn't seem to be in good spirits. I mean, he pushed me aside. I expect he just wanted to avoid me, for fear I would pester him, but he caught me such a whack across the back of the neck—such a terrific wallop—that it hurt, I can tell you." And he rubbed the back of his neck with an involuntary grin. "Aye," he added, "he certainly has got a lucky hand, no doubt about that!"

They all laughed at Stepan, and after supper they went to bed.

Meanwhile, at that very moment, a giant of a man with a sack over his shoulder and a big stick in his hand was briskly walking without stopping along the T—highway. It was Gerasim. Without looking back, he was hurrying home to his native village, to the place where he was born.

After drowning poor Mumu, he ran back to his box-room, quickly packed some of his belongings in an old horse-cloth, tied it up in a bundle, hoisted it over his shoulder, and off he went. He had observed the road carefully when he was being taken to Moscow; the village from which his mistress had fetched him was only about fifteen miles off the high-way. He walked along it with a sort of invincible courage, with a desperate and at the same time joyous determination. He walked on, his chest thrown out, his eyes fixed eagerly straight before him. He was in a hurry, just as though his old mother were waiting for him at home, as though she were calling him to come back to her after long wanderings in foreign parts among strangers.

The summer night that had just fallen was still and warm: on one side, where the sun had set, the rim of the sky was still white and covered with a faint flush of the last glow of the vanishing day; and on the other side a blue-grey twilight was already rising up. The night was coming from there. The call of the quails in their hundreds could be heard all round; corncrakes were calling as they chased each other. Gerasim could not hear them, nor could he hear the del-icate, rustling nocturnal whisperings of the trees, past which his strong legs carried him; but he could smell the familiar scent of the ripening rye, which was wafted from the dark fields; he could feel the wind, which flew to meet him— the wind from home—beating caressingly against his face and playing with his hair and beard; he saw the whitening road before him, the road that led to his home, straight as an arrow; in the sky he saw stars without number, lighting him on his way; and he strode along, strong and bold like a lion, so that when the rising sun threw its first rosy light upon the sturdy young fellow who had only just got into his stride, about thirty miles already lay between him and Moscow. . .

Two days later he was at home in his little cottage, to the great astonishment of the soldier's wife who had been quartered there. After saying a prayer before the icons, he at once went to see the village headman. The headman was at first taken aback; but the haymaking had only just started: Gerasim, a first-class worker, was given a scythe, and he went to mow in his old way, so that the peasants were struck with wonder as they watched his arms sweeping and raking together the hay.

Meanwhile, in Moscow, they discovered Gerasim's flight a day after he had gone. They went to his box-room, ransacked it, and informed Gavrilo. The latter came, had a look round, shrugged his shoulders, and decided that the dumb man had either run away or drowned himself with his silly dog. The police were informed and the old lady was told. The old lady was very angry. She burst into tears and gave orders that he was to be found at all costs. She kept saying that she had never ordered the dog to be destroyed and finally told off Gavrilo so thoroughly that he just kept shaking his head all day, murmuring, "Well!" until Uncle Tail made him see reason by saying to him, "Well *what*?"

At last news of the arrival of Gerasim in the village came from the country. The old lady calmed down a little; at first she gave orders for him to be sent back to Moscow immediately; then she declared that such an ungrateful man was of no use whatever to her. However, she died soon after this, and her heirs had other things to think of beside Gerasim; they let their mother's other servants go free on the payment of an annual tax.

Gerasim is still living, a lonely bachelor in his lonely cottage; he is strong and healthy as before; he does the work of four men as before; and he is grave and staid as before. But neighbours have noticed that since his return from Moscow he completely stopped associating with women—he will not even look at them—nor does he keep a single dog. "Still," the peasants say to each other, "good luck to him! What does he want to get mixed up with women for? As for a dog, what does he want a dog for? No thief will venture into his yard for any money!" Such is the fame of the titanic strength of the dumb man.

1852

The Deaf Mute
by Guy de Maupassant

In this story we encounter another Gerasim. The deaf man's name this time is Gargan, and he does not live in quite as pleasant surroundings as does Gerasim, but he, like Gerasim, must kill the one he loves because of the vulturism of his fellows, and accept a life of total isolation afterwards. Gargan, like Gerasim, is silent but extraordinarily noble—his story, though full of pathos, is the story of triumphant human dignity.

But what a contrast his story provides to the "frame" in which it exists. In fact, the very point of the story is that contrast, and the sense of irony such as contrast evokes. The "frame" is written by a French aristocrat in a rather offhand, leisurely fashion. He seems to "lean and loaf at his ease" as he writes. He hunts woodcock, reads books, and writes letters to his friends in Paris (the "story" itself, in fact, is supposed to be a letter to a friend in Paris). There is nothing of "human murk" in his writing—it is breezy and light, long on detail, short on feeling. He writes with careless humor ("We take our places in a strange sort of hunting wagon that my father had constructed long ago. Constructed is the only word that I can use in speaking of this monstrous carriage, or rather this earthquake on wheels." "When we are installed, John, my servant, throws us our three terriers, Pif, Paf, and Moustache. Pif belongs to Simon, Paf to Gaspard, and Moustache to me. They look like three crocodiles covered with hair.") All the world is right and orderly to him—it is the world of the eighteenth century: "whatever is, is right."

Here we are then, master Picot and I, in the little woods, where the leaves fall with a sweet and continued murmur, with a dry murmur, a little sad, for they are dead. It is cold, a light cold which stings the eyes, the nose, and the ears, and powders with a fine, white moss the limbs of the trees and the brown, plowed earth. But there is a warmth through all our limbs under the great sheepskin. The sun is gay. . . . It is good to hunt in the woods on fresh mornings in winter.

Could anything ever disturb this man? Does he have the faintest awareness of any misery or pain? He says of the leaves that it is "a *little* sad, for they are dead." He would probably say the same about the peasants with whom he hunts: it is a little sad, for they are poor. And then he would turn to other thoughts.

The irony is that such a man, oblivious to tragedy, should tell the tragic story of Gargan and his wife "Drops." It is a horrible story, full of anguish, violence and wasted lives. It is "real life," far removed from the placid, untroubled life of the idle rich man who narrates the story. At the end, he shows how little he has been affected by the story he himself has told.

As for me, my dear friend, I listened to this adventure to its close, *much moved,* and have related it to you in gross terms in order not to change the farmer's story. But now there is a report of a gun from the woods, and the formidable voice of Gaspard is heard growling in the wind, like the sound of a cannon:

"Woodcock! There is one."

And this is how I employ my time, watching for the woodcock to pass, while you are also going to the Bois to see the first winter costumes. (emphasis added)

He claims to have been "much moved" by the story, but it is obvious this is merely a manner of speaking, for his mind immediately turns to other things. His is the mind of the aristocracy as de Maupassant saw it: closed to the misery of the people who make his ease possible. It is out of such contrast that revolution springs.

Of interest to us, however, is that de Maupassant chose a deaf man, as had Turgenev, to represent the suppressed masses, the peasant class. What is notable about this is that both Turgenev and de Maupassant apparently realized that the most frustrating thing for a deaf person is not failing to hear, but failing to be heard by other people. Both Gerasim and Gargan are literally and figuratively without a voice, unable to speak out and to convey the misery of their existence, or to change anything except through direct brutal action. Both Gerasim and Gargan, as symbols of the suppressed masses of Russia and France, show a basic nobility, but both must suffer alone, denied even the simplest of human pleasure, that of companionship.

The interest in deafness for both writers, then, is in its symbolic value for their political and literary interests. For both of them, a deaf person is the most suppressed of people. In these two stories, then, the upper classes seem to have been blamed for the misery of the masses, and that misery was sometimes most powerfully portrayed by using a deaf character, a person totally unable to stand up for himself because he is totally unheard. In the twentieth century, the conditions of technology are often blamed by writers of the misery of the masses, and, again, deaf characters are used to represent that misery. Instead of suppression, however, the deaf characters in twentieth century fiction show the effects of isolation, the new illness of society. Just as a deaf character often serves best to portray suppression, so he often serves best to portray isolation also.

But do either Gerasim or Gargan show us much about the deaf experience itself? They do in the sense of what we learn of the last century. But at the same time, we know little of the thoughts of either Gerasim or Gargan—they are representative characters, not real people. In fact, of the four writers of the nineteenth century we have included, only de Musset seems to have had the deaf experience itself in mind when he included deaf characters in his story.

THE DEAF MUTE

My DEAR friend, you ask me why I do not return to Paris; you will be astonished, and almost angry, I suppose, when I give you the reason, which will without doubt be revolting to you: "Why should a hunter return to Paris at the height of the woodcock season?"

Certainly I understand and like life in the city very well, that life which leads from the chamber to the sidewalk; but I prefer a freer life, the rude life of the hunter in autumn.

In Paris, it seems to me that I am never out of doors; for, in fact, the streets are only great, common apartments without a ceiling. Is one in the air between two walls, his feet upon stone or wooden pavement, his view shut in everywhere by buildings, without any horizon of verdure, fields, or woods? Thousands of neighbors jostle you, push you, salute you, and talk with you; but the fact of receiving water upon an umbrella when it rains is not sufficient to give me the impression or the sensation of space.

Here, I perceive clearly and deliciously the difference between in doors and out. But it was not of that that I wish to speak to you.

Well, then, the woodcock are flying.

And it is necessary to tell you that I live in a great Norman house, in a valley, near a little river, and that I hunt nearly every day.

Other days, I read; I even read things that men in Paris have not the time to become acquainted with; very serious things, very profound, very curious, written by a brave,

125

scholarly genius, a foreigner who has spent his life studying the subject and observing the facts relative to the influence of the functions of our organs upon our intelligence.

But I was speaking to you of woodcock.

My two friends, the D'Orgemol brothers, and myself remain here during the hunting season awaiting the first frost. Then, when it freezes, we set out for their farm in Cannetot, near Fécamp, because there is a delicious little wood there, a divine wood, where every woodcock that flies comes to lodge.

You know the D'Orgemols, those two giants, those Normans of ancient times, those two males of the old, powerful conquering race which invaded France, took England and kept it, established itself on every coast of the world, made towns everywhere, passed like a flood over Sicily, creating there an admirable art, struck down kings, pillaged the proudest cities, matched popes in their priestly tricks and ridiculed them, more sly than the Italian pontiffs themselves, and above all, left children in all the beds of the world. These D'Orgemols are two Normans of the best stamp, and are all Norman—voice, accent, mind, blond hair, and eyes which are the color of the sea.

When we are together we talk the patois, we live, think, and act in Norman, we become Norman landowners, more peasants than farmers.

For two weeks now, we have been waiting for woodcock. Every morning, Simon, the elder, will say: "Hey! Here's the wind coming round to the east, and it's going to freeze. In two days they will be here."

The younger, Gaspard, more exact, waits for the frost to come before he announces it.

But, last Thursday he entered my room at dawn, crying out:

"It has come! The earth is all white. Two days more and we shall go to Cannetot."

Two days later, in fact, we do set out for Cannetot. Certainly you would have laughed to see us. We take our places in a strange sort of hunting wagon that my father had constructed long ago. Constructed is the only word that I can use in speaking of this monstrous carriage, or rather this earthquake on wheels. There was room for everything inside: a place for provisions, a place for the guns, place for the trunks, and places of clear space for the dogs. Everything is sheltered except the men, perched on seats as high as a third story, and all this supported by four gigantic wheels. One mounted as best he could, making his feet, hands, and even his teeth serve him for the occasion, for there was no step to give access to the edifice.

Now, the two D'Orgemols and myself scaled this mountain, clothed like Laplanders. We have on sheepskins, wear enormous, woolen stockings outside our pantaloons, and gaiters outside our woolen stockings; we also have some black fur caps and white fur gloves. When we are installed, John, my servant, throws us our three terriers, Pif, Paf, and Moustache. Pif belongs to Simon, Paf to Gaspard, and Moustache to me. They look like three crocodiles covered with hair. They are long, low, and crooked, with bent legs, and so hairy that they have the look of a yellow thicket. Their eyes can scarcely be seen under their eyebrows, or their teeth through their beards. One could never shut them into the rolling kennels of the carriage. Each one puts his own dog under his feet to keep him warm.

And now we are off, shivering abominably. It is cold, and freezing hard. We are contented. Toward five o'clock we arrive. The farmer, master Picot, is expecting us, waiting before the door. He is also a jolly fellow, not tall, but

127

round, squat, vigorous as a bulldog, sly as a fox, always laughing, always contented, knowing how to make money out of all of us.

It is a great festival for him when the woodcock arrives. The farm is large, and on it an old building set in an apple orchard, surrounded by four rows of beech-trees, which battle against the winds from the sea all the year.

We enter the kitchen where a bright fire is burning in our honor. Our table is set against the high chimney, where a large chicken is turning and roasting before the clear flame, and whose gravy is running into an earthen dish beneath.

The farmer's wife salutes us, a tall, quiet woman, wholly occupied with the cares of her house, her head full of accounts, the price of grain, of poultry, of mutton, and beef. She is an orderly woman, set and severe, known for her worth in the neighborhood.

At the end of the kitchen is set the long table where all the farm hands, drivers, laborers, stableboys, shepherds, and woman servants sit down. They eat in silence under the active eye of the mistress, watching us dine with master Picot, who says witty things to make us laugh. Then, when all her servants are fed, Madam Picot takes her repast alone at one corner of the table, a rapid and frugal repast, watching the serving maid meanwhile. On ordinary days she dines with all the rest.

We all three sleep, the D'Orgemols and myself, in a bare, white room, whitewashed with lime, containing only our three beds, three chairs, and three basins.

Gaspard always wakes first and sounds the echoing watchword. In half an hour everybody is ready, and we set out with master Picot who hunts with us.

Mr. Picot prefers me to his masters. Why? Without doubt because I am not his master. So we two reach the woods by the right, while the two brothers come to the attack by the left. Simon has the care of the dogs, all three attached to the end of a rope.

For we are not hunting woodcock but the wolf. We are convinced that it is better to find the woodcock than to seek it. If one falls upon one and kills it, there you are! But when one specially wishes to meet one, he can never quite bring him down. It is truly a beautiful and curious thing, hearing the loud report of a gun, in the fresh morning air, and then, the formidable voice of Gaspard filling the space as he howls:

"Woodcock—There it is."

As for me, I am sly. When I have killed a woodcock, I cry out: "Wolf!" And then I triumph in my success when we go to a clear place for the midday lunch.

Here we are then, master Picot and I, in the little woods, where the leaves fall with a sweet and continued murmur, with a dry murmur, a little sad, for they are dead. It is cold, a light cold which stings the eyes, the nose, and the ears, and powders with a fine, white moss the limbs of the trees and the brown, plowed earth. But there is warmth through all our limbs under the great sheepskin. The sun is gay in the blue air which it warms scarcely at all, but it is gay. It is good to hunt in the woods on fresh mornings in winter.

Down below, a dog is loudly baying. It is Pif. I know his thin voice, but it ceases. Then there is another cry, and then another; and Paf in his turn begins to bark. And what has become of Moustache? Ah! there is a little cry like that of a chicken being strangled! They have stirred up a wolf. Attention, master Picot!

They separate, then approach each other, scatter again, and then return; we follow their unforeseen windings, coming out into little roads, the mind on the alert, finger on the trigger of the gun.

They turn toward the fields again, and we turn also. Suddenly, there is a gray spot, a shadow, crossing the by-path. I aim and fire. The light smoke rises in the blue air and I perceive under a bush a bit of white hair which moves. Then I shout, with all my force, "Wolf, wolf! There he is!" And I show him to the three dogs, the three hairy croco-diles, who thank me by wagging their tails. Then they go off in search of another.

Master Picot joins me. Moustache begins to yap. The farmer says: "There must be a hare there at the edge of the field."

The moment that I came out of the woods, I perceived, not ten steps from me, enveloped in his immense yellowish mantle and wearing his knitted, woolen cap such as shep-herds wear at home, master Picot's herdsman Gargan, the deaf-mute. I said "Good morning," to him, according to our custom, and he raised his hand to salute me. He had not heard my voice, but had seen the motion of my lips.

For fifteen years I had known this shepherd. For fifteen years I had seen him each autumn, on the border, or in the middle of the field, his body motionless, and always knitting in his hands. His flock followed him like a pack of hounds, seeming to obey his eye.

Master Picot now took me by the arm, saying:

"Did you know that the shepherd killed his wife?"

I was stupefied. "What Gargan—the deaf-mute?"

"Yes, this winter, and his case was tried at Rouen. I will tell you about it."

And he led me into the underbrush, for the shepherd knew how to catch words from his master's lips, as if he heard them spoken. He could understand only him; but, watching his face closely, he was no longer deaf; and the master, on the other hand, seemed to divine, like a sorcerer, the meaning of all the mute's pantomime, the gestures of his fingers, the expression of his face, and the motion of his eyes.

Here is his simple story, the various, somber facts as they came to pass:

Gargan was the son of a marl digger, one of those men who go down into the marlpit to extract that kind of soft, dissolving stone, sown under the soil. A deaf-mute by birth, he had been brought up to watch the cows along the ditches by the side of the roads.

Then, picked up by Picot's father, he had become the shepherd on his farm. He was an excellent shepherd, devout, upright, knowing how to find the lost members of his flock, although nobody had taught him anything.

When Picot took the farm, in his turn, Gargan was thirty years old and looked forty. He was tall, thin, and bearded— bearded like a patriarch.

About this time a good woman of the country, Mrs. Martel, died very poor, leaving a girl fifteen years old who was called "Drops," because of her immoderate love for brandy.

Picot took in this ragged waif, employed her in light duties, giving her a home without pay in return for her work. She slept under the barn, in the stable, or the cowhouse, upon straw, or on the manure-heap, anywhere, it mattered not where, for they could not give a bed to this barefoot. She slept, then, no matter where, with no matter whom, perhaps the plowman or the stable boy. But it happened soon that she gave her attention to the deaf-mute and coupled herself with him in a continued fashion. What united these two miserable beings? How have they understood each other? Had he ever known a woman before this barn rover, he who had never talked with anyone? Was it she who found him in his wheeled hut and seduced him, like an Eve of the rut, at the edge of the road? No one knows. They only know that one day they were living together as husband and wife.

No one was astonished by it, and Picot found it a very natural coupling. But the curate heard of this union without a mass and was angry. He reproached Mrs. Picot, disturbed her conscience, and threatened her with mysterious punishments. What was to be done? It was very simple. They must go and be married at the church and at the mayor's. They had nothing, either one of them: he, not a whole pair of pantaloons, she, not a petticoat of a single kind of cloth. So there was nothing to oppose what the law and religion required. They were united, in an hour, before the mayor and the curate, and believed that all was regulated for the best.

Now, it soon became a joke in the country (pardon the villainous word) to make a deceived husband of this poor Gargan. Before she was married, no one thought of sleeping with "Drops," but now each one wished his turn, for the sake of a laughable story. Everybody went there for a little glass behind the husband's back. The affair made so much noise that even some of the Goderville gentlemen came to see her.

For a half pint "Drops" would finish the spectacle with no matter whom, in a ditch, behind a wall, anywhere, while the silhouette of the motionless Gargan could be seen knitting a stocking not a hundred feet from there, surrounded by his bleating flock. And they laughed about it enough to make themselves ill in all the cafes of the country. It was the only thing talked of in the evening before the fire; and upon the road, the first thing one would ask:—"Have you paid your drop to 'Drops'?" Everyone knew what that meant.

The shepherd never seemed to see anything. But one day the Poirot boy, of Sasseville, called to Gargan's wife from behind the mill, showing her a full bottle. She understood and ran to him laughing. Now, scarcely were they engaged in their criminal deed when the herdsman fell upon them as if he had come out of a cloud. Piorot fled at full speed, his breeches about his heels, while the deaf-mute, with the cry of a beast, sprang at his wife's throat.

The people working in the fields ran toward them. It was too late; her tongue was black, her eyes were coming out of her head, the blood was flowing from her nose. She was dead.

The shepherd was tried by the Judge at Rouen. As he was a mute, Picot served as interpreter. The details of the affair amused the audience very much. But the farmer had but one idea: his herdsman must be acquitted. And he went about it in earnest.

At first, he related the deaf-mute's whole story, including that of his marriage; then, when he came to the crime, he himself questioned the assassin.

The assemblage was very quiet.

Picot pronounced the words slowly: "Did you know that she had deceived you?" and at the same time he asked the question with his eyes in pantomime.

The other answered "No" with his head.

"Were you asleep in the mill when you surprised her?" And he made a gesture of a man seeing some disgusting thing.

The other answered "Yes" with his head.

Then the farmer, imitating the signs of the mayor who married them, and of the priest who united them in the name of God, asked his servant if he had killed his wife because she was bound to him before men and before heaven.

The shepherd answered "Yes" with his head.

Picot then said to him: "Come, tell us how it happened."

Then the deaf-mute reproduced the whole scene in pantomime. He showed how he was asleep in the mill; that he was awakened by feeling the straw move; that he had watched quietly and had seen the whole thing.

He rose, between the two policemen, and brusquely imitated the obscene movement of the criminal couple entangled before him.

A tumultuous laugh went through the hall, then stopped short; for the herdsman, with haggard eyes, moving his jaw and his great beard as if he had bitten something, with arms extended, and head thrown forward, repeated the terrible action of a murderer who strangles a being.

And he howled frightfully, so excited with anger that one would think he believed he still held her in his grasp; and the policemen were obliged to seize him and seat him by force in order to calm him.

A great shiver of agony ran through the assembly. Then master Picot, placing his hand upon his servant's shoulder, said simply: "He knows what honor is, this man does."

And the shepherd was acquitted.

As for me, my dear friend, I listened to this adventure to its close, much moved, and have related it to you in gross terms in order not to change the farmer's story. But now there is a report of a gun from the woods, and the formidable voice of Gaspard is heard growling in the wind, like the sound of a cannon:

"Woodcock! There is one."

And this is how I employ my time, watching for the woodcock to pass, while you are also going to the Bois to see the first winter costumes.

· TWO ·

THE TWENTIETH CENTURY

INTRODUCTION

In the twentieth century, especially in the last ten years, deaf characters have begun to appear more often in literature, and in more kinds of roles. It appears that deaf characters work well in the imagination of writers who are trying to transmit a sense of the modern condition as they see it—its absurdity, its alienating pressures, its destruction of the individual, its smothering of the voice of one against many. It seems that a large segment of people today see themselves as victims and therefore feel they too are "deaf" in the sense of being ignored, not heard, lost in a world which they cannot understand. And so, by a strange twist of fortune, one who has always been an outsider (the deaf person), suddenly becomes accepted, but only because everyone else feels as much an outsider as he—it is a backhanded way of achieving acceptance, and probably not very welcome to most deaf people.

That we find more deaf characters in fiction now than ever before may seem at first encouraging, but when we consider the *kinds* of characters these are, we wonder if we are blessed or not. Consider the deaf narrator of *The Gypsy's Curse* by Harry Crews, for example: he is truly a grotesque creature. He has almost no legs, but has huge arms; he cannot speak because of a hole in the top of his mouth, but has an uncanny ability to read lips; he lives in a gym with a broad-chested old man of prodigious strength who once had his head rolled over by a car, with an insane old fighter who keeps counting himself out in his last, long ago prize fight, and with a young fighter who fights in basketball shoes and swimming trunks and always gets knocked silly. And so on—the absurd and grotesque aspects of the book go on and on until you either get sick to your stomach or throw the book out the window. Is it about deafness as such? Hardly.

137

Or consider the book, *Dummy*, by Ernest Tidyman: the story of a deaf black man in Chicago who had never learned to communicate at all, in any way, and who therefore, when accused of murder, presents a unique and disconcerting legal dilemma. Can such a man be tried? This book is far ahead of *The Gypsy's Curse* in treating deafness, but, still is really about something other than deafness.

And then there is the modern classic of literature about the deaf, *In This Sign*. Here we find Janice and Abel Ryder, both deaf. There is no question that the book is about deafness and that the author, Joanne Greenberg, knows much about the "deaf world." However, the Ryders are such pathetic people through so much of the book that the book is often rejected by deaf readers as unrealistic, if not downright insulting. The Ryders' ignorance of the world, to be sure, is a product of their poor education, and the inability or unwillingness of the world to communicate with them, but that ignorance, at the same time, is so extreme (Janice doesn't have the slightest idea of what it means to be pregnant even after she is married, for example) that deaf readers feel ashamed in reading of it, and cannot accept that half a century ago such ignorance among deaf people might not have been so rare.

Even John Singer, the deaf protagonist in *The Heart is a Lonely Hunter*, who is neither ignorant nor grotesque, still does not inspire admiration, and is hardly someone with whom a deaf reader would wish to identify. His isolation and frustration in life are so extreme that one not only does not identify *with* him, but can barely stand to read *about* him. In the end, he kills himself. And it does not matter that he was perhaps merely representative of how the author, Carson McCullers, sees the individual in society, he is still a *deaf* man, and he is yet another deaf character who does not inspire the reader but who, instead, brings despair.

There is another book written for young readers by Veronica Robinson called *David in Silence* which, despite its intention for young readers, has been one of my favorites for years. In this book we find a realistic description of a young deaf boy's introduction to hearing society, and some insightful treatment of the deaf experience. When David comes to a new town and meets the hearing children on the block, we find the distrust that hearing people often feel toward deaf people because the handicap is not visible but which yet is so profoundly influential—there is something disconcerting about a person who is apparently normal but yet who acts so strangely. And we find also the typical mistakes and clumsiness in David's efforts to be accepted among the hearing children on the block. Finally, the distrust flares into hostility and the hearing children start chasing David as they would a hunted beast: as for David, he is, of course, nearly crazy with fear and confusion. He is suffering from a too sudden immersion into hearing society (he had pretty much stayed at home before). His total disorientation is symbolized by his retreat before the angry hearing children into a dark tunnel where he becomes completely lost. In the end, after escaping from the tunnel, he is finally accepted provisionally. David is, however, someone many deaf readers can identify with (it is usually the favorite book at Gallaudet in the course "The Deaf in Literature").

Another book appeared recently with a deaf protagonist: *The Acupuncture Murders* by Dwight Steward. Perhaps because Mr. Steward had spent some time with the National Theatre of the Deaf researching it, this book deals with the problems of the deaf in a more sympathetic and understanding way than *Dummy* or *The Gypsy's Curse*, the two other recent "best sellers" dealing with deafness. Sampson Trehune, who is forty-four at the time of the story, is the hero and has been deaf since the age of nine. As is true of so many deaf characters in novels, he can read almost anyone's lips with little or no error—despite a disclaimer at the beginning of the book that the actual perceived dialogue has been "normalized," in reality what we read in the book is the product of not a lip reader but a mind reader.

The story is a murder mystery, spiced up by the topic of acupuncture and of deafness. It includes a lot of interesting sidelights into the deaf experience for the hearing reader (e.g., when Sampson forgets to lock the bathroom door behind him, someone knocks, enters on getting no response, and then is embarrassed and outraged that Sampson said nothing) but there is no question that Sampson is a rather unrepresentative deaf person. He was born rich (which is unrepresentative of everyone), is extremely bright, has no deaf friends (except one tailor mentioned briefly), speaks well enough to be understood almost universally, and, finally, solves a major crime through brilliant detective work. Not necessarily unbelievable, but certainly unrepresentative. It was

139

not intended as a treatise on deafness, of course, but as pleasurable reading, and there must be added pleasure for the deaf reader who can vicariously enjoy the insults and invective that Sampson habitually deals out to the hearing people around him.

Judging from these examples of the recent books dealing in one way or another with deafness, we find that deaf characters are used to heighten interest, to represent the plight of the individual in a technocratic society, or simply to express a sense of the absurd. (Eugene Ionesco wrote a play called *The Chairs* and at the end of the play he introduces a deaf narrator who, of course, is totally ineffectual as narrator although he does succeed in creating a sense of absurdity, which probably was the aim anyhow.) In the first group of books, using deafness to heighten interest, the interest may be in deafness itself (as with *In This Sign* and *David in Silence*) or it may be in minorities, or just simply in people who are different. Now past the terribly destructive cultural process known as "the melting pot," American society seems more able and willing to accept differences among its components, and we now find legitimate interest in ethnic, racial, and religious differences, and interest also in people who are different because of handicapping conditions. The second purpose for which deaf characters are used, to represent the condition of all individuals in modern society (as in *The Heart is a Lonely Hunter* or *Dummy*) is intriguing in that the differences between deaf people and hearing people are diminished—these books maintain that, after all, many people today feel victimized, and many people feel isolated, and many people feel they have no voice. The third purpose for which deaf characters have been used recently is not very welcome to those of us involved in deaf education: that of attempting to portray a sense of the absurd, or of the grotesque, in life (as in *The Gypsy's Curse* or "At the Dances of the Deaf-Mutes").

It is apparent, however, that for whatever purpose deaf characters are used, deafness has become an accepted and more widely used literary subject in recent years. The possibilities of the imaginative treatment of what David Wright calls "a disability without pathos" and characterized by "buffoonery," are just beginning to be known, and it may be that out of the current and future crop of literature about deafness, we may all begin to grasp more profoundly all the implications in what we have called "the deaf experience."

Why It Was W-on-the-Eyes
by Margaret Montague

EDITORS' PREFACE

Margaret Montague's charming story of Charlie Webster at his deaf school is always a favorite with the students in our Deaf in Literature class. This is a real story, about the real deaf experience, with real deaf people in it, and the real conditions under which most deaf people grow up.

In this story, there is an underlying argument which directs the characters and action to a very specific end: that of proving that oral training has value. This is proven by what seems like a highly unique situation: Charlie Webster's mother is blind and therefore can't communicate at all with her deaf son because he has never learned to talk. During the course of the story, Charlie does learn a word, and, for the first time, Charlie's mother hears her son "talk" to her. It is a joyful moment.

In the story, the person who was opposed to oral training is convinced by this episode that oral training does, indeed, have value. On first blush, we wonder at such a conclusion because, after all, how many deaf children have blind mothers? Is that one rather unique situation enough to justify the oral training of all deaf children?

However, there is more to this than that first blush. It all begins to have more weight to it when we realize that the whole world of hearing people is, in effect, blind, blind at least to signs, for how many hearing people will ever know signs? In this sense, Charlie's mother symbolically stands for the whole world of the hearing. If deaf people are going to communicate with them they must learn to speak or at least to use the language of the hearing world.

It is a rather simple story, with a simple message, but still, a message about a task that has inspired more debate and demanded more effort than any other task in all the schools for deaf people everywhere in the world. In this story, then, we are at the heart of the deaf experience.

WHY IT WAS W-ON-THE-EYES

"I wonder why the children's sign for little old Webster should be W-on-the-eyes," Miss Evans speculated. "There's nothing peculiar about his eyes, except perhaps that they're the brightest pair in school."

Miss Evans was the new oral teacher in the Lomax Schools for deaf and blind children, and she was speaking of Charlie Webster, one of the small deaf boys in her class.

That was his sign, W, made in the manual alphabet, with the hand placed against the eyes. Everybody in the deaf department at Lomax had his or her special sign, thus saving the time and trouble of spelling out the whole name on the fingers.

Clarence Chester, the big deaf boy who had finished school, but still stayed on working in the shoe-shop, was the one who made up the signs for the new pupils and teachers. He was rather proud of his talents in this direction, and took the pains of an artist over every sign. They were usually composed of the initial letter of the person's last name placed somewhere on the body, to indicate either some physical peculiarity, or else the position held by that person in school. Mr. Lincoln, for instance, who was the superintendent, had L-on-the-forehead, to show that he was the head of the whole school, and no one else, of course, could have L as high up as that—not even Mrs. Lincoln. She had to be contented with L-on-the-cheek. So, in the same way, Miss Thompson, who was the trained nurse, had T-on-the-wrist, because it was her business to feel the children's pulses.

When Miss Stedman, the new matron for the deaf boys, came, she should have had S-on-the-chest, as Clarence made a habit of placing all the matrons' initials on their chests; but unfortunately, S in the manual alphabet is made by doubling up the fist, and Clarence explained to her that if a boy hits himself on the chest with his fist he is sure to hit that middle button of his shirt, and make a bruise. He had to make this rather complicated explanation in writing because Miss Stedman was new to the sign-language and finger-spelling, and he had received his education at Lomax before articulation was taken up there, and was therefore, of course, a mute. So, on account of the button, S-on-the-chest had to be abandoned. But Clarence looked at Miss Stedman, and, for all that they called her a matron, she was very young and small, and had delicately rosy cheeks, so he smiled a little, and then made the letter S and the sign for pretty. And Miss Stedman went away quite satisfied, and showed every one her sign, being innocently unaware that every time she did so she was announcing that she was pretty. When her education in the sign-language had progressed sufficiently for her to discover the real meaning of her sign she was overcome with confusion, and begged Clarence to change it. But he said he never (*never*! NEVER! made vehemently with his hand) changed a sign after it was once given; besides, by that time all Miss Stedman's little deaf boys had got hold of it and no power on earth could have detached it from their fingers.

But, to go back to Charlie Webster, as Miss Evans remarked, there was nothing peculiar about his eyes, and therefore why his sign should be W-on-the-eyes, caused some small curiosity, but not enough to make any of the teachers or matrons take the trouble to look into the matter. Among themselves, of course, they did not speak of him as W-on-the-eyes: they called him Webster, or Charlie Webster, or most of all, perhaps, "little old Webster," because he was only nine, and everybody in the place adored him.

They may have adored him for that enchanting smile of his, a smile which curved his ridiculously eager little mouth, flooded from his dancing eyes, and generally radiated from the whole expressive little face of him. Or, perhaps, it was because he was so affectionate; or again it might have been because he was so handsome, so alert and gay, and always, moreover, appeared to be having such a good time. Whatever came little old Webster's way seemed always to be the most exciting and delightful thing that had ever happened to him, and whether it was a game to be played, a lesson to be learned, or a person to be loved, he did it with all his might, and with all his heart. Perhaps, after all, the real reason for the world's adoring him was that old classical one for the lamb's devotion to Mary,—he loved the world.

Another thing which sorted him out somewhat from among the other sixty or seventy deaf boys of the school was his fondness for the blind children. It is impossible to imagine any two sets of persons so absolutely shut off from one another as blind people and deaf mutes. It is only through the sense of feeling that they can meet; and for the most part at Lomax, sixty blind children, and more than a hundred deaf ones, move about through the same buildings, eat in the same dining-room, and, to some extent, play in the same grounds, with almost no intercourse or knowledge of one another. They move upon different planes. The deaf child's plane is made up of things seen, the blind child's of things heard. It is only through things touched that their paths ever cross, and surely only the economy and lack of imagination of the past could have crowded two such alien classes into one establishment. But little old Webster had built a bridge of his own over these almost insurmountable barriers, and through the medium of touch had carried his adventures in friendship even into the country of the blind.

Some of the blind boys knew the manual alphabet and could talk to him on their fingers, and by feeling of his hands could understand what he said to them; but with most he had to be satisfied with merely putting his arm about their shoulders and grunting a soft little inarticulate "Ough, ough!" which was no word at all, of course, merely an engaging little expression of his friendship and general good feeling. The blind children recognized him by these little grunts, and accepted things from him which they would never have tolerated from any of the other "dummies," as they called the deaf mutes. Webster was their passionate champion on all occasions. Once, when a deaf boy threw a stone which by accident hit one of the blind boys on the forehead, inflicting a bad cut, Webster flew into a wild fury of rage, and attacked the deaf boy with all the passion of his nine years. Afterwards, he tore up to the hospital where his blind friend was having the cut dressed, and snuggling his face against him grunted many soft "oughs, oughs," of sympathy. But the little deaf boy he had thrashed had to come to the hospital to be tied up as well, for little old Webster was no saint, and once he set out to fight, he did it, as he did everything else, with all his heart.

"I declare," Miss Stedman announced wearily one evening in the officers' dining-room, "if Charlie Webster keeps on I shall just *have* to report him to Mr. Lincoln. He's been fighting this whole blessed afternoon—just one boy right after another."

"Oh," cried Miss Thompson, the trained nurse, "then *that* was the reason there was so many of the little deaf boys up in the hospital this afternoon with sprained thumbs, and black eyes, and so on!"

"Exactly," Miss Stedman confirmed her, "that was Webster's doing—the little scamp! It's because of his shirts. Whenever his mother sends him a new shirt, and he puts it on, he has to fight almost every boy in his dormitory."

"But why? What's the matter with his shirts?" Miss Evans, the oral teacher, demanded.

"Oh, they're the funniest looking things! I don't see what his mother can be thinking of. They look as though they'd been made up hind-side before, and the sleeves are never put in right, and are always too tight for him. Of course, the other children laugh at every fresh one, and that just sends him almost crazy, and he flies at one boy after another. He knows, himself, that the shirts aren't right, but he just *will* wear them in spite of everything. I tried once to get him to put on one from the school supply, and, goodness! I thought he was going to fight me!"

It was at this time that Miss Evans asked why Webster's sign was W-on-the-eyes. Miss Stedman said she thought Chester must have given him that because he was so good to the blind children. That explanation satisfied Miss Evans, but was not, as it happened, the right one.

Little old Webster came to Lomax when he was only seven, two years before they began to teach articulation and lip reading to the children there. His education began therefore with manual method, and by the time he was nine there was hardly a sign that he did not know, or a word that he could not spell with his flying fingers. But he was a little person who craved many forms of self-expression, and he often looked very curiously, and very wistfully, at hearing people when they talked together with their lips. The year he was nine, which was the year of this story, they began the oral instruction at Lomax, Miss Evans being

engaged for this purpose, and being given by Clarence
Chester the sign of E-on-the-lips, to show that she was the
person who taught the children to speak. She had to face
some opposition in getting the new method established.
The older children found it harder than the familiar signs,
and, for the most part, shut their minds persistently against
any attempt to make them speak.

Many of the teachers, also, were opposed to the oral
form of instruction. There was Miss Flyn, for instance. She
had taught deaf children for ten years with the sign-
language, and did not see any reason for abandoning it now.
And, for all her plumpness, and soft sweetness of face, Miss
Eliza Flyn was a firm lady, once her mind was thoroughly
made up. Her argument was that though articulation and
lip-reading might be a wonderful thing for a few brilliant
children, the average deaf child trained in a state school
could never get much benefit from it. "Lip-readers are born
and not made," she maintained stoutly. "It's as much a gift
as an ear for music, or being able to write poetry."

"Any deaf child with the proper amount of brains, and
normal sight, can be taught to articulate and read the lips,"
Miss Evans returned, with equal stoutness, for she was
"pure oral," and could almost have found it in her heart to
wish that the sign-language might be wiped off the face of
the earth. There she and Miss Flyn came to a polite dead-
lock of opinion in the matter.

But whatever others might think, little old Webster apparently had no doubts of the advantage of the oral method.
As soon as he found out what it was all about, he flung
himself into the new study with even more than his usual
zest and enthusiasm. Watching Miss Evans' lips with a
passionate attention, his brown eyes as eager and as dumb
and wistful as a little dog's, he attempted the sounds over
and over, his unaccustomed lips twisting themselves into

all sorts of grotesque positions, in his effort to gain control over them. He always shook his head sharply at his failures, fiercely rebuking himself, and immediately making a fresh attack upon the word or element, working persistently until Miss Evans' nod and smile at length rewarded him, upon which his whole little face would light up, and he would heave a weary but triumphant sigh. His zeal almost frightened Miss Evans, and while she constantly spurred all the other children on to using their lips instead of their eager little fingers, Webster she tried to check, fearing that his enthusiasm might even make him ill.

Early in the school term, when he had not been in Miss Evans' class much above a month, little old Webster received a postcard from his father saying that his parents expected to come to Lomax to see him in a week or so. Webster almost burst with delighted expectancy. He showed the card to every deaf child who could read, and interpreted it in signs and finger-spelling to those who could not; he permitted his blind friends to feel it all over with their delicate inquiring fingers, and gave every teacher and officer the high privilege of reading,—

DEAR LITTLE CHARLIE:—

Your mother and I expect to come to Lomax to see you Friday of next week.

Your loving father,
CHARLES WEBSTER,

while he stood by with those dancing eyes of his, which frequently said more than speaking people's lips. He carried the card in triumph to Miss Evans, and when she had read it he made the sign for mother, and she nodded and said that was nice, taking care of course to speak rather than sign. But his little eager face clouded over, and there appeared on it that shut-in and baffled expression which it sometimes wore when he failed to make himself understood. He repeated the sign and put his hand to his lips pleadingly. Then she realized what he wanted.

"Why, bless his heart, he wants me to teach him to say mother!" she exclaimed delightedly, and sitting down on the veranda steps, for it was out of school hours, she then and there set to work drilling him in the desired word, saying it repeatedly, and placing his hand against her throat that he might feel the vibrations of sound. At last, watching her lips intently, making repeated efforts doomed to failure, shaking his head angrily at himself each time, and renewing the attempt manfully, he did achieve the coveted word. To be sure it was not very distinctly said at first, and was broken into two soft little syllables, thus, "mo-ther"; but his little face shone with the triumph of it. And then in gratitude he said, "Thank you" very politely to Miss Evans, having learned those two words before in his articulation. He said them in his best voice, carefully placing one small conscientious finger on the side of his nose, which gave him a most comically serious expression, but was done to be sure that he had succeeded in putting the proper vibration into his "Thank you."

"Such foolishness!" Miss Eliza Flyn snorted, passing along the veranda at this moment. "What's the good of one word? And he'll forget it anyway by to-morrow!"

But little old Webster held manfully to that hard-won word which his love had bought. Every morning when he entered the classroom he said, "Mo-ther" to Miss Evans with his enchanting smile, so that she began to be afraid that he had confused the meaning of the word, and was calling her mother. On the day, however, that she permitted him to tear the leaf from the school calendar—a daily much-desired privilege—she was reassured on this point, for having torn off the proper date he turned up the other leaves swiftly until he came to the day on which his parents were expected, and putting his finger on the number he said, "Mo-ther, mo-ther," and then in quaint fashion he pointed to the calendar leaf, and then to himself, and locking his forefingers together, first in one direction and then in the other, he made the little sign for friend, meaning that he was friends with that day because it would bring him his mother.

He said the word repeatedly, in school and out. He even said it in his sleep. The night before his mother was to come, when Miss Stedman paid her regular visit to the dormitory where all the little deaf boys were asleep, Webster sat suddenly bolt upright in his bed, his eyes wide-open, but unseeing with sleep, and cried out, "Mother!"

"Goodness!" Miss Stedman commented to herself. "I'll be glad when his mother does come! He'll go crazy if he doesn't get that word off his tongue soon."

The next day—the great, the miraculous day—little old Webster was in a veritable humming-bird quiver of excitement. He jumped in his seat each time the door opened, and when, at length, Miss Flyn actually came to announce that his father and mother had really arrived, he leaped up with a face of such transcendent joy, that his departure left Miss Evans' class-room almost as dark as if the sun had passed under a cloud. So much of pure happiness went with him that, with a smile on her lips, Miss Evans let her fancy follow him on his triumphant way, and for fully three minutes, while she pictured the surprise in store for the waiting mother, she permitted her "pure oral" class to tell each other over and over on their fingers that "E.F." (Miss Flyn's sign) had come to take W-on-the-eyes to see his father and mother, before she awoke to the fact and sternly recalled their runaway language from their fingers to their lips.

In the meantime, gripping Miss Flyn's hand tight, little old Webster went on eager tiptoe feet down the passageway leading into the reception-room. Miss Flyn could feel the vibration of excitement in his fingers as they rested in hers, and her own sympathetic heart went a beat or two faster in consequence. But almost at the reception-room door he dropped her hand suddenly and stopped dead, his face gone a despairing white, and a lost, agonized look in his eyes. For a moment, he stared about him in passionate bewilderment, then, bursting into a storm of tears, he turned to run back to Miss Evans' room. But Miss Flyn caught him firmly and, forcing him to look at her, signed, "What is it?" He made the sign of mother, and then passed his open hand despairingly across his forehead in the sign for forgotten, and Miss Flyn realized that through over-excitement or some trick of a tired brain, his precious word had all at once slipped from him. He looked up at her, and old "signer" though she was, she could not resist the appeal of his tragic little face. Stooping down, she pronounced the lost word, placing his hand against her throat. Remembrance rushed into his eyes, and his face lit like a flame. "Mo-ther! Mo-ther!" he cried, and putting both hands tight against his mouth as if to hold the word in place, he fled down the hall and into the reception-room and flung himself upon a woman who sat very still, her waiting, listening face turned toward the door.

"Mo-ther! Mo-ther!" he cried, his arms tight about her neck.

She gave a sharp, an almost hysterical cry. "*Charlie!*" she screamed. "Is that Charlie? Is that my deaf baby talking?"

She tore his arms from about her neck, and held him away from her, while her eager, trembling fingers went to his lips and felt them move once more, framing the wonderful word.

"It *is* Charlie! It is my little deaf and dumb baby talking!" she cried. And then she went into a wild babble of mother words,—"My baby! My lamb! My darling, precious baby!"—crying and kissing him, while the tears ran down from her eyes. And little old Webster, his word now safely delivered to the one person in all the world to whom it belonged, relapsed once more into his old soft, inarticulate grunting of "Ough, ough!" nuzzling his face close against hers, and laughing gleefully over the splendid surprise he had prepared for her.

And after one astounded, comprehending look, Miss Flyn turned, and, racing down the hallway, burst into Miss Evans' classroom and caught that teacher by the arm.

Little old Webster's mother is *blind*!" she cried. "She's *stone blind*! She's never seen Webster in all her life.—She's never heard him speak until this minute! They've never been able to say *one word* to each other.—She's blind, I tell you! And *that's* why Webster's sign is W-on-the-eyes—Clarence Chester must have known,—and that's why he fought every boy who laughed at the funny way his shirts were made—he knew his mother couldn't see to make them right! And—and—" Miss Flyn choked, —"and *that's* why he's nearly killed himself trying to learn to speak. There's never been any way they could talk to each other except by feeling! She's had to wait nine years to hear him say Mother! And—and," Miss Flyn wound up unsteadily, "you needn't preach to me any more about articulation for—I'm converted!"

And with that she went out and banged the door behind her, and all the children's fingers flew up, to ask Miss Evans in excited signs what E.F. was crying about.

King Silence
by Arnold Payne

EDITORS' PREFACE

The following is a brief excerpt from the novel *King Silence*
by Arnold Payne. It is the only part of the novel that has
much value either in literary terms or for our purposes in
this anthology, but in these few pages how much is said! It
is incredible to think that a person would first find someone
to communicate with at the age of seven! Of course, other
characters in this anthology have lived their whole life in
total isolation, but that was in the nineteenth century, after
all, and in distant lands. Gilbert Stratton (the boy in this
excerpt) is a young deaf boy of our own time, or nearly our
own time. All readers, especially deaf readers, can easily
sympathize with his overwhelming joy and his sense of utter
relief to find that finally he will have friends with whom he
can communicate and who have all shared his experience
in life. This much we all accept and understand.

The only disturbing aspect in this excerpt is that Payne
falls into the old error among hearing authors when they
use deaf characters of imputing heroic qualities to their
characters. In this excerpt we find Gilbert waiting patiently
in the office of his new school "as the deaf have always
waited." He is lonely, but he has learned to accept his
loneliness, says Payne, "as the deaf accept all their trials."
There is a certain condescension in this idealization of deaf
people—it is as if deaf people are not real people, but
wooden images. There is also a certain guilt involved, I
suspect, that a hearing author cannot use a deaf character

153

but he must somehow make that character a superior being. Such are the problems of hearing authors trying to portray the deaf experience: the attitude of the non-handicapped person toward the handicapped person is to care for that person in the abstract, not as he or she is. A person in a wheelchair once told me that the worst experience for her in public was that people refused to look at her.

FROM KING SILENCE

"Born deaf?"

"Born deaf."

The reply was flashed, as quickly as it was uttered, by means of the manual alphabet to Mr. Gordon, who nodded and bent again over the application form before him.

He was interested in the written replies to the usual printed question, for here was a boy who was born deaf, and yet Mr. Gordon knew that his parents were not cousins, nor were their parents before them. Intermarriage with relations sometimes means deafness for those yet unborn, "unto the third and fourth generation." But sometimes even congenital deafness is inexplicable to our limited intelligence. Perhaps it is that the "works of God may be made manifest."

And the child—he was only seven—stood silent, lonely, passive, patient, with eyes apparently looking vacantly at the opposite wall, as deaf children will when others are talking of them. For though they hear nothing they know perfectly well when the conversation is about themselves.

And Gilbert Stratton waited while the mother who loved but did not understand him, and the headmaster who did not love as much but did understand better, conversed together; waited in an office surrounded with maps that were unintelligible, books that were meaningless, figures that conveyed nothing, while people spoke words which were inaudible to him and which would have been incomprehensible even if audible; waited, as the deaf always have waited, but will not have to wait much longer, perhaps.

Lonely he had always been, lonely with an intensity of loneliness utterly unknown to those around him and unrealised even by his parents. But he had accepted it as the deaf accept all their trials, and they are many. It was part of his lot.

But suddenly, as he still stood apparently looking at nothing, he saw the door slowly open and a boy a year younger than himself quietly enter. He walked aimlessly, as it seemed, with head down and hands behind him, in that shy way which children of six have when they wish to be unnoticed. Pausing when opposite to Gilbert on the other side of the room, he remained with head averted till he knew the cursory glances of the seniors present were no longer directed towards him, and then he cautiously raised his eyes and fixed them on the deaf boy's face.

The latter saw it all, and as soon as he felt that he was unobserved by anyone else he allowed his glance to meet that of the other. In an instant the younger, with enquiry stamped on every feature, flicked his right index finger to his ear, then to his mouth, and then pointed at the deaf boy, asking, as plainly as words could say it, "Are you deaf and dumb?"

Utterly taken aback at being addressed in the only method of communication he understood, Gilbert nodded, open-eyed.

With a smile the other again pointed to ear and mouth, and then, alternately clenching his fists and opening his hands with fingers extended several times, and finally pointing through the door, conveyed the news that there were many more deaf and dumb in another room beyond.

Mrs. Stratton at that moment turned her head, and instantly the faces of both boys were as impassive as blocks of marble.

For a few moments Gilbert remained thus gazing straight in front of him. But the delight of the sudden revelation that there was someone here who talked in a language he could comprehend, the language of natural gesture, and that there were many more in that same house who were deaf—deaf like himself—surged with such force through his bewildered brain that his lip quivered. It meant—nay, what did it not mean to him? There were boys and girls in that house who could sympathise, could literally feel as he did, who had passed through what he had passed through, who had seen persons come up to them and look at them curiously and turn to others and mouth inaudibly about them, who had seen their own mothers sorrowfully join in the talk about them, who had had doctors prying and peering into their ears and nose and mouth, and talking, unheard by them, to their fathers about it all, but who had never found anyone to tell them what all the talk was about, had never met anyone who had ever shown any suspicion that they, poor children, could feel any pain at being examined and discussed and kept in ignorance as to what it all meant. There were children there who had experienced all this just as he had, who knew what he knew—the sensitiveness, the shame, the loneliness which was almost intensified by his own parents' attitude. For his love for his father and mother, and their love for him, made their failure to understand and sympathise all the harder to bear.

He was no longer alone! His head swam and he bit his lip. The long and bitter training of past years had made him outwardly unemotional, but the pent-up feelings within him refused to be suppressed. His lips quivered and quivered again; his frame shook. He clenched his hands tightly in an unconscious pride and rebellion against showing these strangely uncomprehending people what he felt, but the strength of his emotion was too great. He suddenly buried his burning face in his hands and burst into tears.

"Poor boy!" exclaimed Mrs. Stratton, as she took him into her embrace; "he feels the parting for us."

Which was perfectly true, of course. But which was not the whole truth.

Mr. Gordon quietly went on reading the form before him. Unknown to the two children he had seen their brief conversation out of the corner of his eye, and he understood what Mrs. Stratton did not. For he was deaf himself, and had passed all but the first ten years of his life among the deaf. Presently, to divert attention from the deaf child, he turned and asked—for he could speak—

"Has any examination been made on Gilbert, Mrs. Stratton?"

"Oh yes, several times. We took him to a doctor in London twice, and our own doctor has seen him often. But they both said they could do nothing."

The reply was finger-spelled with amazing rapidity to the principal by Mrs. Gordon.

"Did they give you no advice?" asked Mr. Gordon.

The Key
by Eudora Welty

EDITORS' PREFACE

The deaf couple in "The Key" are deaf so as to emphasize their separation from the world, their separation brought on by romantic and wishful thinking about a future that will never come. In this story, they miss their train to Niagara Falls, where they expect that after years of marriage they will finally find what it means to hear (or what it means to be alive?). But Albert and Ellie "missed their train" long ago, and always will, for what they are both seeking is something they can never find: a miracle that will change their lives and bring them love and happiness.

Their desperation, their aloneness in the world (two against the world), is emphasized by their deafness but not caused by it. The young man who drops the key understands their hopeless desperation, knows the strange symbolic hope that Albert finds in the key, and knows as well how meaningless his gesture of also giving Ellie a key is, and he therefore walks away from the couple with a feeling of self-loathing for reinforcing their absurd dream of a miraculous escape from their lives.

"The Key," then, is about deafness, and it is not—it is, to the extent that deaf people may often be cut off as were Albert and Ellie, may often place unrealistic hope in something happening someday to rescue them and change their lives, may often feel intense suspicion of the world. But the story is about all people who live such lives of "quiet desperation"—one need not be deaf to fall into such a life.

Albert and Ellie are a truly pathetic couple, but not because of the way they see life and themselves and other people. Their lives are wasted because of fantasy and dreams that replace life itself. They will be, symbolically, always waiting for their train to come and it will never come.

THE KEY

It was quiet in the waiting room of the remote little station, except for the night sounds of insects. You could hear their embroidering movements in the weeds outside, which somehow gave the effect of some tenuous voice in the night, telling a story. Or you could listen to the fat thudding of the light bugs and the hoarse rushing of their big wings against the wooden ceiling. Some of the bugs were clinging heavily to the yellow globe, like idiot bees to a senseless smell.

Under this prickly light two rows of people sat in silence, their faces stung, their bodies twisted and quietly uncomfortable, expectantly so, in ones and twos, not quite asleep. No one seemed impatient, although the train was late. A little girl lay flung back in her mother's lap as though sleep had struck her with a blow.

Ellie and Albert Morgan were sitting on a bench like the others waiting for the train and had nothing to say to each other. Their names were ever so neatly and rather largely printed on a big reddish-tan suitcase strapped crookedly shut, because of a missing buckle, so that it hung apart finally like a stupid pair of lips. "Albert Morgan, Ellie Morgan, Yellow Leaf, Mississippi." They must have been driven into town in a wagon, for they and the suitcase were all touched here and there with a fine yellow dust, like finger marks.

Ellie Morgan was a large woman with a face as pink and crowded as an old-fashioned rose. She must have been about forty years old. One of those black satchel purses hung over her straight, strong wrist. It must have been her savings which were making possible this trip. And to what place? you wondered, for she sat there as tense and solid as a cube, as if to endure some nameless apprehension rising and overflowing within her at the thought of travel. Her face worked and broke into strained, hardening lines, as if there had been a death—that too-explicit evidence of agony in the desire to communicate.

Albert made a slower and softer impression. He sat motionless beside Ellie, holding his hat in his lap with both hands—a hat you were sure he had never worn. He looked home-made, as though his wife had self-consciously knitted or somehow contrived a husband when she sat alone at night. He had a shock of very fine sunburned yellow hair. He was too shy for this world, you could see. His hands were like cardboard, he held his hat so still; and yet how softly his eyes fell upon its crown, moving dreamily and yet with dread over its brown surface! He was smaller than his wife. His suit was brown, too, and he wore it neatly and carefully, as though he were murmuring, "Don't look— no need to look—I am effaced." But you have seen that expression too in silent children, who will tell you what they dreamed the night before in sudden, almost hilarious, bursts of confidence.

Every now and then, as though he perceived some minute thing, a sudden alert, tantalized look would creep over the little man's face, and he would gaze slowly around him, quite slyly. Then he would bow his head again; the expression would vanish; some inner refreshment had been denied him. Behind his head was a wall poster, dirty with time, showing an old-fashioned locomotive about to crash into an open touring car filled with women in veils. No one in the station was frightened by the familiar poster, any more than they were aroused by the little man whose rising and drooping head it framed. Yet for a moment he might seem to you to be sitting there quite filled with hope.

Among the others in the station was a strong-looking young man, alone, hatless, red haired, who was standing by the wall while the rest sat on benches. He had a small key in his hand and was turning it over and over in his fingers, nervously passing it from one hand to the other, tossing it gently into the air and catching it again.

He stood and stared in distraction at the other people; so intent and so wide was his gaze that anyone who glanced after him seemed rocked like a small boat in the wake of a large one. There was an excess of energy about him that separated him from everyone else, but in the motion of his hands there was, instead of the craving for communication, something of reticence, even of secrecy, as the key rose and fell. You guessed that he was a stranger in town; he might have been a criminal or a gambler, but his eyes were widened with gentleness. His look, which traveled without stopping for long anywhere, was a hurried focusing of a very tender and explicit regard.

The color of his hair seemed to jump and move, like the flicker of a match struck in a wind. The ceiling lights were not steady but seemed to pulsate like a living and transient force, and made the young man in his preoccupation appear to tremble in the midst of his size and strength, and to fail to impress his exact outline upon the yellow walls. He was like a salamander in the fire. "Take care," you wanted to say to him, and yet also, "Come here." Nervously, and quite apart in his distraction, he continued to stand tossing

161

the key back and forth from one hand to the other. Suddenly it became a gesture of abandonment: one hand stayed passive in the air, then seized too late: the key fell to the floor.

Everyone, except Albert and Ellie Morgan, looked up for a moment. On the floor the key had made a fierce metallic sound like a challenge, a sound of seriousness. It almost made people jump. It was regarded as an insult, a very personal question, in the quiet peaceful room where the insects were tapping at the ceiling and each person was allowed to sit among his possessions and wait for an unquestioned departure. Little walls of reproach went up about them all.

A flicker of amusement touched the young man's face as he observed the startled but controlled and obstinately blank faces which turned toward him for a moment and then away. He walked over to pick up his key.

But it had glanced and slid across the floor, and now it lay in the dust at Albert Morgan's feet.

Albert Morgan was indeed picking up the key. Across from him, the young man saw him examine it, quite slowly, with wonder written all over his face and hands, as if it had fallen from the sky. Had he failed to hear the clatter? There was something wrong with Albert. . . .

As if by decision, the young man did not terminate this wonder by claiming his key. He stood back, a peculiar flash of interest or of something more inscrutable, like resignation, in his lowered eyes.

The little man had probably been staring at the floor, thinking. And suddenly in the dark surface the small sliding key had appeared. You could see memory seize his face, twist it and hold it. What innocent, strange thing might it have brought back to life—a fish he had once spied just below the top of the water in a sunny lake in the country when he was a child? This was just as unexpected, shocking, and somehow meaningful to him. Albert sat there holding the key in his wide-open hand. How intensified, magnified, really vain all attempt at expression becomes in the afflicted! It was with an almost incandescent delight that he felt the unguessed temperature and weight of the key. Then he turned to his wife. His lips were actually trembling.

And still the young man waited, as if the strange joy of the little man took precedence with him over whatever need he had for the key. With sudden electrification he saw Ellie slip the handle of her satchel purse from her wrist and with her fingers begin to talk to her husband.

The others in the station had seen Ellie too; shallow pity washed over the waiting room like a dirty wave foaming and creeping over a public beach. In quick mumblings from bench to bench people said to each other, "Deaf and dumb!" How ignorant they were of all that the young man was seeing! Although he had no way of knowing the words Ellie said, he seemed troubled enough at the mistake the little man must have made, at his misplaced wonder and joy.

Albert was replying to his wife. On his hands he said to her, "I found it. Now it belongs to me. It is something important! Important! It means something. From now on we will get along better, have more understanding. . . . Maybe when we reach Niagara Falls we will even fall in love, the way other people have done. Maybe our marriage was really for love, after all, not for the other reason—both of us being afflicted in the same way, unable to speak, lonely because of that. Now you can stop being ashamed of me, for being so cautious and slow all my life, for taking my own time. . . . You can take hope. Because it was I who found the key. Remember that—I found it." He laughed all at once, quite silently.

Everyone stared at his impassioned little speech as it came from his fingers. They were embarrassed, vaguely aware of some crisis and vaguely affronted, but unable to interfere; it was as though they were the deaf-mutes and he the speaker. When he laughed, a few people laughed unconsciously with him, in relief, and turned away. But the young man remained still and intent, waiting at his little distance.

"This key came here very mysteriously—it is bound to mean something," the husband went on to say. He held the key up just before her eyes. "You are always praying; you believe in miracles; well, now, here is the answer. It came to me."

His wife looked self-consciously around the room and replied on her fingers, "You are always talking nonsense. Be quiet."

But she was secretly pleased, and when she saw him slowly look down in his old manner, she reached over, as if to retract what she had said, and laid her hand on his, touching the key for herself, softness making her worn hand limp. From then on they never looked around them, never saw anything except each other. They were so intent, so very solemn, wanting to have their symbols perfectly understood!

"You must see it is a symbol," he began again, his fingers clumsy and blurring in his excitement. "It is a symbol of something—something that we deserve, and that is happiness. We will find happiness in Niagara Falls."

And then, as if he were all at once shy even of her, he turned slightly away from her and slid the key into his pocket. They sat staring down at the suitcase, their hands fallen in their laps.

The young man slowly turned away from them and wandered back to the wall, where he took out a cigarette and lighted it.

Outside, the night pressed around the station like a pure stone, in which the little room might be transfixed and, for the preservation of this moment of hope, its future killed, an insect in amber. The short little train drew in, stopped, and rolled away, almost noiselessly.

Then inside, people were gone or turned in sleep or walking about, all changed from the way they had been. But the deaf-mutes and the loitering young man were still in their places.

The man was still smoking. He was dressed like a young doctor or some such person in the town, and yet he did not seem of the town. He looked very strong and active; but there was a startling quality, a willingness to be forever distracted, even disturbed, in the very reassurance of his body, some alertness which made his strength fluid and dissipated instead of withheld and greedily beautiful. His youth by now did not seem an important thing about him; it was a medium for his activity, no doubt, but as he stood there frowning and smoking you felt some apprehension that he would never express whatever might be the desire of his life in being young and strong, in standing apart in compassion, in making any intuitive present or sacrifice, or in any way of action at all—not because there was too much in the world demanding his strength, but because he was too deeply aware.

You felt a shock in glancing up at him, and when you looked away from the whole yellow room and closed your eyes, his intensity, as well as that of the room, seemed to have impressed the imagination with a shadow of itself, a blackness together with the light, the negative beside the positive. You felt as though some exact, skillful contact had been made between the surfaces of your hearts to make you aware, in some pattern, of his joy and his despair. You

165

could feel the fullness and the emptiness of this stranger's life.

The railroad man came in swinging a lantern which he stopped suddenly in its arc. Looking uncomfortable, and then rather angry, he approached the deaf-mutes and shot his arm out in a series of violent gestures and shrugs.

Albert and Ellie Morgan were dreadfully shocked. The woman looked resigned for a moment to hopelessness. But the little man—you were startled by a look of bravado on his face.

In the station the red-haired man was speaking aloud— but to himself. "They missed their train!"

As if in quick apology, the trainman set his lantern down beside Albert's foot, and hurried away.

And as if completing a circle, the red-haired man walked over too and stood silently near the deaf-mutes. With a reproachful look at him the woman reached up and took off her hat.

They began again, talking rapidly back and forth, almost as one person. The old routine of their feeling was upon them once more. Perhaps, you thought, staring at their similarity—her hair was yellow, too—they were children together—cousins even, afflicted in the same way, sent off from home to the state institute. . . .

It was the feeling of conspiracy. They were in counter-plot against the plot of those things that pressed down upon them from outside their knowledge and their ways of making themselves understood. It was obvious that it gave the wife her greatest pleasure. But you wondered, seeing Albert, whom talking seemed rather to dishevel, whether it had not continued to be a rough and violent game which Ellie, as the older and stronger, had taught him to play with her.

"What do you think he wants?" she asked Albert, nodding at the red-haired man, who smiled faintly. And how her eyes shone! Who would ever know how deep her suspicion of the whole outside world lay in her heart, how far it had pushed her!

"What does he want?" Albert was replying quickly. "The key!"

Of course! And how fine it had been to sit there with the key hidden from the strangers and also from his wife, who had not seen where he had put it. He stole up with his hand and secretly felt the key, which must have lain in some pocket nearly against his heart. He nodded gently. The key had come there, under his eyes on the floor in the station, all of a sudden, but yet not quite unexpected. That is the way things happen to you always. But Ellie did not comprehend this.

Now she sat there as quiet as could be. It was not only hopelessness about the trip. She, too, undoubtedly felt something privately about that key, apart from what she had said or what he had told her. He had almost shared it with her—you realized that. He frowned and smiled almost at the same time. There was something—something he could almost remember but not quite—which would let him keep the key always to himself. He knew that, and he would remember it later, when he was alone.

"Never fear, Ellie," he said, a still little smile lifting his lip. "I've got it safe in a pocket. No one can find it, and there's no hole for it to fall through."

She nodded, but she was always doubting, always anxious. You could look at her troubled hands. How terrible it was, how strange, that Albert loved the key more than he loved Ellie! He did not mind missing the train. It showed in every line, every motion of his body. The key was closer—

closer. The whole story began to illuminate them now, as if the lantern flame had been turned up. Ellie's anxious, hovering body could wrap him softly as a cradle, but the secret meaning, that powerful sign, that reassurance he so hopefully sought, so assuredly deserved—that had never come. There was something lacking in Ellie.

Had Ellie, with her suspicions of everything, come to know even things like this, in her way? How empty and nervous her red scrubbed hands were, how desperate to speak! Yes, she must regard it as unhappiness lying between them, as more than emptiness. She must worry about it, talk about it. You could imagine her stopping her churning to come out to his chair on the porch, to tell him that she did love him and would take care of him always, talking with the spotted sour milk dripping from her fingers. Just try to tell her that talking is useless, that care is not needed . . . And sooner or later he would always reply, say something, agree, and she would go away again. . . .

And Albert, with his face so capable of amazement, made you suspect the funny thing about talking to Ellie. Until you do, declared his round brown eyes, you can be peaceful and content that everything takes care of itself. As long as you let it alone everything goes peacefully, like an uneventful day on the farm—chores attended to, woman working in the house, you in the field, crop growing as well as can be expected, the cow giving, and the sky like a coverlet over it all—so that you're as full of yourself as a colt, in need of nothing, and nothing needing you. But when you pick up your hands and start to talk, if you don't watch carefully, this security will run away and leave you. You say something, make an observation, just to answer your wife's worryings, and everything is jolted, disturbed, laid open like the ground behind a plow, with you running along after it.

But happiness, Albert knew, is something that appears to you suddenly, that is meant for you, a thing which you reach for and pick up and hide at your breast, a shiny thing that reminds you of something alive and leaping.

Ellie sat there quiet as a mouse. She has unclasped her purse and taken out a little card with a picture of Niagara Falls on it.

"Hide it from the man," she said. She did suspect him! The red-haired man had drawn closer. He bent and saw that it was a picture of Niagara Falls.

"Do you see the little rail?" Albert began in tenderness. And Ellie loved to watch him tell her about it; she clasped her hands and began to smile and show her crooked tooth; she looked young: it was the way she had looked as a child.

"That is what the teacher pointed to with her wand on the magic-lantern slide—the little rail. You stand right here. You lean up hard against the rail. Then you can hear Niagara Falls."

"How do you hear it?" begged Ellie, nodding.

"You hear it with your whole self. You listen with your arms and your legs and your whole body. You'll never forget what hearing is, after that."

He must have told her hundreds of times in his obedience, yet she smiled with gratitude, and stared deep, deep into the tinted picture of the waterfall.

Presently she said, "By now, we'd have been there, if we hadn't missed the train."

She did not even have any idea that it was miles and days away.

She looked at the red-haired man then, her eyes all puckered up, and he looked away at last. He had seen the dust on her throat and a needle stuck in her collar where she'd forgotten it, with a thread running through the eye—the final details. Her hands were tight and wrinkled with pressure. She swung her foot a little below her skirt, in the new Mary Jane slipper with the hard toe.

Albert turned away too. It was then, you thought, that he became quite frightened to think that if they hadn't missed the train they would be hearing, at that very moment, Niagara Falls. Perhaps they would be standing there together, pressed against the little rail, pressed against each other, with their lives being poured through them, changing. . . . And how did he know what that would be like? He bent his head and tried not to look at his wife. He could say nothing. He glanced up once at the stranger, with almost a pleading look, as if to say, "Won't you come with us?"

"To work so many years, and then to miss the train," Ellie said.

You saw by her face that she was undauntedly wondering, unsatisfied, waiting for the future.

And you knew how she would sit and brood over this as over their conversations together, about every misunderstanding, every discussion, sometimes even about some agreement between them that had been settled—even about the secret and proper separation that lies between a man and a woman, the thing that makes them what they are in themselves, their secret life, their memory of the past, their childhood, their dreams. This to Ellie was unhappiness.

They had told her when she was a little girl how people who have just been married have the custom of going to Niagara Falls on a wedding trip, to start their happiness; and that came to be where she put her hope, all of it. So she saved money. She worked harder than he did, you could observe, comparing their hands, good and bad years, more than was good for a woman. Year after year she had put her hope ahead of her.

And he—somehow he had never thought that this time would come, that they might really go on the journey. He was never looking so far and so deep as Ellie—into the future, into the changing and mixing of their lives together when they should arrive at last at Niagara Falls. To him it was always something postponed, like the paying off of the mortgage.

But sitting here in the station, with the suitcase all packed and at his feet, he had begun to realize that this journey might, for a fact, take place. The key had materialized to show him the enormity of this venture. And after his first shock and pride he had simply reserved the key; he had hidden it in his pocket.

She looked unblinking into the light of the lantern on the floor. Her face looked strong and terrifying, all lighted and very near to his. But there was no joy there. You knew that she was very brave.

Albert seemed to shrink, to retreat. . . . His trembling hand went once more beneath his coat and touched the pocket where the key was lying, waiting. Would he ever remember that elusive thing about it or be sure what it might really be a symbol of? . . . His eyes, in their quick manner of filming over, grew dreamy. Perhaps he had even decided that it was a symbol not of happiness with Ellie, but of something else—something which he could have alone, for only himself, in peace, something strange and unlooked for which would come to him. . . .

The red-haired man took a second key from his pocket, and in one direct motion placed it in Ellie's red palm. It was a key with a large triangular pasteboard tag on which was clearly printed, "Star Hotel, Room 2."

He did not wait to see any more, but went out abruptly into the night. He stood still for a moment and reached for a cigarette. As he held the match close he gazed straight ahead, and in his eyes, all at once wild and searching, there was certainly, besides the simple compassion in his regard, a look both restless and weary, very much used to the comic. You could see that he despised and saw the uselessness of the thing he had done.

Talking Horse
by Bernard Malamud

EDITORS' PREFACE

This strange allegory presents us with a talking horse, Abramowitz, and his deaf master, Goldberg. The allegory makes special use of Goldberg's deafness to intensify the feelings of frustration that Abramowitz experiences in trying to free himself of Goldberg's control.

Goldberg refuses to allow Abramowitz to ask questions, and then refuses to answer if Abramowitz does ask a question. In this way, Malamud is able to give us a sense of what many people feel intuitively—life is unfair and does not ever let us know *what* is happening to us. Abramowitz feels trapped (also a common feeling) because Goldberg keeps him in a ridiculous circus routine to make their living, a routine that Abramowitz finds stupid and boring (like many jobs). Abramowitz feels trapped inside himself, that is, he suspects maybe he is a man inside a horse. Allegorically, there is a free, living person trapped inside a body that performs a dull job and that does not get answers to the important questions of life. We all feel that way at times—we go through the days, performing, feeling bored, trapped, exploited, and yet we go on, even though we know there is another person inside us trying to get out. Abramowitz is like that.

Another aspect of the allegory is that Abramowitz, being a horse, is, of course, stronger than Goldberg, who is a mere human. And so Goldberg could not really stop Abramowitz if Abramowitz wanted to break away from Goldberg. And therefore we are led to the conclusion that Abramowitz is really a partner to his own imprisonment, as we all are who refuse to strive for our freedom.

And what does Goldberg's deafness add to this allegory? Since Abramowitz must speak for Goldberg, and Goldberg controls Abramowitz, and since Goldberg at the end strangely disappears, we suspect that Goldberg is not meant as a real person but represents an authority figure whom Abramowitz carries around in his head—again, something we all do. A parent, teacher, priest, anyone who had influenced us or all of them put together—these are the authorities we carry around with us all the time and who keep us bound to their rules and ideas, even after we leave them and see them no more. Goldberg controlled Abramowitz but only because Abramowitz allowed it.

Goldberg's deafness, then, is a way of making him allegorically a creature of Abramowitz' compulsive obedience. His deafness and muteness rob Goldberg of a sense of real existence because he can communicate only through other people. (De Musset had seen this aspect of deafness also when he referred to Camille, in "Pierre and Camille," as "the phantom of a being.")

The story is a story of Abramowitz' struggle to free himself of this creature who controls him like a puppet. Goldberg's deafness makes us feel, directly, the effort of this struggle, for it makes us understand Goldberg's unapproachability, and it makes his aloofness and distance more palpable.

Abramowitz' suspicion that he is not really a horse—not *just* a horse, that is—but perhaps a man, or a man inside a horse, cannot be confirmed, however, until he begins to rebel against Goldberg. He does and finally succeeds in his rebellion by emerging not as horse *or* man, but as centaur, half man and half horse.

Centaurs represented the wild, natural life to the Greeks, so when Abramowitz becomes a centaur, we are to take it that he has finally been liberated from his compulsive obedience to the Goldberg in his life, and that he has finally come to life. He is described as a "free centaur" at the end, the emphasis being on both "free" and "centaur"—he is free of the authority he had carried in his head, and he is thus a "centaur," strong, natural, alive.

TALKING HORSE

Q. Am I a man in a horse or a horse that talks like a man?
Suppose they took an X-ray, what would they see?—a man's
luminous skeleton prostrate inside a horse, or just a horse
with a complicated voice box? If the first, then Jonah had
it better in the whale—more room all around; also he knew
who he was and how he had got there. About myself I have
to make guesses. Anyway after three days and nights the
big fish stopped at Nineveh and Jonah took his valise and
got off. But not Abramowitz, still on board, or at hand,
after years; he's no prophet. On the contrary, he works in
a sideshow full of freaks—though recently advanced, on
Goldberg's insistence, to the center ring inside the big tent
in an act with his deaf-mute master—Goldberg himself,
may the Almighty forgive him. All I know is I've been here
for years and still don't understand the nature of my fate;
in short if I'm Abramowitz, a horse; or a horse *including*
Abramowitz. Why is anybody's guess. Understanding goes
so far and not further, especially if Goldberg blocks the
way. It might be because of something I said, or thought,
or did, or didn't do in my life. It's easy to make mistakes
and it's easy not to know who made them. I have my theories, glimmers, guesses, but can't prove a thing.

When Abramowitz stands in his stall, his hoofs nervously
booming on the battered wooden boards as he chews in his
bag of hard yellow oats, sometimes he has thoughts, far-off
remembrances they seem to be, of young horses racing,
playing, nipping at each other's flanks in green fields; and
other disquieting images that might be memories; so who's
to say what's really the truth?

I've tried asking Goldberg but save yourself the trouble.
He goes black-and-blue in the face at questions, really up-
tight. I can understand—he's a deaf-mute from way back;

he doesn't like interference with his thoughts or plans, or the way he lives, and no surprises except those he invents. In other words questions disturb him. Ask him a question and he's off his usual track. He talks to me only when he feels like it, which isn't so often—his little patience wears thin. Lately his mood is awful, he reaches too often for his bamboo cane—whoosh across the rump! There's usually plenty of oats and straw and water, and once in a while even a joke to relax me when I'm tensed up, but otherwise it's one threat or another, followed by a flash of pain if I don't get something or other right, or something I say hits him on his nerves. It's not only that cane that slashes like a whip; his threats have the same effect—like a zing-zong of lightning through the flesh; in fact the blow hurts less than the threat—the blow's momentary, the threat you worry about. But the true pain, at least to me, is when you don't know what you have to know.

Which doesn't mean we don't communicate to each other. Goldberg taps our Morse code messages on my head with his big knuckle—crack crack crack; I feel the vibrations run through my bones to the tip of my tail—when he orders me what to do next or he threatens how many lashes for the last offense. His first message, I remember, was NO-QUESTIONS. UNDERSTOOD? I shook my head yes and a little bell jangled on a strap under the forelock. That was the first I knew it was there.

TALK, he knocked on my head after he told me about the act. "You're a talking horse."

"Yes, master." What else can you say?

My voice surprised me when it came out high through the tunnel of a horse's neck. I can't exactly remember the occasion—go remember beginnings. My memory I have to fight to get an early remembrance out of. Don't ask me why unless I happened to fall and hurt my head or was otherwise stunted. Goldberg is my deaf-mute owner; he reads my lips. Once when he was drunk and looking for a little company he tapped me that I used to carry goods on my back to fairs and markets in the old days before we joined the circus.

I used to think I was born here.

"On a rainy, snowy, crappy night," Goldberg Morse-coded me on my skull.

"What happened then?"

He stopped talking altogether. I should know better but don't.

I try to remember what night we're talking about and certain hazy thoughts flicker in my mind, which could be some sort of story I dream up when I have nothing to do but chew oats. It's easier than remembering. The one that comes to me most is about two men, or horses, or men on horses, though which was me I can't say. Anyway two strangers meet, somebody asks the other a question and the next thing they're locked in battle, either hacking at one another's head with swords, or braying wildly as they tear flesh with their teeth; or both at the same time. If riders, or horses, one is thin and poetic, the other a fat stranger wearing a huge black crown. They meet in a stone pit on a rainy, snowy, crappy night, one wearing his cracked metal crown that weighs like a ton on his head and makes his movements slow though nonetheless accurate, and the other on his head wears a ragged colored cap; all night they wrestle by weird light in the slippery stone pit.

Q. "What's to be done?"

A. "None of those accursed bloody questions."

The next morning one of us wakes with a terrible pain which feels like a wound in the neck but also a headache. He remembers a blow he can't swear to and a strange dialogue where the answers come first and the questions follow:

I descended from a ladder.

How did you get here?

The up and the down.

Which ladder?

Abramowitz, in his dream story, suspects Goldberg walloped him over the head and stuffed him into his horse because he needed a talking one for his act and there was no such thing.

I wish I knew for sure.

DON'T DARE ASK.

That's his nature; he's a lout though not without a little consideration when he's depressed and tippling his bottle. That's when he taps me out a teasing anecdote or two. He has no visible friends. Family neither of us talks about. When he laughs he cries.

It must frustrate the owner that all he can say aloud is four-letter words like geee, gooo, gaaa, gaaw; and the circus manager who doubles as ringmaster, in for a snifter, looks embarrassed at the floor. At those who don't know the Morse code Goldberg grimaces, glares, and grinds his teeth. He has his mysteries. He keeps a mildewed three-prong spear hanging on the wall over a stuffed pony's head. Sometimes he goes down the cellar with an old candle and comes up with a new one though we have electric lights. Although he doesn't complain about his life, he worries and cracks his knuckles. Maybe he's a widower, who knows? He doesn't seem interested in women but sees to it that Abramowitz gets his chance at a mare in heat, if available. Abramowitz engages to satisfy his physical nature, a fact is a fact, otherwise it's no big deal; the mare has no interest in a talking courtship. Furthermore Goldberg applauds when Abramowitz mounts her, which is humiliating.

And when they're in their winter quarters the owner
once a week or so dresses up and goes out on the town.
When he puts on his broadcloth suit, diamond stickpin,
and yellow gloves, he preens before the full-length mirror.
He pretends to fence, jabs the bamboo cane at the figure
in the glass, twirls it around one finger. Where he goes
when he goes he doesn't inform Abramowitz. But when he
returns he's usually melancholic, sometimes anguished, didn't
have much of a good time; and in this mood may hand out
a few loving lashes with that bastard cane. Or worse—
makes threats. Nothing serious but who needs it? Usually
he prefers to stay home and watch television. He is fasci-
nated by astronomy, and when they have those programs
on the educational channel he's there night after night,
staring at pictures of stars, quasars, infinite space. He also
likes to read the *Daily News*, which he tears up when he's
done. Sometimes he reads this book he hides on a shelf in
the closet under some old hats. If the book doesn't make
him laugh outright it makes him cry. When he gets excited
over something he's reading in this fat book, his eyes roll,
his mouth gets wet, and he tries to talk through his thick
tongue, though all Abramowitz hears is geee, gooo, gaaa,
gaaw. Always these words, whatever they mean, and sometimes gool goon geek gonk, in various combinations, usually
gool with gonk, which Abramowitz thinks means Goldberg.
And in such states he has been known to kick Abramowitz
in the belly with his heavy boot. Ooof.

When he laughs he sounds like a horse, or maybe it's
the way I hear him with these ears. And though he laughs
once in a while, it doesn't make my life easier, because of
my condition. I mean I think here I am in this horse. This
is my theory though I have my doubts. Otherwise, Goldberg is a small stocky figure with a thick neck, heavy black

brows, each like a small mustache, and big feet that swell up in his shapeless boots. He washes his feet in the kitchen sink and hangs up his yellowed white socks to dry on the whitewashed walls of my stall. Phoo.

He likes to do card tricks.

In winter they live in the South in a small, messy, one-floor house with a horse's stall attached that Goldberg can approach, down a few steps, from the kitchen of the house. To get Abramowitz into the stall he is led up a plank from the outside and the door shuts on his rear end. To keep him from wandering all over the house there's a slatted gate to just under his head. Furthermore the stall is next to the toilet and the broken water closet runs all night. It's a boring life with a deaf-mute except when Goldberg changes the act a little. Abramowitz enjoys it when they rehearse a new routine, although Goldberg hardly ever alters the lines, only the order of answer and question. That's better than nothing. Sometimes when Abramowitz gets tired of talking to himself, asking unanswered questions, he complains, shouts, calls the owner dirty names. He snorts, brays, whinnies shrilly. In his frustration he rears, rocks, gallops in his stall; but what good is a gallop if there's no place to go, and Goldberg can't, or won't, hear complaints, pleas, protest?

Q. "Answer me this: If it's a sentence I'm serving, how long?"

Once in a while Goldberg seems to sense somebody else's needs and is momentarily considerate of Abramowitz—combs and curries him, even rubs his bushy head against the horse's. He also shows interest in his diet and whether his bowel movements are regular and sufficient; but if Abramowitz gets sentimentally careless when the owner is close by and forms a question he can see on his lips, Goldberg punches him on the nose. Or threatens to. It doesn't hurt any the less.

All I know is he's a former vaudeville comic and acrobat. He did a solo act telling jokes with the help of a blind assistant before he went sad. That's about all he's ever tapped to me about himself. When I forgot myself and asked what happened then, he punched me in the nose.

Only once, when he was half drunk and giving me my bucket of water, I sneaked in a fast one which he answered before he knew it.

"Where did you get me master? Did you buy me from somebody else? Maybe in some kind of auction?"

I FOUND YOU IN A CABBAGE PATCH.

Once he tapped my skull: "In the beginning was the word."

"Which word was that?"

Bong on the nose.

NO MORE QUESTIONS.

"Watch out for the wound on my head or whatever it is."

"Keep your trap shut or you'll lose your teeth."

Goldberg should read that story I once heard on his transistor radio, I thought to myself. It's about a poor cab driver driving his sledge in the Russian snow. His son, a fine promising lad, got sick with pneumonia and died, and the poor cabby can't find anybody to talk to so as to relieve his grief. Nobody wants to listen to his troubles, because that's the way it is in the world. When he opens his mouth to say a word, the customers insult him. So he finally tells the story to his bony nag in the stable, and the horse, munching oats, listens as the weeping old man tells him about his boy that he has just buried.

Something like that could happen to you, Goldberg, and

you'd be a lot kinder to whoever I am.

"Will you ever free me out of here, master?"

I'LL FLAY YOU ALIVE, YOU BASTARD HORSE.

We have this act we do together. Goldberg calls it "Ask Me Another," an ironic title where I am concerned.

In the sideshow days people used to stand among the bearded ladies, the blobby fat men, Joey the snake boy, and other freaks, laughing beyond belief at Abramowitz talking. He remembers one man staring into his mouth to see who's hiding there. Homunculus? Others suggested it was a ventriloquist's act even though the horse told them Goldberg was a deaf-mute. But in the main tent the act got thunderous storms of applause.

Reporters pleaded for permission to interview Abramowitz and he had plans to spill all, but Goldberg wouldn't allow it. "His head will swell up too big," he had the talking horse say to them. "He will never be able to wear the same size straw hat he wore last summer."

For the performance the owner dresses up in a balloony red-and-white polka-dot clown's suit with a pointed clown's hat and has borrowed a ring-master's snaky whip, an item Abramowitz is skittish of though Goldberg says it's nothing to worry about, little more than decoration in a circus act. No animal act is without one. People like to hear the snap. He also ties an upside-down feather duster on Abramowitz's head that makes him look like a wilted unicorn. The five-piece circus band ends its brassy "Overture to William Tell"; there's a flourish of trumpets, and Goldberg cracks the whip as Abramowitz, with his loose-feathered, upside-down duster, trots once around the spotlit ring and then stops at attention, facing clown-Goldberg, his left foreleg pawing the sawdust-covered earth. They then begin the act; Goldberg's ruddy face, as he opens his painted mouth to express himself, flushes dark red, and his melancholy eyes under black brows protrude as he painfully squeezes out the abominable sounds, his only eloquence:

"Geee gooo gaaa gaaw?"

Abramowitz's resonant, beautifully timed response is:

A. "To get to the other side."

There's a gasp from the spectators, a murmur, perhaps of puzzlement, and a moment of intense expectant silence. Then at a roll of the drums Goldberg snaps the long whip and Abramowitz translates the owner's idiocy into something that makes sense and somehow fulfills expectations; though in truth it's no more than a question following a response already given.

Q. "Why does a chicken cross the road?"

Then they laugh. And do they laugh! They pound each other in merriment. You'd think this trite riddle, this sad excuse for a joke, was the first they had heard in their lives. And they're laughing at the translated question, of course, not at the answer, which is the way Goldberg has set it up. That's his nature for you. It's the only way he works.

Abramowitz used to sink into the dumps after that, knowing what really amuses everybody is not the old-fashioned tired conumdrum, but the fact it's put to them by a talking horse. That's what splits the gut.

"It's a stupid little question."

"There are no better," Goldberg said.

"You could try letting me ask one or two of my own."

YOU KNOW WHAT A GELDING IS?

I gave him no reply. Two can play at that game.

After the first applause both performers take a low bow. Abramowitz trots around the ring, his head with panache held high. And when Goldberg again cracks the pudgy whip, he moves nervously to the center of the ring and they go through the routine of the other infantile answers and questions in the same silly ass-backwards order. After each question Abramowitz runs around the ring as the spectators cheer.

A. "To hold up his pants."

Q. "Why does a fireman wear red suspenders?"

A. "Columbus."

Q. "What was the first bus to cross the Atlantic?"

A. "A newspaper."

Q. "What's black and white and red all over?"

We did a dozen like that, and when we finished up, Goldberg cracked the foolish whip, I galloped a couple more times around the ring, then we took our last bows.

Goldberg pats my steaming flank and in the ocean-roar of everyone in the tent applauding and shouting bravo, we leave the ring, running down the ramp to our quarters, Goldberg's personal wagon van and attached stall; after that we're private parties till tomorrow's show. Many customers used to come night after night to watch the performance, and they laughed at the riddles though they had known them from childhood. That's how the season goes, and nothing much has changed one way or the other except that recently Goldberg, because the manager was complaining, added a couple of silly elephant riddles to modernize the act.

A. "From playing marbles."

Q. "Why do elephants have wrinkled knees?"

A. "To pack their dirty laundry in."

Q. "Why do elephants have long trunks?"

Neither Goldberg nor I think much of the new jokes but they're the latest style. I reflect that we could do the act without jokes. All you need is a talking horse.

One day Abramowitz thought he would make up a question-response of his own—it's not that hard to do. So that night after they had finished the routine, he slipped in his new riddle.

A. "To greet his friend the chicken."

Q. "Why does a yellow duck cross the road?"

After a moment of confused silence everybody cracked up; they beat themselves silly with their fists—broken straw boaters flew all over the place; but Goldberg in unbelieving astonishment glowered murderously at the horse. His ruddy face turned black. When he cracked the whip it sounded like a river of ice breaking. Realizing in fright that he had gone too far, Abramowitz, baring his big teeth, reared up on his hind legs, and took several steps forward against the will. But the spectators, thinking this was an extra flourish at the end of the act applauded wildly. Goldberg's anger apparently eased, and lowering his whip, he pretended to laugh. Amid continuing applause he beamed at Abramowitz as if he were his only child and could do no wrong, though Abramowitz, in his heart of hearts, knew the owner was furious.

"Don't forget WHO's WHO, you insane horse," Goldberg, his back to the audience, tapped out on Abramowitz's nose.

He made him gallop once more around the ring, mounted him in an acrobatic leap onto his bare back, and drove him madly to the exit.

Afterwards he Morse-coded with his hard knuckle on the horse's bony head that if he pulled anything like that again he would personally deliver him to the glue factory.

WHERE THEY WILL MELT YOU DOWN TO SIZE.

"What's left over goes into dog food cans."

"It was just a joke, master," Abramowitz explained.

"To say the answer was O.K., but not to ask the question by yourself."

Out of stored-up bitterness the talking horse replied, "I did it on account of it made me feel free."

At that Goldberg whacked him hard across the neck with his murderous cane. Abramowitz, choking, staggered but did not bleed.

"Don't, master," he gasped, "not on my old wound."

Goldberg went into slow motion, still waving the cane.

"Try it again, you tub of guts, and I'll be wearing a horsehide coat with fur collar, gool, goon, geek, gonk." Spit crackled in the corners of his mouth.

Understood.

Sometimes I think of myself as an idea, yet here I stand in this filthy stall, my hoofs sunk in my yellow balls of dreck. I feel old, disgusted with myself, smelling the odor of my bad breath as my teeth in the feedbag grind the hard oats into a foaming lump, while Goldberg smokes his panatela as he watches TV. He feeds me well enough, if oats are your dish, but hasn't had my stall cleaned for a week. It's easy to get even on a horse if that's the type you are.

So the act goes on every matinee and night, keeping Goldberg in good spirits and thousands in stitches, but Abramowitz had dreams of being out in the open. They were strange dreams—if dreams; he isn't sure what they are or come from—hidden thoughts, maybe, of freedom, or some sort of self-mockery? You let yourself conceive what can't be? Anyhow, whoever heard of a talking horse's dreams? Goldberg hasn't said he knows what's going on but Abramowitz suspects he understands more than he seems to, because when the horse, lying in his dung and soiled straw, awakens from a dangerous reverie, he hears the owner muttering in his sleep in deaf-mute talk.

Abramowitz dreams, or does something of the sort, of other lives he might live, let's say of a horse that can't talk, couldn't conceive that idea; is perfectly content to be simply a horse without problems of speech. He sees himself, for instance, pulling a wagon load of yellow apples along a rural road. There are leafy beech trees on both sides and beyond them broad green fields full of wild flowers. If he were that kind of horse, maybe he might retire to graze in such fields. More adventurously, he sees himself a racehorse in goggles, thundering along the last stretch of muddy track, slicing through a wedge of other galloping horses to win by a nose at the finish; and the jockey is definitely not Goldberg. There is no jockey; he fell off.

Or if not a racehorse, if he has to be practical about it, Abramowitz continues on as a talking horse but not in circus work any longer; and every night on the stage he recites poetry. The theater is packed and people cry out oooh and aaah, what beautiful things that horse is saying.

Sometimes he thinks of himself as altogether a free "man," someone of indeterminate appearance and characteristics, who, if he has the right education, is maybe a doctor or lawyer helping poor people. Not a bad idea for a useful life.

But even if I am dreaming or whatever it is, I hear Goldberg talking in *my* sleep. He talks something like me:

As for number one, you are first and last a talking horse, not any ordinary nag that can't talk; and believe me I have got nothing against you that you *can* talk, Abramowitz, but on account of what you say when you open your mouth and break the rules.

As for a racehorse, if you take a good look at the broken-down type you are—overweight, with big sagging belly and a thick uneven dark-brown coat that won't shine up no matter how much I comb or brush you, and four hairy, thick, bent legs, plus a pair of slight cross-eyes, you would give up that foolish idea you can be a racehorse before you do something very ridiculous.

As for reciting poetry, who wants to hear a horse recite poetry? That's for the birds.

As for the last dream, or whatever it is that's bothering

you, that you can be a doctor or lawyer, you better forget it, it's not that kind of world. A horse is a horse even if he's a talking horse; don't mix yourself up with human beings if you know what I mean. If you're a talking horse that's your fate. I warn you, don't try to be a wise guy, Abramowitz. Don't try to know everything, you might go mad. Nobody can know everything; it's not that kind of a world. Follow the rules of the game. Don't rock the boat. Don't try to make a monkey out of me; I know more than you. We got to be who we are, although this is rough on both of us. But that's the logic of the situation. It goes by certain laws even though that's a hard proposition for some to understand. The law is the law, you can't change the order. That's the way things stay put together. We are mutually related, Abramowitz, and that's all there is to it. If it makes you feel any better, I will admit to you I can't live without you and I won't let you live without me. I have my living to make and you are my talking horse I use in my act to earn my living, plus so I can take care of your needs. The true freedom, like I have always told you, though you never want to believe me, is to understand that and live with it so you don't waste your energy resisting the rules; if so you waste your life. All you are is a horse who talks, and believe me, there are very few horses that can do that; so if you are smart, Abramowitz, it should make you happy instead of always and continually dissatisfied. Don't break up the act if you know what's good for you.

As for those yellow balls of your dreck, if you will behave yourself like a gentleman and watch out what you say, tomorrow the shovelers will come and after I will hose you over personally with warm water. Believe me, there's nothing like cleanliness.

Thus he mocks me in my sleep though I have my doubts that I sleep much nowadays.

In short hops between towns and small cities the circus moves in wagon vans. The other horses pull them, but Goldberg won't let me, which again wakes disturbing ideas in my head. For longer hauls, from one big city to another, we ride in red-and-white-striped circus trains. I have a stall in a freight car with some nontalking horses with fancy braided manes and sculptured tails from the bareback riders' act. None of us are much interested in each other. If they think at all they think a talking horse is a show off. All they do is eat and drink, piss and crap, all day. Not a single word goes back or forth among them. Nobody has a good or bad idea.

The long train rides generally give us a day off without a show, and Goldberg gets depressed and surly when we're not working the matinee or evening performance. Early in the morning of a long train-ride day he starts loving his bottle and Morse-coding me nasty remarks and threats.

"Abramowitz, you think too much, why do you bother? In the first place your thoughts come out of you and you don't know that much, so your thoughts don't either. In other words, don't get too ambitious. For instance what's on your mind right now, tell me?"

"Answers and questions, master—some new ones to modernize the act."

"Feh, we don't need any new ones, the act is already too long."

He should know the questions I am really asking myself, though better not.

Once you start asking questions one leads to the next and in the end it's endless. And what if it turns out I'm always asking myself the same question in different words? I keep on wanting to know why I can't ask this coarse lout a simple question about *anything*. By now I have it figured out Goldberg is afraid of questions because a question could show he's afraid people will find out who he is. Somebody who all he does is repeat his fate. Anyway, Goldberg has some kind of past he is afraid to tell me about, though sometimes he hints. And when I mention my own past he says forget it. Concentrate on the future. What future? On the other hand, what does he think he can hide from Abramowitz, a student by nature, who spends most of his time asking himself questions Goldberg won't permit him to ask, putting one and one together, and finally making up his mind—miraculous thought—that he knows more than a horse should, even a talking horse, so therefore, given all the built-up evidence, he is positively not a horse. Not in origin anyway.

So I came once more to the conclusion that I am a man in a horse and not just a horse that happens to be able to talk. I had figured this out in my mind before; then I said, no it can't be. I feel more like a horse bodywise; on the other hand I talk, I think, I wish to ask questions. So I am what I am, which is a man in a horse, not a talking horse. Something tells me there is no such thing even though Goldberg, pointing his fat finger at me, says the opposite. He lives on his lies, it's his nature.

After long days of traveling, when they were in their new quarters one night, finding the rear door to his stall unlocked—Goldberg grew careless when depressed—acting on belief as well as impulse, Abramowitz cautiously backed out. Avoiding the front of Goldberg's wagon van he trotted across the fairgrounds on which the circus was situated. Two of the circus hands who saw him trot by, perhaps because Abramowitz greeted them, "Hello, boys, marvelous evening," did not attempt to stop him. Outside the grounds, though exhilarated to be in the open Abramowitz began to wonder if he was doing a foolish thing. He had hoped to find a wooded spot to hide in for the time being, surrounded by fields in which he could peacefully graze; but this was the industrial edge of the city, and though he clop-clopped from street to street there were no woods nearby, not even a small park.

Where can somebody who looks like a horse go by himself?

Abramowitz tried to hide in an old riding-school stable and was driven out by an irate woman. In the end they caught up with him on a station platform where he had been waiting for a train. Quite foolishly, he knew. The conductor wouldn't let him get on though Abramowitz had explained his predicament. The stationmaster then ran out and pointed a pistol at his head. He held the horse there, deaf to his blandishments, until Goldberg arrived with his bamboo cane. The owner threatened to whip Abramowitz to the quick, and his description of the effects was so painfully vivid that Abramowitz felt as though he had been slashed into a bleeding pulp. A half hour later he found himself back in his locked stall, his throbbing head encrusted with dried horse blood. Goldberg ranted in deaf-mute talk, but Abramowitz, who with lowered head pretended contrition, felt none. To escape from Goldberg he must first get out of the horse he was in.

But to exit a horse as a man takes some doing. Abramowitz planned to proceed slowly and appeal to public opinion. It might take months, possibly years, to do what he must. Protest! Sabotage if necessary! Revolt! One night after they had taken their bows and the applause was subsiding, Abramowitz, raising his head as though to whinny his appreciation of the plaudits, cried out to all assembled in the circus tent, "Help! Get me out of here, somebody! I am a prisoner in this horse! Free a fellow man!"

After a silence that rose like a dense forest, Goldberg, who was standing to the side, unaware of Abramowitz's passionate cry—he picked up the news later from the ring-master—saw at once from everybody's surprised and star-tled expression, not to mention Abramowitz's undisguised look of triumph, that something had gone seriously amiss. The owner at once began to laugh heartily, as though what-ever it was that was going on was more of the same, part of the act, a bit of personal encore by the horse. The spec-tators laughed too, and again warmly applauded.

"It won't do you any good," the owner Morse-coded Abramowitz afterwards. "Because nobody is going to be-lieve you."

"Then please let me out of here on your own account, master. Have some mercy."

"About that matter," Goldberg rapped out sternly, "I am already on record. Our lives and livings are dependent one on the other. You got nothing substantial to complain about, Abramowitz. I'm taking care of you better than you can take care of yourself."

Maybe that's so, Mr. Goldberg, but what good is it if in my heart I am a man and not a horse, not even a talking one?"

Goldberg's ruddy face blanched as he Morse-coded the usual NO QUESTIONS.

"I'm not asking, I'm trying to tell you something very serious."

"Watch out for hubris, Abramowitz."

That night the owner went out on the town, came back dreadfully drunk, as though he had been lying with his mouth under a spigot pouring brandy; and he threatened Abramowitz with the trident spear he kept in his trunk when they traveled. This is a new torment.

Anyway, the act goes on but definitely altered, not as before. Abramowitz, despite numerous warnings and var-ious other painful threats, daily disturbs the routine. After

Goldberg makes his idiot noises, his geee gooo gaaa gaaw, Abramowitz purposely mixes up the responses to the usual ridiculous riddles.

A. "To get to the other side."

Q. "Why does a fireman wear red suspenders?"

A. "From playing marbles."

Q. "Why do elephants have long trunks?"

And he adds dangerous A.'s and Q.'s without permission despite the inevitability of punishment.

A. "A talking horse."

Q. "What has four legs and wishes to be free?"

At that nobody laughed.

He also mocked Goldberg when the owner wasn't attentively reading his lips; called him "deaf-mute," "stupid ears," "lock mouth"; and whenever possible addressed the public, requesting, urging, begging their assistance.

"Gevalt! Get me out of here! I am one of you! This is slavery! I wish to be free!"

Now and then when Goldberg's back was turned, or when he was too lethargic with melancholy to be much attentive, Abramowitz clowned around and in other ways ridiculed the owner. He heehawed at his appearance, brayed at his "talk," stupidity, arrogance. Sometimes he made up little songs of freedom as he danced on his hind legs, exposing his private parts. And at times Goldberg, to mock the mocker, danced gracelessly with him—a clown with a glum-painted smile, waltzing with a horse. Those who had seen the act last season were astounded, stunned by the change, uneasy, as though the future threatened.

"Help! Help, somebody help me!" Abramowitz pleaded, but nobody moved.

Sensing the tension in and around the ring, the audience sometimes booed the performers, causing Goldberg, in his red-and-white polka-dot suit and white clown's cap, great embarrassment, though on the whole he kept his cool during the act and never used the ringmaster's whip. In fact he smiled as he was insulted, whether he "listened" or not. He heard what he saw. A sly smile was fixed on his face and his lips twitched. And though his fleshy ears flared like torches at the gibes and mockeries he endured, Goldberg laughed to the verge of tears at Abramowitz's sallies and shenanigans; many in the big tent laughed along with him. Abramowitz was furious.

Afterwards Goldberg, once he had stepped out of his clown suit, threatened him to the point of collapse, or flayed him viciously with his cane; and the next day fed him pep pills and painted his hide black before the performance so that people wouldn't see the wounds.

"You bastard horse, you'll lose us our living."

"I wish to be free."

"To be free you got to know when you are free. Considering your type, Abramowitz, you'll be free in the glue factory."

One night when Goldberg, after a day of profound depression, was listless and logy in the ring, could not evoke so much as a limp snap out of his whip, Abramowitz, thinking that where the future was concerned, glue factory or his present condition of life made little difference, determined to escape either fate; he gave a solo performance for freedom, the best of his career. Though desperate, he entertained, made up hilarious riddles: A. "By jumping through the window." Q. "How do you end the pane?"; he recited poems he had heard on Goldberg's radio, which sometimes stayed on all night after the owner had fallen asleep; he also told stories and ended the evening with a moving speech.

He told sad stories of the lot of horses, one, for instance, beaten to death by his cruel owner, his brains battered with a log because he was too weakened by hunger to pull a wagon load of wood. Another concerned a racehorse of fabulous speed, a sure winner in the Kentucky Derby, had he not in his very first race been doped by his avaricious master who had placed a fortune in bets on the next best horse. A third was about a fabulous flying horse shot down by a hunter who couldn't believe his own eyes. And then Abramowitz told a story of a youth of great promise, who, out for a stroll one spring day, came upon a goddess bathing naked in a stream. As he gazed at her beauty in amazement and longing she let out a piercing scream to the sky. The youth took off at a fast gallop, realizing from the snorting, and sound of pounding hoofs as he ran, that he was no longer a youth of great promise but a horse running.

Abramowitz then cried out to the faces that surrounded him, "I also am a man in a horse. Is there a doctor in the house?"

Dead silence.

"Maybe a magician?"

No response but nervous tittering.

He then delivered an impassioned speech on freedom for all. Abramowitz talked his brains blue, ending once more with a personal appeal. "Help me to recover my original form. It's not what I am but what I wish to be. I wish to be what I really am which is a man."

At the end of the act many people in the tent were standing wet-eyed and the band played "The Star-Spangled Banner."

Goldberg, who had been dozing in a sawdust pile for a good part of Abramowitz's solo act, roused himself in time to join the horse in a bow. Afterwards, on the enthusiastic advice of the circus manager, he changed the name of the act from "Ask Me Another" to "Goldberg's Varieties." And wept himself for unknown reasons.

Back in the stall after the failure of his most passionate,

most inspired, pleas for assistance, Abramowitz butted his head in frustration against the stall gate until his nostrils bled into the feedbag. He thought he would drown in the blood and didn't much care. Goldberg found him lying on the floor in the dirty straw, half in a faint, and revived him with aromatic spirits of ammonia. He bandaged his nose and spoke to him in a fatherly fashion.

"That's how the mop flops," he Morse-coded with his blunt fingertip, "but things could be worse. Take my advice and settle for a talking horse, it's not without distinction."

"Make me either into a man or make me either into a horse," Abramowitz pleaded. "It's in your power, Goldberg."

"You got the wrong party, my friend."

"Why do you always say lies?"

"Why do you always ask questions you can't ask?"

"I ask because I am. Because I wish to be free."

"So who's free, tell me?" Goldberg mocked.

"If so," said Abramowitz, "what's to be done?"

DON'T ASK I WARNED YOU.

He warned he would punch his nose; it bled again.

Abramowitz later that day began a hunger strike which he carried on for the better part of a week; but Goldberg threatened force-feeding with thick rubber tubes in both nostrils, and that ended that. Abramowitz almost choked to death at the thought of it. The act went on as before, and the owner changed its name back to "Ask Me Another." When the season was over the circus headed south, Abramowitz trotting along in a cloud of dust with the other horses.

Anyway I got my own thoughts.

One fine autumn, after a long hard summer, Goldberg washed his big feet in the kitchen sink and hung his smelly white socks to dry on the gate of Abramowitz's stall before sitting down to watch astronomy on ETV. To see better he placed a lit candle on top of the color set. But he had carelessly left the stall gate open, and Abramowitz hopped up three steps and trotted through the messy kitchen, his eyes flaring. Confronting Goldberg staring in awe at the universe on the screen, he reared with a bray of rage, to bring his hoofs down on the owner's head. Goldberg, seeing him out of the corner of his eye, rose to protect himself. Instantly jumping up on the chair, he managed with a grunt to grab Abramowitz by both big ears as though to lift him by them, and the horse's head and neck, up to an old wound, came off in his hands. Amid the stench of blood and bowel a man's pale head popped out of the hole in the horse. He was in his early forties, with fogged pince-nez, intense dark eyes, and a black mustache. Pulling his arms free, he grabbed Goldberg around his thick neck with both bare arms and held on for dear life. As they tugged and struggled, Abramowitz, straining to the point of madness, slowly pulled himself out of the horse up to his navel. At that moment Goldberg broke his frantic grip and, though the astronomy lesson was still going on in a blaze of light, disappeared. Abramowitz later made a few discreet inquiries, but no one could say where.

Departing the circus grounds he cantered across a grassy soft field into a dark wood, a free centaur.

At the Dances of the Deaf-Mutes
by Walter Toman

EDITORS' PREFACE

"At the Dances of the Deaf-Mutes" is an allegory, in which the deaf and blind people represent two types of people who are different, who cannot communicate very well between themselves, but who find a ceremonial way of communication. As such, the story is a psychological study of human communication.

Perhaps the two groups, the deaf and the blind are men and women, or two separate nationalities (it is difficult to be sure for clues are scarce in the story), but what seems to be important in the story is the nature of the communication that is possible: the dance itself. Outside of the dances, the deaf and blind could not communicate. It may be that ceremonial communication (the dance) is all that is possible—in another short story Walter Toman (the author) describes a man and woman in love who constantly stay in armor, more transparent allegory about communication (or lack thereof) between people.

Toman, despite his interest in communication, obviously knew little of sign language, for at one point in this story he remarks that sign language "offers too little release for angry feelings." To those of us who have any inkling of the dramatic force of sign language, this statement is absurd.

In any case, this story does get to one of the key aspects of the deaf experience, the limitations of all forms of human communication. Toman sees it as essentially non-personal, as stylized and ritualized. At the same time, however, it achieves beauty of movement and harmony.

AT THE DANCES OF THE DEAF-MUTES

When the deaf-mutes were still putting on their dances by themselves, they had a number of difficulties. I need not point out that they could not hear the music. Nor did they feel it with their chests, as vibration, as some assert. At first people thought that the floor rumbled from the drum-beats (which were especially strong here, by design) and that the deaf-mutes perceived these reverberations. But the only thing they really seemed to feel were their own treads under which the floor shook, and although these steps started out in the same rhythm, there was mad confusion soon after the beginning of every number. If they had danced a quadrille, they might have stuck it out longer, but the modern dances, with their wonderful gyrations of limbs and body, quickly got the rhythm all mixed up. Their eyes were not able to separate the dance steps as such from the many superimposed motions of the entire body, and not just the rhythm was lost. Because of the fact that soon all were hopping around on their own, they bumped into one another to a much greater extent than other dancers who get their beat from the music. They stepped on one another's feet, tore their stockings and trouser cuffs, insulted one another in the language of deaf-mutes, and, since this communication offers too little release for angry feelings, they very often became violent. It got to the point where an ambulance (and later two of them) had to maintain a regular shuttle service between the dance hall and the first-aid station.

People had tried to change things. One of the most obvious ways was to impart the beat to the dancers by means of lights. An apparatus was constructed which made the dance-hall lights sway in the rhythm of the music. However, this irritated the musicians as well as the deaf-mutes.

199

The latter complained of feeling nauseated and dizzy, but they probably would have got used to it if the musicians hadn't walked out first, claiming that the light-changing device was working too mechanically and interfering with their playing. Thereupon they had a member of the band regulate the rhythm of the lights, but now the musicians, too, discovered that they were getting nauseated. It wasn't so hard any more to keep in rhythm, and that probably gave them the opportunity to pay attention to their bodily sensations. At any rate, they began to feel so sick that they walked out again, and the management finally had to look around for a new rhythm device. They also tried to keep the dance-hall lights constant and to have only the red emergency lights flash rhythmically, but the success or, rather, the failure was the same. Some engineers had been hired to construct a dance floor that could be made to vibrate at will to the rhythm of the music, and the first blueprints had already been submitted. They even considered doing without a band entirely, but the first hint of this brought such a protest from the deaf-mutes that the idea was abandoned. "The band is the last thing we can do without," said the deaf-mutes. So the management went back to the plans for a vibrating dance floor, but then things happened quite differently.

The deaf-mute Peter Perz had invited a blind girl, Ilse Weninger, to one of the dances of the deaf-mutes, and she not only could hear the music of the band but was also a very talented dancer and musician. The two had in a short time become a team so splendidly attuned to each other that one deaf-mute couple after another stepped to the edge of the dance floor and watched them. Stimulated by the beautiful couple, the band played more and more fierily, and when Peter and Ilse were dancing solo, the musicians applauded after every number. The deaf-mutes, seeing them clap, soon did likewise, and suddenly another deaf-mute rushed forward and took the blind girl out of Peter's arms. Peter submitted to this, himself motioned to the band, and a new dance began. The other deaf-mute, too, quickly adapted himself to the blind girl, and now, in ever increasing succession, all the deaf-mutes wanted to dance with her. Even the deaf-mute girls wooed her, and at the very next dance the deaf-mutes and the blind joined together.

Now the affair became a pleasure for the musicians, too, for they saw a reaction to their playing, and the project of the vibrating dance floor was dropped. The deaf-mutes learned extremely fast, especially the girls, but the men, too; and at the dances the blind people received eyes, as it were. From now on there was sheer bliss, and if communication between the blind and the deaf-mutes had not been so difficult away from the dances (for the blind could not see their partners speak and the deaf-mutes could not hear theirs), there would have been many a union for life. But this difficulty was not insuperable. For example, Peter Perz took special lessons in voice projecting, Ilse Weninger learned sign language, and the two became a pair. Others tried to do the same thing, but because of their lesser intelligence did not succeed. Most of them, when they had reached a suitable age, married one of their own kind. But at their dances they exchanged partners, and henceforth these affairs were a sheer delight.

• THREE •

FROM DEAF AUTHORS

INTRODUCTION

In this section, five deaf authors describe the experience of being deaf. Needless to say, these writers get down to the essentials of the day-to-day experience.

It is interesting to compare the viewpoints in this section with those in the previous sections. In those sections, the deaf characters are all manifestations of the writer's views of society or of life in general. Perhaps the deaf character represents a superior moral position, or represents the suppressed mass, or the alienated mass, or any of the other ways in which deaf characters have been used by hearing authors. Rarely does a hearing writer concern himself or herself with the actual experience of being deaf—for example, hearing authors generally create deaf characters who can lipread anyone from any angle in any kind of light, which is an impossibility as anyone who has tried it knows.

The aspect most common to these five writers (except for Terry, who, though deaf himself, did not write much about deafness) is that of defiance and this aspect, interestingly, we find in the sections by hearing writers also. There is a certain pride in facing the difficulties that life throws at you and standing up to them. Ballin entitled his autobiography *The Deaf Mute Howls*—and, indeed, he does. A deaf English poet, David Wright, deaf since the age of seven, but still an accomplished poet and Oxford graduate, also shows the defiance I speak of. In his poem, "Monologue of a Deaf Man," Wright says

"The injury, dominated, is an asset:
It is there for domination, that is all."

In his book, *Deafness* (which, because it is still in print, we have not excerpted), he says

So far as cripples are concerned pity is no virtue. It is a sentiment that deceives its bestower and disparages its recipient. Helen Keller hated it, and she was blind as well as deaf. Its acceptance not only humiliates, but actually blunts the tools needed to best the disability. To accept pity means taking the first step towards self pity, thence to the finding, and finally the manufacture, of excuses. The end-product of self-exculpation is the failed human being, the victim. As the cliche runs—"victim of circumstances beyond his control"—as if anybody were in control of circumstances.

Defiance—refusal to accept the subtle traps of the world.

Miron, in Relgis' account of the loss of hearing, finds his own key to survival in defiance: hounded by his old friends, Miron, who has just become deaf (and thus the hounded), accepts the treatment for a few long moments but then something within him rebels.

The strength returns to his body as though stimulated by the lash of a whip. Electrified by revolt, the heritage of so many generations which have struggled against humiliation and slavery—Miron, with a bound, rises to his feet. His ardent and piercing glance is fixed upon the eyes of the evil child who had howled into his ear. The first revolt of human dignity, always the same, is revindicated in its simple grandeur, unknown to children and in which their parents do not believe.

And Miron, his eyes burning, his forehead raised, his hands clenched, walks away, holding in check the group wavering between ferocity and fear.

John Kitto, the deaf English writer of the nineteenth century who wrote *The Lost Senses*, does not show such an open rebellion, but rebel he does. At an early age, after he had lost his hearing, he was put into a job that nearly destroyed his will—it was a grueling physical job that left him only enough time to fall exhausted into bed at night, but it was felt that, being deaf, he was suited only for this kind of job. That he forced himself to continue learning during this employment, and that he eventually found a profession in spite of the great effort he had to expend, is another testimony to the value of defiance for the deaf person—defiance of the victim role thrust upon deaf people by those who imagine themselves to be benefactors.

Wiggins and Ballin also demonstrate defiance, as is mentioned in the prefaces before each of the selections. Defiance is a healthy reaction—it avoids the chance of becoming a mere "victim" of life, as David Wright points out, and the choice between defiance and playing victim is a central part of the deaf experience.

The Lost Senses
by John Kitto

EDITORS' PREFACE

John Kitto, an English missionary of the last century, wrote
this autobiography in mid life. He had lost his hearing early
in life, though postlingually, and tells us of the difficulties
he had in finding a niche in life because of the prejudices
against deaf people. It should be interesting to all our deaf
readers who have struggled much of their life with English
to find that Kitto finally settled upon writing as one of his
professions. He was almost as audacious in this decision as
was David Wright, a modern English poet who is deaf, who
not only decided to become a writer but a poet, and, not
only that, but a translator as well (the only other deaf person
we know who has had the gall to translate professionally is
one of the people who has his name on the front cover of
this book). Wright has become successful in all his ventures
in spite of his deafness, and Kitto was also, although not to
quite the degree that Wright is.

The excerpts from Kitto give us another side of the world
of the deaf in the nineteenth century that we encountered
in the first part. Kitto is no Gerasim or Gargan, for sure,
since he obviously was well established in the world and
hardly the isolated "natural man" that Gerasim and Gargan
were. In Kitto's account we find out about the most hopeful
signs for the advancement of deaf people in his time. His
is a practical account, a realistic appraisal of the life of an
educated deaf person (albeit one who could speak, and who
could use English well) in the last century. It should be

interesting to compare this account with the ones that follow it, they all having been written more recently, when deaf people were becoming more impatient with accepting second class citizenship.

FROM THE LOST SENSES

• INTRODUCTION •

I became deaf on my father's birthday, early in the year 1817, when I had lately completed the twelfth year of my age. . . .

The circumstances of that day—the last of twelve years of hearing, and the first of twenty-eight years of deafness, have left a more distinct impression upon my mind than those of any previous, or almost any subsequent, day of my life. It was a day to be remembered. The last day on which any customary labour ceases,—the last day on which any customary privilege is enjoyed,—the last day on which we do the things we have done daily, are always marked days in the calendar of life; how much, therefore, must the mind not linger in the memories of a day which was the last of many blessed things, and in which one stroke of action and suffering,—one moment of time, wrought a greater change of condition, than any sudden loss of wealth or honours ever made in the state of man. . . .

On the day in question my father and another man, attended by myself, were engaged in new slating the roof of a house, the ladder ascending to which was fixed in a small court paved with flag stones. . . . In one of the apartments of the house in which we were at work, a young sailor, of whom I had some knowledge, had died after a lingering illness, which had been attended with circumstances which the doctors could not well understand. It was, therefore,

209

concluded that the body should be opened to ascertain the cause of death. I knew this was to be done, but not the time appointed for the operation. But on passing from the street into the yard, with a load of slates which I was to take to the house-top, my attention was drawn to a stream of blood, or rather, I suppose, bloody water, flowing through the gutter by which the passage was traversed. The idea that this was the blood of the dead youth, whom I had so lately seen alive, and that the doctors were then at work cutting him up and groping at his inside, made me shudder, and gave what I should now call a shock to my nerves, although I was very innocent of all knowledge about nerves at that time. I cannot but think it was owing to this that I lost much of the presence of mind and collectedness so important to me at that moment; for when I had ascended to the top of the ladder, and was in the critical act of stepping from it on to the roof, I lost my footing, and fell backward, from a height of about thirty-five feet, into the paved court below.

Of what followed I know nothing. . . .

In this state I remained for a fortnight, as I afterwards learned. These days were a blank in my life, I could never bring any recollections to bear upon them; and when I awoke one morning to consciousness, it was as from a night of sleep. I saw that it was at least two hours later than my usual time of rising, and marvelled that I had been suffered to sleep so late. I attempted to spring up in bed, and was astonished to find that I could not even move. The utter prostration of my strength subdued all curiosity within me. I experienced no pain, but I felt that I was weak; I saw that I was treated as an invalid, and acquiesced in my condition, though some time passed—more time than the reader would imagine, before I could piece together my broken recollections so as to comprehend it.

I was very slow in learning that my hearing was entirely gone. The unusual stillness of all things was grateful to me in my utter exhaustion; and if in this half-awakened state, a thought of the matter entered my mind, I ascribed it to the unusual care and success of my friends in preserving silence around me. I saw them talking indeed to one another, and thought that, out of regard to my feeble condition, they spoke in whispers, because I heard them not. The truth was revealed to me in consequence of my solicitude about the book which had so much interested me in the day of my fall. It had, it seems, been reclaimed by the good old man who had sent it to me, and who doubtless concluded, that I should have no more need of books in this life. He was wrong; for there has been nothing in this life which I have needed more. I asked for this book with much earnestness, and was answered by signs which I could not comprehend.

"Why do you not speak?" I cried; "Pray let me have the book."

This seemed to create some confusion; and at length some one, more clever than the rest, hit upon the happy expedient of writing upon a slate, that the book had been reclaimed by the owner, and that I could not in my weak state be allowed to read.

"But," I said in great astonishment, "Why do you write to me, why not speak? Speak, speak."

Those who stood around the bed exchanged significant looks of concern, and the writer soon displayed upon his slate the awful words—"YOU ARE DEAF."

Did not this utterly crush me? By no means. In my then weakened condition nothing like this could affect me. Besides, I was a child; and to a child the full extent of such a calamity could not be at once apparent. However, I knew not the future—it was well I did not; and there was nothing to show me that I suffered under more than a temporary deafness, which in a few days might pass away. It was left for time to show me the sad realities of the condition to which I was reduced.

Time passed on, and I slowly recovered strength, but my deafness continued. The doctors were perplexed by it. They probed and tested my ears in various fashions. The tympanum was uninjured, and the organ seemed in every respect perfect, excepting that it would not act. Some thought that a disorganization of the internal mechanism had been produced by the concussion; others that the auditory nerve had been paralyzed.

They poured into my tortured ears various infusions, hot and cold; they bled me, they blistered me, leeched me, physicked me; and, at last, they put a watch between my teeth, and on finding that I was unable to distinguish the ticking, they gave it up as a bad case, and left me to my fate. I cannot know whether my case was properly dealt with or not. I have no reason to complain of inattention, of my own knowledge; but, some six months after, a wise doctor from London affirmed that, by a different course at the commencement, my hearing might have been restored. He caused a seton to be inserted in my neck; but this had no effect upon my deafness, although it seems to have acted beneficially upon the general health. Some years after, Mr. Snow Harris, with a spontaneous kindness, for which I am happy to be able at this distant day to express my obligations, put my ears through a course of electrical operations. He persevered for more than a month; but no good came of it: and since then nothing further has been done or attempted. Indeed, I have not sought any relief; and have discouraged the suggestions of friends who would have had me apply to Dr. This and Dr. That. The condition in which two-thirds of my life has been passed, has become a habit to me—a part of my physical nature: I have learned to acquiesce in it, and to mould my habits of life according to the conditions which it imposes; and have hence been unwilling to give footing for hopes and expectations, which I feel in my heart can never be realized. . . .

The disinclination which one feels to leave his warm bed on a frosty morning, is nothing to that which I experienced against any exercise of the organs of speech. The force of this tendency to dumbness was so great, that for many years I habitually expressed myself to others in writing even when not more than a few words were necessary; and where this mode of intercourse could not be used, I avoided occasion of speech, or heaved up a few monosyllables, or expressed my wish by slight motion or gesture;—*signs*, as a means of intercourse, I always abominated; and no one could annoy me more than by adopting this mode of communication. In fact, I came to be generally considered as both deaf and dumb, excepting by the few who were acquainted with my real condition; and hence many tolerated my mode of expression by writing, who would have urged upon me the exercise of my vocal organs. I rejoiced in the protection which that impression afforded; for nothing distressed me more than to be asked to speak: and from disuse having been superadded to the preexisting causes, there seemed a strong probability of my eventually justifying the impression concerning my dumbness which was generally entertained. I now speak with considerable ease and freedom, and, in personal intercourse, never resort to any other than the oral mode of communication. . . .

• DISQUALIFICATIONS •

It will require no great weight of argument or force of illustration to demonstrate that one who is deaf labours under a highly disqualified condition. In much of that in which lieth the great strength of man, he is impotent; for the great race of life he is maimed; and his daily walk is beset with petty humiliations, which bear down his spirit by the consciousness, which he is never allowed to forget, that he is, in one most essential respect,

"Inferior to the vilest now become."

If a man without the advantages of any but self-acquired education, without the smiles of fortune, and without those well-doing connections from whom alone can be expected services which strangers will not render in helping him over the rough places of this career: if, in the face of want, trouble, and moral isolation, such a man struggles forth into the light from the outer darkness by which he was surrounded, and takes a position of honour and usefulness, we count that he has done a great thing; and we deny not that he who has among a thousand competitors distanced many possessed of all the advantages which he has lacked, must have done so by the exercise of great energies, unbounded hope, and unusual force of character.

If this be the case with one who, whatever be his outward circumstances, has at least been in full possession of all the faculties which minister to success in life—what hope is there for one who sits in utter DEAFNESS; which *by itself*, will be readily admitted to be by far a greater privation and disqualification than any which mere circumstances can bring? What hope is there for *him*, even though he be surrounded by the external helps which the other wants? And what if these two classes of disqualification, the first tremendously difficult, and the other all but insuperable—what if BOTH are the lot of the same man? Is there any hope for him? "No hope for this world:" would be the answer of a thousand voices; yet, thank God, this answer would be wrong. I, perhaps, have as much right as any man that lives, to bear

214

witness that there is no one so low but that he may rise; no condition so cast down as to be really hopeless; and no privation which need of itself shut out any man from the paths of honourable exertion, or from the hope of usefulness in life. I have sometimes thought that it was possibly my mission to affirm and establish these great truths: and if my experience tends in any way to this result, I shall not have lived in vain. . . .

When my health was restored, I was no longer required to resume my former labours, and it is now clear to me, that I was considered to have been rendered useless by my affliction. I had thus much leisure thrown upon my hands. . . . Very cheerless was the lot that seemed then to lie before me. Had I not already become an incumbrance which only love could bear, and which even love would not be able to bear always? Did it not appear as if at the feast of life no place was left for me? And did it not seem even more than could be expected that, by some humble employment, I might be just able to relieve others from the burden of my support?

If the reader spares one moment to take a glance over the occupations by which men live and thrive, he will be surprised to find how few there are, for which the condition to which I was reduced would not operate as a serious disqualification. To all trades, consisting of buying and selling, hearing is most essential; to all professions it is still more necessary; and there are not many kinds of handicraft in which it could be easily dispensed with. Still, there are some kinds in which even one who is deaf might contrive to get on, through the occasional help and ever-ready sympathy which I am happy to believe that handicraft-workmen are apt to show—at any expense of time or labour—towards an afflicted brother. But even handicraft-labour seemed closed against one who was deaf. The branches are few to which deafness would not be an insurmountable bar, and in these few a premium would be necessary. And, even with a premium, who would readily encumber himself with a deaf apprentice, when he might have a choice of those in full possession of all their senses? Taking all these matters into account, it seems that the utmost usefulness to which one in this position could feasibly aspire, would be that of redeeming himself from entire uselessness by doing *something* towards his own maintenance; and that this alone would be so difficult as, under all the circumstances, to become a great and meritorious achievement. . . .

For many years I had no views towards literature beyond the instruction and solace of my own mind; and under these views, and in the absence of other mental stimulants, the pursuit of it eventually became a passion which devoured all others. I take no merit for the industry and application with which I pursued this object—none for the ingenious contrivances by which I sought to shorten the hours of needful rest, that I might have the more time for making myself acquainted with the minds of other men. The reward was great and immediate. . . . An undefinable craving was often felt for sympathy and appreciation in pursuits so dear to me; but to want this was one of the disqualifications of my condition—quite as much so as my deafness itself; and in the same degree in which I submitted to my deafness, as a dispensation of Providence towards me, did I submit to this as its necessary consequence. It was, however, one of the peculiarities of my condition, that I was then, as I ever have been, too much *shut up*. With the same dispositions and habits, without being deaf, it would have been easy to have found companions who would have understood me, and sympathised with my love for books and study— my progress in which might also have been much advanced by such intercommunication. As it was, the shyness and reserve which the deaf usually exhibit, gave increased effect to the physical disqualification; and precluded me from seeking, and kept me from incidentally finding, beyond the narrow sphere in which I moved, the sympathies which were not found in it. As time passed, my mind became filled with ideas and sentiments, and with various knowledges of things new and old, all of which were as the things of another told to those among whom my lot was cast. The conviction of this completed my isolation; and eventually all my human interests were concentrated in these points,— to get books, and, as they were mostly borrowed, to preserve the most valuable points in their contents, either by extracts, or by a distinct intention to impress them on the memory. When I went forth, I counted the hours till I might return to the only pursuits in which I could take interest; and when free to return, how swiftly I flew to immure myself in that little sanctuary, which I had been permitted to appropriate, in one of those rare nooks only afforded by such old Elizabethan houses as that in which my relatives then abode. . . .

It at first seemed so great an idea that I should cease to be utterly helpless, that it took some time before I could contemplate this prospect in any other relations than those which bore upon my own condition. As nearly as the matter can be now traced, the progress of my ideas appears to have been this:—Firstly, that I was not altogether so helpless as I had seemed. Secondly, that notwithstanding my afflicted state, I might realize much comfort in the condition of life in which I had been placed. Thirdly, that I might even raise myself out of that condition into one of less privation. Fourthly, that it was not impossible for me to place my own among honourable names, by proving that no privation formed an insuperable bar to useful labour and self-advancement. Lastly, I became dissatisfied with this conclusion; and took up the view that the objects which I had by this time proposed to myself would be unattained, unless the degree of usefulness which I might be enabled to realize, were not merely *comparative* with reference to the circumstances by which I was surrounded, but *positive*, and without any such reference. To do what no one under the same combination of afflictive circumstances ever did, soon then ceased to be the limit of my ambition: and I doubted that I should have any just right to come before the world at all, unless I could hope to accomplish something which might, on the sole ground of its own merits, be received with favour. . . . My greatest and most successful labour was placed before the public without any name; and although the author's name has been attached to later works, it has not been accompanied by any information concerning the circumstances which have now been described. As therefore the public has had no materials on which to form a sympathizing, and therefore partial, estimate of my services, and has yet received them with signal favour, I may venture to regard the object which I had proposed to myself as in some sort achieved. . . .

The nature of my affliction unfitted me for any other sphere of usefulness than that of literature. This conviction was the more strongly pressed upon me by every attempt which was made to cultivate other fields of useful occupation. I am, however, somewhat in fear lest it should seem that I consider deafness a *qualification* for literature. This is very far indeed from the impression I wish to convey, which is, that to me, deafness was *less a disqualification* for literature than for any other pursuit to which I could turn: but even in the pursuits of literature, deafness is a greater hindrance and disqualification than those unacquainted with such pursuits would easily imagine.

If literature were nothing but closet-work, it might be all well. But the pursuit is not confined to this. It involves, or should involve, intimacy with men of similar pursuits, and it involves business often of a delicate and perplexing nature. But the moment the deaf student rises from his desk, and goes forth into the business of the world, in which so many other men find their element, his strength departs from him. The intense consciousness of this disqualification, makes him shy and reserved, indisposed to move personally beyond the walls of his library and the limits of his domestic circle. This, in many ways, affects unpleasantly his circumstances, and neutralizes many of the advantages which belong to the position he may have attained. He is too much disposed to maintain all intercourse, and to transact all business, by writing; and he is hence, in his best estate, bare of those personal friendships, in which other men find strength and solace, and by which their objects in life are much advanced. Nothing useful or encouraging occurs in the daily intercourse of life—no new ideas are started, and brightened by the collision of different minds—no hints are gathered,—no information obtained—and no openings for usefulness are heard of or indicated. When it is considered how much of what a man hears and says in his personal intercourse with others, especially in the intercourse of studious men, influences his own career and determines his course of action—the disadvantages of this utter self-dependence will be readily perceived, although their full extent can only be estimated by the sufferer. He stands too much alone: and although his literary intercourse may be copious and extensive, he lives in the feeling that there is no stay for him but in the care of Heaven, and in his own right hand. If he stumbles in his career, there is no one who has personal interest enough in him to take the trouble to help him up; and if difficulties at times beset his path, he must work his own way through them, unhelped and unencouraged. . . .

If the disqualifying influences of entire deafness operate to this extent against the formation of personal connections, it may easily be apprehended that these influences are still more detrimental in those matters of business, which even literature involves. The business in which a man of letters is interested, lies chiefly with that large, various, and influential body of commercial men, through whom his intercourse with the public is carried on. To one or two members of this body I owe much; and so far as my knowledge extends I believe it to contain a larger proportion of considerate and liberal-minded men than could be easily found in any other class of the community. Still, they are men of business; and every point which goes to form *that* character, is so much a point of repulsion to the deaf; and every point which goes to make up the personal position of a deaf man, is so much a point of repulsion to them, that feelings of cordiality, the foundation of which lies chiefly in personal intercourse, can seldom exist between them. Men of business have also a feeling that affairs can be transacted much better by personal interviews than in writing; and I have no doubt that this is the fact. But even a personal interview with one who is deaf involves the necessity of writing, or of some equally slow process of intercommunication; and this is apt to become wearisome, and to involve a loss of time, which men of business habits do not relish. In fact, there is no concealing it, that the deaf man is likely to be regarded as a bore. Sensitively alive to this danger, he will perhaps depart, leaving his business unfinished; or if he concludes it best to sit it out at all hazards, he cannot but feel that he has engrossed too much of time considered precious, and that his visit has been received as a penal infliction. He will, however, be more likely, under the painful consciousness of this difficulty, to manage as much as possible of his intercourse by letter. This will be to him a substitute for an interview, a written talk, and it will therefore be long. But he learns that men of business have a dread of long letters, and will not sufficiently consider that the ten minutes' reading which is offered to them, is in reality offered as a substitute for the much larger demand upon their time which a personal interview would require. It is likely, that under the influence of this consideration he will write briefly; and will then feel that the statement he has offered has almost the same relation to an interview between unafflicted men, as the summary of a chapter in a book has to the chapter itself. If his business reaches a satisfactory conclusion under these circumstances, well: but if not, he will be apt to consider the failure as owing to that affliction, which so greatly limits his personal influence, by excluding him from the advantages of those easy and incidental conversations in which so much of the real business of the world is transacted. . . .

• COMMUNICATIONS •

There is perhaps no fact which more strongly illustrates the unprofitable nature and limited extent of my early intercourse with the external world than this—that I was six years deaf before I knew that there existed any mode of communication with the fingers. A gentleman then happening to accost me on the fingers, and finding that I was unacquainted with this mode of intercourse, taught it to me on the spot. This manual talk was much less known at that time than it has since become; and I did not for a good while find much use in it. Very few of the persons whom

I for some years knew, employed it in expressing themselves to me: and I never used it myself, having always, as
the reader has been informed, *written* whatever I had to
say, till the use of the vocal organs was recovered: the case
is much altered in this respect now. All my own household,
and all those with whom I am in habits of personal intercourse, make use of their fingers. Indeed, even my little
ones, in their successive infancies, have early taken to *imitating* this mode of communication. They begin while yet
in arms, falling to finger-talking whenever they see me—
from mere imitation: and at a somewhat later stage, when
they have begun to talk, it is truly affecting to see that,
after having tried to make me understand their wishes in
the ordinary way, they will stand up into my face with
infinite seriousness, and resting in the full confidence that
I have understood them, or ought to have done so. But if
they find that I have not apprehended them, the operation
is with equal gravity repeated, until I either guess what is
the matter, or direct their attention to some other object.
I should add, that if the little creatures are so placed as to
be unable to engage my attention by touching me, they
call to me, and on finding that also unavailing, blow to me,
or, if that also fails, stamp upon the floor; and when they
have by one or other of these methods attracted my eyes,
begin their pretty talk upon the fingers. One of the least
patient of them, used to stamp and cry herself into a vast
rage, in the vain effort to engage my attention. It is very
singular that these practices have been taken up by all of
them in succession, like natural instincts, without having
learned them from one another.

It may be somewhat out of place, but now that I touch
upon this matter, there is a constraint upon me to indicate
the fact that—I never heard the voices of any of my children. The reader of course knows this; but the fact, as stated

in plain words, is almost shocking. Is there anything on earth so engaging to a parent, as to catch the first lispings of his infant's tongue? or so interesting, as to listen to its dear prattle, and trace its gradual mastery of speech? If there be any one thing, arising out of my condition, which more than another fills my heart with grief, it is THIS: it is to *see* their blessed lips in motion, and to *hear* them not; and to witness others moved to smiles and kisses by the sweet peculiarities of infantile speech which are incommunicable to me, and which pass by me like the idle wind.

As I have said, the finger-talk has become much more common now; especially among ladies, who, as I have been told, find it useful at school, as an inaudible means of communication, and for that purpose teach it to one another. Man, proud man, not needing it for this purpose, seldom knows it at all in youth; and in after life seems to regard it as too small an attainment to be worthy of his attention. Or, perhaps he over estimates the difficulty of an acquirement, which any one may make in a quarter of an hour, and prefers the use of the instruments with which he is familiar—the pen or pencil—to the adoption of a new one, in the use of which, he must at the first incur the humiliation of making a few blunders, and of being somewhat unready. Whatever be the cause, the result is, that of twenty educated men perhaps not more than one will be found possessed of this accomplishment, whereas, perhaps, not more than eight or ten in twenty educated ladies are without it.

For long communications, writing is doubtless best; but for incidental purposes, which are far more numerous, the finger-talk is better. The advantages are these:—that the fingers are, so to speak, always at hand, and can be used with almost as much spontaneity as the tongue; whereas for writing, various implements are required—the production and preparation of which distress the deaf man with a painful consciousness of the difficulty of communicating with him, and of the trouble he is giving. Another thing is, that the finger language can be used with as much freedom in walking or riding as under any other circumstances, which with writing is far from being the case. How vividly do I remember the pleasant and informing intercourse which has in this way, at different times, been carried on with friends, throughout the live-long day, as we rode, side by side, for months together, over the plains of Asia. How greatly did not our caravan companions—the natives of the country,—marvel at it, as at one of the mysteries which might have been hidden under the seal of Solomon. And how pleasant was it to behold the reverence and admiration of THE USEFUL irradiate their swart countenances, when the simple principle of the art was explained to them, and it was shown to be as available for their own languages— Arabian, Persian, Turkish,—as for any other.

It is another recommendation of the manual alphabet, that the use of it is a less conspicuous act than that of writing; in company it excludes, or seems to exclude, the deaf man less from the circle of coversation than writing would; and in the streets, it attracts less attention than stopping to write. It also, upon emergencies, supplies a mode of communication in the dark: for as the letters are formed by the play of the right-hand fingers upon the left, it is manifest that a person who wishes to communicate in darkness, has only to work with the fingers of his right hand upon the left hand of his friend to convey the information he requires. The process is indeed tedious and sometimes uncertain; but it suffices for such concise intimations as in the dark can be alone necessary. I must confess, that I have on all occasions eschewed darkness with too much earnestness, to have found much use in this property of finger-talk: but it has nevertheless been sometimes useful, especially in travelling by night. The really practised finger-talkers, prefer that mode of communication with the deaf before writing; as they can form the words faster than the most rapid writer, with less effort, and certainly with less waste of materials.

The inconveniences in the use of the fingers are more obvious to the talkee than to the talker. The perfection of a dactylogist is to form the characters with rapidity and distinctness. In beginners, the desire to be distinct often produces a tedious slowness; and in proficients, the rapidity of action which habit occasions often produces indistinctness. To acquire rapidity, and yet retain distinctness, is what few can manage; but these are the few to whom the deaf man delights to attend. . . .

The finger-talker has little notion of the difficulties which occur in following his operations. The distress which I have myself experienced frequently, in the consciousness of having missed a word or two, has often been very great. The connection of the sentence is broken, and its exact purport lost, and the question is whether to put your friend to the trouble of repeating his communication (a very different thing from asking the repetition of a verbal statement), or to allow it to be supposed that you have understood, when the communication does not seem to have been of importance, or such as requires a direct answer. . .

Of *signs*, as a medium of intercourse, I have but limited acquaintance, and of the artificial system, taught at the asylums, none. In my own intercourse signs have not been needed, save with the uninstructed deaf and dumb, and with persons unable either to write or to use the finger-language. With both these classes my intercourse has been small, because I could gain or impart nothing useful by it, and because I have the strongest aversion to modes of intercourse which attract the attention and curiosity of others.

As soon, therefore, as a person has attempted to communicate with me by signs, I have ceased to have any other object than to make my escape. I have sometimes been accosted by persons after the system of the asylums; and, without being able to recognize many of the signs, I have been shocked at the too marked movements which they involved. This is stated simply with reference to my own impressions; for the very circumstances which rendered them unprofitable and annoying to me, might make them the more fitting medium of intercourse for the born deaf and dumb, or those who have occasion to communicate with them. . . .

Signs may be termed *natural*; but the naturally deaf do not stop here with this language of pantomime. When they are fortunate enough to meet with an attentive companion or two, especially where two or more deaf persons happen to be brought up together, it is astonishing what approaches they will make towards the construction of an artificial language. I mean that by an arbitrary sign, fixed by common consent or accidentally hit upon, they will designate a person or thing by that sign; which, from henceforth, is used by them as a proper name. It is remarkable that although in the first instance of inventing and applying these sign-names (if I may call them so), they are generally guided by some prominent, but, perhaps, by no means permanently distinguishing mark, such as (in the case of a person) a particular article of dress being worn, the first time of becoming acquainted; an accidental wound, though it leave no scar; or peculiarity of manner, &c. . . .

It so happened, that, before my own deafness, I had a boyish acquaintance with a born deaf-mute, running wild about the streets, and entirely uninstructed. The untameable violence of his character was, however, so opposed to the quietness of my own temper, that I rather shunned and dreaded him, than courted his friendship. For some years I lost sight of him; but eventually, after I had become deaf, we were again brought into closer contact then ever, and I had ample opportunities of studying his characteristics, and of comparing my own condition with his. I then found that he was understood to have become able to read and write; and as he was far from unintelligent, but, on the contrary, one of the sharpest lads I ever knew, I supposed that it would be in my power to communicate with him in writing; but I found that he could be induced to write nothing beyond his own name, and the words of any copy from which he had been taught to write; and when I placed before him a written question or communication, it was lamentable to see how hopelessly he groped over it, without the most dim perception of the meaning, though he was acquainted with the letters of which the sentence was composed. But when another undertook to express the same thing to him by signs, it was wonderful to see how his blank and somewhat fallen countenance lighted up, and how readily he apprehended the purport of the communication thus made to him. The signs were of his own devising, and had mostly been learned from him by the lads with whom he associated. I observed, however, that if a lad had something to express for which no existing sign was sufficient, this lad would invent a new one for the occasion, or would persevere in trying several, till he hit upon one which the deaf-mute could understand. The sign thus invented, was usually adopted by the latter into his system; and if, when used by him, it was not easily understood, he could refer to the inventor, whose explanation would soon render it current. I was myself eventually obliged to adopt this mode of intercourse with him, and to acquaint myself with his system of signs. It was, in some respects, wonderfully ingenious, in others strikingly significant, and in some grossly simple, from the absence in his mind of any of that acquired delicacy, which teaches that there are facts which will not admit of the most direct and significant description. Upon the whole, it exhibited a vast amount of curious contrivances and resources, for getting over the difficulties which must necessarily occur in making manual signs the representatives of facts or ideas.

That part which stood for proper names seemed to me very interesting, and engaged much of my attention. They proceeded exactly upon the system so well described by Dr. Watson. The lad's sign for my name was to put his fingers to his ears; and for his own to put his forefingers to his ears and his thumbs towards his mouth, at the same time. There were many lame persons within the range of his knowledge; and the different kinds of lameness were discriminated with highly mimetic accuracy, to designate the different persons. There was one man who was both lame and in the habit of occasionally blowing, in a somewhat marked manner. The blowing furnished a mark for this person; but if this were not sufficient, the blowing and lameness were *both* indicated in such a manner that no one acquainted with the original could be longer under any doubt. The lameness alone would not have done as a sign, since another exhibited a similar lameness. Another person was designated by his manner of brushing up his hair; others, by habits of smoking or taking snuff, by the shape of the nose, by peculiarities of temper or manner, and even by trades, professions, and habits of place. I observed that to avoid a perplexing multiplicity of such signs, females and young people were, for the most part, designated by reference to their relationship to the head of the family, and translated into words would stand thus,—the wife of Longnose; the first, second, or third son, or daughter, of Longnose, etc.

With respect to names of *places*, I discovered nothing of the kind in his range of signs. He had a movement of the hand for indicating distances, and the more numerous and prolonged were these movements the more distant was the place he wished to indicate; and as his local knowledge was limited to a few miles, his indications were generally understood.

The knowledge of signs which I picked up in this way, proved of some use to me when in foreign parts and especially when among people who, from the habit of seeing persons of neighbouring nations whose language they only partially or not at all understood, were much in the habit of using signs as a substitute for or as an assistant to oral language. Thus my occasional resort to signs, for incidental communication in streets, bazaars, villages, and caravanserais, caused me to seem to them rather as a foreigner ignorant of their language, than as deaf; and the resort to signs had no strangeness to them or attracted that notice from others which it never fails to do in this country. From this ready apprehension of signs, I found more facilities of communication than might have been expected—more than perhaps would be open to one possessed of hearing but only partially acquainted with the language: for such a person would be more disposed to blunder along with his attempts at speech, than to resort to the universal language of signs. These also are the only circumstances in which I ever used or attended to signs without reluctance.

The signs used by the Orientals to express universal acts and objects, I found not to be materially different from those which my former deaf-mute companion had employed; but those which were founded upon local or national customs and Moslem observances, I found much difficulty in comprehending, till these customs and observances had become familiar to me by residence in the East.

With all this help from signs, however, travel is to a deaf man not without its dangers and difficulties. I cannot better show this than by exhibiting the incidents of one day, which all bear more or less upon this subject.

I was staying at the village of Orta Khoi on the Bosphorus, about six miles above Constantinople, of which it is one of the suburbs, and was in the frequent habit of going down to the city and returning by water. One morning on which I had determined to go, it threatened to rain; but I took my umbrella and departed. On arriving at the beach it appeared that all the boats were gone, and there was no alternative but to abandon my intention, or to proceed on foot along a road which manifestly led in the right direction, at the back of the buildings and yards which line the Bosphorus. I had not proceeded far before it began to rain, and I put up my umbrella and trudged on, followed, at some distance behind, by an old Turk in the same predicament with myself: for it should be observed, that, at and about Constantinople, the people are so much in the habit of relying upon water conveyance, that there is less use of horses than in any Eastern town with which I am acquainted. Nothing occurred till I arrived at the back of the handsome country palace of Dolma Baktche, the front of which had often engaged my attention in passing up and down by water. Here the sentinel at the gate motioned to me in a very peculiar manner, which I could not comprehend. He had probably called previously, and in vain. Finding that I heeded him not, he was hastening towards me in a very violent manner, with his fixed bayonet pointed direct at my body, when the good-natured Turk behind me, who had by this time come up, assailed me very unceremoniously from behind, by pulling down my umbrella. After some words to the sentinel, I was suffered to pass on under his protection, till we had passed the precincts of the imperial residence, where he put up his own umbrella, and motioned me to do the same. By this act, and by the signs which he had used in explanation of this strange affair, I clearly understood that it was all on account of the umbrella. This article, so useful and common in rainy climates, is an ensign of royalty in the East; and although the use of it for common purposes has crept in at Constantinople, the sovereign is supposed to be ignorant of the fact, and it may not on any account be displayed in this presence, or in passing any of the royal residences.

That day I was detained in Pera longer than I expected; and darkness had set in by the time the wherry in which I returned reached Orta Khoi. After I had paid the fare, and was walking up the beach, the boatmen followed and endeavoured to impress something upon me, with much emphasis of manner, but without disrespect. My impression was that they wanted to exact more than their fare; and as I knew that I had given the right sum, I, with John Bullish hatred at imposition, buckled up my mind against giving one para more. Presently the contest between us brought over some Nizam soldiers from the guard-house, who took the same side with the boatmen; for when I attempted to make my way on, they refused to allow me to proceed. Here I was in a regular dilemma, and was beginning to suspect that there was something more than the fare in question; when a Turk, of apparently high authority, came up, and after a few words had been exchanged between him and the soldiers, I was suffered to proceed.

As I went on, up the principal street of the village, I was greatly startled to perceive a heavy earthen vessel, which had fallen with great force from above, dashed in pieces on the pavement at my feet. Presently, such vessels descended, thick as hail, as I passed along, and were broken to sherds on every side of me. It is a marvel how I escaped having my brains dashed out; but I got off with only a smart blow between the shoulders. A rain of cats and dogs, is a thing of which we have some knowledge; but a rain of potter's vessels was very much beyond the limits of European experience. On reaching the hospitable roof which was then my shelter, I learned that this was the night which the Armenians, by whom the place was chiefly inhabited, devoted to the expurgation of their houses from evil spirits, which act they accompanied or testified by throwing earthen vessels out of their windows, with certain cries which served as warnings to the passengers: but that the streets were notwithstanding still so dangerous that scarcely any one ventured out while the operation was in progress. From not hearing these cries, my danger was of course two-fold, and my escape seemed something more remarkable: and I must confess that I was of the same opinion when the next morning disclosed the vast quantities of broken pottery with which the streets were strewed.

It seems probable that the adventure on the beach had originated in the kind wish of the boatmen and soldiers to prevent me from exposing myself to this danger. But there was also a regulation preventing any one from being in the streets at night without a lantern: and the intention may possibly have been to enforce this observance, especially as a lantern would this night have been a safeguard to me, by apprising the pot-breakers of my presence in the street.

The adventures of this one day will serve for a specimen of numberless incidents, showing the sort of difficulties which a deaf man has to contend with in distant travel. The instances evince the insufficiency of mere signs as a means of communication, unless in some matter in which there is a prepared understanding, as in buying or selling. This mode of intercourse necessarily fails, when, as in the cases cited, it is made the exponent of customs unknown to one of the parties in that intercourse. Signs must in all cases be an imperfect vehicle for the communication of abstract ideas; and we see the proof of this in the distressing dearth of matter in the letters and other writings of the deaf-mutes, who have learned the use of written language through the medium of signs. In ideas they are not necessarily deficient, unless so far as a deficiency arises from the want of real education and substantial reading. But they want the power of expression; and hence are necessitated to confine themselves to a few simple matters which they know they can express, like a foreigner in speaking a language which he has but imperfectly acquired. This painful narrowness of range is much overlooked by cursory observers, in their surprise and admiration at finding the deaf and dumb in possession of *any* means of communication with others. There are no doubt exceptions, as in the cases of Fontenay, Massieu, Clerc, and a few more, who attained a great command of written language. But these were the exceptions of men of genius, of whom it would be in vain to expect to see more than two or three in a hundred years. And by "genius," in this application, is understood that ardour for a given object—say knowledge—with that force of character in the pursuit of it, which enable men to rise over difficulties that seem insurmountable. Through such ardour and force of character, these men made themselves "extraordinary," by bringing their attainments nearly up to the mark of middle class education among those who have hearing and speech. The same degree of energy and force of character necessary to bring them to this point, would have made them not only "extraordinary" but "great"—would have procured for them immortal names, if they could have started from the level of average attainments among men. The cause of deaf and dumb education is made to rest too much upon the examples of such men. But their cases are exceptional, and as infrequent as cases of first-rate genius in the world at large: and to be convinced of this, we need only to note the woeful difference between their compositions, and the letters of the most proficient pupils of the Asylums, as published in the Reports. These incoherent compositions, which seem to be chiefly made up of recollections of Scripture and reading books, give a most deplorable idea of the condition of which *this* is almost the ultimate attainment; and yet, the lower idea we form of that condition, the greater will be our satisfaction at even the exceeding limited resources which this sort of education opens to them. Much more than has been done for them might perhaps be effected, if this education had been suited more to their real condition, than directed to the production of effects calculated to strike public attention.

Signs are undoubtedly the proper language of the deaf and dumb; and it is equally the mode of communication among those who, by ignorance of each other's language, are virtually dumb to each other. I have stated that in my own experience abroad, signs were best understood and most used in those places where the population was much mixed, or which were much the resort of strangers. This observation is corroborated by a curious fact recorded in 'Observations on the Language of Signs,' by Samuel Akerly, M.D., read before the New York Lyceum of Natural History, in 1823. . . .

"Philosophers have discussed the subject of a universal language, but have failed to invent one; while the savages of America have adopted the only one which can possibly become universal. The language of signs is so true to nature, that the deaf and dumb from different parts of the globe will immediately on meeting understand each other. Their language, however, in an uncultivated state, is limited to the expression of their immediate wants, and of the few ideas which they have acquired by their silent intercourse with their fellow-beings. As this manner of expressing their thoughts has arisen from necessity, it is surprising how the Indians have adopted a similar language when the intercourse between nations of different tongues is usually carried on by interpreters of spoken language.

"If we examine the signs employed by the Indians, it will be found that some are peculiar, and arise from their savage customs, and are not so universal as sign language in general; but others are natural and universally applicable, and are the same as those employed in the Schools for the Deaf and Dumb, after the method of the celebrated Abbé Sicard."

It was very probably some indistinct rumours concerning this people, which led the Abbé Sicard to conceive the possible existence of a nation of deaf-mutes. The following passage from one of his books is cited in Dr. Orpen's 'Anecdotes and Annals:' —"May there not exist in some corner of the world an entire people of deaf-mutes? Well, suppose these individuals were so degraded, do you think that they would remain without communication and without intelligence? They would have, without any manner of doubt, a language of signs, and possibly more rich than our own; it would be, certainly unequivocal, always the faithful portrait of the affections of the soul; and then, what should hinder them from being civilized? Why should they not have laws, a government, a police, very probably less involved in obscurity than our own?"

This excellent man was very clearly of opinion, which he constantly avowed, that signs were the proper language of the deaf-mutes. And it would appear, that if their own happiness and comfort only were considered, much of the time and labour which is wasted in other and to them foreign objects, might be advantageously employed in completing and enriching the language of artificial signs. Their own estimation of signs is evinced by the hilarity and *abandon* with which they communicate with one another by them, as compared with the restraint and hesitation which they manifest in the use of written, or still more, in which they *imitate* vocal language. . . . In the Sixth Report of the American Asylum at Hartford, Connecticut, the following occurs as the answer of a deaf-mute to the question—"Which do you consider preferable—the language of speech or of signs?" Answer—"I consider to prefer the language of signs best of it, because the language of signs is capable of to give me elucidation and understanding well. I am fond of talking with the deaf and dumb persons by signs, quickly, about the subjects, without having the troubles of voice: therefore the language of signs is more still and calm than the language of speech, which is full of falsehood and troubles."

The more attentively this answer is considered, the more suggestive it will appear: and the last phrase, in particular, evinces that the difficulty and sense of labour in expressing an idea, which those who have hearing connect with the use of manual signs, are referred by the deaf-mutes to the use of oral language—so far as it is known to them in their own experience. . . .

This clearly expresses the impression that signs are the proper language of the deaf and dumb, and there is a manifest disposition to prefer it to writing, with a vague impression of its being inferior only to speech as used by those who have hearing, and preferable to speech as used by the deaf and dumb.

The result of the testimony as furnished, by the educated deaf-mutes *themselves*, is—that oral speech is of little if any use to them, and not worth the labour which the acquisition has cost; that reading and writing, although difficult, are useful and important as a means of acquiring knowledge; but that signs are the proper instrument of their *intercourse*, and the only one they can use with pleasure. It may also be collected that the chief attraction of writing is, that it may enable them to communicate with persons at a distance. They accordingly betake themselves to this employment of their acquisition with eagerness; but they appear soon to break down under the paucity of ideas and facts, which is the most afflictive circumstance of their condition; and if religiously educated, they fill their paper with matter taken from the Scriptures. To the friends of those unfortunates, it must be most interesting to peruse their simple effusions; but to the public, most of the letters which have been offered as signs of advancement in the first class scholars, are melancholy displays of deficiency and feebleness.

My own estimate is in accordance with that which has been stated, as the one which the deaf-mutes themselves form of signs and of writing, and oral language. Signs will be their means of intercourse among themselves; writing (including of course reading and the fingers) their instrument for acquiring knowledge, and for their intercourse with those beyond their own class; but speech, learned with so much difficulty, and used with so much effort and reluctance, can never be of much, if any, use to them. Its only value would be to qualify them for intercourse with those who can hear and speak; but it does nothing of the kind: for that deafness alone is a sufficient bar against such intercourse, is shown by my own experience, as related in this work. It proves this at least: but, in other respects, it must be remembered that in my case speech was recovered merely, and not created. And if in that case there was so much reluctance to speak and difficulty in speaking, how much more in the case of the born deaf-mutes. And joining my own experience to that of others, I am thoroughly convinced that writing and signs are abundantly sufficient for all the intercourse to which a deaf-mute is equal. . . .

But it is an idle dream to hope to restore such persons entirely to society. Deafness—the same cause which has cut me off from society, from the enjoyment of which I am by nothing else disqualified—would alone, even though they spoke with the tongue of angels, suffice to exclude them from it. My own present facility of speech stands me in little stead, beyond the walls of my own house. I do not find real occasion for it ten times in a year. . . .

• SOCIETY •

If one who is deaf has any respect for himself, and for his own feelings, as well as for the real comfort of others, he will not be solicitous to bring himself into that unequal condition which his presence, say at a dinner party, imposes; nor is it clear that one whose condition is socially so unequal to that of others, has any right to introduce into such company the anomaly which his inability to take part in the flow and windings the conversation involves. Those around him will be uneasy if they neglect him; and will yet feel that in attending to him they are making a sacrifice of some part of their own enjoyment in "the flow of soul" around. Under such circumstances, it is surely a social duty in the deaf to avoid company, in the assurance that by going into it, or gathering it around him, he is only a stumbling-block to the pleasure of others, and is only laying up for himself a store of mortification and of regret for those terrible disqualifications which, in the solitude of his chamber, or in the presence of his trained domestic circle, he may half forget.

Still there are occasions in which even one who is deaf cannot without apparent affectation or show of neglect, avoid "putting in his appearance" on such occasions: and the feeling of what would under ordinary circumstances be considered due to his social position, will be stronger than the perception of his unfitness for this portion of its obligations. This, with the apprehension that others will not give enough thought to the matter to allow for any marked evasion, or to appreciate his reasons for it, will sometimes tempt him to the daring act of quitting the sober light of his shaded reading lamp for the full blaze of wax candles. If the party be his own, he will get on better, although his responsibilities are greater, than when it is another's; for, in the former case, all of the persons composing it will be known to him, in the latter only a few. If the company which he joins is brought together by and at the house of a friend, the ease of the deaf guest will be proportioned to the number of personal acquaintances, or at least of known faces, which he is able to recognize. A glance at the company will satisfy him of his position in this respect, and assure him of the ground on which he stands. I have usually on such occasions endeavoured to seat myself near the person whom, of all my acquaintance present, I know to be the most expert dactylogist, and able in a quiet way to attend to me without appearing to neglect the company. When this choice of a victim for the evening has been managed with reasonable skill and judgment, one great part of the difficulty and embarrassment of an anomalous position is over. The person thus selected has, by the fact of that selection, a somewhat onerous task imposed upon him: but he invariably submits quietly to his fate; and if at first he does wince a little, he soon regains his good humour, and discharges his task with feeling and spirit, and gets animated by a desire to impart to me some share of the enjoyment which is circulating through the room.

The right of enlistment for this special service is never disputed, nor is there any appeal from it. It is one of the few offices remaining in this country, which the person to whom it is offered is not at liberty to decline. The right of making it, is supported by a tacit understanding on all sides, that it is the best thing that can be done for the general benefit, and for my own in particular. My individual benefit is clear: and, for the company, it is convenient to be able to feel that there is some one to attend to me, when they are disposed to abandon themselves to the general current of conversation; and one through whom such of them as may not happen to know the finger alphabet, may be able to exchange some words with me. The unfortunate recruit himself is the only one who has any reason to complain. And he does not complain: for there must have been a singular failure of discrimination if the selection has fallen on one in whose good humour and willingness for the service reliance may not be placed.

The duty which practically devolves upon this obliging person is, to keep his client apprised of the general current of the conversation, and to exhibit in some detail, the salient points which from time to time produce such animation in the company as to awaken his curiosity and interest. . . .

This, however, so far as I am concerned, depended on the kindly co-operation of one man, and although that man was, in the time of my greatest need, taken from me, it is well to have the opportunity of noting in one's tablets

—"That there is such a feeling."

This person was the one with whom—far beyond all others—I most enjoyed private intercourse, from a number of common sympathies in literature, from his excellent talents and strong powers of observation, from his being able to impart much of the kind of information, floating about in society, to which I had no other means of access; from the striking points of view in which his lively fancy invested, and the singular phosphoric light which is left for a moment upon, every subject on which it rested. And then, which was his crowning gift—he had, beyond all the persons I ever knew, the talent of giving to his finger-talk much of the distinctness, the emphasis, the intonation, the collo- quial ease of oral language: and all these peculiar endow- ments, so admirably suited to my wants that I might have wandered over the globe without finding another like him, were animated and *applied* by a distinct and vivid appre- ciation of my condition, and by a sort of friendly gratification in the knowledge of the enjoyment which he knew that he was capable of imparting to me. This prevented the exer- tions necessary to any prolonged intercourse with me, from being in any way burdensome to him; and indeed, I have reason to think that, notwithstanding the inequality of all intercourse between the hearing and the deaf, the enjoy- ment was, in some degree, reciprocal; although to him there was open intercourse necessarily much more plea- surable than any which a solitary deaf man could offer, while to me there was nothing on earth comparable to, or in rivalry with, the enjoyment which he was capable of af- fording.

I have specified this, that it may be the better understood what a relief and resource it was to me when this friend was present at such a party as I have just described. Every thing went right the moment he appeared. He at once threw an aegis over me, under which I not only found shelter from the social difficulties of my temporary position, but became able to receive much satisfaction from the com- pany, and perhaps to impart a little. He took, as by instinct, his place between me and the company, and gave new life to both. His voluble tongue became at the service of the party, and his equally voluble fingers at mine; and occasionally both could be going at once on different subjects. I am certainly persuaded that he heard separately with both ears; and I am in doubt that he did not see separately with both eyes. At all events, the facility with which he managed an under current of talk with me, while taking his full share in that of the company, was truly wonderful. He also *indicated* to me the general current and windings of the conversation, and *detailed*, with rare tact, the particular points which might suggest the whole, or which involved any strong or witty remark. This was a rare qualification for me. In general, when you see the company visibly amused or interested, and ask to know the cause, the chances are that the person to whom you apply thinks it *not worth* repeating on his fingers; and so even at the end of a long sitting, which appears to have been animated, you apply to one of your own domestic circle for a report of the subjects which have engaged attention, you will probably find that nothing has made a sufficiently distinct impression to seem worth recording. This is one great annoyance in the estate of the deaf. He is confined to the solid bones, the dry bread, the hard wood, the substantial fibre of life; and gets but little of the grace, the unction, the gilding and the flowers, which are to be found precisely in those small things which are "not worth" reporting on the fingers.

The friend of whom I have spoken, understood this; and he was not backward to impart to me the casual intimation and light remark, while still warm and volant from the speaker's mouth, and animated by the gleam of his countenance. In his esteem, nothing that was large enough to please, was too small for the fingers; and this feeling, on his part, was not the least of the things which, taken together, constituted the charm of his society to me.

In the attempt to take part in the current conversation without engrossing it entirely, one who is deaf will encounter some curious difficulties. It has been my own custom to inquire from time to time what turn the conversation has taken, and then, perhaps, the general drift, or some pointed observation which may suggest it, is reported to me. I am then prompted to make an observation on that subject, which I may, perhaps think striking or suggestive; but the difficulty is how to discharge it. The eyes are thrown round the circle again and again, to catch a moment when no one else is speaking. But nothing is harder to catch than this. After long watching for the happy moment in which a sentence may be thrust in, it may seem at last to be secured. Every tongue is at rest. Then I begin, when a start of divided attention, a look wandering from me to another, apprises me that the ball of conversation had again been struck up in another part of the circle in the brief interval of an eyeblink, and I find myself involved in the incivility and rudeness of having interrupted another, perhaps a lady, and have to drop, with confusion of face, the work I had taken up, or else to give it utterance under circumstances of apology and pressure, which magnifies into mortifying importance, and therefore renders abortive, what was designed only as an airy remark or jocular illustration.

If, however, it so happens that I do succeed in launching by observation without such utter wreck at the outset, I have often the humiliation of finding that it has become stale by keeping, and that it applies to a subject which the rapid current of oral talk has left a mile behind. In both cases, although the remark may have been perfectly impromptu, that is, may have occurred at the very moment the intimation was made to you, the time which has passed till the opportunity for giving it utterance occurs, will necessarily give one the appearance of having been all this while concocting what turns out to be no great matter after all. Sometimes, however, the very reverse of this happens: and the observation may prove to be very same which is being made, or has just been made, or is just about to be made, by another of the party. This singular coincidence is much more frequent than the uninitiated would imagine. It merely shows how two minds set upon the same track may reach the same point together. And even this is only in appearance; for while the other party utters what he has then first conceived, I necessarily utter what I had some time before conceived, and had waited an opporunity to deliver. The coincidence of utterance is still, however, singular, and is sometimes so much the same, even in form of words, as to call forth many merry exclamations of "You hear!" "You hear!" "You are found out!" etc. And, in truth at the first glance such a fact will convey this impression, although the second will show that no one possessed of his hearing would say the same thing that another was saying or had just said.

Under such circumstances as have been here described, a strange craving arises for that lesser talk which no person thinks it worth while to repeat to one who is deaf, and which indeed no such repetition can adequately convey. I sigh to hear the talk of children to each other; and have a strong desire to be in a condition to pick up the wisdom and the foolishness that cry in the streets. If I am walking with a friend, nothing surprises me more than his indifference to the street-talk which is passing in all directions. I speculate within myself upon the intimations of condition, and the insights of feelings and character, which might be gathered from the expressions which must smite the ear in the streets. . . . In doing this, deafness is felt to be a great

hindrance and discouragement; for a thousand distinguishing traits of individual character, must needs be lost to one
who is unable to catch up the forms and habits of expression,
which are as identifying and as characteristic as the personal
manner and the countenance. To illustrate this deficiency
and the sense of privation which it conveys, I may ask the
reader whether in the stories of Mr. Dickens, the numerous
characters are not identified and fixed in the mind more
by their manner of speech than, as characters, by the de-
scriptions of their conduct and personal appearance? It cannot be denied that their talk goes far to make up the idea
which we form of those characters. But the deaf student of
living character, is in precisely the same case as would be
the student of the characters in Boz, who should be acquainted with no other copy of the tales, than one in which
all the talk is blotted out. . . .

• MISCELLANEOUS •

I cannot pretend to any permanent regret in connection
with the absence of vocal or other sounds. There are indeed
times when I felicitate myself on the quiet which I am able
to enjoy in my study, in the midst of all the noises which,
as I am told, the voices of my children and knockings at
the door produce. This is, however, but an incidental benefit; even as a man is secure from a surfeit who never dines:
and is therefore of little weight in an estimate of the general
condition. And now that I have touched on this point, I
will not hesitate to denounce with indignation the cold and
miserable comfort of those, who seem to think it a kind of
compensation for the loss or absence of a sense, that one
is no longer exposed to some matters of annoyance, which
the wide range of the organ must now and then embrace.
What is this but to comfort a man with a wooden leg by

the assurance that corns will no more afflict his toes; that his feet can be no more cold; and that he saves much in shoe leather? It is surely spare comfort to the deaf man, that the same calamity which shuts up to him the world of uttered thoughts, and from the sweet concords of the universe, also excludes an occasional noise or discordance; and to the blind, that the same lost sense which might enable them to look

> "Abroad through nature, to the range
> Of planets, suns, and adamantine spheres;"

might also light upon the annoyance of a dunghill or of a dead carcase. . . .

It is my conviction, that the human mind is incapable of any permanent, unredeemed, feeling of affliction. Under this, the mind or body must soon give way, and yield the relief of madness or of the grave. It there were any physical calamities over which the mind might be supposed to brood with more abundant and abiding sorrow than any others, they should be deafness and blindness: but the blind are proverbially cheerful, and the deaf, although less hilarious, do not rest in abiding depression. My own experience is this. It has been already stated, that at first, and in early boyhood, the enjoyments which hearing offered were necessarily too limited and too indistinctly appreciated, to occasion much, if any, regret at the loss I had sustained. But afterwards, when I became more truly aware of my real position, coupled as deafness was with other downcasting influences, my mind gradually became

> "Sicklied o'er with the pale cast of thought;"

and habitually rested in most sombre views of life, and of my own position and prospects in it. When, however, I was enabled to realize the pleasant consciousness that my solitary studies had not been altogether in vain, and that I might come as an invited guest, and not a beggar, to the feast of life, my views and feelings underwent a rapid change, and my average temper has become by far more cheerful than melancholy, and much more sanguine than despondent. It remains, however, that, from my course having lain so much alone and apart, I am less than most men able to endure the frets and annoyances from the outer world to which life is incident, and from which my own career has been by no means exempt. Under the nervous sensitiveness which is thus produced, many things oppress, grieve, and overpower me, which probably a man moving about among the activities of life, would heed but little.

The regrets arising *directly* from the sense of privation are by no means so common as might be supposed, and are seldom experienced with any intensity, save in the presence of some strongly exciting cause. . . .

In a preceding chapter I have described the usage respecting proper names among deaf-mutes. My own experience with reference to such names could not there be introduced, as it had no direct relation to the subject of the chapter; but it is too remarkable to be left unrecorded.

A person in the full enjoyment of his senses is in the habit of constantly hearing the names of persons with whom he is even in a slight degree associated, or whom he is in the habit of seeing frequently. The reverse of this is the case with the deaf. A person's face often becomes as familiar to him as that of one of his own family, before he is acquainted with his name; and when a name is given to him, in the way of formal introduction or in answer to direct inquiry, it is in most cases imparted to him but once, and therefore does not make that distinct impression which frequent repetition produces. It is hence often forgotten beyond recovery; and this is a circumstance which not seldom occasions much confusion and embarrassment, and sometimes may prove the source of unpleasant feeling to those who do not sufficiently consider the peculiar difficulties of the deaf condition. An example which made a vivid impression upon my own mind will illustrate this.

On my last return from the East, I was detained for some time at a port on the Black Sea, waiting for a vessel in which to proceed to Constantinople. During this time I remained with the British Consul, in the receipt of those gentlemanly hospitalities to which many travellers before and since have been eager to acknowledge their obligations. Among the permanent inmates were two gentlemen whom I met at every meal, and from whom I received much local information and many kindnesses. Some years after I was privileged to meet the Consul in London; and in the course of conversation inquired after these gentlemen. One of them I had no difficulty in naming, as his name had intermediately come under my notice as the correspondent of a scientific journal; but the name of the other, with whom I had had far more communication, had utterly escaped me, although his person and manner were most vividly before me. Unaware of this, I proceeded to inquire concerning "Mr."——— and there I found myself at a dead halt, which distressed me beyond measure, as calculated to suggest that I had but a very faint recollection of one who had shown much kindness to me. The name itself seemed indeed at the tip of my tongue; but it would not quit my mouth; and after a pause of nervous anxiety, I was constrained to indicate the person as "the gentleman with the silver snuffbox;" resorting in fact to an oral *sign*, to express the name which I was unable to recover.

Now I had been in circumstances in which, if possessed of hearing, this gentleman's name would have been heard by me at least ten times a day during three or four weeks, so that it could not have failed to occur most readily to me on all future occasions; but the fact being, that it had only once or twice been brought before me in all that time, and that I never met with it in the intervening years, sufficiently accounts for the lapse of recollection. But it was not likely that this point would be considered by the person who witnessed my hesitation; and I have often since recurred to this incident with much annoyance, which would have been greatly increased had I supposed it likely that the gentleman whose name was in question, should ever become acquainted with the fact of my imperfect recollection. . . .

There is one point of difference between the deaf and the blind which does not appear to have received all the attention it deserves, although it seems better calculated than any other single circumstance which could be produced to illustrate the disparity of their intellectual condition. This is the prominence of poetical tendencies in the blind, and the utter absence of such tendencies in the deaf. The cause of this remarkable difference is not very recondite. The blind have a perfect mastery of words, and their sole reliance upon the ear, as the vehicle of pleasurable sensations, renders them exquisitely alive to harmonious sounds and numbers. Add to this, that in the absence of the resources in reading, etc., which hearing allows, it must be a most interesting occupation and solace to the blind, to be able to occupy themselves in poetical compositions, in marshalling their ideas, and in constructing and polishing their verse. During those hours in which they must necessarily be left to their own resources, the time thus employed must move more pleasantly away than in any other intellectual exercise which could be devised.

But the deaf man, having external resources from visual impressions, will not take the same degree of interest in this as a mental exercise, even supposing him equal to it. But he cannot be equal to it; for he not only *wants* all the peculiar resources of the blind man for this kind of occupation, but his disqualifications for it are in direct antagonism to the qualifications of the other. In the first place he wants words; and then he has in a painfully literal sense, *no ear* for numbers. For want of oral guidance in hearing others speak, it is next to impossible that he should have that knowledge of quantity and rhyme which is essential to harmonious verse. He would also be unsafe in his rhymes: for rhyme lies in assonances which can often only be determined by the ear; and verse will require words which one who became deaf in early life will never have heard. It is, therefore, not wonderful that the deaf-mutes, and those who have become deaf in childhood, never do attempt to contend with these difficulties, which seem absolutely insuperable. I am utterly ignorant of any verse—for I will not venture to call my own such—written by any persons under such circumstances. With those who become deaf after adult age has been attained, the case may be different—although I am not aware of any poetry which even such persons have given to the world. . . .

• MASSIEU AND OTHERS •

I have already more than once adverted to this celebrated pupil of the Abbé Sicard; and as he, beyond all deaf-mutes, possessed the power of explaining his own condition, I shall, in this place, introduce the details which he has given; and, in proceeding, offer some remarks upon them.

The author of a little book, called 'La Corbeille de Fleurs,' relates that he was anxious to have from Massieu some particulars concerning his childhood, and induced him to furnish in writing the following history of his first years.

"I was born at Semens, in the canton of St. Macaire, department of La Gironde. My father died in the month of January, 1791; my mother lives still. In my country we were six deaf-mutes, of the same paternal family, three boys and three girls. Until the age of thirteen years and nine months, I remained in my country, where I never received any instruction.

"I expressed my ideas by manual signs, or by gestures. The signs which I at that time used to express my ideas to my parents, and to my brothers and sisters, were very different from those of the instructed deaf-mutes. Strangers never understood us, when we were expressing to them our ideas; but the neighbours understood us.

"I saw oxen, horses, pigs, dogs, cats, vegetables, houses, fields, vines; and when I had seen all these objects I remembered them well." . . .

"Before my education, while I was a child, I knew neither to read or write. I desired to write and read. I often saw young boys and girls who were going to school, and I desired to follow them." . . .

"I begged of my father, with tears in my eyes, permission to go to school. I took a book and turned it upside down to mark my ignorance. I put it under my arm as if to go out; but my father refused me the permission I requested, making signs to me that I should never be able to learn anything, because I was deaf and dumb." . . .

"Then I cried very loud. I again took the books to read them; but I neither knew the letters nor the words, nor the phrases, nor the periods. Full of vexation, I put my fingers in my ears, and demanded with impatience of my father to have them cured.

"He answered me, that there was no remedy. Then I was disconsolate. I quitted by father's house and went to school, without telling my father. I addressed myself to the master, and asked him by signs to teach me to read and write. He refused me roughly, and drove me from the school. This made me cry much; but my purpose I gave not up. I often thought of writing and reading. I was then twelve years old; I attempted alone to form with the pen the writing signs." . . .

"In my childhood, my father made me make prayers in gestures, evening and morning. I threw myself on my knees, I joined by hands and *moved my lips* in imitation of those who speak when they are praying to God. At present I know there is a God, who is the creator of heaven and earth. In my childhood I adored the heavens, not God. I did not see God, I did see the heavens.

"I did not know whether I had been myself made, or whether I made myself.

"I grew tall. But if I had not known my instructor Sicard, my mind would not have grown as my body, for my mind was very poor; in growing up I should have thought the heavens were God.

"Then the children of my age did not play with me, they despised me. I was like a dog. I amused myself alone in playing at ball, or marbles, or running about on stilts.

"I knew the numbers before my instruction,—my fingers had taught me them; but I did not know the figures. I counted with my fingers, and when the number passed ten, I made notches on a stick.

"During my childhood, my parents sometimes made me watch a flock; and often those who met me, touched with my condition, gave me money.

"One day a gentleman who was passing took a liking to me. He made me go to his house, and gave me to eat and drink.

"Afterwards, when he went to Bordeaux, he spoke about me to M. Sicard, who consented to take charge of my education.

"This gentleman wrote to my father, who showed me his letter; but I could not read it. My relations and neighbours told me what it contained. They informed me that I should go to Bordeaux. They though it was to learn to be a cooper; my father said to me that it was to learn to read and write.

"I set out with him for Bordeaux. When we arrived there, we went to visit M. l'Abbé Sicard, whom I found very thin.". . . .

"I commenced by forming letters with my fingers. In the space of many days, I knew how to write some words. In the space of three months I knew how to write many words. In the space of six months I knew how to write some phrases. In the space of a year I wrote well. In the space of a year and nine months I wrote better, and I answered well to questions that were proposed to me.

"It was three years and six months that I had been with M. l'Abbé Sicard, when I set out with him for Paris.

"In the space of four years, I became like the *entendans-parlans*."

The narrator proceeds to state, that he asked Massieu some questions which might tend to throw still further light on his condition.

"Before your instruction, what did you think that people were doing when they looked at each other and moved their lips?"

"I thought they were expressing ideas."

"Why did you think so?"

"Because I recollected that some one had spoken of me to my father, and he had threatened to have me punished."

"You thought, then, that the motion of the lips was one

way of communicating ideas?"

"Yes."

"Why, then, did you not move your lips to communicate yours?"

"Because I had not sufficiently watched the lips of the speakers when they spoke; and because people told me my noises were bad. As they told me my defect was in my ears, I took some brandy, poured it into my ears, and stopped them with cotton." This was manifestly done in imitation of persons whom he had seen so treat their ears in temporary deafness from cold.

"Did you know what it was to hear?"

"Yes."

"How had you learned that?"

"A hearing female relative, who lived at our house, told me that *she saw with her ears a person whom she could not see with her eyes*—a person who was coming to my father. The hearing *see with their ears* during the night a person who is walking." . . . It is certain that no *proper* idea of a sound can be entertained by those who never heard it—whatever be the degree of their "education." . . .

Other points in the conversation with Massieu involve some interesting disclosures.

"What were you thinking about while your father made you remain on your knees?"

"About the heavens."

"With what view did you address to it a prayer?"

"To make it descend at night to the earth, in order that the plants which I had planted might grow, and that the sick might be restored to health."

"Was it with ideas, words, or sentiments, that you composed your prayer?"

"It was the heart that made it. I did not yet know either words, or their meaning, or value."

"What did you feel in your heart?"

"Joy, when I found that the plants and fruits grew. Grief, when I saw their injury by the hail, and that my parents still remained sick."

At these last words of his answer, Massieu made many signs, which expressed anger and menaces. The fact, as I have been informed (says the narrator), was, that during his mother's illness, he used to go out every evening to pray to a particular star, that he had selected for its beauty, for her restoration; but finding that she got worse, he was enraged, and pelted stones at the star.

"Is it possible that you menaced the heavens?" said we, with astonishment.

"Yes."

"But from what motive?"

"Because I thought that I could not get at it to beat it and kill it, for causing all these disasters, and not curing my parents."

"Had you no fear of irritating it?"

"I was not then acquainted with my good master, Sicard, and I was ignorant what this heaven was. It was not until a year after my education was commenced that I had any fear of being punished by it."

"Did you give any figure or form to the heavens?"

"My father had made me look at a large statue, which was in the church of my country. It represented an old man with a long beard; he held a globe in his hand. I thought he lived above the sun." . . .

"Did you know who made the ox, the horse, etc.?"

"No: but I was curious to see them spring up. Often I went to hide myself in the dykes, to watch the heaven descending upon the earth, for the growth of beings. I wished much to see this."

"What were your thoughts when M. Sicard made you

trace, for the first time, words with letters?"

"I thought that the words were the images of the objects
I saw around me. I learned them by memory with the
utmost ardour. When I first learned the word GOD, written
with chalk on a board, I looked at it very often, for I believed
that God caused death, and I feared him very much."

"What idea had you then of death?"

"That it was the cessation of motion, of sensation, of
chewing, of the softness of the skin, and of the flesh."

"Why had you this idea?"

"Because I had seen a corpse."

"Did you think that you should always live?"

"I thought there was a heavenly land, and that the body
was eternal." . . .

Massieu's abilities, when fully instructed, were chiefly
evinced in the written answers to questions put to him by
strangers. Most of them were good, and some wonderfully
fine. The following are specimens of their quality:—

"What is hope?"
"Hope is the blossom of happiness."

"What is the difference between hope and desire?"
"Desire is a tree in leaf, hope is a tree in blossom,
enjoyment is a tree in fruit."

"What is gratitude?"
"Gratitude is the memory of the heart."

"What is time?"
"A line that has two ends,—a path that begins in the
cradle and ends in the tomb."

"What is eternity?"
"A day without yesterday or to-morrow; a line that has
no end."

"What is God?"

"The necessary Being, the sun of eternity, the mechanist of nature, the eye of justice, the watchmaker of the universe, the soul of the universe."

The acute and dangerous question, "Does God reason?" is said to have been put to him by Sir James Mackintosh. The answer was—

"Man reasons, because he doubts; he deliberates, he decides: God is omniscient; he never doubts; he therefore never reasons."

This seems to us the best answer Massieu ever gave. It will be observed, that most of the others, which are among the best specimens of his peculiar talent, are properly translations into words of picture language. They are illustrations, similitudes, not always very distinct. He seldom attempts an abstract definition, and when he does so he usually fails. . . .

These admired answers seem to us to afford painful evidence of the labour and contrivance which even such a man as Massieu had to employ in affixing ideas to words. It was obviously an intellectual exercise in which he took pleasure; and this bore him on to the success which he eventually achieved, and which few others can be expected to attain. The traces of this process of intellection in his answers, give to them a kind of misty grandeur, well calculated to engage attention and to excite admiration. . . .

Massieu's idea of hearing as "auricular sight" has already been examined: and it has been shown that the born deaf cannot possibly have any correct idea of sound. These conclusions are corroborated by all which has been elicited from other persons in that condition. One who had been educated in an American institution was asked—

"Before instruction, how did you feel when you saw that there was a striking difference between yourself and other folks?"

"I sometimes felt surprised to see them speak quickly. I examined their tongues, speaking. I thought their tongues were not like my tongue. I wished to speak easily. I was sorry that I was deaf and dumb. I disliked to make signs."

"What idea have you of sound; or what do you think sound is like?"

"I cannot think what sound is like."

It would, however, seem this person at first conceived that the mere *motions* of the tongue communicated ideas visually perceived: and that when undeceived in this respect, was unable to substitute any other idea. Another, when asked the same question, respecting the difference between himself and other people, answered—

"I was much surprised at the speech of the folks, when I saw them speaking. I had much desire to speak and hear, but I could not speak and hear: but I thought that somebody had stolen my hearing when I was a young boy."

Of *Music*, it appears that even the educated deaf-mutes can only form any notion by reference to its *apparent* effects upon others who can hear. Observe how the writer of the following escapes from the painful attempts to define what he does not understand, to rest upon the tangible idea of the tarantula.

"Music is a copy or rule of voice. When a person sings, he looks in a musical book, and sings according to the musical rule. I am told that music is very lively. I know it is far more delicious than the fine food or drink. It is wonderful that music has the virtue of exciting the heart. It inspirits persons who are discouraged or look downcast. Martial music makes the soul brave. Melancholy music drops the tears from the eyes of persons. Many persons are transported by the sweet music. It is especially more striking that the sweet music is the sovereign remedy against the craziness caused by the bite of the tarantula,—a great and poisonous spider. Having been bitten by the spider a person becomes crazy. A number of musicians are immediately called. They play upon musical instruments before him. He is moved by hearing the sweet music. It removes his fatal craziness, and he becomes quiet, and is delivered from death. He cannot recognize his past craziness. The music casts the recollection of his craziness into oblivion. But the music cannot heal the deaf and dumb of this fatal craziness. But the deaf and dumb should be very careful, and flee from the tarantula. The deaf and dumb cannot enjoy music because they are destitute of the organ of hearing: but they should be contented because they can be moved by poetry, while they read poems." . . .

Many long years have passed since I have abandoned the slightest hope which I might once have entertained, of ever more hearing a sound in this world. I have almost ceased to desire it. . . .

Besides, the condition in which three-fourths of life have been passed, has become in some sort natural to me. . . . I fear that I should run wild under the influence of so great a change; and that I should be no longer able to maintain the sedentary life which I have hitherto led, or keep up the habits of close application and incessant study, in which I have been enabled to find many sources of satisfaction and the means of some usefulness. . . . Still, if I *knew* that any operation or application would awaken the aural nerve from its long rest, and restore the lost sense to me, I should probably think it my duty to risk the consequences of that great joy at which I tremble—not because I value it not, or because I do not appreciate it, but because I rate it so highly as to fear that the mind might be overwhelmed, and established habits broken up, by the mighty influx of new sensations, new ideas, and new hopes. . . .

London, 1848

A Voice from the Silence
by Howard L. Terry

EDITORS' PREFACE

The following excerpt is more notable for its being written
by a deaf author than for its insight into deafness or for its
literary merit. Howard L. Terry is the only published deaf
novelist, but he rarely wrote about deafness or used deaf
characters, the character in this story, Jack Harlow, being
the only important one. And, indeed, even with Harlow
we learn very little of how Terry viewed the deaf experience. Harlow is merely an incidental character in the novel
and useful as a deaf character *per se* only because he was
able to read Gibbs' lips without Gibbs knowing.

However, we can forgive Terry his avoiding the subject
of deafness. This novel was written over a half century ago
when public interest in handicapped people or in minority
groups of any sort was still dormant. The primary concern
in America at that time was in assimilating the scattered,
wildly heterogeneous patchwork quilt of American society
into a unified whole—it was the time of the "melting pot"
and the diminution of differences, not a time like today of
the search for ethnic roots, of black pride, of the Jewish
Defense League, or of Indians going back to the tribe. Little
wonder that Terry, although deaf himself, still wrote novels
about the lives of "mainstream" Americans rather than about
people who were at that time forgotten citizens: the deaf.
It is enough that a deaf man was able to write and publish
novels; we cannot ask that he also crusade at a time when
such a crusade would probably, if you will pardon us, have
fallen on deaf ears.

261

FROM A VOICE FROM THE SILENCE

Where Gibbs got his original capital, no one knew, but he
did get it and lent it at ten per cent, and even more when
he had some poor farmer at his mercy, getting richer as
time passed. No one that had good security need fear to
ask for a loan. He was rarely away from town, and then
only as far as the county seat, except when called by business demands. He was careful of his speech, yet ready to
joke; sharp in all business transactions, acquainted with
every one for miles around, stingy, uncharitable, unloving.
He smiled at the young ladies, but had never been known
to call on one socially. To increase his bank account had
been his sole aim; to enjoy his gain, or to use it for the
common good was never in his mind. Greed of gain, as
time passed, had developed into a mania, a mental disease.
In physical make-up Gibbs was short and square set, with
a firm chin and well set features. In dress he was always
neat, but cared nothing for fashion. He was a man in whom
no one could pick a legal flaw. He followed a calling if not
uplifting, allowed by law; he troubled no one, and he was
agreeable in conversation when not angered.

"Duncan," began Gibbs, drawing his chair up to the table
and filling his plate with yesterday's leftovers, "Duncan,
the Mutual has got me—got most of my notes, and there
is no use to expect any more business so long as this com-
bine is running. The only good thing that I have left is the
Woodcraft eighty, and it isn't lawfully mine at that, you
know." He looked out of the window as a caution. "Now,
you are the only one that knows how things stand, and if
we don't act at once we'll lose the land." He looked around
in his usual cautious manner, and seeing the front door
slightly ajar, got up and locked it. "There," he said, re-
seating himself, "now we can feel safe. That squab, Jene

Anderson, has made fools of us. Nevertheless, I can't help admire him—ain't afraid of any one, good at plannin' and executing.

"Now it's our turn. Listen, Tom!" Gibbs set down his knife and fork, and looking calmly into his companion's face, went on: "All these twenty years, or nearly twenty, your life's been in my hands, since that hour when you, in your haste and recklessness, laid Buck Martin low. A single word from me would have got you hanged." Duncan shuddered. "Excepting me, not a soul either in this country or on earth, for that matter, ever knew who killed Buck Martin—unless I lie. I protected you, and stood by you, and helped you make money, and now, Tom Duncan, it's up to you to return the kindness—your note's due!" Gibbs paused, still looking straight into the now pale face of Duncan. Then, almost involuntarily his eyes turned toward the window, and at that moment a youth appeared. It was Jack Harlow, and he beckoned Gibbs to open the door.

Startled by the sudden appearance of a third person, and most decidedly alarmed, Gibbs instinctively motioned Jack to go away; but the boy insisted on seeing him.

"Let me in—I must see Mr. Duncan at once. Open the door!"

Assuming their usual composure, the two men stepped to the kitchen door and admitted Jack. It was still early— not quite seven o'clock—and the men stared at the heavily breathing boy. Jack had run all the way from his home.

"Mrs. Duncan is sick—poisoned. Get home—as—quick— as—you—can—Mr. Duncan!"

"Good God!" cried Duncan, throwing up his hands in alarm, and stepping across the room for his hat.

"Hold!" cried Gibbs, grabbing him. "Here's sympathy and help if it's true; but by hell ye can't go till ye promise."

Duncan turned a wrathful face on his tormentor.

"Let him go" cried Jack, staring at Gibbs who still held his man. "I tell you, his wife's sick. Oliver 'phoned all over trying to find you, Mr. Duncan, and I came to Linn to hunt you."

It was so, and Oliver's efforts to telephone to Gibbs had failed because Gibbs was sound asleep and was not disturbed by the ringing of the telephone.

"Sit down there!" ordered Gibbs, addressing Jack, and pointing to a chair. He followed up his command by pushing the startled boy into the seat.

"We'll go in a rig, Tom; be calm, an' we'll get out in no time. Listen! This boy—Jack Harlow—is deaf as a post; I can talk an' no fear. He's a tightening his hold on May Martin, an' you ought to know it. He'll get her yet an' at the proper time if he don't act at once. You killed her father—May's father." Jack's eyes were riveted on the speaker's face. "Your life's in my hands. Ye promised me that day in the cabin you'd stick by me, and now it's up to you to do it—I repeat. Marry Oliver to May—force the girl to do it, if necessary; then buy the land—her—Sam's land, of me an' we'll mine it. Promise!"

"Ain't in my power!" glared Duncan, his better nature rebelling against the idea of the awful injustice. He jerked away.

"Then by heaven, Tom Duncan, you shall hang!"

"Damn ye!" Tom leaped at the glaring man, and Jack, springing to his feet, threw himself between them. Then suddenly calming themselves, the two men broke into a mock laugh in an ineffectual effort to deceive Jack.

"I'll do it—I swear," and Duncan slapped Gibbs on the back good-naturedly.

Gibbs drew forth from his pockets a pad and a pencil and wrote a plausible excuse for their behavior, and showed it to Jack. He then hurried out to get his horse; but suddenly

changing his mind, he saddled the animal instead of hitch-
ing him to the buggy, whereupon Duncan leaped into the
saddle and galloped away.

Jack slipped away without a word. His head was all a-
whirl.

As the boy went homeward he was quick to notice that
the town had heard of the poisoning, at least so he judged,
for the people stood in little groups discussing the matter.

"It's ptomaine pizzen," explained a knowing old woman.
"She eat canned stuff. Dr. Woods is out there."

"I hear Tom wasn't to home," voiced another.

"D'ye reckon she'll die? I heerd that kind of pizzen is
powerful bad."

"Naw," assured Parsons. "Dr. Woods can save her."

And so they gossiped and speculated, none dreaming
that Duncan himself had been so near them, nor of the
little affair that had just transpired over at Gibbs'. Tom's
departure had not been seen because the Gibbs cottage
was not in sight from the store.

Jack made post-haste for his home. He hurried across
lots, passed the station where the operator was just opening
up his office, and evading his notice, ran under the shipping
shed that stood high on piles, and gained the road on the
other side of the tracks. Jack's heart beat like a trip hammer;
he had read the men's lips! He had grasped the full significance of what Gibbs had said. Duncan a murderer—the
murderer of May's father—for nearly twenty years a mystery! Gibbs a rascal and a schemer of the boldest type! May
to be forced into marrying Oliver! Never! But what meant
all this? Here was a new world of things, and very bad
things, at that. Like a bolt from a clear sky the awful intelligence had struck the boy, and like an earthquake shook
his peace of mind; his brain swam as he hurried along. Far
ahead of him he could see the dust and the flying hoofs as

the horse bearing Duncan along flew over the ground, and he wished that he, too, were mounted. Gradually, however, he became calmer, and he resolved to hold his secret until he could decide what was best to do. Setting himself to that resolve, he walked calmly along and arrived home in a steady state of mind. He went to work as usual. The next day, without breathing a word about his discovery, he joined the party for the outing narrated in the foregoing chapter.

The Deaf Mute Howls
by Albert Ballin

EDITORS' PREFACE

This excerpt from *The Deaf Mute Howls* tells us more about the deaf experience than almost anything written before it. Its chief value, beyond having been written by a deaf man, is that it reveals to use the rage that many deaf people feel against a world that is so constantly unfair. Ballin, to be sure, did not suffer as did the fictional characters Gerasim and Gargan (in *Mumu* and "The Deaf Mute"), who were totally isolated, but he did suffer from a special kind of frustration: he was *in* the hearing world, but he was not *of* it. The rage of Ballin's frustration appears especially in regard to oralism and signs, for it is, of course, through a certain degree of oral training that deaf people are able to get by in the hearing world. Ballin lived in the hearing world, that is, he was able to make it, but there is in this biography a thinly veiled resentment, a seething rage almost, because of the extraordinary difficulties he had to undergo for the sake of making it. He loved and hated his hearing friends at the same time.

Nowhere is Ballin's poignant ambivalence more apparent than when he talks about Alexander Graham Bell. His feelings toward Bell were obviously strong, but it is hard to tell if he loathed or loved him. At first we hear Ballin talking of Bell (whom he had met in Europe) in this way: "there never existed a more gracious, more affable, more fun-loving or jollier fellow on this sorry old globe than Dr. Bell." But after a few pages, we find this diatribe against the oralists, which, of course, included Bell:

To be fair and just I must concede a high motive and perfect honesty of purpose to SOME of the oralists. But insofar as results are concerned one may as well concede the same to Tomas Torquemada of the infamous inquisition, or to the witch hunters, and burners of heretics. So deep-rooted is the prejudice against the sign-language among some classes, that it approaches a form of persecution.

Until his death, Alexander Graham Bell, the inventor of the telephone, headed the oralists. Because of his great fame, wealth, and his having been a teacher of the deaf in his youth, he was able to exert a powerful influence in spreading the propaganda of the oral method. As a matter of fact, had Mr. Bell not invented the telephone and won fame and wealth, his views on the subject would have had no more force and weight than a goose feather in a tornado, for among eminent, experienced educators of the deaf he was considered a mere tyro in this field of education.

This is a fairly strongly-worded indictment of Bell. Yet Ballin spent a lot of time with Bell, became almost a member of the family, and used to engage in banter about the relative merits of sign and lip reading. Ballin must have been flattered to be valued so highly by Bell, and he obviously liked the man, but inside there burned a flame, and it comes out at times, as in this excerpt:

He spent a considerable part of his wealth and time on his favorite theory concerning the deaf. It was his hobby. Still, his expenditures and energies were, I believe, sadly misspent. In fact they have brought misery to the ones he loved and wanted most to help.

Ballin can't quite make up his mind to love or hate Bell, just as he had been unable to do with the hard of hearing friend in school. In fact, in all of this excerpt we find ambivalence, a suggestion of great pent-up feelings that don't know how to get out. The rage appears, but a sense of duty quickly comes to the fore, and Ballin qualifies his rage. Ballin was clearly mad at the world—as well he might be.

Ballin is the first deaf person to really speak out among the characters and authors in this book. Figuratively speaking, I see Ballin as the suppressed Gerasim, Gargan, Sophy, Camille, even the suppressed Terry, our deaf author who did not really speak of deafness, all these suppressed characters representing the suppressed deaf people of the world finally finding their voice, but that voice (*The Deaf Mute Howls*), in the person of Ballin, stumbles a little, contradicts itself, can't quite put its rage into proper expression—it attempts to right all wrongs in one fell swoop (after all, it's had centuries of backlog to make up for) and therefore ends up righting no wrongs because it protested too much, was too unsure of itself, was still bound in the chains of deaf Uncle-Tomism. The "howl" is only a muted one—it is too apologetic, too ambivalent.

Even in the issues this excerpt mentions, we find contradictions and unreasoned statements born of the rage Ballin put into his writing. One of the most intriguing and explosive is the question whether sign language interferes with the learning of English. Ballin dismisses such a suggestion out of hand, but, in his anger, fails to see some of the complications involved. There is by now a vast literature regarding this issue, but, in general, we would probably now all agree that free and open communication all during the years growing up, be it with the hands, the voice, or the elbows, is essential to language development in children. In this sense, it is probably better for a deaf child to have deaf parents than hearing parents unless the hearing parents are fluent in sign language. In this way, the deaf child is getting language training immediately. It is the language itself that is important, not *which* language.

Ballin also questions the practice of "herding together" deaf children for their education and rearing. Again, Ballin in his rage-produced ambivalence fails to mention some of the more complicated concerns in this regard, either. For those deaf children who can make it in a hearing school, in general it is better to go to a hearing school if their aim is education. If their aim is companionship and a feeling of being part of the world, however, they had better choose to grow up with their fellows. Or if the child is smart enough to compete on unequal terms in a hearing school, but still tends to feel inferior, even without the consideration of friendship, probably that child would be better off among deaf children. And so on. The considerations are enormously complex, and even Ballin must have had some idea that they were, but instead he simply lashes out—he simply howls.

At another point Ballin talks of Gallaudet graduates working as common laborers (I am quick to point out, as a Gallaudet professor myself, that this is, to my knowledge, no longer the case), suggesting that education for the deaf is hardly worthwhile (though Ballin, I'm sure, would not care to forsake his!) because society is so insensitive and prejudiced toward deaf people. And, of course, he was right, but the solution certainly is not to stop educating deaf people but to start educating hearing people.

Ballin's rage next is directed against the movie industry for taking up "talkies." Here, he is beside himself, so much so that he falls into a totally unreasonable declaration that the "talkies" will never last. Again, his anger is justified, for the silent movies offered one moment when the deaf people of the time were equal to everyone else. In this one medium, at least, they could share experiences with hearing people. And now it was being taken away. And so Ballin rages at the studios, blaming the post-World War I "hysterical mood" for the adoption of such a foolish innovation.

Finally, Ballin takes on the whole world of the hearing for not learning finger spelling, thereby forcing deaf people to try to read lips, a skill which Ballin apparently was never able to master. As before, we sympathize with Ballin, but expecting that the whole world will learn finger spelling on the chance that a deaf person may someday be around is patently absurd.

Ah! How poignant is this whole outburst. How pathetic! In it we see the hopelessness facing the deaf people of even fifty years ago. How does one react to a world totally stacked against one? How else? With a howl of rage. Ballin was healthy. He was right to rage. He had every reason to do so. And even today that howl continues. Deaf people are no longer content to wait and accept as the seven year old Gilbert Stratton did in Payne's *King Silence*. Just as he found out, deaf people are not alone against the world—there are others. And where there are others, there is hope. Where there is hope, suppression is no longer possible.

FROM THE DEAF MUTE HOWLS

• I MAKE "PROGRESS" •

After several years, I reached the point where it was assumed I was able to wrestle with grammar. But, consistent with my earlier childish resolution, I simply allowed words to float and swirl heedlessly around my head, making no effort to grasp them. Resolution may not be the correct term to apply to this case, for my ambition to advance myself in other directions was never quenched. Nothing was really the matter with my brain, unless we except the referred-to inexplicable atrophied centers connected with the acquirement of language. English—my mother tongue—seemed to be forever soaring miles and miles beyond reach of my comprehension. It would not or could not penetrate my head.

Nouns, adjectives, adverbs, and all their ungodly relatives gyrated and squirmed like witches on a stormy Sabbath eve to bewilder and ache my poor head. I simply sat back, looking on with a blank stare as though in a torpor, my mental eyes closed tight. I was feeling too spiritually worn out to even wish to think. These lessons were infinitely more confusing to me than conjugating irregular French verbs would be to you. You would, at least, have your English grammar at hand to help you. I had no background—nothing to guide me.

271

I was taught some smatterings of history, geography, arithmetic, etc., but as usual, I was too mentally atrophied to take interest in the ever-multiplying number of hard words, their complex, intricate meanings, and their innumerable secondary colors, shades, and tones. But I made marvelous progress in understanding stories when rendered in SIGNS. They were then interesting, enthralling, though I could remember but very few names of persons, places or dates.

My teachers had, by now, abandoned trying to make me recite my lessons in writing. To them I was a hopeless case of laziness, obstinacy or sheer stupidity. They felt like the farmer who tries to make the horse drink against its will.

Fagged out by the dull monotony of futile exercises in the class room, I welcomed with delight the recesses and other dismissals from my lessons. I ran, played and forgot the little I had "learned" at school. In our talks, we, the deaf-mutes, never communicate except by signs—only signs. It is to us, the most natural, easiest and sweetest language. Spelt words are entirely tabooed among ourselves. Even persons and places are given distinctive signs of their own. The few cases where this is not practical are rare. You may be surprised to know that nearly every City, State and Country has its own sign.

Matters stood thus until the entrance of a SEMI-MUTE pupil into my class. It was then that something unusual transpired. But the influence he had over me must be treated separately and referred to later.

In an earlier chapter I have outline the difference between a DEAF-MUTE and a SEMI-MUTE; a difference as great as that of a warbling canary and a bull-dog. The deaf-mute is such as I have described my composite self. The other, having become deaf when over six years old, his brain has attained a development that enables him to retain unimpaired, the memories of what he had heard and learned through his ears. He is much easier to teach, almost as easy as any normal child.

Many of the semi-mutes who came to my school lost their hearing at ages as late as ten, fifteen, and some when eighteen and over. Many of them had gone through schools for the hearing, some to High School, a few to College. They were the pets of the teachers and officers. In fact, they were used as decoys to deceive and delude the indiscriminate and gullible public.

The semi-mutes, I will repeat, number 20 percent of all the deaf. When my school had 500 pupils, it had approximately 400 deaf-mutes and 100 semi-mutes. It was always the latter 100 who were the SHOW-PUPILS at public and private exhibitions. They were the only ones shown to visitors and parents of deaf children applying for admission. The officers never explained the differences between these two classes—if such explanation could be avoided. They deliberately impressed the visitors that these SEMI-MUTES were the same as all the other pupils and that they owed all their education wholly to the school. No wonder then that the visitors were amazed and charmed over their mastery of English, extensive knowledge of History, Geography, Current Events. The showing was almost as good as at any school for the hearing. Usually, what astonished the visitor, was the proficiency these pupils showed in VOCAL SPEECH. Their speech is plain, natural and perfect in modulation. Such visitors returned home and broadcast the glad tidings of the miracles they witnessed, and lauded to the skies the "wonderful" system of instruction given to all the deaf children!

Occasionally visitors come upon a deaf-mute pupil, and find him DUMB, in all that the word dummy implies. But the institution officers are never embarrassed; they are veterans at the game, and are ready with stock explanations. The favorite ones are that these "dummies" are "exceptions," "unfortunate victims of diseases or accidents that impaired both their hearing and mental faculties at the same time." "Born that way, my dear Madam;" "vicious by nature, my dear Sir;" "stubborn in his refusal to learn;" "born idiot;" "offspring of degenerate foreigners;" "a product of the slums," and other like deceptions that seem to fit the individual cases.

Because of this method of humbugging, the public is neither wise nor safe. The system is prolific of wrong reactions. Such an exhibition of decoys create impressions in the minds of parents that the school can impart ARTICULATE SPEECH to their deaf-mute children. Have they not seen with their own eyes, heard with their own ears, the wonderful "orally-taught" DEAF AND DUMB pupils? They are definitely "sold" upon such a system of instruction.

Instead of accepting the explanation and advice of the officers who say that their children will be benefitted by the "combined method" which uses the manual alphabet and signs, the parents threaten to place their children in a school which claims ability to teach vocal speech to ALL through the pure-oral method.

Honest officers have yet to yield, much against their own judgement, and allow the pure-oral method to creep in, until finally it crowds out the combined system. I say they have to because otherwise the school would be closed. This pure-oral method was beginning to assume supremacy in the school of which I was a pupil. Of this method I shall speak at the proper place and time.

• STRUGGLE WITH LANGUAGE •

One of the greatest wrongs inflicted on deaf children is their enforced herding together under one roof. In these quarters they do not contact the customs, habits, or life of the normal human beings with whom they must associate after leaving school. Under the one roof, they are kept in close contact with one another day in and day out for fifteen years or longer. Like most children, they learn more from one another in five minutes than they do in a whole week from their teachers. And what do they learn? Your imagination can easily conjecture the correct answer. Most assuredly not good language or manners. In this existence, they form uncouth mannerisms, peculiarly their own. Mannerisms that tend to drive them farther apart from their future hearing neighbors.

But there are always some stray rays of brightness in the murky blackness of institutional life for the deaf-mutes. One is the presence in their midst of the semi-mutes who are helpful without realizing it. Their limited help shows the value to be gained by such contacts, for the semi-mutes are next door to the hearing.

Now I shall present as an example my personal experience upon meeting a semi-mute after I reached my fourteenth year.

At this period there came to my school, and into my class, the semi-mute alluded to in a former chapter, a boy whom I shall call Tom Wolf. He was fourteen and had become deaf the previous year. Since the age of six he had been going to a public school for the hearing. It was his great superiority in the mastery of English and general knowledge that inspired admiration, awe, and envy, in us—the poor "dummies." He was one of the first to awaken my latent ability as a scholar. He and I were good friends and bitter enemies, by turns. At first he was not amiable, for he was disgusted with his new environment, believing, no doubt, that he had been cast into a crazy house. His sentiments on meeting his schoolmates were of withering scorn and disdainful contempt. He believed them to be too idiotic to learn anything in the class rooms. He did not realize until long afterwards the tremendous handicaps suffered by the deaf-mutes.

This Tom Wolf was an unusually smart chap; and he did a great deal in leading me on the right road to learning. One reason why he helped me to a betterment in manners and improvement in language was because he played upon my sensitiveness to ridicule. I preferred by far to be knocked down and pummelled than to be laughed at, and it was Tom's whim to be merciless in his laughing and sneering. Today I thank him.

But, alas, this disposition of mine was rare among the other scholars. The other pupils bitterly resented Tom Wolf's derision and air of superiority—detested him for a conceited "high brow"—and wiped up the floor with him. In time, Tom learned to keep his mouth shut, and to cease airing his opinions of his companions' mental calibre. He had to come down a peg or two, and effect a reconciliation in order to keep at peace and play with his schoolmates.

In spite of the deaf-mute's predicament as a scholar, he does try to learn, particularly when he finds himself under obligations to communicate with hearing people, or to write letters to home folks. As he always thinks in pictures or ideas, he tries to marshal the few words he can muster in a manner he thinks would convey what is in his mind and the results are often very strange and grotesque. Let us examine a specimen or two:

"A horse black big catch I jumped back and rided evening last yesterday."

It will be noticed that the words are arranged according to their importance in the mind of the speaker. The horse is first, its color comes next, then size, and so on to the end.

On account of his indifferent success with grammar the deaf-mute mixes his words and tenses with abandon.

"I will you head strike if no stops me trouble. If you next time second you seize collar coat throw window out."

More expressive than elegant, but quite correct in sequence of action.

Idioms, and different meanings of the same words are lost on the average deaf-mute—they slide from him like water off the back of a duck. In consequence, many an innocent, harmless situation, terminates almost tragically with him. Here is a specimen:

One day, a sweet little girl received a letter from home which threw her on the floor in convulsions. She kicked, and broke into uncontrollable sobbing and crying. After several futile attempts to pacify her, and to ascertain the cause, she declared (in signs) that she had, unintentionally, killed her dear little brother. She pointed to the accusing line in the letter, which read:

"The beautiful fountain pen you sent to Jackie tickled him to death."

Another illustration, one that happened outside the school:

A fine young man (deaf-mute) was calling on his (hearing) sweetheart. She wrote on his pad, "Make yourself at home." Whereupon he went white, jumped on his feet, quaking from head to foot, hurriedly put on his hat, and rushed out of the house, resolved never to return.

A certain deaf-mute went into a stationery store to buy some writing paper. He tried to describe with his clumsy gestures the size and kind he wanted. The clerk caught on to the meaning after a while, and wrote, "Foolscap?" An awful scrimmage followed immediately.

Should the deaf-mute become entangled with the law, he finds himself in a sorry mess, for he often gives wrong answers to puzzling questions. He will say "No," when he means just the contrary. When our legal verbiage is so complicated that many hearing persons are confused, what chance has a poor deaf-mute? Recently, in Los Angeles, one was arrested and charged with a heinous breach of law. When he was examined by the police the conversation had to be carried on in writing and he committed himself in black and white with statements that incriminated him beyond reasonable doubt. He was faced with imprisonment for fourteen years. Fortunately he secured the services of a clever interpreter, the daughter of a deaf-mute couple. After questioning him for a short time she realized that he was entirely innocent of the alleged crime. Through patient, persistent explanation she convinced the judge and the accused was set at liberty. Afterward the judge confessed he was impressed by the deaf-mute's intelligence, and could not understand how such a man could blunder in answering simple questions. Incidentally, it might be mentioned that the judge was not left with a very high opinion of the institutions that are supported by the state and expected to provide an adequate education for the deaf.

In the examples I have presented I have introduced characters whose understanding of English was on a par with my own, before the advent of Tom Wolf at my school.

• PURE ORALISM •

The pure-oralists are those so-called experts who claim that all the deaf children can be taught to articulate correctly, and speak good English, WITHOUT THE AID OF THE SIGN LANGUAGE. It is their pet theory that the sign language is a handicap to the deaf child while at school. They point the finger of scorn at examples such as I have presented in earlier chapters, and offer them as proof that the sign language makes the child think only in signs, and is responsible for his neglect of English. But they forget to state that the graduates of the oral schools are, as a rule even more deficient in English. They affect to ignore the fact that the deaf-mute child, because of his affliction, thinks from the cradle up only in pictures and ideas which, by instinct, are his most natural substitute for speech.

To you who have read closely it should now be obvious that it is not the sign language that is responsible for the poor English of the deaf-mute. His use of signs is no more to blame than is the pencil in your hand when you write.

Oralists in their efforts to suppress the use of signs practically bind the arms of the child, thereby gagging it, so it may not express itself naturally. BUT EVEN THESE METHODS CANNOT ABOLISH THE USE OF THE SIGN LANGUAGE. The attempts to suppress it hinder graceful, upright growth and development, and are worse than no schooling at all. The enlightened deaf people ascribe to the methods of the oralists the uncouth, grotesque, slovenly antics and grimaces made by children reared in their schools. These children ALWAYS invent their own signs in spite of all efforts at suppression. They are the sort that shock and prejudice the prudes against the proper and correct use of the sign language.

To be fair and just I must concede a high motive and perfect honesty of purpose to SOME of the oralists. But insofar as results are concerned one may as well concede the same to Tomas Torquemada of the infamous inquisition, or to the witch hunters, and burners of heretics. So deeprooted is the prejudice against the sign language among some classes, that it approaches a form of persecution.

Until his death, Alexander Graham Bell, the inventor of the telephone, headed the oralists. Because of his great fame, wealth, and his having been a teacher of the deaf in his youth, he was able to exert a powerful influence in spreading the propaganda of the oral method. As a matter of fact, had Mr. Bell not invented the telephone and won fame and wealth, his views on the subject would have had no more force and weight than a goose feather in a tornado, for among eminent, experienced educators of the deaf he was considered a mere tyro in this field of education.

It was Li Hung Chang, I believe, who said, "It is not WHAT is said, but WHO said it that counts." This truism also explains why we have so many misfits sitting in judgement and clothed with power to rule over the destinies of others.

In time the oralists, headed by the great Dr. Bell, drove the Combined System adherents to the wall. They were encouraged by the misguided parents who were crazy to hear their children prattle a few words more than just "papa" and "mama." For results, the semi-mute decoys were put on exhibition, where they posed as ORALLY-TAUGHT deaf and dumb pupils. At this point I must make it plain that these decoys were not aware of the use to which they were being put. They did not learn of it until long after they had left school. Then it was that they raged and fumed.

Let me proceed to explain how they teach articulation by telling a little of my own experience as an orally-taught pupil, for I became one at another school in another state.

The first steps were to make me shape my mouth so, place my tongue such and such a way, and then make a sound by studying the movements of my teacher's mouth and by passing my hands over his throat or nose. If the letter F was to be pronounced I was made to place my upper teeth on my lower lip, and then to blow at a scrap of paper lying on the back of my hand. If the letter were a V, I had to add a sound. The letters M, B, and P looked so much alike when formed by the lips that I was confused in knowing which of the three letters my teacher was asking me to articulate. The R, Ng, K, etc., were so modestly concealed within the throat, that I thought I should dive into my teacher's mouth and locate them. This entire process or method is both tedious and discouraging. I might also add that it was a bit disgusting when the teacher had partaken of onions.

You would better appreciate the difficulties of lip reading if you were to try talking with a friend without uttering a sound; or have your friend speak aloud behind a glass partition that excludes the sound of his voice. Under these conditions try to understand his message to you by watching the play of his lips. Even with the background of experience acquired by having had the use of ears and tongue in gaining an understanding of correct pronunciation and in building a vocabulary—advantages that a deaf-mute lacks—you will soon perceive the utter nonsense of educating a deaf-mute by such a method.

Some deaf-mutes do remarkably well in reading the lips. But these are the few who have devoted years and years of constant, persevering study and practice. But even they cannot understand every word spoken, unless the subject is commonplace and they are able to catch the key words and then guess the rest. To accomplish all this the individual must be prepared to neglect other branches of learning, such as History, Literature, Languages, Science, etc. Furthermore, he must come of a family who have the means to support him throughout the years. But what about the others who have to go to work for a living? Certainly the institutions supported by the state are not for the small number of prodigies who have the means to devote their life to study.

While taking my lessons in articulation, I learned that very few words in English are pronounced as they are spelt. I found that gh must be pronounced like f—laugh–laff; enough–enuff; league–leeg, and so on without number. To succeed under this condition I would have to carry a pronouncing dictionary under my arm, and break off in my conversation to hunt the word and find out how it should be enunciated.

The best lip reader requires certain well-defined conditions to read even tolerably well. The speaker must face him in a good light, at a distance of not more than fifteen feet, and move his lips broadly, slowly, and deliberately. Let the speaker turn his head sideways, talk a little too fast, or mumble carelessly, and it is goodnight so far as the listener is concerned. If a speaker attempts to address an assembly of lip readers, he may as well harangue to a blank wall. If he reads aloud out of a book it will be equally futile.

The semi-mute dislikes lip reading more than does the deaf-mute. It is no doubt the inability of the semi-mute to equal the deaf-mute as a lip reader that is responsible for this. The reason the deaf-mute is his superior is because of his keenness of sight. This may be the operation of the law of compensation of which we often hear. But when it comes to speaking orally the semi-mute is superior to the deaf-mute. There are, of course, exceptions to this general rule—but they are few.

I met several soldiers who were deafened by explosions. They carried pads and pencils with which to carry on conversation. They preferred this method to learning lip reading. Does this need any explanation?

If there exists any deaf-mute who had been taught orally and who can pass as a hearing person, I must say that I have never seen or read of him. If you have heard of such, I can safely bet that the odds are a thousand to one that the person is a semi-mute.

I remember how ambitious I was to learn to articulate, and my teachers thought pretty well of my abilities. My voice, I believe, was no worse than that of the average deaf-mute (at least it was not harsh enough to make a trolley car jump its tracks), but I could never learn to pronounce correctly, to modulate my voice or to make it sound natural. I cannot, even now, make my B sound different from P, my D differ from T, and my R is always missing. Because of these deficiencies I often make queer blunders that either amuse or disgust my hearers. Let me relate an incident or two to illustrate the "brilliant" results of my education in articulation:

I made a social call on a lady friend while she was giving a tea party to a large circle of acquaintances. She was on the point of sending her maid to make some purchases when it occurred to me that I wanted a package of cigarettes. I asked her if I could have the maid bring me a box of a brand then in vogue called "Duke's Best." I spoke vocally. To my astonishment the whole company broke out laughing. Upon my request to be enlightened, she reluctantly told me that I pronounced my request like this:

"Pleeze keet me a-ah pox of dogs pest."

At another time and place I tried vocally to deliver my holiday greetings: "I wish you a Merry Christmas." In spite of my efforts the sentence sounded like:

"Eye wisch yeo-u a-ah Mary kiss my—"

My mistakes, deplorable though they were, were mild and innocuous compared to those made by others—some of which are downright obscene—though not so intended by the speaker. Under such conditions can you imagine how women feel about it when they learn how such blunders have changed the meaning of their speech. You can appreciate why they would blush with mortification, and disappear. After such experiences no amount of entreaty, persuasion or threats can persuade them to again open their mouths to utter another word in public this side of eternity. All their long years of toil in school, all their sacrifices of subjects more worth while than oral speech and lip reading, are for nothing.

I could go on interminably citing other examples of the disastrous results of the present system of "education;" but I will bring this chapter to a close with one more tale— one that is almost unthinkable.

For the moment I shall stuff your ears with wax so you cannot hear a sound, and I shall ask you to imagine yourself a deaf-mute, my pupil, whom I am teaching by the oral method. I must also ask that you have never heard music before. Now I take you into a room where for the first time you see a Paderewski seated before a piano, playing one of the classics. I command you to watch sharply. Next I urge you to lay your hands on the piano to feel the vibrations. You obey me because I am your master, ready to reward or punish you. I insist that your eyes must become your ears. My deepest regret is that I cannot help you to smell the music. You watch the pianist move his hands gracefully across the keyboard and watch his nimble fingers as they strike the keys. He brings his hands down with a thundering crash. Then his fingers and hands barely move as he comes to an andante passage. His body seems to swing and sway rhythmically. After this performance I make you sit before the piano and order you to reproduce the same composition as accurately, and with the same musical taste as he rendered it. You will fail at first. But you must not become discouraged. Brace up, and try it again. You will win out at the end of fifteen, twenty-five, or maybe a thousand years. IT WILL BE YOUR OWN FAULT IF YOU FAIL!

This you say is ridiculous. Oh, no! No more ridiculous than the extravagant claims made by some of the oralists as to their ability to teach the deaf children any and all things, and so well that they will be fully restored to the society of hearing people.

• THE GRADUATE •

Today the deaf-mute graduates and goes into the world poorly equipped and prepared for the task of taking care of himself. During his life at school, every one of his actions have been regulated by rules designed more for the benefit of his teachers than for himself. He has so long been denied the right to think for himself that he is now an automation with no initiative of his own. He is conscious that in leaving school he is "free," but he does not know what to do with his freedom. He is dazed. He feels like the long-term prisoner or slave suddenly liberated from captivity. With the habit of childlike dependence upon others bred into his soul, he seeks sympathy and help from his fellow-unfortunates. Usually he is guided to the parsonage of some Church for the Deaf, where the parson is a deaf man with a sympathetic understanding of his kind. After looking into the case with care, this good parson tries to find employment for the graduate, a heart-breaking task, because of the deep-rooted prejudice against employing deaf-mutes. Unless the graduate is more skillful than the average hearing man doing the same kind of work, it goes pretty hard with him.

The school he just left teaches several trades, such as tailoring, baking, printing, cabinet-making, carpentry, shoemaking, and a few others; but the methods taught are all so antiquated that the pupils are seldom able to handle modern tools or machines. The schools cannot be blamed for this, for industry is constantly introducing new machinery and methods, and the schools have not the finances to follow suit. The one I attended had a large printing equipment. It was set up over sixty years ago, and has been changed but slightly since then. The graduate from that shop had to begin as a "printer's devil," and learn all over again.

But a small percentage of the graduates follow the trades they learned at school. The majority, unless they have well-to-do relatives to help them, are half starved before they become proficient at a trade that does not call for the use of the English language.

A few deaf-mutes possess talent for highly skilled work like Commercial Art, Carving in wood, clay or marble, Architectural Draughting, Decorative Painting, Illustrating. This is found even among the most illiterate. But the poor devil is up against it good and plenty if he is ignorant of English while working at one of these arts. Sometimes he is employed on trial. He receives in writing instructions as to what he is to do. Often he cannot understand them. If he turns to his fellow-workers for explanation, he finds that none of them know the sign language, and therefore cannot help him. He scratches his head, makes wild guesses, and goes ahead, taking desperate chances. He makes mistakes. The boss tears his hair and kicks him out, vowing never again to employ another "dummy." This poor "dummy" then has to give up his cherished vocation, and wash dishes, help the janitor, scrub floors, or undertake some other form of menial labor.

Is it not a pity that he did not find a boss who could understand the sign language? If he had, both might have prospered together happily. But, alas, such employers are as scarce as hens' teeth.

There are, today, many graduates from Gallaudet College working side by side at manual labor, with deaf-mutes from Russia, Poland, Germany, Italy, and other countries, who can scarcely scrawl their own names. They grumble at their lot, and ask, with wonder, what is the use of higher education, if all it fits one for is making bed-springs, auto tires, etc. Often the foreigner draws higher wages. Many of them never went to any school, but they did receive thorough training at some trade like tailoring, cutting garments, carving, engraving on copper, stone or steel, and similar trades that require extraordinary dexterity.

There are rare cases where genius, by sheer force of ambition, pride or unusual opportunities, overcomes all handicaps and rises in spite of, not because of, institutional life and training. It is also strange that most of the artists among the deaf are found in Europe, where schools for their kind are few and considered inferior to those in this country.

The deaf-mute does not wish to be an object for compassion. He craves neither pity nor charity. Should you be approached by anyone extending his hand to you for alms on account of his deafness, it is high time for you to yell for the police, for the chances are ninety-nine out of one hundred that the pan-handler is an imposter. The deaf-mute has pride and believes himself as good as any man alive. All he asks for, nay, DEMANDS, as his birthright, is to be respected and treated as an equal and be given an equal chance in this life. He does not want to be discriminated against because of his impediment.

• ALEXANDER GRAHAM BELL •

I was fortunate in having had for my father an artist—a lithographer to be exact. He took me out of school when I

was sixteen, which is five years earlier than is usually allotted to a pupil for graduation. I am certain it was this
step that saved me from becoming a confirmed dummy,
because the older one grows, the harder it is for him to
change acquired habits. But my father did not take me from
school because he mistrusted the system. He simply decided that I could not begin any too soon to learn drawing
and painting, for he desired me to become a painter of
pictures. He put me in the studio of an Italian artist, and
also had me attend Cooper's Union in New York. A year
later, I entered the studio of the great H. Humphrey Moore.

To me it was indeed a strange world. I could not have
felt more different if I had been magically transported to
another planet. After some intimate association with hearing people, mostly art students, I began to perceive that I
was different from them in endless ways. At first I was
positive I was right, and they dead wrong. I was stubborn
in adhering to the odd ways of thinking and acting, which
I had acquired while at school. I wondered, with a sinking
heart, why I was shunned and left severely alone. I had to
go through much pondering before I realized it was I who
was at fault—that I was a thorough-going dummy in my
habits, behavior, ideas, language, character, outlook on life—
all of which made me repulsive to my new acquaintances.

It was the perseverance of my family who had by this
time learned enough of the manual alphabet to talk with
me, that helped me to mend my ways. But it proved a slow
process for I had to unlearn what I had been taught and
acquired at school, and it is human nature for one to cling
tenaciously to early acquired prejudices and habits. Frankly,
I rejoice that I left school while very young, while my mind
was still flexible enough to absorb new and better influences. The known effect of childhood impressions on later

life should convince the serious-minded of the need of the right schooling for the deaf.

As I manifested signs of talent in my art work, some rich relatives sent me to Europe for intensive study. There I lived for three full years without meeting a single deaf-mute. I did not purposely avoid them. I merely did not seek them out; and I never missed their company.

On the third day after my arrival in Paris, I was sauntering along the beautiful Avenue des Champs-Elysees. My eye caught the sign, "Restaurant Ledoyen." Without further ado I strolled inside. With cheerful nonchalance, I ordered a sumptuous repast, including a full quart bottle of heady old wine.

As was to be expected, the fumes went to my head, and all objects around me swam and floated giddily. Finally I gesticulated to my waiter to make out my bill. My gestures attracted the attention of a fine looking, portly, black bearded man sitting at a table just behind mine. He beckoned my waiter, and asked him if I were a deaf-mute. Upon receiving the latter's affirmative nod, he walked over and seated himself at my table. At first he spoke orally. I shook my head, and pointed to my ear—the sign a deaf man usually makes to indicate his impediment.

"Parlez-vous francais?" spelt he on his fingers.

I again shook my head.

"Are you English?"

I shook my head emphatically, and spelled on my fingers, "I'm an American!"

"So am I." He laughed and shook my hand. Then he gave me his card. I could not read the fine print, it was too blurred by the alcoholic fumes in my head. I nodded gravely as if I understood and put it in my vest pocket. Then I handed him my card.

After some desultory conversation through which I fumbled foolishly, I begged his pardon for my appearance, remarking that I was not accustomed to European climate.

"Yes, I can see that plainly enough," he laughed.

I tried to rise, but my legs wobbled, and I sank helplessly back into my chair. I had to ask him to kindly pay my bill, handing him my pocketbook, saying, "I can't make out these silly pale blue French bank notes!"

He courteously complied with my request. Moreover, he ordered a fiacre, and brought me to my hotel. Thereafter all was a blank until I recovered consciousness next morning and found myself in my hotel room, suffering from a ringing headache. I recalled the meeting with a fellow countryman, and jumping out of bed I sought his card. It read "Alexander Graham Bell."

Oh, oh!

The next day I received a note from him, inviting me to join him at dinner at his hotel.

"Are you acclimated?" were his words of greeting upon my arrival. What a jolly host he was. What a glorious evening I spent with him. Afterward he was fond of recounting to others the ludicrous manner by which we met. I usually countered by twitting him over his use of the sign language, which he affected to detest, but which was responsible for bringing us together.

I saw him several times while in Paris; we parted company when I moved on to Rome. But within the month he was in Rome and we met again—and several times thereafter. He was, I learned, on the point of setting out for Egypt with his family, consisting of his lovely wife who was as deaf as I, two sweet daughters, one of three and the other five, their maids, governesses, private secretary, valets de place, valets de chambre, guides, footmen, etc., (mostly the etc.). Included in the party was his venerable father, Melville Bell, who had prepared charts, with diagrams of the tongue, lips, throat, nose and other organs of speech. His object was to describe their positions in speech and thereby assist in teaching articulation to deaf children. The party was later increased by the arrival of Col. J. Gardiner Hubbard, Dr. Bell's father-in-law, and his own retinue. What an immense company. I asked the doctor if he were aware how much the jaunt to Egypt would cost him. He acted as if he were alarmed, and asked me how much it would. I exclaimed, "Why, it can't be less than $10 a day for each person." I counted fifteen in his party alone, and added, "Oh, fully $150." He pretended to be dismayed and turned to consult his secretary for a few minutes; after which he assured me, "He (meaning the secretary) tells me that we are getting about $100,000 a month. I guess we can stand the racket." I was so dumbfounded that I blurted out, "If that's true, you can certainly include me in your party!"

"Sure," he answered, "Come along if you like!"

But that trip was never undertaken, for shortly afterwards both his daughters were stricken with scarlet fever, and they were very ill indeed. In fact they nearly lost their hearing. This illness detained the family at Rome for three months. When the children recovered, it was then too late in the season to continue to Egypt. They turned north towards Nice and from there on home to America.

Their stay in Rome afforded me opportunities to become more intimate with the doctor. He was always busy, trying to invent something else. He had, at the moment, a bulky mass of machinery or apparatus. He said that he was trying to produce sound by light.

"To make the deaf hear by light?" I facetiously inquired.

"No, no! I don't know yet to what purpose it may be put, if successful. All great inventions are like children, we never can tell what they will turn out to be until they are grown."

His favorite hours of labor were during the night from 8:30 to 4 a.m. "Until five or six when my wife is not looking on," he used to say with a merry wink.

I should record now that there never existed a more gracious, more affable, more fun-loving or jollier fellow on this sorry old globe than Dr. Bell. His character was without blemish. Still, it does not necessarily follow that his ideas or judgement on all things was infallible. In criticizing his theories on the education of the deaf, I have not the slightest intention to impute insincerity on his part. He was absolutely honest in his beliefs. But his beliefs were, in my opinion, and the opinion of many others, altogether wrong. His love and sympathy for the deaf were boundless, and should never be questioned. He spent a considerable part of his wealth and time on his favorite theory concerning the deaf. It was his hobby. Still, his expenditures and energies were, I believe, sadly misspent. In fact they have brought misery to the ones he loved and wanted most to help.

Though a confirmed pure-oralist, Dr. Bell was a fluent talker on his fingers—as good as any deaf-mute—and could use his fingers and arms with bewitching grace and ease. His wife was charming, beautiful and intelligent. Though a DEAF-MUTE in the sense I have defined, she was a comparatively fine lip reader. But it is with regret that I cannot say one word in praise of her articulation. Even today I find it difficult to convince others that she could not spell on her fingers or make signs. I never saw her do either. In conversing with her, I moved my mouth without making any sound, and she always answered IN WRITING; an anomaly of social intercourse between two deaf-mutes. She understood every word I spoke, if I moved my mouth broadly, deliberately, and if the topics were commonplace. One evening I begged Dr. Bell to spell orally one word, to see if she could catch it. I selected FUJIYAMA (the holy mountain of Japan). He rebelled, explaining that that word was foreign. But finally he yielded to my entreaty. He took her on his lap, and pronounced each letter slowly and repeatedly, "F. ef, not ve, just fu, fu—eye, ah ah—ama." It took him some minutes, but she later succeeded in spelling the whole word correctly in writing.

He turned around to me with a triumphant light in his eyes, and smiled as though to say, "Now you see!"

I shrugged and spelt on my fingers, "Why waste minutes, when spelling the word on the fingers will take but seconds?" He also shrugged, and waved aside my sly thrust as inconsequential. Then began a heated argument:

"That is a mere persiflage in contradiction of the psychoanalysis and final diagnosis of the vertical parallelogram on the reasoning, as differentiated from the horizontal—and—"

These are not his exact words, but to me they sounded equally intricate and involved. Perhaps you, too, have encountered some learned pedagogue who obscured his arguments with unintelligible, scientific jargon. Like myself, you were probably ashamed of your ignorance, and of your inability to pay back in like coin. Therefore you assumed an air of wisdom and answered, "You are right—perfectly right, my dear Sir. I understand perfectly." Then glancing at your watch you added: "But please excuse me. I've an important engagement. Good night!" And then you scooted.

I "scooted" that night. I was so young and inexperienced—twenty—that I could not possibly answer such a torrent of eloquence. But in my heart I was not at all convinced by his argument. Then and there I resolved not to again hurt his feelings and bring upon my head another avalanche of jaw-breaking words.

• THE SIGN LANGUAGE BEAUTIFUL •

For many years, more for amusement than for any serious purpose, I improvised some new features for the sign language. They were along the lines of picture painting in the air. You may recall what I said about the habit of deaf-mutes, from infancy, thinking only in pictures. The transition from pictures to signs is, for me, so smooth and natural that I always preferred signs to writing—a habit from which I have never entirely broken away. In fact, I can always express through signs in five minutes what would take me a whole day of racking, mental wrestling to translate into words. In the end, my words would not be one-tenth as graphic. To me self expression in words has been hopelessly difficult. I have found I am not the only deaf-mute in this position.

When you learn the sign language, as I hope you will, you will be astonished to find how much more readily you can express your ideas. Words will seem slow and ponderous. When you become an expert you will be able to spell the alphabet as fast manually as orally.

The true sign language is nothing more or less than DRAWING PICTURES IN THE AIR. A careless, slouchy sign maker will make poor pictures with his hands, fingers, arms and facial expressions. A carefully trained "speaker" goes through his gestures deliberately and artistically. His pictures then become plain and are pleasant to look upon. The better he draws in the air, the more beautiful and more impressive become his pictures.

The pure sign language is as different from the slang as the awkward gambols of a waltzing elephant from the graceful, airy undulations of a Pavlova.

In spite of the stifling atmosphere of institutional life, the deaf do not lose their instinct for rhythm.

If you should attend a ball or social gathering of the deaf where dancing is indulged, you will be surprised to find a number of them going through a Fox Trot with grace and rhythm. Then you ask how they do it without hearing music. Someone may tell you that they feel vibrations through the floor. This in my opinion is sheer nonsense. They are guided solely by imagination and a latent sense of rhythm.

Many of the deaf are fond of rendering in signs, songs and hymns. They perform according to instinct, without training or coaching from artists. Lack of culture makes their "singing in signs" unsatisfactory. They believe they must "sign" the verses as they are printed—word for word. What they should do is to communicate ideas and not emasculate their expressions and emotions by an attempt to follow words.

Shortly before I married I became acquainted with a clever teacher of the Delsarte System of Expression and Pantomime. While there is no resemblance between it and the Sign Language of the Deaf, we both recognized good points in the two methods. We even undertook to blend the two. After some rehearsals we succeeded in a measure that won enthusiastic comment from hearing audiences.

I adopted this new combination as a child to raise and nurture. I improvised gestures that were a combination of the language of the deaf, and the "signs" of the Indians, Italians, French, etc. I tried to make them take the form of well defined pictures, without sacrificing expression or emotion. My aim was to make them intelligible to everyone, even to those who had seen stories rendered in signs.

By the time my oldest child reached her eighth year, I had taught her to sing in signs the hymn, NEARER, MY GOD, TO THEE , using the sign method that I had worked out. I made her blend one gesture into another, until every verse resembled what we might call "visible music." It was not dissimilar to the rhythm of Greek dancing.

Confident that she could render the hymn in public, I had her "speak" at a few Church gatherings of the hearing. As to the results, I will quote from articles that appeared in newspapers:

The most impressive rendering of NEARER, MY GOD, TO THEE, that the writer has ever witnessed, was by little Marion Ballin. I have seen it rendered by past masters of Delsartan gestures, and of our own beautiful language of signs, but none has approached the reverential beauty and grace given by little Miss Ballin. (*Deaf-Mutes Journal*, May, 1905.)

I have heard from a dozen different sources how a little eight-year-old girl, the hearing daughter of a deaf-mute father, an unusually gifted sign maker and brilliant thinker, and the mother, also a gifted woman, and a highly rated musician, made an audience of deaf people gasp in astonishment when she recited, in signs, the hymn, NEARER, MY GOD, TO THEE, accompanied on the piano by her mother. Those who saw the really wonderful exhibition, say that they never saw anything like it before, and that no deaf-mute, to whom the language of signs comes most natural, ever approached her in grace, ease or clearness.

But it is not to be wondered at, for the child inherits from her parents all the characteristics of both. She makes signs as graphically as her father does, and from the music her mother furnished, she infused melody into her expression. (Fragment of an article by Alex. L. Pach, in the *Silent Worker*, June, 1905.)

On other occasions I recited songs, such as LOCHINVAR, STAR SPANGLED BANNER, etc. In paraphrasing THE MARSEILLAISE I chose the original French version by Captain Rouget de l'Isle. I believe I succeeded in my attempt to make of it a real motion picture. You know that a painting on canvas, if skillfully executed, needs no translation into any other language. It is a poor artist who has to put on a label.

The following quotations speak for themselves:

. . . Mr. Ballin's hands flashed with a dramatic gesture as he opened the meeting with THE MARSEILLAISE in the sign language. He rocked the babe in his arms and rolled up the tyrant in a ball and cast him out from the stage with such violence that a little man chewing a cigar in the front row nearly swallowed the butt in his terror.

Mr. Ballin called the citizens together with a magnificent sweep of his hand that thrilled the audience and ended with a vivid piece of acting which brought a burst of applause from his listeners.

. . . And after the banquet, Mrs. Terry introduced a visitor from New York—Albert Ballin, a brilliantly dramatic deaf-mute, who kept them in ecstasies of delight with his busy fingers, and "sang" them THE MARSEILLAISE with such dramatic gestures that I vow I could hear the marching feet, the beating of the drums, the war cries of the French, and see the flag in the breeze.

The "speaker" also had considerable to say about the numerous signs and gestures of the directors, actors and their hearing audiences, which often mean something different to the deaf. He considered it the duty of the industry to study the language of the deaf—

many of which are infinitely more interpretive of the real emotions than the forms now in use to portray the silent drama. (Alma Whitaker, in the *Los Angeles Times*, May 11, 1924.)

• COMING TO CALIFORNIA •

With high hopes and ambition, I packed what little I possessed in wordly goods into my grip, and boarded the good ship, FINLAND, to sail for California, the home of our beloved Cinema Child.

Some deaf friends came to wave me God-speed on my hazardous venture. Here I must mention a feature that is often seen, but whose significance is seldom considered. As the ship was unmoored, and started on her long voyage, her passengers and their friends on the dock were yelling their parting farewells, using their hands as megaphones; but all their vocal exchanges were drowned by the steam sirens, clanging bells, stentorian orders of the ship-officers, shouts of the seamen, and the general bedlam. My deaf friends and I were never harassed by this ear-splitting clamor. For us it did not exist. We went on conversing, using our fingers and arms, missing not one word. I believe the last message I flashed off on my fingers was:

"You can see that our deafness is a blessing in disguise. Now we have the laugh on the hearing, and can pity their helplessness? What?"

Came the answer:

"Right you are, old man! Bon voyage and good luck to you!"

Our conversation was soon cut short by the warping of the ship around to the other side. We could have gone on talking at a distance far beyond ear-shot. Our system was far better than that of the signal wig-wagging of sailors on a war-ship.

I now propose to plunge into an account of my adventures in the motion picture world.

I received a splendid welcome at the Ince Studio (now Pathe). Mr. Ince knew and appreciated my purpose in coming, and gave me complete freedom of the studio, and facilities to study all details at close range. I visited other studios where I was welcomed and assisted in my work. From that time dates my affiliation with the industry. I served as a writer for periodicals and magazines, teacher of signs to the acting fraternity, and as a painter of portraits. At various times I was used as an actor in minor bits. In fact, were I to permit myself to digress, I could fill several volumes with accounts of my interesting experiences.

One of the most striking curiosities, a downright anomaly in this industry, is the utter lack of directors who can talk fluently on their fingers. I searched diligently, and found only one. He spells slowly and rheumatically on his fingers, and no more. All the directors I have met are friendly, very fine gentlemen, supremely clever in their work. Nevertheless, it does look odd from my point of view that they should not know this sign language—THE LANGUAGE SO NECESSARY TO PICTURE-MAKING.

With the exception of two or three actors, like the late Lon Chaney, who are children of deaf-mute parents, practically everyone connected with the industry, from the highest producer down to the lowly sweeper, is blissfully (?) ignorant of the sign language. Lon Chaney declared in published articles that he was thankful for his knowledge of signs, and believed that much of his success was due to that knowledge.

In watching the production of pictures, I noticed a great deal of waste in time and money because of this lack of knowledge of signs. The following is an illustration:

I witnessed a scene where the heroine was fleeing in an automobile. She was crouching at the wheel, turning her head every minute or two to watch her pursuers. The car was actually at a standstill. In the background was a canvas with pictures of fields, trees, shrubbery, telegraph poles, turning swiftly on revolving cylinders, to give the illusion that the car was moving. To intensify the illusion, four men, two at either end, jumped up and down on planks attached to the car, making it appear is if the car were driving along a rough road. In front of the car out of camera range, a motor driven propeller blew wind at the car, fluttering the heroine's hair and ribbons in the breeze. The illusion of the car rushing at full speed turned out perfectly on the screen. By an oversight, the girl's hair and ribbons were stuck fast inside her coat. The director bellowed directions through his megaphone, ordering her to loosen her hair and ribbons; but the din created by the aeroplane machine was too deafening for her to hear him. He had to stop the camera, walk up to her, and explain what he wanted; and then make a retake.

At the conclusion, I wrote on my pad. "You are a h--- of a director. If you knew how, you could have made signs to the girl to loosen her hair and be spared the retake."

The director, a good-natured friend, glared at me; then his scowling features melted into a broad grin. He nodded admission that I was just in my criticism.

I also saw mob scenes, cow-boys and soldiers shooting guns, houses on fire, battle scenes and other scenes that produced terrific din, drowning all vocal orders. In the handling of such scenes, signs would have been invaluable.

The time may come when we shall have no more use for directors or players who are ignorant of the sign language than we would for carpenters who don't know the use of a hammer or saw.

At a certain studio, during a dissertation on my favorite topic, I made some remarks, characterizing the bulk of motion pictures as rank bunk, insulting the intelligence of the American people. One actor laughingly declared that "stories are written by, of, and for dumb-bells." The director retorted, "about eighty per cent of the American people are morons, the class that pays and supports the movies; we have put across some highbrow stuff (naming several truly great stories), and they were financial failures." Another actor nodded gravely and added, "We have to cater to the tastes of the morons or go out of business altogether."

There is a good deal of sense in these remarks, when viewed from the old, unsound theory that most people are low in mentality and tastes. But the accusation is erroneous. I must repeat my conclusions, that the great majority of the people are really intelligent; but too many, about sixty per cent, are "unschooled" in the sense I have already defined.

Those who cannot read the words thrown on the screen lose the story—they become disgusted and bored, and, thereafter refuse to see such shows. This has been plainly proved by the crowds that flock to see Charlie Chaplin's pictures. Those he had made fifteen years ago are popular today. They are pictures—NOT WORDS. The bunk offered by some producers will always keep away self-respecting spectators who can read. Ignoring the fundamental causes of diminishing box office receipts, many producers have the idea that they can repair the damage by offering pictures that are sillier and more salacious. They act like the man who fell into quick-sand—the harder he struggled the faster he would sink. Hence the poor Cinema is becoming anaemic and sickly.

There has boomed suddenly into our midst an innovation

called the TALKIE, which reproduces the human voice, music and all sounds. The producers and exhibitors have scrambled after it headlong, spending hundreds of millions with a lavish hand. Though far from perfected, the device, like a mother-in-law, is likely to remain with us. Now that oral speech has reached the screen it is expected to help the box office. It may for a time—but will it last? Will the success be permanent? I doubt it. We are still in a hysterical mood; a natural sequence after the Great War. The instant success of the "Talkie" does, however, show the need of a substitute for the endless WORDS that formerly were written on the screen. Speech does help a goodly number of the so-called "unschooled." It also succeeds in driving away all the deaf and hard-of-hearing. And how these bemoan the passing of the silent movie. It was counted among their few blessings. It entertained and helped to keep them cheerful. "But it brings in the blind," remarked a publicity man to me. Smart of him, perhaps, but he forgets that the deaf pay admission fees; the blind don't.

The "Talkie" restricts theatre attendance to those understanding the one language. It turns away those to whom the tongue is foreign. It may be all right, even commendable, to utilize music and all other appropriate sounds to enhance illusions of reality, but we can very well eliminate monologues, dialogues and all orally spoken words that have to be translated into many tongues to reach the world. At the best, dialogue retards and slows down action, one of the greatest charms of motion pictures. The Cinema will fall short of its ideal if it does not make itself universal; and it can never be universal unless it is understood everywhere on the globe.

We have been living in the jazz age too long; we are exhausted, sick of the incessant clamor worthy only of savages. Does the Talkie threaten us with more just when we are beginning to yearn after repose?

When we sit down to read and enjoy a story, the book in our hands does not shriek from every page with all varieties of type-screaming capitals, italics, copious foot-notes. It would irritate and disgust us and we would throw it into the fireplace. A good story is best when couched in plain, clean type, clearly and simply phrased, leaving plenty of room for imagination. Many of the old silent pictures have been eminently successful; they linger in our memories like good books. It is the kind of work that we ought to preserve and improve.

Charlie Chaplin, the famous comedian, knows a good deal about the signs and makes excellent use of them without making of them a distinct language. You never see him open his mouth to utter one syllable; his sub-titles are few and short. We know he regrets having to use any at all. His pictures are, in consequence, never in need of translation. From them he has made a fortune that he well deserves.

As I was penning the above lines, I came across an article entitled, "Charlie Chaplin Attacks the Talkies." It appears in the magazine, *Motion Pictures*, for May, 1929. I am quoting from it:

"You can tell 'em I loathe them," he said. "They are spoiling the oldest art in the world—the art of pantomime. They are ruining the great beauty of silence. They are defeating the meaning of the screen, the appeal that has created the star system, the fan system, the vast popularity of the whole—the appeal of beauty. It is beauty that matters in pictures—nothing else. The screen is pictorial. Pictures. I am not using the talkies in my new picture. I am never going to use them. For me, it would be fatal. I can't understand why anyone who can possibly avoid it, does use it; Harold Lloyd, for instance."

Mr. Chaplin knows his subject thoroughly and can speak about it with authority. Frankly, I count him one of the staunchest supporters of the movement this book proposes to launch. We need the influence of a few more men like him to help overcome the ignorance and baseless prejudices that handicap progress.

In speaking of the ignorance on this subject, let me separate it from the indifference that is responsible for what the deaf-mute is and for woes that pursue him throughout his whole life. To make clear the presence of this ignorance among those supposed to possess intelligence, I will relate an experience in one of the studios where I met many who were most learned, and generous.

When I first met the very charming Miss Betty Compson, she asked me, during an interview:

"Can you read the lips?"

I answered, "No, I can't."

"Why not?" she demanded.

My reply was, "Can you spell on your fingers?"

"No," came the quick response.

I smiled, as I repeated her own words, "Why not?"

"Why should I?" she asked. "I never meet any deaf people."

When I did not answer she continued, "Let me tell you that I have a very dear friend who is a great actress on both the stage and screen. She was so sensitive when her hearing became affected that she learned to read lips so well that nobody knows about her trouble. Her name is Louise D——."

(I felt like saying, Oh, Louise, how can you read the lips when your back is turned, or when the klieg lights are in your eyes? How can you read the lips of your director when his mouth is hidden behind a megaphone? It is difficult enough for anyone to pretend to be a deaf-mute; but for a deaf person to conduct herself as one who hears—well, it has me stumped. But I could not embarrass sweet Betty with inquiries along such lines.)

"That is very fine," I replied, "How old was she when her hearing began to fail?"

"I am not sure. Perhaps thirty."

"You see," I explained, "she could hear and talk like you until she was thirty, and then lip reading was all she had to learn. You don't seem to realize that it takes a deaf child fifteen, twenty, sometimes even twenty-five years of hardest labor, and the sacrifice of all other branches of learning to even attempt to talk orally and to read the lips. Even after years of study and work he is likely to fail in the end. All these years are given to save you and those like you some thirty minutes of your whole life. Is it fair to ask this of the deaf when a few minutes would enable you to spell on your fingers and communicate with him?"

Betty looked surprised and pained. She turned to speak with her friends. Then she wrote on my pad with tears trickling down the pencil point:

"We never looked at the thing in that light before. I am so ashamed of myself and beg your pardon."

Like most others, she was merely ignorant of this much-slighted subject. I meet others like her every day, innocent and perfectly sincere in asking me the same questions—never suspecting that they are asking a question no less absurd than, "Can you dance blindfolded on a swinging rope in a stormy night?"

It has taken me a year to compile this book, after almost a lifetime of careful thinking. During the years I have repeatedly been asked the question that was put to me by Miss Compson. It is rather discouraging.

When I first met Mary Pickford, she also asked me this heart-breaking question, "Can you read the lips?" I hope to be forgiven for replying, "No, I only kiss them when they are sweet like yours." Of course, she excused me by laughing merrily.

Muted Voices
by Eugene Relgis

EDITORS' PREFACE

In this chapter from Relgis' fictionalized autobiography, we see Miron (Relgis' stand-in) experiencing the first day in the world as a deaf person. The prose reflects the disorientation that one experiences with the loss of hearing. Miron's former friends, seeing him acting in a strange way, begin to attack him as beasts of prey would a wounded game animal, and it is Miron's reaction to his torment that provides the high point of this chapter.

Miron reacts in a way that is similar to the reactions of other deaf characters included in this anthology, be they fictional or biographical characters, and in a way that we have pointed to consistently—it is the reaction of proud and angry defiance. From the story at the beginning of the book by de Musset, where we find some sense of defiance toward the feelings of isolation and frustration of exclusion from so many things , to the story of the talking horse near the end of the book, where Abramowitz rebels in the end to set himself free, from start to finish and everywhere in between there is defiance—the refusal to buckle under, the upwelling of human dignity, the choice of freedom over victimization.

Arguing for defiance is the one most consistent theme in the book, and the reaction that all authors seem to point to as the solution to affliction of all sorts. As Hemingway has pointed out, man can be destroyed, but he cannot be defeated. It is this rebellious spirit that we find in Gerasim, in Gargan, in Ballin, in Wiggins, in Kitto, and in Relgis (via

Miron). Miron is taunted, physically abused, is down on the ground, his head in a swirl, tears in his eyes, caught in a nightmare of horrors, yet he rebels defiantly, stands and walks away with his head in the air. It is this spirit which is the salvation of all deaf people (Defoe's deaf hero Duncan Campbell had it in large measure as does Sampson Trehune, the deaf detective in *The Acupuncture Murders*). It is this spirit that modern authors see as the salvation of all people living in our time, and it is for this reason, perhaps, that deaf characters have grown so numerous in the last quarter century.

FROM MUTED VOICES

• THE TEARS OF REVIVAL •

From the threshold of the door Miron gazes into the street. Supported on one hand, his head a little bowed, he remains as though on the edge of a precipice, hesitating to go on. The street frightens him. It no longer wears its former pleasant aspect; the houses no longer have their air of familiarity with indulgent or smiling aspects; the gates seem severe, isolating the flowering gardens; the orchards heavy with fruit where together with his playmates he gave free course to his illusions and his ectasies. He glances to the left—and the facades of the houses seem like the dams of some dried-up, dusty canal, burying itself among other heaps of somber masses above which the sterile hill sheds rivers of pulverized stone. He looks to the right—and, over the street he sees the vault of the foliage of chestnut-trees. A green confusion; the jumbled sensation becomes irritating when his glance settles upon the large waves of the beech-wood, beyond the horizon; and the forest seems hostile to him.

Things are no longer animated by the fervent imagination; his glances no longer probe to their core; his childish senses no longer drink from thousands of springs. Everything rests immobile beneath the triumphant sun. Throughout the serenity of his convalescence the same irritating sensation whispers: Why is the street dull and the forest void of lure? A faint odor of slow decay emanates from all sides. How distant does his life of yester-year seem to him! However, he recalls nothing precisely. It was as though he had strayed across enchanted lands; the picture of happiness fell away like golden motes falling among rays. Remnants of dreams vaguely palpitated in his breast. Scarcely comprehended calls vibrated within him, but he no longer sees them in surrounding things. Why does everything seem to him passive, exhausted, enigmatic?

And the sun pours down its torrid heat. A crushing silence reigns over all; the very air seems to grow heavier and heavier and with its overheated miasmas it seems to paralyze the murmurs from the gardens and the woods. Silence crawls along the dust of the street. Everything irritates him; the vehicles, the carriages, the men passing near him like apparitions. Something seems lacking even in them. Something which was inseparable at every step, every expression, every turn. Men and vehicles pass silently and the pavement does not resound nor do the walls prolong any echo. Why at this hour when the daily work begins, does not the factory-whistle ring out any longer strident and imperious?

Everything is enervated with the heat; the fatigued glances of Miron plunge into the cloudless sky; how empty that sky is—like a glassbell under which forgotten flowers slowly wither. . . . His irritation increases. Shudders run through his legs, a weakness softens his organs and more and more does he feel a lump in his throat which forces him to breathe quickly and deeply. He pants—and a transitory giddiness makes everything around him waver. Within the heart of Miron this sadness increases. Something agonizing, dark, lamentable insinuates itself within him. He is not yet aware of his sadness—the tenacious chimera which flutters its wings before his face and irritates his nerves is repaid with blood. He knows her not as yet, the dark goddess, but he feels as though her empire has been extended to the most hidden recess of his being.

And the street is sad, and the woods equally so, and the passersby also seem sad. Without accounting for this to himself, this persistent irritation urges him to the street. One step, two, three . . . and the pavement burns and the rebellious stone repulses him. He feels himself borne along of his own accord, a body which is not made for the soul inhabiting it. He goes on mechanically, stealthily among the hedgerows; his gaze penetrates to strange courtyards. He turns the street; he feels a stranger and lost in realms which had formerly been his.

And always the same all-pervasive, infinite silence. Suddenly, crossing the street, he stops, petrified; a cart with galloping horses passed by almost touching him. His breast is suddenly filled with an oppressive warmth; his heart, ready to burst; fright sends prickles down the back of his neck, throughout his body; he can scarcely stand. The furious image of the driver calling after him loudly seemed like the grimacing symbol of Danger—of the multiple terror which he felt had permeated the hostile landscape surrounding him.

The driver disappeared in clouds of dust, and Miron still remained in the middle of the street, still seeming to see the lightning-flashes hurled by malignant eyes. Presentiments crowded within him like black crows on a tree stripped of leaves. He was ready to yield to the mute despair which burned his eyeballs when the blow of a fist on his back made him tremble,—the same sensation of just a while ago, when he had been almost crushed by a cart, seized him in its envenomed claws. Before him the loud laughter of Ermil with a red face glistening with sweat and an unruly mop of hair was exploding the surrounding peace. The laughter grew ever louder, changing into joyful bursts of satisfaction. Miron stared at him alarmed.

"Are you all right now?" and as the question remained unanswered, Ermil grew calm. For a few moments Miron's frightened face embarrassed him. But his glee broke out anew. Seizing Miron by the arm, Ermil began to run, dragging him after him. It seemed as though perfidious chasms opened under his feet; instinctive efforts exhausted the attenuated body. When he stopped in the vast and vague territory where his band habitually reigned, Miron was like a prey in the midst of savage beasts. His hands were pressed against his breast which was heaving in waves of terror; his eyes shining with their feverish regard unconsciously lighted upon the figures which surrounded him. His old playmates examined him with a devouring curiosity, healthy and provocative.

Here, then, is Miron once more among them! But he appears so lamentable who had so often been the head of his band! He regarded them with unvarying fright; beneath the familiar forms he found the hostile spirit which he had formerly found only in things. Their curiosity afflicted him; his cheeks burned with shame; it seemed as though he were clad in some ridiculous garment of many colors. The malevolent sarcasm of the boys wounded him. His glance passed from one to the other with a supplication. He would have desired to take refuge somewhere, in some obscure corner, to bury himself in oblivion and in silence, as in his sick-room, dimmed with shutters. Oh, to escape from this op-pressive circle!—and then he fixed his gaze upon the ground obstinately. Dozens of hands pulled him, pushed him, shook him, and he often perceived joyous figures; mouths wide open, but their shouts did not carry to him, in tones of triumph.

The conduct of Miron began to puzzle them all. Their reproaches to which he did not respond were followed by raillery—subtler and steelier with children because more spontaneous and direct. Miron felt it; the laughter pierced him like poisoned arrows. After the sufferings of the body, the first mental pangs made their appearance. The pleasure of the beast which holds his prey between his talons, the atavistic pleasure of torture excited the group of children. They struck him, turned him about, upset him. Paralyzed with terror and pain, Miron abandoned himself to their hands, crushing the tears back beneath his eyeballs. For his modesty took refuge in these tears which none ought to see; it was all that remained to him in his loss; only his tears; with the remainder of his strength he forced himself to restrain his tears, the crystal fruits of his soul. In the vortex of his suffering, in all the heaviness of revealed evil, Miron had instinctively found the sole refuge: he felt it burning in the depths of his being. . . . "Let's play leap-frog!"

Miron is seized by the nape of the neck, almost broken in two, his head upon his breast. And one behind the other the boys begin to leap. Fists fall heavily upon his back and he feels their weight passing over him—the weight of bod-ies evil and inexorable, which leap unceasingly. And Miron, stiff, panting, sweating, trembling with exhaustion. A strange pride brought him upright after every yielding—the fear of a new torture held him there with bursting sides. And the boys jumped on and on—and their fists pommelled him vigorously and his living, voracious, joyful load grew heavier and heavier. The blood strummed with redoubled force in his temples and breast; hot and cold shudders agitated him, his knees knocked together. His inordinately dilated eyes see the black whirlpool of the precipice . . . suffering formless and limitless,—and suddenly he sinks down like an animal beneath the blow of a club. The boys, whose ferocious and ignorant joy find form in shouts augmented with burst of laughter, stamp their feet, howl. Miron with his face on the ground moans; his jaws clenched, his fingers clutching the grass.

One of the boys, Ermil himself, bent over close to Miron's ear. For he had finally discovered the shameful infirmity, the pivot of an entire destiny, the soubriquet which sums up a man. Ermil began to shout the word in Miron's ear. He cried it ever more loudly, seized with the fury of an absurd passion; he shouted with an accent of ferocious defiance, unaware of how Satanic was his furious desire to be heard:

"Deaf! You are deaf! You are deaf! . . ." and his howls penetrated to the wounded ears, striking at the numb nerves.

The echo of his voice pierced the obscured consciousness of Miron. A sensation he had not felt for a long time, the subtle, sonorous vibration reverberated throughout his prostrate being. The sound pierced him in magic waves. This was what he had missed for several weeks, this was what all things and all beings had lacked. He hears!—echoes lost in the shadows—and it seems to him that he revives. He hears! . . . and how strange the obstinately howled syllables seem to him! The echoes resound within him rolling among grimacing forms—and at last the MEANING of the word descends upon him like a lightning-stroke.

The strength returns to his body as though stimulated

by the lash of a whip. Electrified by revolt, the heritage of so many generations which have struggled against humiliation and slavery—Miron, with a bound, rises to his feet. His ardent and piercing glance is fixed upon the eyes of the evil child who had howled into his ear. The first revolt of human dignity, always the same, is revindicated in its simple grandeur, unknown to children and in which their parents do not believe.

And Miron, his eyes burning, his forehead raised, his hands clenched, walks away, holding in check the group wavering between ferocity and fear.

At home, in the rear of the garden, prone upon the grass, Miron weeps with his head in his hands. He weeps the tears he held back there in the arena of his first humiliation. He weeps over his first conscious sorrow. The tears liberate him from the mists of ignorance; he emerges purified by them. The man within him is revealed as a reality which has been hidden by appearances and tossed about by the blind impulses of life. At present, poor creature, he feels himself diminished in his own forces, amidst temptations and numerous perils. He feels himself altogether entire— and, oblivious of everybody, even his mother, Miron bathes his soul anew in the tears of solitary suffering.

He weeps, but no longer because of humiliation endured, through sterile pride or despair at having been lessened by a sense. He weeps because sorrow brings knowledge of self. He weeps because Love, hidden in every human heart, only reveals itself through tears: the first sorrow lays bare in the nascent consciousness of the child, the infinite yet fertile sufferings of the humanity which has preceded him and the humanity in the midst of which he lives.

No Sound
by Julius Wiggins

EDITORS' PREFACE

The following excerpt from *No Sound* by Julius Wiggins, present editor and publisher of the *Silent News* ("America's Most Popular Newspaper for the Deaf"), contains numerous insights into the deaf experience. Wiggins was, of course, unusually successful for a deaf person of his time, and so has reason to write of his life. He does not record the difficulties, the embarrassments, the rejections which he must have experienced; instead we find successes and good times.

There is, however, the experience of the hope for a medical miracle bringing his hearing back, and the episode with the hearing aid. In this connection, we find what probably seems startling to hearing people: deaf people who have never heard don't wish to hear and couldn't handle it if they did. This is startling because we have all been duped by the television episodes where a person who has been blind all his life, or deaf, suddenly, through some miracle, regains his or her lost sense. We all cry, the character in the drama cries, all is right with the world, and we go to bed, happy in the thought that there really is justice in the world. What we forget is that sensory data must be processed by our brain and *translated into* meaningful perception: a person who has never heard before or seen before would undergo great trauma trying to re-adjust to a world in which a flood of new, totally confusing sensory data crashed in upon the brain. The only analogy I can think of for a "normal" person is if suddenly that person gained an intense sensitivity to radio waves, TV signals, radar, telephone transmission, gamma rays, xrays, and so on, and was therefore constantly bombarded with signals that were contradictory, overwhelming, totally confusing. It would take maybe a year or two, assuming the experience did not bring on insanity, to begin to develop a filtering and "descrambling" mechanism. As Wiggins points out, deaf people do not want to hear (for who would, given the kind of experience I've just described?), they merely want to know what's going on.

What Wiggins makes us aware of is the obsession with sound and hearing that hearing people develop when they come in contact with deaf people. The lack of hearing is what hearing people notice, of course, so it is understandable, but still no less exasperating. People always notice obvious differences: differences in skin color, differences in facial features—but, just as people cannot change their skin color or ethnic background, neither can they change their lack of hearing, and to remind people of that which makes them "different" certainly doesn't help smooth human relationships. Black people don't want to be white; deaf people don't want to hear. This is simple, or seemingly so, for one is what one is, but for the dominant majority it is a truth that is impossible to understand or remember. Deaf people don't want to know that they will be treated decently only if they can seem like hearing people (lip reading, learning speech, using only English), they want to know that they will be treated decently because they are human, with all the rights to life that any other human has. Otherwise, how condescending it is or how belittling—but there have always been enough Uncle Toms trying to be white, or hearing, to perpetuate such condescension. What the Uncle Toms don't realize is that Uncle Tomming offers a fake promise: even after one becomes "white" or "hearing," one still is not accepted—if anything, one is even more despised, and now not only by the majority, but by his own group as well.

From this brief excerpt, we see that Wiggins was (and still is) a happy person. We do not find laments at not being accepted by hearing people. We do not see him pining away at the back of concert halls, longing for just one sweet note to inspire his soul. We do not see him wandering the streets, hoping to gain some sense of the hustle and bustle he so sadly misses (as does John Singer in *The Heart is a Lonely Hunter*). And this is an important point, for we find deaf characters in fiction who are used to personify the loneliest and most isolated characters that authors can imagine. If an author wishes to create the most pathetically isolated person he or she can, often what comes to mind is a deaf character, as we have seen, and will see, in this anthology. It is a clever conceit, and, for most readers, appropriately moving. But, when applied to most real deaf people it is terribly misleading. The experience that Wiggins describes in this excerpt is not fiction—it all happened, more or less (as Mark Twain would say), and it was not by any means unrepresentative. Wiggins is not a fluke—one need only glance through the recently published *Notable Deaf Persons* (Florence B. Crammatte, ed., Washington, D.C., 1975, G.C.A.A.) to confirm *that*!

"Pierre and Camille" and "Doctor Marigold" were both stories with "happy" endings because Camille and Sophy both had hearing children; even if one accepts that this constitutes a happy ending, *No Sound* is still a much happier story, for Wiggins is a person who has not suffered from feelings of inferiority—he does not seem to have grown up with the idea that being deaf was shameful and that he must try to become a hearing person. We all know that individual happiness, in part, entails becoming aware of one's limitations, accepting them, and making the most of our strengths. This is as true for deaf people as for anyone else—and so to constantly hold out the promise of hearing to a deaf person is a mere taunt and only retards or destroys the chances for him or her to grow into a mature adult.

FROM NO SOUND

Levaint was paying me seventy dollars a week whereas I had been earning sixty-five at Creed's. True, the taxes were higher and I was paying for lodgings and food—something I had not done before. However, I knew that when I got used to the machine and achieved speed, I would earn more. I knew that from the others, who made much more money. In a month I asked for a raise, but was put off with, "No, not now, later." I waited and waited. Christmas came with the usual slack season and the temporary layoffs.

I met my mother's friend one day for lunch and I told him about my anxiety over the layoff. He advised me not to give it a thought. "You wait and see," he said. "They will be calling you back after New Year's and hiring new men to replace those who have skipped."

But I did not go back to Levaint's. Instead I 'skipped' to a new job at higher pay. I was learning my way around and had become adjusted to New York ways. I only stayed three weeks in that place because the job and the people were dull and the work irregular.

One day I met my Aunt's brother-in-law. Wandering about in the fur market, he had overheard a couple of cutters talking about an addition to the factory in which they worked. This meant they'd have to hire more operators, men experienced in mink. My relative spoke to them and pointed me out. One of the cutters was also the hiring foreman. He came over and asked me whether I could work on mink. When I assured him I could and told him where I had been working, he took me to Fishbach and Roxenberg on West Thirtieth Street. After a trial they told me they liked my work, although I was a bit slow. However, they hired me. I asked for a hundred and fifty dollars, which everyone else was getting. They gave me a hundred and twenty-five dollars with promises of a raise.

I was doing first class stitching on curves, a specialist's work. Ordinary straight operators made a hundred and fifty dollars. Therefore, in accordance with union rules, I should have started from a hundred and fifty dollars, but because I was the youngest operator in the place, they must have felt they could take advantage of that. However, after awhile, they did increase my wage.

I worked with Fishbach and Roxenberg for about three years, the longest time I had ever remained with one company. About fifty people were employed there and about a dozen worked exclusively on mink. I got along well and particularly liked the hiring foreman and chief cutter, but he was only on a one-year contract. When the year was up, he decided not to renew it, so he trained the second cutter to take his place. The new foreman offered mink sewers training in cutting. It meant a reduction in pay while learning. Therefore, I turned the offer down. Some time later, when Father came to New York, I told him about it. He groaned and told me I was a dunce. The reduction in pay was nothing, compared with the benefits to be gained from learning a job which would have greatly increased not only my earnings but my knowledge of the artistic side of my craft. It would also have meant naming my own price, wherever I worked. I realized my mistake, but it was too late, now.

The new head cutter was in the habit of running to the boss with all kinds of little complaints. So, one day, when we were in the restaurant for lunch, I heard quite a lot of mean gossip. The head cutter made a derogatory remark about me and I retaliated by writing him that he spent most of his time kissing a select portion of the boss's anatomy. He folded the note up carefully and took it to the boss. Whereupon he came roaring in and fired me.

I went to my union agent, who was a nice guy, and told him what had happened. The agent put on his hat and coat and took me back to the shop. There he pointed out to the boss that the cutter had insulted me verbally but as I couldn't talk, I had to write the things others constantly got away with orally. Anyway, the union agent continued, this had occurred at a restaurant and not at work, so there were no grounds for firing me. The boss cooled down and recognized the validity of the union man's argument. He rehired me, and I went back to work.

About this time my mother came to New York to see how I was getting on. During her visit she called on some distant relatives, who had hitherto not known I was deaf. They told her about another young deaf relative who had been cured by a specialist and advised us to see him.

"After all, you have nothing to lose," they said.

I thought it a lot of nonsense, but parents don't like having their children different from other people's. It makes them feel like failures. So I agreed. After all, there might be something to it.

The specialist had a whole building near Fifth Avenue. We spent all day there going from technician to specialist and back again. There were many, many tests! At length, the doctor called us in, fussed with some papers on his desk, and said regretfully that surgery would be useless, but a very special hearing aid might help me. I honestly felt relieved, because that kind of hoping is a strain on deaf people. Besides, hearing people think deaf people want to hear. It is not so, because we don't mind not hearing. We just want to know what is going on around us and we do manage that, usually very well. But of course, Mother was quite disappointed, although she tried not to show it. We left the doctor's building and never discussed it again.

Earlier that year I had learned at the Hebrew Association of the Deaf that there was a night school for deaf people at the Washington Irving High School. Before leaving for New York, Father had advised me to attend night school, therefore when it was time to register for classes, I went along with some other deaf.

I found that there were three classrooms set aside for the deaf. There was an English class on speech improvement subjects, as needed by the various pupils, which was held three times a week.

I had been attending for about six months when my father came to New York. I took him with me one night and he watched the work with much interest. After class I introduced him to my teacher, who asked him many questions about my general background. She thought it a shame I hadn't been educated sufficiently and held that my speech could have been better. She then told him about a doctor who specialized in speech training for the deaf. She also recommended that I wear a hearing aid for a little while at least, so that I could become acquainted with sound. Before we left, we had the doctor's address and also that of a hearing aid dealer who was operating in the Hard-of-Hearing Club on Lexington Avenue. We followed her advice and went to both the doctor and the club.

This club forbade its members to use the sign language and had a display of hearing aids. I also found that there were classrooms with hearing aids for small children to practice listening. After testing, the hearing aid man fitted the ear piece by first stuffing some soft material into my ear and then, when he had removed it, put on earphones like those worn by radio operators. He turned knobs, watched dials and wrote notes on a card. Finished at last, he told me to return in a week, when the aid would be ready.

I came as arranged and was instructed on how to place the aid in my ear and how to use it. I was told about the off, on, high, and low settings. The doctor's fingers made noises on the table, he rattled papers and they made noises.

My shirt rubbing against the receiver of the hearing aid made noises. Then I got into the elevator and the noise of its descent frightened me a little. Yet these were very small sounds which I accepted easily, but the blast of noise which hit me when I stepped into the street was horrible. Busses roared, brakes on cars screeched, horns blared—all very hard to bear. But it was odd that the noise of people's feet as they walked, greatly surprised me.

As was my custom, I took the subway home. I was already feeling dizzy and miserable, when the subway train roared into the station. It was practically unbearable. Inside the train, the never ending din began to give me a violent headache. Home at last, I found that even turning the key in the lock and opening the door made noises. The running water as it came out of the tap, when I filled my water glass, the ice cubes I dropped into the glass, the personal noises of getting ready for bed—all of them were shocking.

The next day, I went to work without the hearing aid, first, because I did not want fellow workers asking questions or staring at me, and second, I wanted to get used to the aid before going anywhere with it.

I did wear it to class, however. My teacher's voice was, of course, a new experience, but I could not hear her as well or understand her speech, as I could other sounds. Perhaps with practice, I hoped, I would manage. On the other hand, I recalled that many mildly deaf people have trouble with understanding people's speech, even with an aid, because, as I learned later, the human voice is too high pitched and changes its tones and volume very rapidly. It is also difficult for the ears of the hearing-handicapped to discriminate between sounds. Coarse sounds, like that of cars, busses and water running, are easy to pick up, because they do not vary in pitch, tone or timing. And I was not just mildly deaf, but actually totally so.

I took the hearing aid to the speech doctor and noted the difference between his speech and mine. His voice continued while he spoke many words. Mine stopped after every word and sometimes after every syllable. This difference was hard to understand. At school, teachers would show us the words divided into sounds and would put a light mark for a weak sound and a heavy stroke for a strong sound over every syllable, as it is done in dictionaries. But this was definitely not the way people spoke. I was surprised and discouraged. Nevertheless, I went on with the speech lessons for quite awhile.

However, I never became accustomed to my hearing aid. The tramp of feet, rustle of papers, knocks on doors, sounds of falling coins and voices I couldn't understand, all seemed to gallop into my poor head like the charge of the cavalry. My headaches became worse and worse until I was finally compelled to give up the hearing aid.

What a blessed relief was the peace and quiet! But one thing I did learn from the hearing aid, was how much I missed. For instance, the sound of music. The fact that there were so many kinds of music was interesting to me.

Nevertheless, had I known what sound and noise were, I never would have bought the aid. Of course, I should have had it when I was very young. But now, it was too late. I could not stand the headaches.

But being deaf did not interfere with social life at all. I discussed various organizations with Mrs. Harris, and she felt that the Hebrew Association of the Deaf was very good. As she was a member, she received the news bulletins published by the Association. Many forthcoming events were listed in it. She also contacted a friend of Hymie's, so I wouldn't have to trouble Harry Goodwin, who lived out in Brooklyn, and being merely hard-of-hearing, had his own circle of friends. But first, she took me to the H.A.D.

It was on West Eighty-fifth Street in an old three-story brownstone, owned by the Association. Mrs. Harris steamed in with me in tow and introduced me around. There were lots of people and they welcomed me warmly. Best of all it was all right to use sign language. When a pause came in the general flicker-flick of fingers, I began to look around.

There were many girls. One in particular caught my eye. She had rather dull blonde hair, fine features and a figure that would drive any unsophisticated male around the bend. I went around the bend so fast I couldn't catch my breath for a month.

This glittering goddess responded. "You're from Canada," she said, and immediately I felt the hay sprouting out all over and it tickled. I swallowed a couple of times and worked up the courage to say "yes" and to ask her how she knew. It turned out that I had dated a friend of hers when I was holidaying in New York. She had shown her my picture and told her that in person I looked like a movie star.

"Which one?" I asked.

"Tony Martin of course," she replied.

Naturally I was flattered. I felt great and asked her for a date.

I took her to dinner and then to the Apollo Theatre which presented excellent foreign films with sub-titles, so good for deaf people.

The next date I called for her at home. We sign-talked and looked at her photo album. She told me about her life in New York. Then, quite suddenly and apropos of nothing in particular, she told how expensive her dress was, and that my suit was not top quality—in fact, cheap.

"Huh!" said I. "This cheap? It's a made to order suit."

She then reached into the pocket of her dress, pulled out a price tag which she must have kept for just such occasions. I got a funny feeling in my stomach like, maybe I could do with some bicarbonate. She carried on in this vein about her expensive clothes and their importance until her mother came in and asked me to stay for supper. But by that time I wanted to get away as fast as possible. So I declined and left, never to return.

I had come to New York to enjoy life and go out on dates but was really too inexperienced to understand what made people tick. Now, that I am older I realize that this girl must have been impressed by me but, being unsure of herself, was trying to impress me the only way she knew how.

I continued to date girls, mainly nice ones, some fun to be with, but not especially interesting. During that time I was introduced to one of Hymie's pals by Mrs. Harris. Although a very young man, he had a superior intellect as well as a good command of language. There also were Mack, Izzie and Art. We formed a sort of group and went stag to affairs when we didn't want to bother with dates.

One night we went to a basketball game between White Plains School for the Deaf and the Perkins Day School. Now, it is not a regular thing for "out-in-the-world" deaf to attend interschool games, but they do sometimes. In this case the group had just dropped in to get off the street for a place to converse. We signed about jobs, Jills and jalopies, the three major topics in the world of the deaf bachelor. One of them asked me how I was doing and I said, "Not so good. This new job at Fishback and Roxenberg pays me only a hundred and twenty-five dollars a week."

"Migosh!" Al signed, "don't bird it to the whole world. Most of us make seventy-five."

I signed, "What? I thought everyone else was earning more than I."

The boys laughed, "He's one of those 'furriers' who was

told New York's pavements were paved with gold."

"And what's more," said another, "he's managing to find it."

Al took me to the Sports Club named Naismith Social and Athletic Club to honor the memory of a popular athlete, who had been killed in an automobile accident. Most of its members were from P.S. 47, an oral day school. The club had a good basketball team which met with the senior basketball teams of other clubs. There also were sports events and planned trips and cruises. It was a really good young people's club—alcohol not permitted.

My sister, Marie, came to visit me that Christmas. I met her at Grand Central Station and to my surprise Sammy was with her. While delighted to see him, he presented me with a problem. I had planned the places I would take my sister, but Sammy would naturally want a different kind of entertainment. I needn't have worried as one of his cousins came to pick him up and I didn't see much of him for the rest of the holiday. Mrs. Harris was willing to have Marie stay with us. She set her up in the living room.

I took Marie to various clubs and introduced her to some of my friends. She was pleasantly surprised at the number of organizations we had and compared them with those in Toronto, quite favorably. Over supper in a restaurant soon after she arrived, Marie told me how things were at home. She said Mother and Father missed me terribly and in the beginning from force of habit Mother used to set my place at the table.

After a week of showing her all the sights of the big town, she returned rather reluctantly to Toronto. New York hath charms!

My circle of friends increased. I dated, attended functions and worked on mink all day long. Al and I remained close and when the Naismith club closed for the summer, we and other members often rented lockers at Washington Baths in Coney Island. We had a pool, handball courts, quoits, tennis, showers and steam baths.

Al shared a locker with me. The Naismith club reserved a handball court but when I took one look at the feverish game, I decided it was not for me. Instead I would go to the beach exit, have my hand stamped with the club symbol in fluorescent ink, and walk on the sand or swim in the ocean.

There were usually crowds of deaf people on the beach and it was fun conversing with them. It was a soft, luxurious life, and Al and I went often. The short way to the baths from the subway station was through the Amusement Park. The first time Al and I were there, an unfamiliar odor distressed me.

"What is that awful smell?" I asked.

"Something to eat," signed Al. "What!" I imagined that we were in a hospital where both staff and patients had come down with some loathsome disease and no one about to clean up.

"Sure," signed Al, "it's pizza. There is hardly anything better-tasting. I'll get you some. You'll like it."

He steered me over to a pizzeria. I eyed the concoction with some distaste, but he made me take a bite. It was not too bad, so I took another and then another. Then I ordered a second wedge.

Every kind of snack, from A to Z, was on sale in Coney Island. The Chinese sold egg rolls, Jews sold knishes and corn on the cob, Nathan's sold the most delicious frankfurters in the world. They are made of good beef from a special recipe which the owner will not divulge. This place, always crowded, was open twenty-four hours a day and was also the only place in the Amusement Park which was open for business during the winter. During the summer there were as many as fourteen men, working at high speed serving the customers. It was a sight to see the crowds lined up and yelling and the waiters moving so fast they seemed to have eight arms each.

One day towards the end of summer, our group was discussing what to do on the Labor Day weekend. We decided on Atlantic City, especially as there was a beauty queen contest there every year on the Labor Day weekend.

Art had a Plymouth convertible and we would share gas and other expenses. On Saturday of Labor Day weekend, we met at the pre-arranged time and place and started south. We drove along admiring the scenery and arrived at Atlantic City about two-thirty in the afternoon. There we went from hotel to hotel all afternoon. "Filled up," was the answer. We then decided to split forces and go looking individually. No success. Disconsolately we gathered at the pre-arranged meeting place. Only Art was missing. He came at last, running. He had found a room.

The hotel was one of the Gay Nineties type, wooden, heavily painted, with double-decker porches running the length of the front and a single dim hall leading from front to back. A flight of stairs led to the upstairs rooms. The odor of age was over-powering. We went up to the desk and the manager, who was doubling as clerk, was very affable. He led us down the hall, past the stairs and through the kitchen to a door at the back, inserted a key in the keyhole, turned it and opened the door.

One glimpse of the interior and we were horrified. There were no windows. The floor was dirty, the walls were filthy, the linen looked muddy and the beds were merely cots.

Art, Al and I were for dropping the whole thing and driving home. Manny, however, pointed out that it was late and it would be foolish to give up all the fun we were going to have just because of sleeping accommodations.

The manager offered to get the bedding changed and the floor washed up. Finally Manny prevailed on us to stay. We went back to the car and collected our gear.

The manager had changed the bed linen and the floor was being washed. At Manny's suggestion we drew lots for the beds. Four scraps of paper with numbers on them were shuffled around in a hat and we all drew. Poor Manny drew the worst of the four cots. We cleaned and dressed up as best we could and went out to supper. That turned out to be good and comforted us somewhat.

After supper we wandered around on foot, looking at people, meeting other deaf, conversing and forgetting our terrible lodgings. Some time after midnight, we grew tired and unhappily dragged ourselves back to our room. We settled down or tried to. During the night I woke and saw that Art's bed was empty. I was too sleepy to think about the reason so I rolled over and went to sleep again. But soon I began to be very uncomfortable. I woke up to find myself sweating profusely. It seems my bed was against the wall near the kitchen stove and the servants were heating it to prepare their own early breakfast.

I got up as Art come into the room from the street. He said he had nearly choked to death on the smell from the mattress, and had gone out to get some fresh air. About eight o'clock we all dressed and went out. After breakfast we asked about the beauty queen contest and were told the judging was taking place at a hotel and the general public wasn't admitted. We met some more deaf people, but they were mainly the same as those from Coney Island. We gave up and, totally disgusted, drove back to New York.

BIBLIOGRAPHY

The annotated bibliography that follows was selected from a master list of some 700 items. Hence, the reader of this book should be cautioned not to regard the list as definitive (something a critic hesitates to admit). Moreover, the bibliography has certain limitations in accordance with the purpose expressed in the introduction to this anthology: All the selections are linked in some way to the deaf experience as reflected in prose works by and about deaf people. Because the anthology omits poetry and the literary efforts of deaf-blind writers (there's one exception to the latter, but her work of fiction depicts a deaf character), no books are cited in these two areas. The reader should also observe that (1) some selections are not annotated because they appear in the anthology or are adequately described in the introductions and prefaces supplied by the editors (the reader should refer to these and, of course, read the selections; such works are preceded by an asterisk), and (2) works produced by writers who have varying degrees of deafness are simply noted with the term (H.I.) for hearing impaired. The bibliography has followed the current fashion of generalizing varying degrees of deafness so as not to complicate an already difficult task.

Any bibliography of deaf literature can never be compiled without acknowledging the previous works and efforts that have preceded it, nor can a complete list of those who share an interest in deaf literature appear here. Nevertheless, I owe a special note of gratitude to Prof. Robert Panara at National Technical Institute for the Deaf (NTID), a leading scholar in this area, for graciously allowing me to share his articles and notes which have enriched my own research. I must also thank Francis C. Higgins, chairman of the Department of Chemistry at Gallaudet College, who has provided and will continue to provide items for any bibliography on deafness and who does so for the sheer love of it. I cannot name the many students who have helped me to compile the master bibliography from which these selections were taken, but I thank them as well. There are numerous reference works of which any bibliographer in deaf literature should avail himself or herself, but unfortunately these are not included here. The reader may be briefly introduced to the subject by referring to Professor Panara's articles in *The Deaf American* and the *American Annals of the Deaf*, Gilbert Braddock's *Notable Deaf Persons*, edited by Florence B. Crammatte, and *The Gallaudet Almanac* (pp. 260–262) published by the Gallaudet College Alumni Association.

Finally, a special note of thanks goes to Dr. Keith Wright, formerly head librarian, and the staff of the Gallaudet College Library, which houses a strong deaf collection, for their special efforts in my behalf, and to Dr. John S. Schuchman for providing me moral and financial support. It is my hope that this partial listing will lead the reader into the vast but interesting area of deaf literature.

DANIEL C. NASCIMENTO, PH.D.

Adams, I. (1928). *Heart of the woods*. New York: Century.

Novel containing a noble portrait of deafness, the wife of a college professor, who triumphs over her hearing loss to enjoy a meaningful life. Emphasis on lipreading skills of heroine in French and English.

Adams, I. (1933). *The dumb man*. New York: Appleton-Century.

Novel containing a major deaf character, Hercule, a fisherman whom the author endows with noble traits of heroism, loyalty, and kindness.

Andrew, P. (1961). *Ordeal by silence*. New York: Putnam.

Novel about a "holy fool," a deaf miracle-worker in Medieval England. By suffering in silence he serves as an example of goodness to men of incontinence, violence, and fraud.

Anonymous. (1896). *In a silent world: The love story of a deaf mute by the author of "Views of English society. . . ."* New York: Dodd, Mead.

Charming narrative written with clarity and strength with unusual (for the time) first person deaf point of view (major character and narrator is a deaf woman). The story is set in America and various parts of Europe, including England and Germany. The book wanders into sentimental romance and ends on a tragic note linked to the heroine's deafness.

Ashley, J. (1973). *Journey into silence*. London: Bodley Head. (H.I.)

Autobiographical account of a member of English Parliament who suffers late onset of total deafness and through perseverance and lipreading skills succeeds as an English politician. No references to signing or manual alphabet.

*Ballin, A. (1930). *The deaf mute howls*. Los Angeles: Grafton. (H.I.)

*Batson, T., & Bergman, E. (Eds.) (1976). *The deaf experience: An anthology of literature by and about the deaf (3rd ed.)*. South Waterford, ME: Merrian-Eddy.

Bennett, H. P. (1973). *Road girl*. Long Beach, CA: Colling.

Colorful autobiography, travel narrative, and account of experiences with deaf daughters.

Bierce, A. (1909). Chickamauga. In *The collected works of Ambrose Bierce: Vol. II. In the midst of life*. New York and Washington, DC: Neale.

Short story in which deaf character (boy) is used as a foil to emphasize the brutality and grotesqueness of war. The boy's deafness is not revealed until the end.

Bishop, W. H. (1902). Jerry and Clarinda. In *Queer people including the brown stone boy*. New York and London: Street & Smith.

Deafness abounds in this quaint tale. Deaf hero, Jerry, after many trials along the way finds happiness in marriage to a deaf school chum, Clarinda. Cast of deaf characters includes an armless deaf friend and a deaf horse. Includes references to and examples of writing problems of deaf. Obvious plot with turns.

Bouilly, J. N. (1818). *Deaf and dumb; or the Abbe de l'Epée. An historical drama founded upon very interesting facts. From the French of J. N. Bouilly with a preface by Laurent Clerc*. Hartford: S. G. Goodrich.

Historical drama mainly noteworthy for its portrait of Abbe de l'Epée, famed teacher of the deaf in France. Plot revolves around the teacher's attempts to aid an abandoned deaf boy who ultimately regains family and riches. Play reveals fact that deafness is no barrier to intelligence or its communication through writing.

Bowen, E. (1968). *Eva Trout: or, changing scenes*. New York: Alfred A. Knopf.

Well-wrought English novel with a wealthy dark heroine who, in second half of book, mysteriously adopts a deaf child in America and brings him back to England. She allows him to lead a life of primitive enjoyment without education until educators in France (oralists) and a friend of the mother (her ex-teacher) open the doors of communication for him. The novel ends on a tragic note when the deaf boy accidentally shoots his "mother."

Burnet, J. R. (1835). *Tales of the deaf and dumb, with miscellaneous poems*. Neward, NJ: B. Olds. (H.I.)

Includes two early tales of Burnet, deaf since eight, on themes of deafness, written in sentimental, religious vein. Author claims these as first "humble attempts" to write about "deaf mutes" in fiction.

Calkins, E. E. (1924). *Louder please!* Boston: Atlantic Monthly Press. (H.I.)

Autobiography of an American deaf man who rises to success in world of advertising and gains the freedom to explore the resources of culture (literature, theatre, art, travel, etc.) denied to most of his deaf contemporaries.

Chagall, D. (1970). *Diary of a deaf-mute*. Los Angeles: Millenium.

Fictional account of a young college student who poses as a deaf-mute to avoid communication with humanity in the back-woods of Maine where he attempts to recapture his honesty. Example of deafness used as a symbolic device.

Clark, B. (Comp.). (1865). *An account of St. Ann's church for deaf mutes, and articles of prose and poetry by deaf mutes.* New York: John A. Gray and Green.

Account is followed by a sampling of prose sketches and poems by deaf writers (John R. Burnet, James Nack, John Carlin, Isaac H. Benedict, Joseph Mount, etc.) of the nineteenth century.

Collingwood, H. W. (1923). *Adventures in silence.* New York: Rural New Yorker. (H.I.)

Lively, well-written biographical account of a deaf man's experiences in "the world of silence" aimed at educating the hearing audience "to understand the affliction" of deafness.

Collins, W. (1861). *Hide and seek.* New York: Peter Fenelon Collier.

Domestic, sentimental novel (part mystery) with deaf central character. First half of novel depicts Victorian modes of educating and rehabilitating the heroine who became deaf as the result of an accident while performing as a child in a circus. Detection of her true identity reserved for second half of novel.

Corbett, S. (1972). *Dead before docking.* Boston: Little, Brown.

Detective novel for youthful readers with a young deaf hero who lipreads his way into the middle of a murder plot.

Creasey, J. [Anthony Morton, pseud.]. (1961) *Deaf, dumb, and blonde.* Garden City, NY: Doubleday.

Detective story that employs a deaf female character who suffers deafness through shock after witnessing the murder of her father and is cured in the same fashion when her uncle is shot to death. She experiences communication problems that aid the machinations of the plot.

*Crews, H. (1974). *The gypsy's curse*. New York: Alfred A. Knopf.

Dallam, J. W. (1848). *The deaf spy*. Baltimore: William Taylor.

Fictional account based on historical and legendary exploits of Deaf Smith, hard of hearing scout and spy for Sam Houston in the war between Texas and Mexico.

Davis, C. (1963, November 9). Silence. *Saturday Evening Post*, pp. 48–55.

Short story of the popular boy-meets-girl formula involving deaf characters who work as linotype operators for a big city newspaper.

Defoe, D. (1720). *The history of the life and adventures of Mr. Duncan Campbell*. . . . London: W. Meers.

Picaresque novel based on the real-life figure of a deaf gentleman in England who overcomes his handicap to be an inspiration to others who are similarly afflicted. Much information on the education of the deaf in the eighteenth century is included.

*Dickens, C. (1900). Doctor Marigold. In *Works of Charles Dickens: Vol. 7. Christmas Stories*. London: Merrill & Baker.

Dinesen, I. (1938). *Out of Africa*. New York: Random.

Author's account of life on a coffee farm in Kenya including a sympathetic sketch of a deaf boy who does not understand why dogs rush to him when he blows his special whistle.

Duthie, J. (1955). *I cycled into the Arctic Circle*. Ilfracombe, England: Arthur H. Stockwell. (H.I.)

Unusual and lively travel narrative by a born-deaf "Scotsman" whose "language and syntax," a reviewer in *The Silent World* has noted, "is entirely that of the born deaf."

Eastman, G. (1974). *Sign me Alice*. Washington, DC: Gallaudet College Press. (H.I.)

Original and amusing play in sign language that turns George Bernard Shaw's *Pygmalion* into a satirical defense of American Sign Language.

Edmund Booth (1810–1905) forty-niner: The life story of a deaf pioneer including portions of his autobiographical notes and gold rush diary, and selections from family letters and reminiscences. (1953). Stockton, CA: San Joaquin Pioneer and Historical Society. (H.I.)

Historical account of a deaf pioneer, totally deaf since eight, who journeys from Iowa to California in 1849 in a search for gold and returns home to Iowa and his deaf wife. Last chapter describes Edmund Booth's role in founding Iowa School for the Deaf and his editorship of abolitionist newspaper.

Faulkner, W. (1956). Hand upon the waters. In *Knight's Gambit*. New York: Signet.

Short story in which a deaf orphan avenges the death of his mentally retarded guardian by killing his guardian's murderer.

Faulkner, W. (1959). *The mansion*. New York: Random.

Sympathetically portrayed major character, Linda Snopes Kohl, is deafened in her twenties by an explosion during the Spanish Civil War. Her deafness serves to isolate her from time and change.

Field, R. L. (1942). *And now tomorrow.* New York: Macmillan.

Romantic novel in which the heroine becomes deaf at twenty-one after an epidemic of meningitis. Her deafness spoils her chances for marriage and happiness until a young doctor comes to her rescue with a miraculous cure.

Fletcher, C. W. (1843). *The deaf and dumb boy, a tale, with some account of the mode of educating the deaf and dumb.* London: J. W. Parker.

Story of a little boy born deaf who gains his hearing at age four with the aid of a "surgeon-aurist" and a loud band playing in a park. Despite the fantastic recovery, the author purports the account to be based on fact and we do get some examples of letters written by deaf people of the times.

Flourney, J. J. (1855). *The big bull in a court house: A tale of horror. By Jacobus, Jackson County, Georgia.* Athens, GA. (H.I.)

Vituperative tract written in dramatic and narrative form which attacks the county in Georgia for denying equality and justice to deaf persons.

France, A. (1926). *The man who married a dumb wife, a comedy in two acts.* (C. H. Page, Trans.). New York: Dodd, Mead.

Comedy about a man whose mute wife becomes so garrulous and voluble (via an operation on her tongue) that he becomes deaf through drugs and charms prescribed by a doctor; hence, the wife goes mad when her railings and scoldings fall on deaf ears.

Greenberg, J. (1966, March). A cry of silence. *Good House-keeping*, pp. 88–89, 170, 172, 186–189.

Short story in which a hearing woman must learn to cope with a deaf husband and sons. One son returns from a drafting school in Chicago with a young deaf wife, a new form of communication—signs—which the wife eventually accepts. Narrative mostly from point of view of hearing woman.

*Greenberg, J. (1970). *In this sign*. New York: Holt, Rinehart & Winston.

Guare, J. (1972). *The house of blue leaves*. New York: Viking.

Award winning mad farcical play that includes a hearing-impaired Hollywood starlet who is ashamed of her deafness and tries to hide her hearing aids.

Harris, E. B. (1956). *Johnny Belinda*. (Adapted by S. Carson and J. Hanau). London: Samuel French

Drama about a young deaf woman set in Prince Edward Island, off Nova Scotia, Canada. She is harshly treated by her father, the community, and especially a roughneck who rapes her. A doctor from Montreal, however, befriends her and teaches her to communicate in sign language. The plot ends melodramatically in a murder trial, but the play stresses the importance of sign language and the deaf heroine's capacity to learn and live a normal life.

Hofsteater, H. T. (1960). Dummy. In R. F. Panara, T. B. Denis, & J. H. McFarlane (Eds.), *The silent muse*. Toronto, Canada: Gallaudet College Alumni Assn. (H.I.)

Short, short story with deaf character whose relationship with a hearing woman comes to a jarring close on her wedding day.

Hubbard, R. (1930) *Queer person*. Garden City, NY: Doubleday, Doran Junior Books.

Simple story of an outcast Indian boy growing up deaf. He communicates in Indian sign language and reads lips. Interest in the book ends when he is cured of deafness. As a deaf Indian he was an evil spirit; as a hearing Indian he gets tribal status.

Hunter, E. [Ed McBain, pseud.]. (1973). *Let's hear it for the deaf man*. Garden City: NY: Doubleday.

One in a long series of novels of New York police detection (87th Precinct) in which one of the running characters, Detective Steve Carella, has a deaf wife. In this novel the deaf man turns out to be a hearing man named Taubman (*Der taube mann*).

Huston, C. (1973). *Deaf Smith: Incredible Texas spy*. Waco, TX: Texian Press.

Definitive life story of Erastus "Deaf" Smith, the hard-of-hearing scout and spy of the Texas revolution, especially under Sam Houston. He became a hero of the victory in San Jacinto and thus a folk hero of the Texas Republic.

*Ionesco, E. (1958). The chairs. In D. Watson (Trans.), *Eugene Ionesco: Plays: Vol. I*. London: John Calder.

Kennedy, M. (1964). *Not in the calendar*. New York: Macmillan.

Simple story about a deaf girl who rises to success as an artist, and her hearing friend who becomes an educator to the deaf.

Kenyon, C. F. (1971). The deaf mute of Kilindir. In *Tales of a cruel country*. Freeport, NY: Books for Libraries Press.

Story in reprint of 1919 collection in which a faithful giant of a deaf servant informs his master that his wife is unfaithful. The deaf man, who has rebuffed the seductive entreaties of the wife, is unjustly cast off by the angry master.

*Kitto, J. (1848). *The lost senses*. Edinburgh: William Oliphant. (H.I.)

Le Pla, F. (n.d.). *The queerness of Ciaran*. Manchester, England: Humane Education Society. (H.I.-Blind)

Deaf-blind author's story about a ten-year-old girl who discovers a hearing-impaired, disfigured boy in the forest and their pact. She teaches him the ways of man, and he teaches her the ways of animals.

Lewis, H. (ca. 1948). *The day is ours*. London: Jarrold.

A moving, if romanticized account of a deaf child and her family as they attempt to deal with deafness and the problems of education (oralism). The conflicts are contrived and the solutions a bit pat, but the novel provides insights into the English system of deaf education.

Lillie, H. (ca. 1970). *The listening silence*. New York: Hawthorn.

Suspense novel concentrating on a young woman who struggles to hide her growing deafness as she learns the truth of her sister's death. Includes several other hearing-impaired characters and a family who cannot adjust to deafness.

*McCullers, C. (1940). *The heart is a lonely hunter*. Boston: Houghton.

McGreevey, G. (1968). *I'm thirsty too!* South Brunswick, NJ: A. S. Barnes. (H.I.)

Funny, sometimes serious autobiography of a hard of hearing woman who endures, if not always prevails, in the country of the hearing.

*Malamud, B. (1973). Talking horse. In *Rembrandt's hat*. New York: Farrar, Strauss.

*Maupassant, de G. (ca. 1923). The deaf mute. In *Complete short stories*. New York: P. F. Collier.

Melville, H. (1949). Fragments from a writing desk. In J. Leyda (Ed.), *The complete stories of Herman Melville*. New York: Random.

Melville's first attempt at storytelling in which a young, romantic hero follows a mysterious and beautiful girl only to discover to his horror that she is "dumb and deaf!" References in his later works reveal a keener insight into deafness and sign language.

*Montague, M. (1915). Why it was w-on-the-eyes. In *Closed doors: Studies of deaf and blind children*. Boston: Houghton.

*Musset, de A. (1907). Pierre and Camille. In M. R. Pellissier (Trans.), *The complete writings of Alfred de Musset: Vol VII*. New York: Edwin C. Hill.

Parsons, F. M. (ca. 1907). *Sound of the stars*. New York: Vantage. (H.I.)

Diary of a deaf girl's adventures with family and friends in Tahiti in the late thirties.

343

*Payne, A. H. (n.d.). *King silence*. London: Jarrold.

Powers, H. (1972). *Signs of silence: Bernard Bragg and the National Theatre of the Deaf*. New York: Dodd, Mead.

The biography of a deaf man born of deaf parents and his rise to stardom as an actor and mime in the National Theatre of the Deaf which he cofounded. Includes an introduction by Nanette Fabray.

*Relgis, E. (1938). *Muted voices*. (R. Freeman-Ishill, Trans.). Berkeley Heights, NJ: Oriole. (H.I.)

Riddell, F. (1934). *Silent world*. London: Geoffrey Bles.

Romantic novel in which a man, deaf from shock since age one, regains his hearing following a car accident at the age of twenty-eight. He reenters the hearing world, rejects his deaf wife, and falls in love with a hearing woman. The deaf wife is left to care for the deaf child of their broken marriage.

Rinehart, M. R. (1919). God's fool. In *Love stories*. New York: George H. Doran.

Story of an ugly deaf hospital attendant with misshapen hands ("Dummy") whose devotion to a young woman brings her together with her boyfriend. "Dummy" receives her parrot in reward. Deaf as grotesque motif.

*Robinson, V. (1966). *David in silence*. Philadelphia: J. B. Lippincott.

Salinger, J. D. (1959). *Raise high the roofbeam, carpenters* and *Seymour an introduction*. Boston: Little, Brown.

In the former of these two narrative pieces, the author draws a short portrait of a little old deaf man to illustrate the ideal of silence as a way of coping with the harsher realities of the modern world.

Scott, W. (1943). *The talisman*. New York: Dodd, Mead.

Classic example of character disguising himself as a deaf person to conceal true identity. Also used in at least one other novel, *Peveril of the Peak*, by Sir Walter Scott.

Seelye, J. (1972). *The kid*. New York: Viking.

Novel of a small western town, late nineteenth century, that includes an African deaf character. The black, deaf man possesses unusual strength and occult powers, but nevertheless comes to a violent end. He communicates by signs to his friend, the Kid.

Shaw, J. G. [Jay Gee, pseud.]. (1912). *John and Elizabeth, a romance in real life*. Preston, England: George Toulmin & Sons.

Romance between John (hearing) and Elizabeth (deaf) that ends on a happy marital note. The novel considers the question of whether or not deafness is hereditary.

Sigourney, L. H. (1833). *Memoir of Phebe P. Hammond, a pupil in the American Asylum at Hartford. Prepared for press by Mrs. L.H.S.* New York: Sleight & Van Norden.

Sentimental vignette of brief life and death of a deaf child by a noted American authoress.

Sigourney, L. H. (1851). *Letters to my pupils with narrative and biographical sketches*. New York: Robert Carter & Brothers.

Contains a sketch of Alice Cogswell (pp. 249–262), famous deaf pupil of Thomas Hopkins Gallaudet and close friend and neighbor of "sweet singer of Hartford," popular American authoress of her time.

Smollett, T. (1956). *Peregrine pickle* (Vols. 1–2). London: J. M. Dent & Sons.

Novel features a misanthropic old Welshman who assists the hero by feigning deafness to expose society's fakers and hypocrites.

*Steward, D. (1973). *The acupuncture murders*. New York: Harper & Row.

*Terry, H. L. (ca. 1914). *A voice from the silence*. Santa Monica, CA: Palisades. (H.I.)

*Tidyman, E. (1974). *Dummy*. Boston: Little, Brown.

*Toman, W. (1959). At the dances of the deaf-mutes. In H. Zohn (Trans.) & D. Ray (Ed.), *The Chicago Review Anthology*. Chicago: The University of Chicago Press.

Tonna, C. E. (1850). *Memoir of John Britt, the happy mute. Compiled from the writings, letters, and conversation of Charlotte Elizabeth*. London: Seeley.

Account of Mrs. Tonna's educational experiences with a boy deaf from birth who died from consumption. Heavy on Christianity.

*Turgenev, I. (1904). Mumú. In I. F. Hapgood (Trans.), *The novels and stories of Ivan Turgenieff: Vol. XI*. New York: Charles Scribner's Sons.

Twain, M. [Samuel Langhorne Clemens]. (1912). *The adventures of Huckleberry Finn*. New York: P. F. Collier & Son.

Especially noteworthy for the Negro slave Jim's moving and dramatic account of his discovery, after punishing his daughter numerous times, that she was deaf. Includes a few other references to deafness.

Wallace, L. (1893). *The prince of India* or *Why Constantinople fell* (Vols. 1–2). New York: Harper & Brothers.

Historical romance in which hero surrounds himself with deaf slaves, two of which are important to the plot and courageous, nobel, and trustworthy in character.

*Welty, E. (1941). The key. In *A curtain of green and other stories*. New York: Harcourt.

West, P. (1970). *Words for a deaf daughter*. New York & Evanston: Harper & Row.

A father's well-written, imaginative account of his deaf and brain-damaged daughter. West is an English poet and novelist.

*Wiggins, J. (1970). *No sound*. New York: Silent Press. (H.I.)

Wojeciechawska, M. (1968). *A single night*. New York: Harper & Row.

Religious novel set in a small village in Spain with a deaf girl who is an outcast in society until she finds meaning and love in caring for a sculpture of the Christ child.

*Wright, D. (1969). *Deafness*. New York: Stein & Day. (H.I.)

Trent Batson, Professor of English and Computer Coordinator in the Writing Center at Gallaudet College, received his doctorate in American Studies from The George Washington University. In 1980 he started a course at Gallaudet College called "The Deaf Culture in America." More recently Dr. Batson began a course, with Clayton Valli, in American Sign Language (ASL) poetry.

•

Eugene Bergman, Assistant Professor of English at Gallaudet College, received his doctorate from The George Washington University. For years he has taught the course, "The Deaf in Literature," for which this book was compiled. Dr. Bergman is author, with Bernard Bragg, of *Tales from a Clubroom*, a successful play about a deaf club. He has been deaf since his boyhood in Poland.

•

Angels and Outcasts, originally published as *The Deaf Experience*, is a unique collection designed for a course in literature by and about the deaf. It offers more than just stories about deafness; it offers good literature. Most importantly, the book contains insights into society's changing attitudes toward deafness over the last two centuries. Introductions to the different parts are provided as well as a preface for each story. The selective annotated bibliography was prepared by Daniel C. Nascimento of Gallaudet College.